WHEN THE APRICOTS BLOOM

ROBERTA FORREST is a British author whose first novel *The Lushai Girl* was shortlisted for the Romantic Novelist Association Award in 1986. She lives in St Weonards, Herefordshire.

ROBERTA FORREST

When the Apricots Bloom

FONTANA/Collins

First published by William Collins Sons & Co. Ltd, 1988
First issued in Fontana Paperbacks 1989
Second impression June 1990

© Roberta Forrest 1988

Printed and bound in Great Britain by
William Collins Sons & Co. Ltd, Glasgow

'Bukra fil mishmish' is Arabic for
'Tomorrow when the apricots bloom'.
It is the promised tomorrow . . .
which may never come.

ONE

Sahara 1936

The boy's laughter echoed strangely from the craggy outcrops of distorted rock above the dry wadi. The December afternoon heat had grown from a dawn frost that for brief minutes before sunrise had given the desert sand a frail crust, strong enough to support the daintier mammals who scavenged its inhospitable surface. Now it was dry, seemingly almost liquid, and the vibrations of the child's voice in the still, hot air produced minuscule avalanches where the sand lay steeply wind-blown beneath the ochre cliffs.

Once, twenty thousand years before, the wadi had contained a river, its shallows reed-filled, its banks overhung by great trees. On lush, rolling hills vast herds of game had wandered and fed, returning at dusk to the refreshing waters which had flowed through the fertile land.

Over the long ages the water-table had dropped, and the river which had tumbled between rich banks now seeped uselessly and hidden a hundred feet beneath the scorched plain. Each day the relentless Sahara sun drew a little of the dying river's moisture towards the harsh surface, and in rare places where soluble minerals met, combined, and crystallized, there formed the desert roses; delicate, exotically beautiful. The boy was searching for them.

His parents' open tourer, a while Delahaye, one of Europe's most expensive motor cars, stood in the shade of one of the grotesque rock pinnacles at the edge of the dirt road. The vehicle's normally gleaming chrome and paintwork was stained with the fine yellow dust which had been its wake since leaving the oasis town of Ghardaia at five am, that morning. It was not yet noon, but there were still over a hundred and eighty tedious miles to drive on grit roads before the Charpentiers would reach their chateau and estates on the fertile Algerian coastal plain at Hadjout. It would be dark by then.

Colette Charpentier, a plumpish but good-looking, twenty-six-year-old woman, her dark eyes and near black hair indicating the mixed Spanish and French ancestry of many of the colonial families, knelt on a tartan car rug a few yards away from the vehicle and began repacking the picnic basket. Beside her slept her two-year-old daughter, Belle, the child's forehead damp with perspiration. Colette fastened the leather strap of the basket, then sat back on her heels. She removed her head scarf and shook the flour-like dust from it, then ran her fingers through her hair; it felt lank, dirty, and she wondered briefly if she should rinse it in water from one of the emergency jerricans carried in the Delahaye's boot. She knew it would be a waste of time, after a few miles it would be as clogged with dust as ever. She stood and lazily stretched herself.

Her son's laughter, distant, caught her attention, and she glanced quickly and nervously at her husband, Christian. He stood beside the car, peering through his binoculars at a guano-stained crag. 'Can you see Vincent?' she asked him. For the colonists, the desert interior of the country seemed to hold a million dangers.

Christian Charpentier, an elegantly slender and aristocratic-looking man, dressed in a khaki bush-jacket and slacks, answered without moving. 'I can see an eagle's nest on the rocks.' He lowered the binoculars reluctantly. 'Vincent? He's in the wadi; I saw him a few moments ago.' He glanced at his wristwatch. 'I suppose we'd better make a move.' Only thirty-two, his years in the fierce Algerian summer sun had already cut fine lines in the deeply tanned skin of his face. He was much fairer than his wife, his pale blue eyes suggesting Nordic forefathers. He dropped the Zeiss into their case and casually tossed them into the back of the tourer. 'There he is,' he nodded in the direction of the dry river bed two hundred yards away.

Although the family's visit to Ghardaia had been intended as a Christmas break for them all, for Christian, the third generation of Charpentier sons to be born in north Africa and now the company chairman, it had been an ideal opportunity to make an inspection of a neglected corner of the multi-billion franc Charpentier empire. Founded by his great-grandfather less than twenty years after France had overcome the country's Turkish rulers in 1830, the Charpentier Company was now one of the wealthiest and most successful in the department.

The ancient desert town of Ghardaia, with its white-washed houses built in traditional Arab style behind crenellated walls, was one of the many staging-posts and depots for the company's trucking fleet. During the colder months of the year when the Sahara was navigable, the Charpentier trucks carried thousands of fifty-litre glass carboys of red wine and as many of orange juice, the produce of the company's own vineyards and orange groves, to the French territories of Niger, Chad and Volta in the south, returning loaded high with sacks of ground-nuts.

To his wife's irritation, she had seen little of her husband during the short vacation, and tending the needs of the two children, alone, and without even the customary assistance of the children's *fatma* and her own house servants, had exhausted and bored her. Like most of the wealthy pieds-noir, she preferred her holidays in the civilization of Europe.

'I don't like Vincent so far away from us, please do something.' Colette sat the awakened Belle upright and wiped the perspiration and dust from the sleepy child's forehead with a handkerchief.

Christian looked towards the wadi, Vincent was now standing on its lip, waving at them.

He shouted to the boy; the sharpness of his voice bringing an irritable whimper from his daughter. 'Come on, time we were going.' His voice echoed back by the rocks, the words repeating until they died, far away, in hidden crevices and caves. Vincent ignored his father's command and beckoned more exaggeratedly. 'Damn the child,' Christian muttered. He began walking towards Vincent, cursing again as fine sand filled the sides of his shoes.

As he drew closer, picking his way through the rubble of decaying rock, he could see his son was excited. Vincent stood on the edge of the wadi, staring downwards, still frantically signalling. Beyond him the shimmering heat turned the desert plain into a vast lake, making distances impossible to judge; the mirage which had traditionally led thirst-crazed travellers to madness.

'For heaven's sake, what is it?' Christian was unable to keep his annoyance from his voice.

Vincent, still a few yards away, answered without turning his head. 'A baby.'

Christian joined his son on the steep bank of the wadi. Fifteen feet below was an outcrop of jumbled boulders, an island in the brown sand of the dry river bed. The boy pointed, but Christian could see nothing in the harlequin shadows of the rocks. 'A baby what?'

'A real baby,' Vincent paused. 'There, under that big piece of stone.'

'You're imagining things. Come along. I don't want to be driving all night. We've been waiting for you.' He took the boy's hand, but Vincent resisted him.

'It's there, Papa. It *was* moving, and I heard it crying.' He sounded desperate; convincing. Christian hesitated. Vincent's voice was begging him. 'There, Papa . . . below that big rock with the crack in it. Just a bit to the right, underneath in the shade.'

Christian could make out a small corner of red cloth. 'It's only a bit of rubbish. Rags some Arabs have thrown away. Come along now.'

'It moved, really. And it did cry out.'

Christian was surprised to see tears of frustration in his son's eyes. 'All right, we'll go down and look.'

'No. We can't.' Vincent gripped his father's hand tighter. 'There's a big snake. I threw a stone at it. It's under the same rock. It'll bite the baby.'

Christian said firmly: 'Stay here, I'll go.'

He scrambled cautiously down over the rock pile, knowing that at this time of the year if there was one snake there might be others. In winter they often gathered together for warmth, separating only to sun themselves at the hottest time of the day. Once, several years previously while on a hunting trip, his Arab guide had shown him a small cave which contained a writhing mass of hundreds of poisonous reptiles. The sight could have been the basis for nightmares.

Vincent questioned him anxiously from above. 'Can you see it now?'

Christian began a negative reply, but a slight movement in the shadow of one of the rocks stopped him. There was a small bundle of red cloth, and as he watched it moved again. 'I can see something,' he admitted.

11

He was now less than a yard away, almost within touching distance but loathe to move closer until he was better able to examine the deep shade; then he saw the snake, a thick-bodied viper, pressed deep into the crevice, its flat head drawn back defensively, against its side.

From the bundle of rags came a dry, inhuman sound; the faint bleat of a distressed animal.

Christian muttered an exclamation: 'Good God!' Perhaps Vincent was right, the rags might conceal a baby but he knew that if he stretched out his hand the viper would certainly strike.

He tapped his trouser pockets searching for the matches he carried to light his pipe, then drew them out with his handkerchief. He rolled the white linen into a ball, weighting it with a pebble, then struck one of the matches and held the flame against the cloth. For a few seconds he blew the embers carefully, before tossing the smouldering handkerchief into the crevice. The viper flinched dangerously, tightening its muscles as Christian backed slowly away, and waited.

Smoke drifted lazily from the shadow of the rock, a faint inadequate haze in the sunlight. Then there was sudden movement. The viper, despite its thick ugly body, slid from the crevice with astonishing speed, searching for purchase on the smooth rock, finding little and dropping onto the sand beneath. In a second it was amongst the broken rubble and then lost beneath the outcrop, only a swerving furrow in the fine sand indicating its path.

Christian was still cautious, still not convinced that the content of the rag bundle could be human; the rags might contain some trapped desert animal which had sought warmth amongst them. He probed carefully with his fingertips before pulling it from the mouth of the small cave, then held it away from his body, teasing the cloth from it as though each fold concealed danger. It was a child, minute, barely alive, already dehydrated, its skin filthy with dried blood and sand.

Colette stared at it for several seconds in disbelief before taking it from her husband. 'It's only hours old; almost dead, poor thing. It needs liquid.' Her voice hardened. 'Damned Arabs, they don't even care about their own children.' She cradled the naked baby protectively in her hands.

Vincent stared, fascinated. He had not seen his sister Belle until she was three-weeks-old, when he had returned from the house of his aunt where he had been sent during the last days of his mother's pregnancy. Belle had been much bigger than this baby, which seemed as wrinkled and gnarled as the old Arabs he saw camped with their wares in the market-places. 'I found it where some Bedouins had been camping last night, Mama. They must have forgotten the baby when they left. Perhaps they'll come back for it?'

His father dropped a hand on the boy's shoulder. 'I'm afraid not. The Bedouin do this sometimes; abandon babies, if they've too many and can't feed them all.'

Vincent was horrified. 'Just leave their babies in the desert? Arabs are so stupid. I hate them.'

Colette spoke with concern. 'She's filthy.' She could see that the baby's mouth was almost clogged by mucous. 'Vincent, get me some water. And one of the towels.' She looked up at her husband, her eyes slightly moist. 'She'll die if we don't do something.'

'I'm afraid it'll die anyway,' said Christian, refusing to give the baby more identity by recognizing its sex. Then he regretted his remark. Between the births of Vincent and Belle, there had been a series of miscarriages which had accounted for the six years difference in ages between

13

brother and sister. Each miscarriage had brought its individual heartbreak to Colette. After Belle's birth, she had been warned that further pregnancies would be dangerous for her health. Most of the Catholic pieds-noir families were large, seven or eight children quite common, and Christian was aware that his wife had felt herself inadequate. Her sister, Françoise, had given birth to four children by the time she was twenty-three, had five now and was a year younger than Colette. After visits to the Charpentier home by the growing number of nephews and nieces, Colette was depressed for days. Christian sounded more optimistic. 'We're only an hour from Laghouat, we'll be able to hand it in at the Gendarmerie.'

Colette reacted angrily. 'She's not a piece of luggage someone has lost.' She began cleaning the baby's face, wiping the inside of its lips gently with a wet corner of the towel. The baby protested silently, its delicate limbs clawing at the hot air, its wrinkled face distorted into a simian grimace of annoyance.

Christian knelt beside her. 'They'll find her a home.' He lifted the heavy jerrican and poured more tepid water onto the towel Colette held towards him.

'Would you trust your new born baby to an Arab gendarme?' she asked coldly. 'He'd simply put her out in the desert again tonight. They don't want extra children, especially someone else's, and particularly Bedouin babies. Besides, they're so superstitious, they'd probably think we'd brought them a devil-child.'

Belle, unaccustomed to being ignored, began crying loudly. Unlike Vincent who had been a lively and active infant, Belle was proving to be a late walker. Probably, Christian had decided, because she really didn't need to move very much. There was always her mother or the *fatma* nearby to attend to her wants. Vincent had been much more independent. Christian lifted Belle onto his

14

knee and the child's sobs ceased instantly with his attention.

Colette frowned. She had hoped the Arab baby would begin sucking the damp corner of the towel so it might get some moisture into its dehydrated body. She tried dropping a small amount into its mouth from the tip of her little finger, but the baby choked as the water ran into its windpipe. She turned it onto its stomach on her lap. It began screaming, a surprisingly powerful, mind-searing sound, high pitched and so continuous that it was as though its minuscule lungs contained a never-ending volume of air.

Christian winced. Why, he wondered, had he agreed to stop at this particular place? Anywhere else on the journey and he would not now be faced by this additional problem. The day had begun relaxed and pleasant enough. He had been looking forward to the drive back to the coast. But Vincent had wanted them to picnic here, the last opportunity he would have to search for desert roses, the rock crystals he collected along with countless fossils, the dried corpses of insects, butterflies, birds' eggs, shells and anything else that attracted his attention. Mentally, Christian shrugged, feeling guilty at his thoughts. Kismet! God's will! Perhaps it was meant to be. He watched Colette, surprised by the primitive maternal interest that the baby's sounds of distress were arousing in his wife. She was rocking the child against her, attempting to silence it with comfort and security. 'The longer we stay here, the less chance it has.'

Colette nodded. She knew that somehow she must keep the baby alive until they reached the château. Once there, the *fatma* would find a wet nurse amongst the women of the Arab field workers. There was Amar's wife, barely fifteen-years-old, Colette had guessed, who had given birth to a child only a week ago. She would certainly be happy to provide milk for a few extra centimes in her husband's wages.

The road improved as they drove northwards, and once past Laghouat it became tarmac. It was cooler now in the evening sun as they climbed steadily through the foothills of the Atlas mountains towards Medea and the spectacular Chiffa Gorge. The children were on the back seat of the Delahaye, Belle asleep once more, lulled by the soft suspension of the heavy vehicle, Vincent still lively, interested in the long views across the changing landscape which was now becoming greener and more colourful against the dark background of tree-covered mountains. The Arab baby's crying had been penetrating and incessant, and its sudden silence was, to Christian, ominous. He looked quickly at his wife seated next to him and saw she was smiling. Her blouse was open to the waist and the wizened baby was sucking contentedly at one of her breasts, its face pressed against her soft, velvet flesh.

She caught his curious stare and blushed quickly. 'I can't give her anything.' She sounded embarrassed. 'But it seems to be making her feel better.'

To Christian's annoyance, the problems raised by the finding of the Bedouin child compounded rather than dissipated on their return to Chateau Beau Lac, for despite all his reasoning Colette firmly refused to part with the baby she had named Maryse.

At first he had expected his wife's fascination for the child to pass, but this did not happen. And something which he found even more difficult to comprehend was that the normal disdain which Colette, in common with most pieds-noir, had for anyone of Arab parentage, she certainly did not extend to Maryse. It was as though a

16

part of Colette's mind refused to accept that the child could be of any blood other than her own.

But Colette was not as insensitive as Christian believed to the reactions she was provoking in her husband. Even to herself the feelings she experienced towards Maryse were inexplicable. It was as though the olive-skinned baby, in a desperate bid for it survival, had cast a mysterious spell upon her, demanding her total love and protection in its weakest days. Compared to the two sturdy babies which she had produced from her own womb, this tiny Bedouin child seemed incredibly fragile and vulnerable, its body and limbs, minute fingers so fascinatingly delicate in an enchanting and already feminine way that its attraction was hypnotic and irresistible.

Apart from the disappointments the miscarriages had given her between the birth of Vincent and Belle there had been little to disturb the serenity of Colette's life. Wealth had protected and cushioned her since her own childhood, and she had been faced with few important decisions. In her late teens she had willingly accepted Christian's proposal, without realizing that their courtship had been as carefully planned by his family as had any other of the Charpentier's many successful business ventures. She had welcomed her duties as the wife of one of the most important businessmen in the Algerian Department and she had enjoyed and maintained the expected luxuries of her household, and had been an elegant hostess and companion to her husband. She had provided Christian with children, not as many as she would have liked, but to her satisfaction he had an heir for the Charpentier name. Now, and for the first time she found herself rebelling, not only against the wishes of her husband but against those of her entire family.

As the days gathered into weeks Christian's views remained unchanged; in his opinion, to bring up an Arab

17

child within a Catholic settler family would be detrimental not only to their own children but to the Arab child herself. Serious problems were bound to result from the differing backgrounds of the two nationalities. Arabs were anathema to the Algerian-born Europeans – the pieds-noir – at any level of their society, and were openly disliked by the majority. To raise an Arab child within such a community, one that would never permit itself to accept her, might prove the worst form of cruelty, bringing heartbreak not only to Colette but eventually to Maryse.

For the first time in her married life, Colette defied her husband, and fought countless battles against relatives seeking to reinforce Christian's views. Although not all her battles were won neither were they lost, and Maryse remained at the Château Beau Lac despite every argument that was presented.

The final decision on the baby's future could only, however, be made by Christian, and he had never before encountered such stubbornness in his wife. In different circumstances he might have found this previously unrevealed trait admirable, but he was now aware that a wedge was being driven between them which must be removed before their relationship was damaged forever.

It was Vincent, however, who convinced his father to agree that Maryse should remain with the Charpentier family. Vincent and his father had been alone together in one of the caves where Christian had been sampling a great oak cask which contained part of the new season's wine. For several minutes Vincent had been unusually quiet and Christian wondered what was going on in the boy's mind.

As his father closed down the cask, Vincent spoke nervously: 'Why do you hate our baby, Papa?'

18

The question surprised Christian. To give himself time to think he wiped the glass he had been using slowly, before replacing it on the top of the cask. 'I don't hate her.'

'She doesn't eat very much,' said Vincent persuasively. He had deliberately eavesdropped on his father's conversations with Colette. 'And if she grows up with us, she won't be Arab any longer.'

Christian lifted Vincent and sat him on the cask. Their eyes were now level and Christian found the boy's stare was slightly disconcerting. 'It's a question of parentage,' he explained, simplistically. 'If you put a mongrel puppy into a kennel of greyhounds, it won't become one, will it?' How could you explain all the difficulties that might lie ahead, to a child, he wondered.

'Our baby isn't a dog, Papa,' Vincent answered him flatly, his eyes still meeting Christian's, who found them uncomfortably penetrating. It was as though he stared into a mirror and saw an image of himself in his own childhood . . . the same skin texture, hair and eye colouring.

'I didn't say she was. But suppose Ahmed . . .' He named one of the old field-workers. 'Suppose he had found you when you were a baby. Would you have liked to live with Ahmed? Wouldn't you prefer to be raised by your own people?'

Vincent had been inside Ahmed's small concrete house which bore no resemblance to Château Beau Lac but was unconvinced by his father's argument. 'That's quite different. His house is horrible. Ours is nice, and the baby is in *our* house.'

'But you know that Arabs are different from us. They live differently, they think differently. They have quite different needs . . . different ambitions.'

'They're sometimes very lazy,' admitted Vincent, remembering past arguments between the foremen and his father. 'But Belle's lazy, too. Mother says that's why she doesn't bother to speak much, or walk. And I could teach Rose not to be lazy.'

'Rose? I thought your mother had named the baby Maryse.'

'Well, I call her Rose,' admitted Vincent, dropping his eyes with sudden boyish embarrassment.

'Why Rose?' Christian sensed he was about to learn the reason for Vincent's interest in the Arab baby.

'Because I found her,' the boy said softly. 'She's really mine, not Mama's. So I named her after the rock crystals; the desert roses.'

In late February, the Arab baby was baptized in the Roman Catholic church of Saint Joseph, in Hadjout, and given the names: Maryse Rose. Only on one point Christian Charpentier remained adamant; he was not prepared to officially adopt the child.

As the first years passed and Maryse Rose grew and developed, sheltered by the wealth and influence of the Charpentier household, few of the problems which Christian anticipated for her had yet materialized. But although Colette seemed unaware of them, the signs of the resentment for anyone of Arab blood, so deep-rooted amongst the settlers as to be almost genetic, were sometimes noticeable to her husband in the eyes of the closest family friends; the signs were usually so concealed as to be almost indiscernible, but they existed. They appeared when Maryse Rose's name was mentioned in casual conversation, and showed even when the child's voice emerged for an instant above those of the group within which she played. The involuntary signs might be faint now, but Christian was aware that the pieds-noir elite had notoriously long memories; they would never forget Maryse Rose's alien background, nor the unique manner in which she was unwittingly embarrassing them.

Despite his early misgivings and reluctance, Christian had grown to love Maryse Rose as much as his own children. She was an easy child to like, warm and affectionate, bright and attentive, who greeted him excitedly whenever he returned to Beau Lac whether his absence had been for days or only a few hours. There was very little in her appearance indicating her Bedouin parentage. She was no darker skinned than most of the settlers' children with their Mediterranean backgrounds, and in fact, the skin on the parts of her body which were not exposed to the sun in her play, was pale, almost sallow and flawless, which Christian knew would be attractive when she reached maturity. Her features, now she was beginning to lose the chubbiness of babyhood, were fine and delicate.

Her foster mother, Colette, had not been so foolish to allow the enchantment for Maryse Rose, which had so dominated her in the first weeks of the child's life, to eclipse the love which she felt for her own children. Once the initial flames of her obsession had quelled she had tried to ensure her affection was equally shared amongst all three. But this sharing had become, unnoticed by Colette, so ritualistic that it seemed unnatural even to the children themselves. It created its own passions, but whereas Vincent quickly became aware that the occasional feelings of resentment he experienced were the result of the idiosyncrasies of his mother, Belle grew intensely jealous of Maryse Rose.

Vincent had never lost the strange possessive feelings he had experienced for Maryse Rose since the day he discovered her in the rocks of the desert wadi, and as the maternal protectiveness of his mother towards the baby faded into more normal parental affection he unconsciously adopted a guardian role. Just as his father's position protected the Arab child in the adult European society, so did Vincent's amongst their children with whom they played.

The French declaration of war against Germany in 1939 and the sudden and unexpected collapse of the allied armies in Europe, brought a reaction from Christian which Colette had never anticipated. After continually refusing to consider the legal adoption of Maryse Rose, he now suggested it should take place as soon as it could be arranged. He had been silent for hours following the broadcast statement that the new French government, under Marshal Petain, would collaborate with the Nazi rulers of France in return for 'concessions' in the form of an 'unoccupied' zone which included Algeria.

Christian was sickened by the disaster which had so quickly overcome France, and disappointed by its weak leadership. He felt ashamed he had not offered to serve in the French army himself as many other settlers had done. But France, then, had seemed so secure, backed by her neighbours and the British; commerce in Algeria and his own political work had appeared more important at the crucial time. Regardless of the German guarantees, he had no doubt what Marshal Petain's 'collaboration' would mean in the years to come. Algeria was strategically important to Nazi Germany, which would need the country's Mediterranean ports and vital desert communications to overpower the allied armies massing against them in Egypt. Christian had suddenly become aware of the dangers a member of his own family might face when Algeria was eventually occupied. The Nazis had already

indicated in Europe how they dealt with those they classi-
fied as 'racial inferiors' and Maryse Rose, as an Arab,
would undoubtedly be placed in that category by the
conquerors despite the reassurances of the French Vichy
government.

He did not discuss the reasons for his decision with
Colette, nor did she question him. He had never been an
overtly emotional man and so she accepted his proposal
with a feeling of satisfaction rather than curiosity. Her
husband's motives made no difference to the legal act
which Colette had wanted since the days when she had
first cradled Maryse Rose in her arms. Now she felt only
the contentment of an ambition finally realized, the total
equality amongst her children that she had sought for so
long.

To the four-year-old Arab child, witnessing the signing
of the legal documents which gave her the right to her
family's name, was a magical event. In her brief memory
it seemed to her that every dispute she had experienced
with Belle had ended with a reminder or jibe that she
was different, an Arab, and not a true member of the
Charpentier family. She had prayed to God to be allowed
to become one of them, and now she was no longer an
Arab but a Charpentier, and French! In her imagination it
was as though she had walked into the airless registration
office of the Prefecture, with its claustrophobic scent of
old books, ink and floor polish, as an ugly pupae which
during the brief civil formality developed into a butterfly.
Afterwards Vincent led her into the busy Algiers street,
holding her hand as though she were a bride emerging
from a church.

Even though she understood he was not her real father
she had always called Christian, Papa. Now the word itself
seemed to hold a far deeper, almost holy significance for
her. As they walked to the waiting car she said the word

23

several times under her breath before finally blurting it out aloud: 'Papa.'

Christian looked down at her, understood, and then smiled. 'Miss Maryse Rose Charpentier,' he said. 'Our little desert rose.'

As Maryse Rose scrambled into their car feeling excited and happy, Belle pinched her.

TWO

October 1954

It had been one of the last of the hot October days, the sun blazing down onto the weathered rocks from a clear azure sky. Maryse Rose lay a few feet from the sea, sheltered from the light breeze by the nearby ruins of the ancient Roman town of Tipaza, whose excavated column-lined walks were now softened by lush olive and orange trees, their branches laden with ripe fruits. She knew this place intimately, and had played here since her childhood; where the long sweeping Tipaza beach began, its sands a wedge of bright gold-dust between the deep blue of the Mediterranean and the distant sea cliffs of the green Atlas mountains.

Like all the young pieds-noir who were swimming in the nearby sea, lazing on the sands or rocks, or dancing on the balcony of the small restaurant below the dunes, her oiled skin had been tanned to deep mahogany. Wide sun-glasses shaded her eyes but she was not asleep, and she could hear the excited voices of her friends as they splashed in the depths of a nearby rock pool retrieving cooled bottles of wine.

She was eighteen-years-old, her slender body lithe and supple, so that she moved with an intriguing feline grace accentuated as she stretched herself lazily in the heat of the sun. Concealed by the lenses of her sun-glasses her eyes were an unusual hazel, set wide above a gently

25

angular face, her nose small but straight-bridged. Her hair was jet black, shining as though it had been oiled. She was conscious now that men watched her, as she lay sunbathing on the rocks, as she walked on the beach, swam in the cooling sea, strolled the boulevards of the city or sat at the tables in the fashionable restaurants or clubs.

The past few weeks of her life had been the most pleasant she could remember; she had come home at last. For two years she had been in boarding school in France, in the small town of Evry – several miles from the suburbs of Paris. She had not disliked the school, but had hated being away from Algeria for so long, away from her family and friends, away from the sun, the sea, and the gentle north African winter climate. She had missed the glorious blooms of the Mediterranean spring, the relaxed and casual atmosphere that existed in its summer heat, the parties, and the dancing. During those impatient years she had returned home only once, and it had been so painful, then, to wrench herself away again that she had decided to remain at Evry until her schooling was finally completed. She had counted the last year day by day on a calendar, like a prisoner awaiting release from jail.

She had gone to the finishing school a girl, and returned a young woman, but only in retrospect had she been able to admit its value; those of her acquaintances who had remained in Algeria seemed still immature, younger than herself in so many ways, while she felt that she had gained in confidence and sophistication.

A shadow moved briefly across her eyelids and she was conscious of someone seating themselves on a nearby outcrop of weathered rock. She prepared herself to be angry if the arrival was accompanied by a shower of sea-water from a wine bottle or some other youthful jape, but remained motionless as though asleep. She had left Belle and their group of friends half an hour before intending to read her book in peace, but the sun and the lunch she had eaten were soporific. The book lay open, cover upwards, on the rock beside her.

'*Bonjour Tristesse* is a stupid title,' said a man's voice. Its unfamiliarity startled her. She opened her eyes and moved quickly to support herself on an elbow. The sharp surface of the rock caught at her skin, making her flinch. The sunlight, even through the lenses of her glasses, temporarily blinded her so she could not see the man. 'I'm sorry, I've made you cut your arm. You're bleeding. Can I help?'

She said: 'No,' curtly, and searched in her beach bag for a tissue. To her annoyance the stranger did not go away.

'I just think that welcoming sadness is not a particularly sensible philosophy.' His voice was deep but gentle, almost sensuous. He had a mainland French accent which she could not immediately identify. She glanced at him. He was in uniform, but his jacket was across his knees and his shirt open to the waist. His kepi was on the rock at his side, but in the fierce sunlight she was unable to judge the colour which would have identified his regiment. Since the recent and humiliating end of the Indo China war Algeria was full of servicemen.

Despite the inexplicable thrill she had experienced as he had spoken, she felt resentful. 'You've read the book?'

'No. It's a girl's book, written for girls.'

'Francoise Sagan is *eighteen*.'

The man chuckled, amused by her defensive response. 'Eighteen is a girl. And eighteen is a rather pretentious age to write books.'

She picked up the novel and turned her back on him, trying to concentrate on the crowded pages. The mock

27

anger she had prepared to defend herself against a friend's intrusion, had become real.

The man spoke softly, his voice serious but still edged with humour. 'Now I've insulted you. *YOU* must be Francoise Sagan, you wrote *Bonjour Tristesse and* you're eighteen.' There was a momentary pause. 'I'm Ernest Hemingway and I just wondered, as we're both literary personalities in a strange country, if we could celebrate my Nobel Prize together this evening, or if you've already made plans perhaps tomorrow?'

His ridiculous approach lessened her anger, but she still felt that his remarks about the age of the author had been a personal slight. In common with most settlers she did not like the French conscripts who, since the end of the Indo China War, were being sent for their service to Algeria; amongst their many other failings they filled the cafes and bars, were usually drunk, and thought every Algerian girl easy prey for metropolitan charm.

She replied curtly in Arabic. 'Bukra fil mishmish.' It was a commonly used expression amongst Algerians, translating as 'tomorrow, when the apricots bloom', but inferring a day which would never arrive.

He repeated the phrase as though memorizing it but failed to understand its meaning, and then continued to tease her. 'I suppose you've heard that the government is refusing to make an official statement about flying saucers, and that there was another one seen over Bordeaux yesterday? There are little green men everywhere nowadays.'

She turned quickly towards him, intending to tell him that she was not enjoying his attention. He had moved slightly, and for the first time she was able to see his face. He would have been handsome, but for a long, deep scar which cut an ugly furrow from above his left eyebrow to below his jaw.

He realized her eyes were examining him, and smiled uncomfortably, the scar tissue pulling at his face and turning the smile into a grimace. 'I fell off my high chair.'

She felt herself blushing.

He stood, casually swinging his jacket onto one shoulder and picked up his kepi. He was tall, athletically slim, his hair crew-cut.

'You don't have to go.' Embarrassed, she realized she had spoken too quickly as if she really wanted him to stay.

He set the kepi squarely on his head and began to climb the gentle slope of brown rocks towards the footpath. After a few paces he turned towards her again. 'You should read Jean-Paul Sartre, Miss Sagan.'

Although Maryse Rose was unaware of it until later, her father, Christian Charpentier, now a Deputy of the National Assembly, had spent that afternoon in the office of Colonel Henri Lefitte of Intelligence Department Three of the Algerian Sûrété.

The office was situated on the western corner of the top floor of an ancient Turkish palace, on the promenade overlooking Algiers harbour. From the ornately carved windows of the former harem quarters, which faced seawards to the north, Colonel Lefitte could watch the comings and goings of the merchant ships which busied the port's quays, the cruise liners briefly releasing their excited tourists to the avaricious bazaars, and the troopships from Marseilles transporting the thousands of nervous conscripts or frustrated veterans, between the depots of the French mainland and their regiments in North Africa.

The Colonel's view from the solitary window in the western wall was of slab-sided modern commercial buildings. Visible above these, because of the rising hillside upon which the city was built, was the conglomeration of the thousands of decrepit tenements, houses, shops, markets, palaces and mosques of the Arab casbah. Most of its inhabitants dwelt in perpetual shade in the maze of narrow, filthy alleyways, passages, high-walled court-yards and tunnels.

The two men had known each other for several years, and Henri Lefitte was a regular visitor to Christian Charpentier's home, but they were not close friends. Some barrier in Christian's mind prevented him from enjoying an intimacy which Henri Lefitte himself believed existed between them.

The men were useful to each other. Christian Charpentier was not only a Deputy, but was recognized as one of the most successful and wealthy businessmen in Algeria, a member of the pieds-noir elite known colloquially to the public and press as 'The Ten'. The Charpentier Company, besides its trucking interests, orange groves and vineyards, owned factories and bottling plants, dockside warehouses and several merchant ships. Colonel Lefitte's bureau, efficient and reliable, and employing a number of pro-fessional intelligence agents as well as several score of Arab informers, was frequently in the position to supply Christian with information far beyond the political re-quirements of a normal Deputy of the Assembly. In return Colonel Lefitte and his wife Suzanne enjoyed a social acceptance amongst the country's grandest families, and this was important to Henri Lefitte; it was his ambition to control the entire Sûreté in Algeria.

The two men were as different in appearance as back-ground. Christian was casually elegant, tall, but now slightly stooped. His pale blue eyes set him apart from most French settlers. His hair had once been fair, but was prematurely white. Although he, like Lefitte, had served with the Free French and after the Allied invasion of

North West Africa had attained a similar commissioned rank of Colonel, Christian had discarded all military attributes the moment the war had ended. He was quietly spoken, of a thoughtful nature, and was normally decisive.

Lefitte had been nicknamed 'the eagle' by his staff. He did not object, even though he knew it was based on his looks rather than his reputation. His eyes were deeply set beneath heavy brows and his nose narrow and slightly hooked. His dress was invariably immaculate and he wore his suits or dinner-jackets as though they were uniforms. His moustache was trimmed with pencilled precision into a thin line, and his black hair, receding at the temples, glistened with perfumed brilliantine. Subordinates described his manner as brusque.

He had invited Christian to his office on the pretext of discussing the problems which had arisen as a result of the recent Orleanville earthquake in which over a thousand people had died. But Lefitte's problem had nothing to do with the earthquake. It was a bomb.

More correctly, it concerned two hundred bombs which he had learnt were hidden in an illegal arsenal in the casbah.

For a few moments after the soldier had left her Maryse Rose had felt guilty, as though her inquisitive stare at his wound had been a deliberate insult. She had not intended it to be so. She had seen far greater scars and disfigurements in the past, but it had been unexpected on a youthful and otherwise attractive European face. She forgot him in the exasperation caused by blood from the deep graze on her elbow staining a favourite sundress as she drove home to Château Beau Lac. The All Saints Eve Ball was only a few days away, and she might now be forced to wear a sticking-plaster on her arm; something

31

which was bound to detract from the image she had planned to present with her carefully chosen Dior gown and the exquisite jewellery Colette, her mother, had agreed to lend her. It was her first All Saints Eve Ball for two years, and more importantly her first as a woman rather than a girl.

She had not seen Vincent since her return from Paris, and was longing to be with him even for the short time of the family reunion; perhaps to impress him a little with her new sophistication. She had been heartbroken when he had first announced his engagement to Madelene. Until then she had been unaware even of his friendship with the girl. It had struck her like the blow of a fist when he had told them all, one weekend when he had returned home from Oran where he had been working in one of the Company's offices. She had been fourteen then, and it had seemed as though the one man in whom she had always been able to place her entire trust and love had betrayed her. Her first meeting with Madelene a few weeks later had been difficult. For her entire life Vincent had been her Charlemagne, her knight. It had been Vincent who had saved her as a baby in the desert, Vincent who had always protected and comforted her as she grew older. Even in the erotic dreams and fantasies of puberty it had been Vincent who cradled her in his arms, lay beside her in secret bowers, and whispered the first words of love into her eager ears.

Only gradually had she been able to accept that the love she had felt for him had been destined to be fruitless. In her early childhood she had prayed that one day she would be permitted to become his real sister, and it was as though God had agreed but with the cruel proviso that she must always remain as such. She had wept at his wedding, not tears of joy but of despair. Perhaps Madelene alone had understood, for gradually they had become close friends, and soon they would all be together for the ball.

When Maryse Rose returned to Beau Lac that evening, Belle took delight in publicly reminding her at dinner of her meeting with the soldier. With habitual cattiness she chose a suitable moment of silence to ensure both her parents' attention.

'Did that soldier ask you for a date?' There was an unnatural casualness, itself a warning to Maryse Rose, in the way she spoke. Belle's dark eyes moved quickly between her parents' faces gauging their reactions. As she had expected her father paused to listen, frowning slightly.

Maryse Rose lied: 'Of course not.' Belle never overlooked the opportunity to compromise her, but although it was often unpleasant Maryse Rose normally refused to allow herself to be provoked. As a child she had been more vulnerable and had retaliated if Vincent had not been present, but she had soon realized that her pique only gave Belle more satisfaction.

Colette raised her carefully-plucked eyebrows towards Maryse Rose. 'It's not very sensible to encourage them. You really must take care; things have changed. Papa warned you when you first came home; these men are used to savagery . . . there are terrible stories in the newspapers every day.'

Belle spoke dramatically to her mother. 'He looked awful, Mama; like a Marseilles criminal. His face was dreadfully scarred.' She gave a dramatic shudder of repulsion.

Maryse Rose's feeling of guilt returned briefly. 'He didn't look awful. Besides, he only spoke to me for a few moments. Quite politely. He said I should read Jean-Paul Sartre.'

'Then he was a socialist thug,' said Belle, triumphantly.

Two years older than Maryse Rose, she was shorter and far plumper; a younger version of her mother, Colette, but with her hair permed into brown curls instead of worn at the older woman's mature shoulder length.

Christian Charpentier who had been silent for most of the meal, put his knife and fork on the china rest beside his plate. 'I think it would be sensible for you girls to avoid the beach for a while . . . *both* of you to avoid the beach.'

'Papa!' Belle who had been hoping for a parental warning for Maryse Rose, had not intended it to include herself. Almost all the weekend social life revolved around the Tipaza beach, and with the winter months ahead the loss of even a single day was a disaster. The Algiers' clubs or the racetrack where their parents spent their time were poor substitutes for the young.

'I'm not talking of danger from soldiers, Belle.' Christian's face was serious, and there was no humour in his eyes. At times, especially if he were angry, they could seem more grey than blue. He turned to Colette. 'I had a chat with Henri this afternoon. The Sûrété is concerned about the likelihood of another uprising.'

Colette blew out her cheeks. 'Pah! The Sûrété! Henri Lefitte is a typical policeman; he sees criminals everywhere. How can he suggest an uprising with the country so full of our soldiers?' She dabbed her lips carefully with a napkin.

'I'm afraid the prestige of the French Army at the moment is more likely to encourage an uprising than discourage one. Cairo radio has been making the most of our poor performance in Indo China for weeks now.'

'But no-one listens to Cairo radio, Papa,' protested Belle. 'It's gibberish!'

'All the Arabs listen,' corrected her father. 'But there's no immediate danger according to Henri, and he has reliable information. But the Department in Paris thinks it could happen in December.'

'The Arabs were well thrashed last time,' observed Colette. 'Surely they wouldn't risk it again?'

'They don't think like us,' Christian reminded her. 'Remember that for them their fate is inevitable, therefore they don't consider risk as we do. But, at least this time we've been forewarned. And we know they don't have much in the way of weapons; a few stolen guns and some homemade bombs.'

'Bombs?' His wife's eyes widened in horror.

'Crude things. Old military plastique stuffed into jam-tins. Two hundred of them, according to one of Henri's men . . . hidden in the casbah. The agent brought one in as a sample,' Christian paused. 'Henri's thinking of returning it with a timer fitted; it would get rid of the illegal arsenal in one go.'

'That would be a terrible thing to do, Papa,' protested Maryse Rose. 'Hundreds of innocent people would be killed; it's so crowded in there.'

'They're going to try to kill us with those bombs,' Belle glared scornfully at Maryse Rose before turning to her father. 'I hope he does it, Papa.'

Maryse Rose spoke angrily: 'Arabs are people.'

'Not people, fig trees,' retorted Belle, using one of the pieds-noir derogatory terms for Arabs and knowing it was an expression Maryse Rose hated.

Christian's eyes silenced her. 'I advised him against it. But I don't believe Henri had any real intention of doing it anyway; François Mitterand would have his head if he did, and Henri knows it.'

Christian's warning to his daughters was forgotten in two or three days. There had been talk of Arab 'uprisings' for as long as they could remember and they seldom came to anything; if they included acts of terrorism against civilians they were brutally put down. Not since 1945, when both the girls had been children, had anything really serious taken place. Now, it was inconceivable that the Arabs, who seemed barely capable of managing even the most simple tasks without European supervision, could organize themselves sufficiently to be anything more than an irritation to the settlers protected by a strong and experienced army.

For Maryse Rose and Belle, the autumn combination of sun, blue sky, and the beaches of Tipaza, remained seductively irresistible. On the 31 October, there had been no necessity for Maryse Rose to telephone her friends to suggest they should meet once more at Tipaza; she had known they would all be there.

It was a relief for her to escape from the chaos which inevitably preceded the All Saints Eve Ball at Beau Lac. She had always hated the preparations which temporarily destroyed the daylight charm and beauty of the château, its gardens and palm groves. In darkness, by the time the first guests arrived, it would all be different and would appear as a fairyland castle, majestically floodlit, the dense, lush palm groves a bewitching forest where thousands of minute coloured lights reflected from the swaying fronds, creating magical grottoes amongst the shadowed trunks. The fountains on the lawns would be phosphorescent rainbows, cascading on the bronze nymphs who played in the shallows, and there would be the music and the elegance of the guests themselves in their ball gowns and dinner-jackets. But at the moment, in the revealing daylight, the château grounds looked no more than an untidy building site, the canvas of the marquees heaped upon the cropped grass, coils of rope, stacks of poles, lorries unloading tables and chairs, gangs of shouting Arab workmen, gardeners attempting to repair the damage as it was caused, panic-stricken house servants, and a director of the catering company, whose task it was to organize the event, pacing the long drive, florid-faced, and looking as though at any moment he would suffer a heart attack.

After breakfasting she drove quickly away from Beau Lac, enjoying the morning breeze as it curled over the low windscreen of the white Mercedes sports, and the roar of the car's powerful engine as its wheels scattered gravel from the loose surface of the winding coastal road. The Mercedes was still a novelty, a gift from her father on her return to Algeria, and she was grateful for the freedom it gave her.

She did not remember the soldier until she was parking the car in the Tipaza dunes.

The unexpected and sudden memory briefly panicked her, and for a few seconds she could see him clearly in her mind just as he had stood watching her, before he had finally strolled away. She now had the strange feeling that although it was he who had left, it was she who had been dismissed, and that he had not been angered by her unintentional scrutiny of his disfigurement, but terribly hurt. When it had happened she had felt guilt, as though she had somehow insulted him. Now she experienced a deeper and more uncomfortable emotion. Once, as a child, she had been playing with a kitten and had accidentally dropped it, breaking its leg. She had not felt guilty then, but had experienced far more chastening and sombre feelings which had remained with her for weeks. She recognized them again.

As she had left her room at Beau Lac, she had placed her unfinished novel, *Bonjour Tristesse*, in her beach-bag intending to complete it while she sunbathed. Now she realized it could no longer be a pleasure; she would be unable to read the book today or at any time in the future without every line reminding her of the young officer, and the manner in which she had unintentionally hurt him. She took the novel from the bag, carried it to where the wind had exposed the rubble of some ancient building, and buried it beneath the sand. But despite the company on the beach the day seemed interminably long. During the afternoon she deliberately lay on the rocks where the soldier had spoken to her, but although now she hoped he might return, only the gentle sounds of the sea and the voices of her friends on the beach disturbed her. By the time she had driven home from Tipaza the sun had set and the glow of lights which illuminated the chateau and its gardens was visible from the darkness of the ramshackle Arab bidonville a mile from Beau Lac.

She ignored the bustling of the house servants, the contractor's hired waiters and bar staff, and went straight to her room. She knew from past balls that for the final two hours, before the arrival of the first guests, it would be a peaceful haven where she could isolate herself and enjoy her own unhurried preparations for the night ahead. She did not ring for her *fatma*, knowing that on this rare occasion the summons was unlikely to be answered, and even if it were, the woman, already busy at some unaccustomed task would be flustered and nervous and would transmit her own confused emotions. Instead Maryse Rose switched on her radio, tuned it until she found soft music from a metropolitan station, and ran her own bath. While it filled she undressed, then washed the salt and sand from her hair. Afterwards she lay in the deep bath for a long time, enjoying its sensuously perfumed water and remembering the many times she had excitedly anticipated the All Saints Eves of past years.

As a child it had been one of the few social events, like Christmas, when she had been allowed to mingle with the adult guests, and bedtime was delayed; and if she was quiet and clever, might even be forgotten. When she and Belle had grown older it had been a time of almost uncontrollable excitement, the subject of countless discussions for weeks before it took place. Most of the young men, the sons of other '*Grand Colon*' families, attended with their parents, and although the girls knew them all there were usually some, less familiar, who were just returning from schools or universities in Europe. To their disappointment the imaginary fantasies the girls created in their anticipation of the ball were seldom realized, and even if they were, inevitably faded with the dawn.

Later, as Maryse Rose began dressing, as leisurely as she had bathed, she heard the first of the guests arrive; when she finally left her room the orchestra was playing and the dance floor within the marquee and the graceful lawns of Beau Lac, were already crowded.

She was aware she had never looked more spectacular, never more a woman than a girl. The Dior gown in pale green silk had been specially imported for her, and contrasting with the pale olive skin of her arms and neck Colette's emerald bracelets and necklace, dragon's eyes of gems in light gold settings, reflected the festive lights as though they were captive night stars.

THREE

The All Saints Eve celebrations were always more exciting for Maryse Rose after midnight when the older guests had drifted towards the relative calm of the château itself, and the ball became a youthful party until daybreak. She had danced almost continuously since her arrival in the marquee earlier in the evening. Now her hair had loosened and was tangled around her shoulders, her gown felt damp with perspiration and little of the sophistication she had sought to attain as she prepared for the ball now remained. The marquee was hot and humid. The evening itself had been warm, and the activity of the dancers who crowded the marquee had raised the temperature by several more degrees. The shirts of the small orchestra on the dais were sweat-stained and they had discarded their formal jackets. Laughter, and conversations shouted above the dance music, carried far beyond the gardens of the château into the surrounding vineyards and orange groves. The air was heavy with perfumes of the dancers, and the countless flowers that decorated the tables. Waiters and waitresses bustled amongst the guests, trays of slender wine glasses balanced perilously.

She was dancing with Vincent, enjoying the effervescent thrill of his arms around her once again, and as the music ended he lifted her from her feet and swung her around until she squealed for mercy, unable to stand for dizziness. He carried her back to the table in his arms, Madelene laughingly applauding his antics.

Belle, sitting beside her latest beau, Francis Levac, the son of a neighbouring vineyard owner, glared across the table at Maryse Rose. 'Look at you, you're a mess. Do you always have to behave like an Arab?'

Madelene, in the late stage of her first pregnancy defended Maryse Rose quickly. 'Reprimand Vincent, not your sister. He's a typical male, as he gets older he becomes more juvenile.'

Vincent laughed and then ruffled his wife's tightly curled auburn hair affectionately. He examined an empty champagne bottle, shook his head in mock disapproval at Madelene, and disappeared towards the bar.

'He forgets I'm drinking for two,' explained Madelene as Maryse Rose flopped exhausted onto the seat next to her.

Maryse Rose leant forward and slipped off one of her shoes. She massaged a foot cramped by the unaccustomed height of the heels she was wearing.

'Miss Sagan . . .' A full glass of white wine was held only a few inches from her lowered face. She took it automatically as she straightened herself, but was so startled to see the soldier who had spoken to her on the Tipaza rocks that she dropped the glass onto the beechwood flooring. It shattered, spraying its contents over his trousers. She was horrified to see him frown quickly with embarrassment, and her own mind became enmeshed in his confusion. He began apologizing but she tried to stop him, desperately seizing the blame.

'No, it's my fault. I caught my elbow.' Although she was flustered his eyes were unexpectedly seductive and she felt that in some strange hypnotic manner she was being cradled by him, held in an intimate embrace, so physical that she could feel the naked warmth of his body against her. She had never experienced the feeling before and momentarily it stunned her.

41

The soldier's eyes began teasing her. 'Don't move,' he said, suddenly authoritative. He stooped beside her and she felt his hand on her foot as he replaced her shoe. His grip was strong and lingered for a moment more than was necessary. He collected the larger pieces of glass, then stood and wrapped them in a serviette before handing them to a passing waiter. His eyes met hers again. 'I should keep your shoes on, there may be a few more splinters.'

'What's happening?' Vincent placed a pair of champagne bottles on the table.

Madelene answered him, her voice bubbling with amusement. 'I'm not sure darling . . . but it's becoming quite interesting.' Her green eyes twinkled, wickedly. 'Someone did some juggling I believe, with a glass of wine.'

'I caused a slight accident,' apologized the soldier.

Madelene smiled mischievously at Vincent. 'I wouldn't say that really; more of an incident.'

'I was just clumsy,' Maryse Rose interjected quickly. It was suddenly important to her that Vincent should like the soldier and that even such a trivial reason as the broken wine glass might influence his judgement. 'And I've soaked his uniform.'

'It's really nothing,' insisted the officer.

'It's really something,' giggled Madelene. 'For heaven's sake Vincent, ask him to introduce himself before the tension becomes completely unbearable.'

The soldier straightened himself slightly, then bowed, half-formally. 'Philippe Viard, Sous-Lieutenant. I'm charmed to meet you all.' His eyes never left Maryse Rose.

Although Philippe had only fleetingly touched Maryse Rose before they began dancing together, she experienced a sense of familiarity in his arms and an unexpected euphoria which carried her far beyond the reality which surrounded her. It was so intoxicating that she did not dare question it for fear it might be lost. All she could do was to allow her emotions to be swirled along, uncontrollably, like specks of sand lifted high above the earth by a fierce desert storm.

Only much later, when he led her from the musky heat of the crowded marquee into the sobering cool of the gardens did she realize that while she had been in his arms, time, for her, had ceased to exist.

When they were in the coloured shade of the illuminated palm grove he turned her to face him and stared down into her eyes. The scar on his cheek, which had seemed so vivid when she had first met him was barely visible in the soft light.

He was about to speak, but she stopped him. 'I don't know anything about you. Only your name.'

'You know I read Jean-Paul Sartre.' There was a strongly masculine depth to his voice.

'And that you think eighteen-year-old authoresses are pretentious.'

'I apologize, my observation was facetious.' His steel grey eyes were beginning to hypnotize her again and she felt as though she was being drawn into a deep mysterious pool.

She forced herself to question him. 'But where are you from? You're not pied-noir.'

'From Caen . . . by a tortuous route. Indo China, Infantry Officers' School at Cherchell, and now the Chiffa Barracks.' He took both her hands.

She tried to keep her voice calm, normal, but his eyes held hers without movement, as if searching for the emotions she was attempting to conceal. 'Before Indo China?'

'Before Indo China is like Before Christ. It's a distant time, not a real place.'

43

She was slipping faster. 'In that time, then?'

'A mother and father who were schoolteachers. My baccalaureate, a job as a clerk in the Electricity Department's offices.' He slid his hands to the upper part of her arms, the touch of his fingers bringing unanticipated excitement. 'Do you know that you're the most beautiful woman I've ever met?'

She did not know how to answer him.

Very gently he drew her closer so that the first touch of their bodies was almost indiscernible, but to her embarrassment she heard herself gasp involuntarily. Then her body and brain seemed to divorce themselves from her control. Without movement she explored him, feeling the strength of his thighs against her, the taut plain of his lean stomach, conscious that her breasts softly yielded to his powerful torso. A million electrified nerves crowded her mind with a chaos of sensual recognition. She had never desired a man before, but now experienced a growing urgency to possess him, a need for him to caress and satisfy her, to become a part of her.

She knew he wanted to kiss her, but the gardens were too crowded. People wandered the paths amongst the trees. Not far away on the trampled lawn a pair of tipsy youths, stripped to their waists, were wrestling, encouraged by the shouts and jeers of their friends. From somewhere in the palm grove she could hear singing.

She wished she were alone with Philippe in the solitude of the night beach at Tipaza where the golden autumn moonlight would be romantic, the crests of silent waves phosphorescent, spinning blue fire towards the sand.

He seemed to read her mind and understand, sharing her need. 'We could drive somewhere. Your home perhaps? Or do you have a chaperone . . . or someone with you?'

'Of course not. But I am at home.'

44

'Here?' He sounded puzzled, and she remembered that Vincent had introduced herself and Madelene only by their christian names.

'I'm Maryse Rose Charpentier.'

He said: 'Oh!' softly.

'Why oh?' She sensed that he had withdrawn from her a little, as though she had somehow offended him.

Before he could answer, the night sky beyond the estate barns was split by a vast pillar of scarlet flame. The ground quivered abruptly and the sudden shock of an explosion blasted the still air. A woman screamed. There was momentary silence which was ended by a long burst of machine-gun fire.

It was so unexpected that Maryse Rose's mind could not identify the danger. Philippe Viard collected her in his arms so forcefully that her breath was crushed from her lungs. She felt herself lifted from her feet and hurled through the branches of a group of small shrubs at the foot of the palm trees. Philippe's body cushioned her fall, but then his weight pressed her deep into the moist earth.

There was a second explosion, briefer and sharper than the first, followed by the distant rattle of stones and debris falling on the roman-tiled roofs of the barns. Philippe's arms tightened around her as she instinctively struggled to free herself. 'Don't move. Lie still.' The hubbub of sound in the marquee was abruptly silenced.

'What's happening?' Her mind seemed to have emptied with shock and she was conscious only of his body against her own, a protective barrier.

'*Fellagha.*' He used the local expression for Arab rebels. 'What's beyond those farm buildings, near the road?'

She forced herself to concentrate. 'A gendarmerie. Not very large, just a few men.' As she spoke one of the cars parked in the château drive revved into life and was accelerated wildly out onto the road, its engine roaring, its wheels skidding noisily.

'Damned fools,' Philippe swore softly. Another couple ran towards a vehicle. Philippe shouted at them: 'Get down, and stay down.' They obeyed him, dropping to the ground beneath the palms. As they did so the lights illuminating the marquee, lawns and palm grove were simultaneously extinguished, plunging the château and its gardens into darkness. 'About time,' he breathed.

'Can we do anything?' Maryse Rose asked. The muscles of her stomach seemed to have contracted. She wanted to be sick.

'Just pray,' said Philippe, grimly. 'There's nothing else we can do. With luck the gendarmerie will have telephoned for help . . . unless the lines were cut.' He paused. Unarmed, he realized there was no way he could assist them. 'There is something *we* could do,' he whispered, thoughtfully.

She began to say: 'What . . .' But as her mouth formed the question, his lips silenced her.

Her resistance was more in her mind than physical, but it seemed to her somehow blasphemous to enjoy his embrace when only a few hundred yards away someone might be dying. But after only a moment, sensing her reluctance, he moved his head so that she was cradled like a child against his shoulder, held securely in his arms.

Within twenty minutes, although it seemed a lifetime for those guests huddled within the marquee or scattered through the palm grove, a military truck carrying a section of young conscripts and their lieutenant lumbered into the château drive and crunched to a halt on the gravel of the turning circle in front of the entrance. A powerful searchlight on the cab roof swung a slow arc of light across the lawns, pausing briefly on each group of crumpled and now icily sober guests, as though its concealed operator was relishing their discomfort.

No guests remained to enjoy the traditional dawn breakfast at Beau Lac. The debris of the night, overturned tables, scattered possessions, bottles, glasses, all the paraphernalia of the ball, lay forlornly as it had been abandoned; only serviettes and paper decorations stirred in the cool morning breeze not yet warmed by the early sun.

Once the grounds and vineyards had been searched by the military patrols, the guests had hurriedly left, fearing for the safety of children or families who had remained at home.

Three of the four gendarmes manning the Hadjout gendarmerie a few hundred yards from Beau Lac had been killed during the rebel attack. To the Charpentier family's horror they learnt that the body of the fourth gendarme had been found only a quarter of a mile farther down the road, bound naked to a telegraph pole by a length of barbed wire; his throat had been cut. All the weapons and ammunition stored in the gendarmerie had been stolen. There appeared to be no rebel casualties nor any sign of the attackers themselves. Leaflets had been scattered throughout the Arab bidonville, and had been nailed to almost every tree along the roadside, proclaiming the intentions of the FLN; national independence by every means until their goal was realized.

As soon as it had become apparent that the rebels had fled, Philippe and three other Tirailleur officers who had been guests at the ball had returned to their unit. There had been barely time for Maryse Rose to bid Philippe goodbye. He had paused momentarily, to wave to her, before sprinting in the direction of a jeep which waited, its engine revving, near the drive gates.

The early morning news bulletin on Radio Algiers confirmed that the uprising was on a far larger scale than any previously experienced. In Algiers itself there had been an attempt to blow up a gasometer and several public buildings; police posts and barracks had been attacked in the city and throughout the country; telephone lines between Kabylia, the Aurés and Algiers were cut in numerous places. Food and tobacco stores had been destroyed and a number of villages in the more mountainous areas had been isolated by the rebels. The French army was already in action.

It was inconceivable to Maryse Rose, as to every other member of her pieds-noir family, that the uprising signalled only the beginning of a long and bitter war. The leaflets dispersed throughout the country by the rebels on All Saints Night, and the proclamations made on their behalf by radio stations in Egypt, Morocco and Tunisia were treated as little more than a joke.

Life barely changed at Beau Lac. In the cities and the towns there were the inevitable reprisals by the pieds-noir, and for days the newspapers were filled with reports of the violence. But Beau Lac, once the shock of the nearby attack had lessened, seemed a peaceful oasis. The constrictions on the younger members of the Charpentier family and their friends, were not only those raised by caution but also by the inclement weather. The Indian summer had been brief, and as if to compensate for its pleasures by mid-November it had become cold and wet with heavy mists blanketing the Mitidja plain, concealing the mountains behind a dreary grey curtain.

Maryse Rose had assumed Philippe would contact her within a few hours of their parting. He did not do so. For the first two or three days she justified his negligence to herself with excuses that he must be on duty, that the

48

telephone connection with the Chiffa Barracks must have been destroyed, or worse, perhaps he was ill.

Her mind retraced every moment she had spent in his company, analyzing every remembered word, his touch, the way he had held and excited her, protected her during the attack, the manner in which his eyes had seemed to penetrate deep inside her to touch her most secret thoughts. She had never considered love before, but now it dominated her thoughts even though she attempted to deny it.

To conceal the reason for the unaccustomed moods which assailed her, bringing her oddly mixed feelings of contentment and sadness, even tears of loneliness and frustration, and to escape Belle's taunts and cruel observations, she feigned sickness, but the solitude of her room did not help: it only lengthened the tedious days.

Gradually, she began to feel hurt and then resentment. Philippe had awakened emotions in her which he was obviously unprepared to fulfil. Perhaps he had acted deliberately, cruelly, to enjoy sadistically the stirrings he had created and which she in childish naivity had believed. She felt he had betrayed her.

Her anger carried her back to the world she had previously enjoyed, the parties and dances that increased in number as the Christmas festive season drew closer, and the planning of one of the family's bi-annual trips to France. Now that she was eighteen she would accompany them and be able to update her wardrobe in the fashionable salons, enjoy the latest productions of the Paris theatres and the hectic social life of her aunt and uncle at their house in Parc Kahn.

Five weeks passed. The day was boring her. There was a tea dance at the Club Anglais which she and a group of friends would attend later that afternoon, but now it was raining, a heavy and oppressive near-tropical downpour that hammered against the windows of the library room at Beau Lac in which she sat reading. The book was *L'Humanité*, the first of de Gaulle's war memoirs, and she was reading it reluctantly; for the past weeks it seemed to be the main subject of conversation at every dinner party she attended. She was finding the book an educational chore rather than a pleasure.

She heard the sound of tyres on the gravel of the drive, but ignored it; vehicles frequently called at Beau Lac and it could be her father returning from a meeting of the Assembly or Belle from her lunch date with Francis Levac.

Ismail, the senior house servant knocked softly on the library door before entering. He had a quiet discreet manner which had earned him the family nickname of 'the undertaker'. He was always polite, courteous, but rarely smiled. Slightly built, he had the hawkish features of the desert Arabs. 'Miss Maryse Rose. A Lieutenant Viard has arrived. Do you wish that I should show him in here?' Guests were rarely entertained in the library.

Philippe! Her initial reaction was one of astonishment. Just as her emotions had calmed he had returned, perhaps to torment her further. The anger which had grown to conceal the deep hurt she had experienced swelled fiercely. She slammed her book closed. Difficult as it might be, Maryse Rose knew she must steel herself to tolerate Philippe's company, determined that the ordeal would be as brief as possible. 'I'll see him in here.'

Ismail acknowledged her request with a slight bow of his head. 'I shall bring tea in five minutes.'

'No,' she said angrily. 'Don't bother. He won't be staying.'

She had only seconds to compose herself before Philippe would enter the room! She must seem indifferent, cold. Why had he come now? It would have been better never to have seen him again. Damn him! She was suddenly conscious that she was wearing no make-up, and a pair of her oldest but most comfortable slacks and a sloppy sweater. Had he come a little later she would have been changed, ready for the tea dance.

'Hello, Maryse Rose.'

He was standing in the doorway, his uniform soaking wet and dripping onto the parquet flooring. He looked as though he had just emerged from a river, thinner than she had remembered, and his face more deeply tanned. His hair was cut so short it seemed he had shaved his head.

He saw her staring at his clothing and spoke, quickly, apologetically. 'I'm in a Jeep. I got caught by the rain . . . no waterproofs. It was like riding a surfboard.'

Maryse Rose had expected her anger to increase when she faced Philippe. It did not. Instead, she felt momentarily that somehow she should mother him, scold him perhaps for risking a chill. I'm stupid she decided. I thought I hated him, but I don't. But I mustn't weaken. She tossed her hair back with a jerk of her head and made her voice icy: 'You should have chosen a better day to drive here. Our autumn was far more pleasant,' she added sarcastically.

'I came as soon as I got back. Just threw my kit into my quarters, then scrounged the vehicle. I've been worried about you; I didn't know what was happening back here.'

Was he acting? Her anger returned explosively. 'Then why haven't you telephoned me? Why haven't you written? Why haven't you . . . anything?' She held the book she had been reading towards him, her hand shaking. 'I'm not one of these, just something you can pick up and lay down as you wish.' She stood and hurled the book across the room. 'You were worried! What about other people's feelings? What about my feelings?' Oh God, she thought instantly, why did I have to say all

51

that? Now he knows that he hurt me. I should have stayed calm and given myself time to think.

Philippe moved closer. 'You've every right to be upset,' he said, softly. 'But not with me. I don't have the independence of a civilian. I have to go where I'm ordered, when I'm ordered. I hoped you'd understand.' He paused for a moment, his grey eyes meeting her own in their hypnotic inquisitive way. 'Two hours after I left you on All Saints Day, my regiment was on its way to Kabylia. That's where I've been until this morning.' He hesitated again. 'I haven't slept in a bed nor eaten off a table in five weeks.'

She was no longer able to sustain her anger. 'But the telephone . . .'

'There were none in the *djebel*, and the lines to the villages have all been cut. We kept in touch with our base by radio.' He was holding a damp package which he now offered her as sheepishly as a schoolboy offering his first flowers to a girl. 'It's not much, but it's all I could find.'

She unwrapped the small parcel carefully, peeling away the soggy wrapping. Silver glinted in the dull afternoon light. It was an antique Arab bracelet, finely engraved, and set with a single row of coral beads so deep scarlet in colour that they seemed to be drops of blood. 'It's very beautiful.' Unintentionally, he had reminded her of her Arab parentage. Few pieds-noir women would wear native jewellery, but she knew she would always treasure this piece.

'These are yours, too.' He fumbled in his tunic pocket and handed her a bundle of envelopes; the ink had run on the wet paper. 'They're letters I wrote to you. I couldn't post them, so I've brought them in person. I wrote whenever I could.' Again there was the hint of schoolboy shyness in his explanation. 'Sometimes while we were resting on patrol; mostly in the evening. I'm afraid some of them are written with a pencil.' She had begun opening one, but he stopped her. 'Don't read them now; read them later.'

He was standing in front of her, less than a yard away, hesitant, as though unable to take the final step that separated them. She knew that somehow she had to help him, help them both. She held the bracelet towards him. 'You must put it on for me.'

He slipped the bracelet gently over her wrist, drew her closer to him. 'I'm soaking wet.'

'I don't mind.' She could smell the warm masculine scent of his rain-damp uniform, and as he kissed her, holding her so tightly that she could feel the moistness of his clothing against the skin of her breasts. The hurt, and loneliness of the past weeks seemed to be drawn from her body.

The day was a kaleidoscope of emotion for her. They ran from the château together, hand in hand, into the torrential rain which instantly plastered their hair to their faces, their clothing to their bodies. They drove laughing, sitting close against each other in the open Jeep, spray lashing the vehicle on the flooded roads, to the deserted Roman town where the olive and orange trees beat the air like flails against the background of the rain-veiled waves.

They raced each other through the worn cobbled streets to the wet sands, waded to their waists in a sea that was warmer than the air, tasted salt on skin in breathless kisses. Their conversation was noisy, exuberant, shouted, overheard only by the sleek terns skimming the shallows at the water's edge.

Neither of them wanted the day to end. They gathered windfall oranges and found shelter in the weathered arch of an ancient temple. She peeled the fruit, the juice mingling with the rain on her hands as she fed the rich flesh to Philippe. When they kissed again, holding each other close and finding comfort in the warmth of their bodies, the kisses no longer tasted of salt, but were sweet and aromatic.

The need to escape with each other remained as the hidden sun faded through the dusk, and the early night became still, silent, dark.

They read each other's thoughts and desires in the tenderness of caresses, so that when Philippe drove the Jeep again it was not towards Beau Lac but Chiffa and the gorge. As they reached the foothills the cloud began to break and a ripe moon cast its romantic light on the majestic forest-clad slopes of the mountain range.

She did not know where he was taking her, nor did she care as long as they remained together. The mountain air was cold, cutting through her wet clothing, and the lights of The Citadelle were inviting as Philippe swung the Jeep into its forecourt; the hotel was almost deserted. During the summer months it was a popular tourist stop, but in autumn and winter was busy only at weekends. Isolated, it stood majestically on a promontory of brown rock which hung above the depths of the gorge, trees and shrubs softening its fortress-like design.

Briefly she wondered how Philippe would explain their dishevelled appearance, the fact that they had no luggage. But as she began to step from the Jeep he caught her in his arms and carried her into the hotel.

An Arab guard leapt from a seat to offer assistance. At the reception desk, a French clerk dozed but was startled into life by their arrival.

Philippe gave him no time. 'We've been drenched by a cloudburst. We'd like a room.'

'Of course, sir.' The clerk's eyes read the uniform badges, identified Philippe's rank, and examined the girl in his arms. 'Your wife, sir?' He spoke with concern, assuming illness.

'Freezing to death!'

Maryse Rose concealed a smile.

The clerk snapped orders to the porter in abrupt Arabic, then slid keys across the desk.

Philippe's strength enthralled her as he carried her up the flight of shallow stairs from the reception area, the porter scurrying to keep ahead. She felt like a bride as he carried her into the room.

Each detail of the room within The Citadelle, like every precious moment of that night, was destined to remain forever in her mind. The paper on the walls was pale gold, embossed with swirling leaf designs; the paintwork, the wardrobes, bedside cupboards and even the head and foot of the bed itself, were coffee-cream, delicately lined and scrolled in sepia. The wall lights were exotic shells, bound in engraved brass and matching the small sparkling Venetian chandelier. The curtains and the coverlet of the bed were chocolate velvet and on the floor beside the bed were Arab hand-woven rugs, garish in the room's peaceful setting, bright squares and diamonds, crimson, blue, fawn, green. And when they were alone, Philippe gently undressed her.

It was so natural, so uncomplicated, that her mind accepted it without questioning. The room was warm after the cold drive in the open Jeep, but even so her skin felt chilled and coarsened by fine goose-pimples on her arms as he removed her wet clothing.

There had been times when she had wondered what it might be like to be naked with her first lover; she had anticipated embarrassment, perhaps mingled with the excitement or impatience of romance. Now she felt none of these emotions, but was calm and at ease.

She was momentarily surprised that he did not kiss her but instead led her by the hand to the bathroom and turned on the shower, testing the water. There was sudden but brief resentment at the realization he was treating her as a child not a woman, and instinctively she pulled away from him, but he held her firmly, the quick anger in her eyes amusing him. 'I'm not prepared to risk you getting pneumonia. You're frozen.'

He adjusted the shower controls then steadied her beneath the hot spray until he felt her relax, then he left her.

The heat of the water flowed through her veins bringing hedonistic comfort. She turned to face the spray, and as she did so felt his arms around her.

They stood together beneath the shower as they had done in the torrential rain of the ancient town that afternoon, but now they were both naked and she could feel the hardness of his lean body against her own soft flesh.

As he towelled her dry she realized that his touch had become more sensual, that his hands were finding the sensitive parts of her body, lingering, caressing, seeking her breasts, nipples, the rounded curves of her hips, buttocks.

She became conscious of her nakedness then, and of her own body, as though before it had been shielded from him by innocence. Questions and uncertainty flickered in her mind. Vincent had once called her scrawny, perhaps Philippe was finding her unattractively thin? Her thoughts swirled in a confused turmoil. How should she respond to his touch? If she did nothing, then he might think she was frigid; but she had nothing to guide her other than the night-time chat of the strict Catholic dormitory, the hinted ecstasies within the novels she had read and the gossip and inferences of her friends. Everything she knew, or thought she had known, was second-hand, probably exaggerated, useless to her now.

There was even a bewildering hint of fear in her mind, for unlike most of the young men amongst her friends, she knew that Philippe would never allow her to dominate him, not even in play. He was strong, mentally as well as physically, and the muscles she could feel beneath her hands rippled like those of a hunting animal, while the air surrounding her seemed to vibrate and throb with his vitality.

Other fears emerged, to dwindle or swell amongst the storm of emotions she was experiencing. She was hating her naivety while praying he would understand that she was giving herself to him, completely and for the first time to any man.

As he had so easily carried her to the room, he carried her to the bed, his lips still against her own. His hands explored her until her already turbulent thoughts became a swirling tempest in which reason and emotions became a chaos of passion.

She felt him open her, his fingertips provoking sensations she had not known existed, galvanic, rapturous, overpowering, concentrating every atom of her being in the one minute area of her impatient body.

She had feared the time when a man would first enter her, but now she was unable to identify that moment in the discomposed eruption of desire and excitement. She was aware only that their bodies were united, their flesh one flesh, their breath linked in long kisses, their limbs entwined. And inside her, she could feel him.

She did not awaken early the next day, but when she did so it was to an horrific nightmare.

She heard the bedside telephone ring and then Philippe answer it. His conversation was brief, muffled by her drowsiness. She felt him swing himself from the bed and heard him dressing.

'What's the matter?' She opened her eyes and sleepily watched him examine himself in front of the mirror. His uniform was crumpled, untidy, splashed with mud.

He glanced at her wryly. 'Something about the Jeep. I have to go down. I won't be long.' He crossed to the bed, leant over her and kissed her, 'I love you.'

She smiled up at him. 'You told me last night. A hundred times.' His words made her feel warm and secure.

He kissed her again.

When he had gone she stretched herself luxuriously, and let her mind relive the tender moments of their past hours together. Philippe had been so gentle, leading her carefully along the unexplored paths. She could find nothing to regret; there had been no misunderstandings, no terrors, no hurt, only the growing strength and depth of their love for each other.

There was a knock at the bedroom door, so positive and determined that it startled her. She assumed that Philippe had forgotten to take the room key with him.

Forcing away her drowsiness she wrapped the coverlet around her shoulders and hurried to welcome the sensual comfort of his arms around her once again, and the exciting touch of his lips against her own. But instead of Philippe a white-helmeted military police officer faced her, his mouth and jaw set taut by anticipation. His cold eyes examined her partial nakedness.

'Miss Charpentier?' His voice was as metallic as his eyes, slicing into her mind like the sharp blade of a knife.

She heard a threat in the tone of his voice which shocked her. She attempted to force the door closed, but he wedged it with his foot.

'Get dressed at once.' He spoke as if he were giving an order to a prisoner.

Shielded from his harsh stare by the door she attempted to find reason in the insanity of the situation. 'Where is Philippe Viard?'

'Lieutenant Viard has been detained.' He softened his voice a little. 'Put some clothes on, please.'

Detained? Did he mean arrested? Why? What was happening? Her mind filled with questions. The idyllic sense of love and security in which she had luxuriated only minutes ago had been replaced by stark panic and disbelief. 'What have you done with him? Why have you come here?'

'Lieutenant Viard will be charged with the unauthorized use of a military vehicle,' the military police officer explained. 'I have personal orders to escort you to your home.'

Anger began to replace the deep feeling of assault she had experienced. 'You have no right to come in here. I do not need an escort.'

The officer's voice regained its authoritative robotic tone. 'Take care. Consider yourself very fortunate that someone has already interceded on your behalf. You've caused us a lot of trouble. Every unit in the area has been searching for you since yesterday evening.'

Maryse Rose was totally unprepared for the scale of the storm which she faced on her arrival at Beau Lac. Her father, mother and Vincent were waiting on the steps of the château as the military truck drew up beneath them. Belle stared from one of the drawing-room windows and Maryse Rose could see the faces of the servants at others.

She could never remember Christian Charpentier so furious before; normally his displeasure showed in an icy coolness beyond which even his political enemies failed to goad him. But after he had thanked the officer who had returned Maryse Rose, he ordered her curtly indoors.

He did not wait until they were alone to berate her, but for the first time in her life did so publicly. It was so unexpected that shame numbed her and drained away what little confidence she had managed to retain as the military truck approached the château. The stern glare of disapproval she could see in Vincent's eyes gave her no comfort and Belle was visibly gloating. Maryse Rose had disgraced them all, her father told her, furiously. Through her irresponsibility she had tortured those who cared for her most. And far worse, as the daughter of one of the most respected and devout Catholic families of the Department she had committed a cardinal sin, and in such a manner that it had already become public knowledge. Within hours it was bound to become the subject for every social gossip in Algiers.

None of the family had slept the previous night. Vincent, who had recently moved back to Algiers, had left the heavily pregnant Madelene, despite the imminence of her labour, to drive to Beau Lac after midnight to help search for Maryse Rose. They had been less concerned then for her moral safety than for her life. That afternoon there had been two bomb explosions in the city, and an army patrol had been ambushed by the FLN only twenty miles from the château during the early evening; all the incidents had been reported on Radio Algiers. When Maryse Rose had failed to return home as darkness fell and Belle had informed them that she had left Beau Lac in a military Jeep, the family had at once feared the worst. Adding to the family's fears was the knowledge that less than six weeks previously two young civilian school teachers had been shot to death by terrorists. The single military vehicle in which Maryse Rose was travelling at night, would surely invite attack.

In desperation, Christian Charpentier had contacted Colonel Henri Lefitte and then Vincent, who had been

60

able to identify the regiment of the officer with whom Maryse Rose had disappeared. Vincent, on his arrival at Beau Lac, had telephoned Philippe Viard's company commander, with whom Vincent had served during his own military service. But apart from the city of Algiers itself, it had been virtually impossible for the military to search the surrounding countryside at night, and the only consolation the family had was that all patrols in the region, and every gendarmerie, had been informed of the missing couple and given the identification number of the Jeep. The first dawn patrol between Chiffa and Medea, had discovered the vehicle in the forecourt of The Cita- delle.

It was only when the family were informed that Maryse Rose was safe, and their first deep feelings of relief dimin- ished, that anger had replaced concern in Christian's mind.

Despite Maryse Rose's tearful apologies, and her at- tempts to explain that the night with Philippe had been an expression of their love for each other, Christian remained adamant; she was forbidden to see Philippe Viard again. Furthermore, as the incident had brought home to her father and mother the difficulty of protecting their daugh- ters in Algeria while the uprising continued, both were to be sent to stay with relatives in France as soon as arrangements to travel could be made.

Belle protested vehemently, feeling that she was being punished yet again for Maryse Rose's irresponsibility. To infuriate her further she was to be separated from her own lover, Francis Levac, at what she considered a critical moment in their relationship. She was certain that in the next few months he would propose to her. The jealousy she had always felt towards Maryse Rose turned to hatred.

FOUR

For Maryse Rose to have claimed that she disliked Paris
would have been a lie. Her Aunt Isabelle, her mother's
oldest sister, and her uncle, Claude de L'Ormeraye, were
charming hosts, and their Napoleonic mansion at Parc
Kahn with its view of the Seine and close proximity to
the fashionable Longchamps racecourse, was a hive of
frequent social gatherings. The place was already familiar
to Belle and Maryse Rose; they had stayed there many
times throughout their lives and Maryse Rose had spent
most of her holidays there while at finishing school. She
was fond too, of her aunt and uncle. Unlike most of the
Charpentier relatives they rarely made her conscious of
her ancestry. By Algerian standards they were liberal and
cosmopolitan, although it was obvious now that they had
been informed of Maryse Rose's fall from grace. Their
own children, two sons and a daughter, had all left home;
the daughter to marry an American in Boston, while one
son was a director of a branch of the family export
company in Marseilles, the other similarly placed on the
board in the Hong Kong offices. Isabelle and Claude de
L'Ormeraye welcomed the return of young voices to their
home.

It soon became obvious to the aunt and uncle that there
was no love lost between Belle and Maryse Rose; the
young women were no company for each other, and
clearly sought to avoid each other if it were possible. As
the weeks developed into months without any improve-

ment in their relationship, the de L'Ormerayes were forced to accept that the deep rift between them was serious enough to be irreparable, despite all their efforts. Even a month in Chamonix for skiing had not helped; the two girls spent the time with separate groups, meeting only when they accompanied their aunt and uncle to meals or parties.

The misery which Maryse Rose had felt both at losing Philippe and leaving Algeria, stayed with her, the Parisian winter making her even more depressed, so that she longed each day for the African sun.

From the moment that Philippe had left her in the bedroom at The Citadelle, she had heard nothing of him. It was as though he had been spirited away ... had perhaps never existed, except in her dreams or the memories she cherished in the present nightmare.

Only the letters he had written during his weeks on patrol maintained the reality of his love. She read each of them until she knew them by heart, sharing the loneliness he had experienced and adding to it her own. There were times of anger and hurt, and of deep despair when she hated the flippancy of Paris and its inhabitants. Sometimes morbid thoughts of death invaded her mind, forcing her to scan the casualty lists in the morning newspapers, terrified that she would see his name.

At first she had been comforted by the thought that somehow their love, now consummated, must eventually bring them together. It seemed impossible to her that such a strength of emotion could fail to do so. But as the time passed and he failed to contact her she began to feel that it was hopeless.

Belle, however, slipped easily into the social whirl of the French metropolis, renewing friendships of her own schooldays, making more through the contacts of the de L'Ormerayes. Her diary was filled with engagements.

63

For Maryse Rose the weeks and days dragged by uselessly. She lingered in her bed in the mornings, took an unnecessarily long time to bath and dress herself, drank slow coffee in the breakfast room and walked her aunt's two spaniels in the Bois de Boulogne until lunchtime. In the afternoon she visited the galleries, churches, shops; usually alone, but sometimes with her aunt. The feeling that she was wasting her life away, grew.

For a time, there seemed to be little official news from Algeria. 'A humorous revolution' was how one of the newspapers referred to the uprising. The fall of the Mendes-France government pushed it even further into the background in the minds of the Parisians and only rarely did the cinema newsreels bother to report what was usually referred to as 'minor incidents in the Algerian Department'. Had it not been for the letters from her father and mother, and occasionally those from Vincent and Madelene, or her closer friends in Algeria, all would have seemed well, making her exile even less bearable.

She had never before considered working. In Algeria it would have been unthinkable for the daughter of one of the wealthiest settlers, and Christian would have forbidden it as fiercely as he had denied her Philippe. Now she began to think of it as a way to ease her increasing frustration.

She scanned the advertisement pages of the newspapers. The thought of working in a shop embarrassed her, and as she was unable to type and had no idea how an office was organized there was no hope of her finding work as a secretary. From the job descriptions in the crowded columns she was too old for a junior clerk and had no experience to become a senior one. It was the distant sound of an ambulance bell which had made up her mind; she would train as a nurse.

The faint amusement which her aunt had shown towards Maryse Rose's announcement that she intended to find work, hardly extended to nursing. She had not realized that her niece was serious when she had first raised the subject. According to Isabelle de L'Ormeraye boredom was to be expected at times and was an inevitable part of a woman's life, and just as it was possible to shake off a winter cold so boredom eventually passed. Besides, how could Maryse Rose be bored in such a city as Paris, where an attractive young woman from a good family was inundated with social invitations? Work was for a quite different class of woman, something to be driven to in financial desperation, and then only acceptable if it was a 'respectable kind of profession'.

Aunt Isabelle tutted in disbelief, shaking her dramatically coiffured head in bewilderment. 'Why not enjoy yourself, like Belle?' she asked, her carefully mascarared eyes moistening at the thought of such an attractive young girl wasting herself behind the walls of some common institution.

Her husband Claude raised his eyes from the morning's newspaper. 'Rubbish! Let her do something useful.' His slightly wavy hair, greying at the temples, and his gold-framed glasses, gave him a distinguished legal appearance.

'What on earth will Christian think?' asked Isabelle, despairingly. 'And Colette will be mortified.'

Claude folded the newspaper on his lap, took off his glasses and slipped them into a slim leather case. 'This is not the eighteenth century Isabelle, and we don't lock our daughters away any more. I think it's a good idea that Maryse Rose should find work, if she wishes.' He glanced around the high-ceilinged room, with its tall windows and elegant empire period furnishings. 'If I was Maryse Rose, I'd probably feel as though I were imprisoned in a morgue. Our own children always did.'

Isabelle smiled at him weakly. 'Yes, perhaps. But darling
. . . nursing!'

To Maryse Rose's amazement she was accepted at her
first interview, and less than a week after she had made
the decision to apply began as a student at the International Hospital only a short walk from Saint Cloud.

In proportions and design, the hospital seemed more
closely related to the ancient Bastille than to a modern
medical centre, and justified her Aunt Isabelle's worse
fears. Built by public subscription before the First World
War, it was uncompromisingly utilitarian. A shallow,
grey-slate roof sat upon four storeys of shiny red brick,
set in a large rectangle of concrete in which subsequent
subscriptions and grants had allowed the board of gover-
nors to build additional wards, laboratories, garages and
extensions. Staff quarters, with the appearance of yet
another prison block, were placed behind the main building across a yard which looked like a military parade
ground and echoed every footstep.

The hours of study were long, but for Maryse Rose the
days at last began to speed by. The work was so hard, often
distasteful and menial, but she overcame the revulsion she
sometimes felt. And as her aunt and uncle had insisted
she continued to live at Parc Kahn rather than in the
student nurse's quarters at the hospital, she usually arrived home exhausted and barely capable of showering
before collapsing on her bed.

She quickly realized that it was virtually impossible to
conceal her family background from her fellow students.
Even though her conversation was smattered by the Arab
words which the pieds-noir used without thought in their
speech, her accent was well-educated, and the most casual
of her clothes were of good quality. But she was soon
accepted. Now, the only luxury she permitted herself

was a small 2CV Citroen which she purchased from her savings, and which she used to explore the countryside beyond the city on her free days.

In August of 1955, the Algerian war flared into sudden prominence with a number of sickening massacres in and around Philippeville. Until then comparatively few civilians had been killed, but in a single day seventy-one European settlers; men, women and children were horribly killed and mutilated. Houses in the small mining town of El-Halia were literally awash with blood. For the 'poor whites' amongst the settler population, many who had no family connections remaining in any European country, migration was not only impossible, but unthinkable.

They retaliated, forming vigilante groups and executing suspected Muslims without trial. The French army's crack regiments hunted gangs of rebels throughout the region.

The FLN, developing as the major Algerian nationalist organization, issued stern orders regarding the treatment of Muslims who remained loyal to the French. 'Kill them . . . take their children and kill them. Kill all those who pay taxes and all those who collect them. Burn the houses of Muslim NCO's who are away on active service with the French army. Kill any person attempting to deflect the militants.'

Maryse Rose was totally absorbed in her studies, delighting in the mental stimulation it provided. The months hurried past and during 1956 the war in Algeria escalated further. The handful of rebels who had led the uprising on All Saints Day now numbered 20,000. The FLN absorbed or eliminated its rival groups and reorganized itself. Amongst the civilian casualties was the Mayor of Algiers, Amedée Froger, shot as he left his house in the rue

Michelin. Five hundred and fifty members of the French security services were also killed; one thousand farms were destroyed, and with them ten thousand acres of crops and four million vines.

But instead of the FLN's successes intimidating the settlers, it hardened them, drew them into closer-knit communities. They fortified their estates, enclosing them in high barbed wire fences, arming their guards and training their families in the use of weapons.

Vincent and Madelene, with their young son, now almost two-years-old, sold their villa in the Algiers suburbs, which had become too dangerous and returned to live at Beau Lac. Vincent never left the château without a pistol either in his waistband or in the glove compartment of his car, whilst a small armoury of shotguns and sporting rifles were now always kept inside Beau Lac itself.

As they had always done, Christian and Colette Charpentier visited France twice a year, spending part of that time in Paris with the de L'Ormerayes, Belle and Maryse Rose. Despite early difficulties it soon became obvious to Maryse Rose that Christian's anger was tempered by his love for her and that she had been forgiven. Her exile, and that of Belle, was now based solely on the dangers their parents saw for them in Algeria. But as her Aunt Isabelle had foreseen, they did not approve of her nursing training, and it was only the intervention of Claude de L'Ormeraye that persuaded them to allow it to continue. Nevertheless, the weeks of their visits were enjoyable and at times Maryse Rose even regretted her work which demanded so many of the hours she would have liked to spend with them.

Her months in France were teaching her far more than simply nursing. They had enabled her to consider her country's problems from new viewpoints. In Algeria she would never have dreamed of reading either socialist or Arab newspapers; they would not have been permitted in Beau Lac. Here, in Paris, she read everything, digesting every fragment of news from the Department. And just as Christian was able to play a part in the community with his political activity, she had become determined to make a more sensible use of her life when it became possible. Just what form this would take she had not yet decided, but there were many possibilities in Algeria for someone with a State Diploma in nursing.

Her second full year in Paris was punctuated by examinations, the now convivial family visits and then the long Parisian winter when the de L'Ormerayes and Belle made their annual pilgrimage to Chamonix; this time Maryse Rose did not accompany them, not only was it impossible for her to arrange the necessary time off from her studies, but she was finding Belle's increasingly predatory behaviour towards any man to whom she was introduced, embarrassing. Belle seemed to be scrambling from one brief affair to another in a desperate attempt to avoid spinsterhood. Francis Levac wrote to her infrequently, and although she made a great show of her pleasure at receiving the letters, and hinted at their contents, the relationship seemed to be stagnating.

There were still occasions when Maryse Rose's thoughts returned to Philippe, and when they did so she was conscious that without him a part of her must remain empty for ever; the love and passion which she had experienced with him would remain unique in her lifetime. But time itself was healing, and now she was seldom lonely. Amongst the students and nursing staff of the International Hospital there was always something to celebrate, although most of the young nurses needed no excuse to hold a party.

*

It was 6.15 am on a July morning in 1957, six weeks before her final examination. The sun was already warm when she was allowed off duty and left the hospital. She was tired; it had been a long night, one when the monotony of routine had been more exhausting than the emergencies which could sometimes occur.

With her were three other students, one of them French, the others an Armenian and a Moroccan; they had all begun their training within a few days of each other, and normally, in the fine weather, they walked to the Metro together. For the first year of their training, the Moroccan girl, Tatiana and the Armenian, Helene, had lived in the students' quarters behind the grim hospital block. Once their probationary period had been completed they had found themselves an apartment at Courbevoie. They were a boisterous friendly couple who had spent so much time in each other's company that they reacted like twin sisters.

The road towards the Metro at Saint Cloud was dirty and noisy, and at this time of the day was busy with trucks and delivery vehicles bringing produce from the west to the shops and markets of the city. Along one section of the road, on its wide pavement, were the market stalls, already busy and cluttering the gutters with scrap boxes, waste paper, discarded vegetables, the salesmen chatting loudly, calling their wares to passers-by. In competition with them and only a few yards away were the shops, small, heavily-stocked; bakers, confectioners, butchers, tobacconists, and the cafés; their tables on the busy pavement pressed back against their dusty windows.

Usually the students stopped at one of the cafés; it gave them an opportunity to relax and chat for a few minutes before they went their different ways at Saint Cloud station. They sat at one of the tables; most were already occupied by men drinking small dark coffees, dipping their lumps of sugar into glasses of cheap brandy.

At the next table to the girls were three young men, all in their early twenties, obviously Arab. They were smartly but casually dressed; not street traders and too informal to be clerks; possibly students. Maryse Rose noticed them only briefly. Paris was full of people of a hundred nationalities, and Arabs could be from a dozen different countries.

A waiter took the girls' orders. Thérèse, the French nurse, began talking of the previous night's work in her ward. One of the three young Arabs turned slightly in his chair and made a comment to Helene. Maryse Rose, listening to Thérèse ignored them. By the time the waiter returned with their coffees, both Helene and Tatiana were involved in animated discussion with the three Arabs.

After a few minutes one of the Arabs interrupted Thérèse and spoke to Maryse Rose. 'You are from Algeria.' It was a statement, not a question.

Thérèse stopped in mid-sentence. Maryse Rose answered the man coolly, resenting his intrusion. 'Yes.' She turned to face Thérèse again.

'I am Algerian, as well,' said the Arab. He moved his chair between the two girls. Thérèse shrugged hopelessly.

Maryse Rose was about to order the man away but as she faced him found herself held by his eyes. They were intense, dark eyes; eyes that reminded her instantly of the passionate race she had left behind.

'She said you were from Algeria.' The man jerked his head in the direction of Helene. 'You are all nurses?'

'Tired student nurses.' Maryse Rose glanced at his hands. They were smooth, well-manicured. His clothes were clean and pressed. He was obviously not one of the thousands of Algerians who laboured in France sweeping streets, mending roads, digging ditches.

71

'You've worked all night?'

She nodded. 'You're students too?'

He smiled at her. 'No. I'm in commerce. I work for myself. Where do you live in Algeria?'

'Hadjout.'

He said: 'Ah, Hadjout,' as though he knew the place, but she guessed he had probably only seen it as the destination of one of the Algiers buses. It was not only his eyes that were intense, Maryse Rosé realized, but his complete expression. He was handsome, straight-nosed, his cheekbones clearly defined; a strong face.

'And you?'

He blew out his upper lip, then said: 'Oran . . . Algiers. Both.'

'They're three hundred miles apart,' observed Maryse Rose.

'I was born in Oran,' said the Arab. 'Now my neighbours are the Hernandez and Perez.' It was a colloquial expression for the European inhabitants of Spanish descent, and identified the Algiers working-class area of Bab-el-Oued.

'I'm falling asleep.' Thérèse signalled the waiter, and searched for change in her purse.

'And I must be going, too,' said Maryse Rose, grateful for an excuse to leave.

The Arab put his hand gently on her arm. 'Stay for a while. Let me buy you another coffee.'

She refused him politely.

As the four girls walked away down the street, he watched them until the early morning shoppers and the market stalls hid them from sight.

The next day he was waiting for Maryse Rose at the gate of the hospital. She was alone. He was leaning against one of the gateposts but straightened himself as she approached. He was tall, broad-shouldered, his hair short and crinkled. He wore a T-shirt with a light cotton jacket hung on one shoulder.

'May I walk you home?' He matched her step.

She said: 'No.' She wished she had waited a few more minutes for Thérèse who had wanted to tidy her locker. Both Helene and Tatiana had a day's leave before commencing the final course.

'May I buy you breakfast, then?'

She was about to refuse him, when he added: 'We Arabs have to stick together in the Metropole.'

His casual identification of her ancestry momentarily confused her. Her entire life had been spent in such close association with Europeans that unless reminded she normally related herself to them without thought. Even when the All Saints Day uprising had taken place she had felt herself as threatened as any other members of her European family or circle of friends. Only Belle deliberately drew attention to her race, and that was so habitual that she ignored it. Not since she had been a child, before her adoption, had it seemed important to her. Did she look so obviously Arab now she was older? She wondered, quickly.

'Well, don't you agree?'

She hesitated before answering him. 'I . . . I suppose so.'

He laughed, and switched from French to Arabic. 'You suppose? You must have been here for too long.' He steered her into the first of the cafés. Even at this early time of the day the bar was crowded, but he led her to a vacant table beneath a smoke-stained mirror that advertized an aperitif. When they sat down, he said. 'I'm Habib. Habib Saadi.' He waited for her to respond.

'Maryse.' She found she was reluctant to give him her full name.

'Just Maryse?'

'Maryse Rose.' She avoided adding Charpentier.

'A Christian first-name.' He signalled a waiter, then ordered coffee and brioche.

When they were alone again Maryse Rose asked: 'Does my religion matter then?' She had not spoken in Arabic for so long that it had become rusty, forcing her to search her mind for the words. As a child she had found it an easy language to learn and spoke it fluently.

'Not to me.' His eyes were examining her.

She pouted. 'But it would to your friends, I imagine.'

'Perhaps, to some. You know the creed; Islam, Arabic, Algeria . . . in that order.' He chuckled. 'I reverse it. When we have Algeria the other two will come naturally.'

'The other two! Algeria! You already have Algeria. Why do Arabs have to fight. Look what's happening at the moment, the battle of Algiers, all those deaths. It's so stupid, so horrible. So unnecessary.'

His dark eyes watching her, half-amused, half-teasing, hardened. 'Stupid? Unnecessary? Why?'

His abrupt change of manner frightened her a little. She said: 'Things have been improving all the time. There's representation in government. There are the elected councils.'

'Elected councils, rubbish! Two electoral colleges.' His voice rose slightly. 'You know how it damned well works; half a million French citizens qualify for the first electoral college, but over nine million of us for the second. Those kind of proportions are ridiculous! You call that *fair* representation? And in any case, every election is rigged by French agents.'

She shook her head disbelievingly.

He reacted angrily, the muscles of his jaw tightening before he spoke. 'They bribe the *caids* to stuff the ballot boxes. They don't even bother to issue registration cards in our villages to enable us to vote. They break up our political meetings, and if nationalist candidates stand for election they're arrested and jailed for years.' He stared at her curiously. 'You don't believe me, do you? I tell you, I've seen it for myself. I've tested it. I've counted people into polling centres . . . yes, counted them in for the entire day, and then compared my number with the figures that they eventually issued. The figures never tallied. Look at the results at Djelfa, not a single vote for a nationalist candidate; not even the candidate's own vote! But the French government candidate managed to get eight hundred votes out of a possible five hundred! The so-called elections are a farce. If you're an opponent of the French regime you can't be elected . . . they make certain you aren't elected. What alternative do they leave us but to fight?'

'But fighting is something you do against soldiers, not defenceless people.' The fire in his voice was infectious, arousing her to defensive argument. The air between them seemed electrified.

'You're incredibly naïve, Maryse. Fighting is something we do to *win* freedom. Haven't you read Carlos Marighela?'

To her surprise his criticism seemed acceptable. She shook her head. 'I've never even heard of him.'

Habib's face was always animated, and the quick changes of expression and moods intrigued her. She could sense a hidden power of leadership, and perhaps, for herself, danger. 'He was a Brazilian freedom fighter. Marighela said the *first* aim of revolution should be to turn political crisis into armed conflict. You must force those in power to take military or police action; action that is as unreasonable as possible, so that all the people are alienated. Then the strength of the revolution grows. If we simply fight the French army, we're playing our war to French rules; it becomes only a few activists against professional soldiers. But by forcing the French to react violently, the road-blocks, the mass searches of the cas-bah, the arrest of innocent suspects, torture, executions, the aerial strikes against our villages, we gain recruits every time, we gain the support of all of our nine million. And this way we will win our liberty.'

'And what will you do with this liberty? Starve?' She found herself deliberately encouraging him to continue his argument and explanation. His enthusiasm was infec-tious, exciting her.

His voice grew more earnest. 'Better to starve in free-dom than in slavery. Every man or woman has a right to freedom, the right to decide their own future, the right to their own land.' He lowered his voice, confidentially. 'They say there is gas in the desert, oil at Hassi Messaoud. And our soil is fertile all along the coast; five crops a year, we can grow! So why should these foreigners exploit *our* land, and *our* people? And where does this money go that they make from us? It goes into their pockets, their banks here in France, or in Switzerland, Spain, Italy. If they build hospitals, then the best are for their people, not ours. The schools! You know what it is like in the schools; they teach us just sufficient to be of use to them. They train us like monkeys!'

He relaxed a little, and his eyes softened. 'Imagine what it could be like. You're a nurse, you know how bad medical services are for us. Imagine modern clinics in every town and village, the best possible equipment, free medication for everyone.'

He caught her eyes and saw her disbelief. 'No, Maryse, I'm not wrong, I'm not exaggerating. The possibility is that the Sahara is one vast oil-field. We can pipe surplus gas to neighbouring countries, or use it to fuel our own power generators and sell electricity. The world will always need energy, and we will supply it. But the revenue, instead of going to buy yachts, grand châteaux, race horses and big cars for foreigners, will go into *our* national fund, for the benefit of *our* people. Instead of them living ten to a room, we'll build them houses; blocks of apartments. And a building programme generates even more work. We'll get rid of unemployment and give our men back their self-respect. We'll educate *all* the people, not just the privileged few. We'll build them schools, universities. We'll train our own specialists; send them abroad to learn the skills. Then we'll build factories to make the goods our people will need. We'll sell the surplus and mechanize our farming; nationalize our land so that it belongs to everyone.' He paused. 'You think we'll starve in our freedom? I think we'll begin to live, Maryse.'

That morning when she had arrived home at Parc Kahn she was unable to sleep, her mind stirred into unaccustomed activity. She lay awake on her bed, sunlight filtering into the room from beyond the long curtains. Distantly, like the sounds of busy insects, was the hum of the traffic on the boulevard.

Her conversation with Habib produced disturbing thoughts. As a child she had often attempted to picture Vincent finding her in the desert. For her, then, that had been the romantic instant of her birth; she had begun to exist only from that moment. But Belle had delighted in comparing her to the rag-clad and dirty Bedouins who wandered into Algiers to beg on the street corners, or the homeless who lived in the squalor of the bidonvilles. They were 'fig trees', 'melons', 'bicots' and in her child's mind it had become impossible to associate herself with them, even distantly. Then, when she was older, her real ancestry had meant little to her; it was far easier for her to accept that she was the daughter of Christian and Colette

Charpentier. The possibility that she could have grown up the child of wandering tribesmen, to have wed at eleven or twelve-years-old and borne children herself by the age of fourteen, had been so incongruous for her that even now it was almost beyond the ability of her imagination. But the reality was that the possibility *had* existed and she would never know why she had been abandoned.

She had always thought that it had been intended that she should die, for had her Arab mother wished to give her even the smallest possibility of life she could have abandoned her baby at the roadside where it might have been found by the driver of a passing truck. But to conceal it beneath a rock three hundred yards from the road, and below the lip of a wadi, was no more than murder.

Or was it? Maryse Rose was startled to perceive for the first time that every emotion she had herself ever experienced was linked by blood to her real mother.

'Bestial!' was how the terrorist murders were frequently described in lurid newspaper reports. 'Callous and cold-blooded'. But surely people who could commit such acts were capable of killing a small child quickly, even though it were one of their own, rather than leaving it to die slowly of thirst and dehydration beneath a rock, shaded from the direct heat of the sun!

Shaded!

Her sudden realization was so overwhelming that instinctively she knew it was correct. She had not been abandoned, but hidden!

Why, was immaterial. Perhaps her father had been disappointed at the birth of a girl-child and her mother was waiting until he had calmed. Perhaps the encampment had been threatened by another tribe; vendettas were common amongst the Bedouin. But whatever the reason, Maryse Rose suddenly understood and with absolute certainty in her mind, that her mother had intended to return for her. The poisonous snake which had been beneath the rock had been no more than a ruse of fate, which when she had so often listened to the story, had seemed to make her abandonment even more cruel; but in the cold night when her Bedouin mother had hidden her the snake would have been dormant, and invisible.

Later, her mother would have come for her . . . and found nothing! There would have been only the tracks of booted feet in the sand above the wadi, perhaps a few scratches on the rocks, a scrap of burnt rag where the snake had been lying. Her Bedouin mother would have attempted to decipher the signs, and then followed the tracks as far as the road, seen the marks of car tyres, picnic scraps. Regardless of the woman's feelings at the loss of her baby she would have been helpless. The mountains and beyond were a world she would not know or understand, and into which she could not venture alone. The nearest police post was several days walk away, and as a desert Bedouin she would trust no-one of authority. She would have been distraught with grief.

For the first time in her life, Maryse Rose felt sadness and pity for her Arab mother.

And the Charpentiers had not rescued her, but stolen her!

That was ridiculous, she thought quickly. To steal implied some form of profit as a motive; they had gained nothing, but had given her everything, including their love.

She heard Habib's voice in her mind and imagined the argument he would present to her if he knew her real background: 'Of course they will have gained, just as the French always gain from us. Colette Charpentier wanted you for purely selfish reasons. She wanted another child of her own and was unable to bear one; you were a surrogate daughter. Of course she gave you her love and you gave far more of yours in return, and you gave her your dependence which she needed. They stole *you* just as they have stolen our country; they love it, but they love it as their own. Maternalism, paternalism, it is the way they rule us and destroy our freedom.'

'I've lacked for nothing,' she said aloud. 'They accepted me as one of them.'

'You lacked for nothing, simply because they have everything,' his voice seemed to say. 'But remember, it was years before Christian Charpentier adopted you. And what happened when you fell in love with one of theirs? They sent you away immediately.'

'That wasn't the reason,' her mind replied desperately. 'I was sent here because Christian was concerned for my safety. Belle was sent too.'

'Then why didn't you hear from Philippe Viard? He loved you, and he would have tried to contact you through them . . . through Vincent if not Christian and Colette. They have all prevented him finding you. And Belle was being courted by Francis Levac; Christian didn't approve of him either. You could see it clearly in his eyes when she mentioned his name. Levac was barely more than a peasant farmer, so hardly a suitable candidate for the hand of Christian Charpentier's real daughter. It was very convenient to move you to the "safety" of Paris. Safety for whom, and from what? We don't kill our own women.'

'You're just trying to confuse me. I know whom I love, and why I love them. And I trust them. Maybe I can't think like an Arab, but that doesn't make me a puppet.'

'One day you will have to decide what you are, Arab, French or puppet. Even if you don't think as an Arab thinks, you will feel as an Arab feels because you are an

Arab. The Arab blood in your veins can never be changed. And I have simply reminded you that you are one of us.'

Her mind was unsettled throughout the day, preventing her from sleeping, so that later when she was working she felt sick with exhaustion. Only the knowledge that it was her last night of the present course, and that for two days afterwards she would be able to rest, enabled her to continue.

Habib was waiting for her again when she left the hospital the next morning. She attempted to ignore him, but to no avail.

'Breakfast?' he asked cheerfully, lengthening his stride as she quickened her pace.

'No thank you, Habib.' She was avoiding meeting his eyes. She glanced quickly along the length of the road hoping she might see a taxi she could hail, but there were none in sight.

'Just coffee then?' He attempted to take her hand but she quickly twisted it from his grip. 'What's the matter?'

'I'm sorry, but I don't want you waiting for me outside the hospital every time I come off duty.'

He grinned at her sheepishly. 'Yes, I'm being unreasonable. You must feel tired. We'll meet somewhere else. Later in the day, when you're rested.'

She had to be firm with him. 'I don't want to see you again.' She began to turn away, but he stopped her.

His face was serious. 'Why?'

She began walking. 'I don't need to give you a reason.'

'I always need reasons. Do you dislike me?'

'No, I don't dislike you.'

'Then I have insulted you? What have I done to upset you?'

'Nothing . . . not intentionally, anyway. Now, please leave me alone.'

He ignored her request. 'So I have done something. What?'

She didn't answer immediately, but then said: 'You confuse me. You make me think too much, and question all the things I value. I don't want to see you again.'

'You're afraid,' he said positively, and there was a challenge in his voice.

She was angry. 'I'm not afraid, but I'm very tired. My body wants rest, and my mind needs peace.'

They were outside the café they had visited the previous day. Habib took her arm again and stopped her. She tried to pull her arm free but he held her strongly. Had it not been for the presence of the street traders and their customers nearby she would have slapped him, but the thought of the public embarrassment it would cause her prevented her.

'One last coffee with me. Five minutes, that's all. Afterwards, if you want, I promise I'll never bother you again.'

'You won't change my mind.' She glared at him furiously.

'I'm not going to try.'

She allowed him to lead her to the café, but as they entered, a man's voice, so loud it was almost a shout, stopped them. 'You two, get out of here.' Behind the bar, an elderly man, his features contorted by emotion, gesticulated wildly.

Neither Maryse Rose nor Habib thought the order had been directed at them. They continued into the bar as its customers turned to watch them.

The pitch of the man's voice rose: 'You damned Algerians. Yes, you two Arabs. Get out of my bar. I'm not having any of you filthy murderers in here.'

Maryse Rose felt the blood drain from her face. She heard Habib begin to protest, then one of the waiters held his arms wide and began motioning them towards the door with his hands as though they were chickens escaped from a coop. The waiter, a diminutive, narrow-faced man, looked apologetic. 'Don't argue with him,' he warned, his voice low. 'Just leave.'

'What have we done?' Habib asked angrily when they were in the street.

'Nothing. At least, not you.' The waiter lowered his eyes to avoid Habib's furious glare. 'The patron heard last night . . . his sister's boy, a conscript. He was killed yesterday in Mers-el-Kebir; a grenade tossed into a bar.' The waiter looked towards Maryse Rose, his eyes examining and recognizing her uniform; it always brought respect from those who lived near the hospital. 'I'm sorry nurse, but please don't come back here.'

Her legs felt weak and she was trembling. For a few moments she thought she was about to faint, but Habib held her arm tightly, supporting her.

'Bastards,' he swore under his breath, then said furiously: 'They don't want to know anything about our war. They don't want to read about it, and don't want to understand it, until it affects them personally. Then all they can do is hate in a pathetic, secondhand manner.' He softened his voice and spoke to her gently. 'There are plenty of cafés around here, we'll go to another one.'

'No, please no.' The thought that a similar incident might occur terrified her. She did not have the courage to take the risk, but she needed somewhere to sit and compose herself before she could continue her journey home.

'My apartment is only two hundred yards away,' suggested Habib, gently. 'It's not much, but it's clean. I've got tea, and fresh mint.' He squeezed her arm reassuringly.

*

The apartment block, built of rendered concrete, was in a narrow street off the main road. There were no elevators, and Habib's flat on the sixth floor was reached by narrow flights of stairs at one end of the building. It had four small rooms, one of which served as both dining room and lounge. Its balcony overlooked a factory and a noisy yard in which scrap vehicles were being dismantled.

Maryse Rose sat in one of the two hard plastic-covered armchairs. She was still feeling badly shaken. She had never before been so humiliated, and the virulence of the café owner's anger had appalled her. In the past two years she had visited the place many times with her friends, and the man had often chatted with them. She even knew his name; Raoul ... Raoul Boursier. She had always thought of him as a jolly, friendly man. She could understand his grief but not his indiscriminate malice.

The sound of a kettle boiling in the kitchen distracted her. There was the clink of glasses and a moment later Habib entered carrying a small tray. She could smell the fragrance of mint as he put a steaming glass in front of her.

'Drink it, it'll help.'

The glass was so hot it burnt her fingertips, and the tea was like thin, sweet syrup but it helped to calm her.

Habib talked, small-talk that required no answers from her, telling her how strange he had found France on his first visit, how unlike it had been to the country of his imagination. He had lowered the pitch of his voice so that it seemed to have a therapeutic quality, and after a few minutes she realized she had once heard an Arab farmworker calming a nervous horse with the same soft, persuasive tone; the tensed muscles of the animal had slowly relaxed, the flattened ears had straightened and after a little while the man had been able to adjust its disturbed harness.

She smiled gratefully at Habib. 'Thank you.' He had seemed so fiery, but there was a kind and understanding side to him. Even his features had softened as he spoke to her.

'For what?' There was a hint of humour in his question.

'For helping. For trying to make me feel better.'

'It's never happened to you before?' He seemed surprised.

She shook her head. 'No.' As he moved, she could see the well-defined muscles of his shoulders beneath his T-shirt. He looked physically very powerful, athletic in a compact way.

He put a hand to his broad forehead in mock amazement. 'You must live in a different world to the rest of us. It's happened to me ever since I was a child. I've been sworn at, cuffed, pushed into gutters. You're more vulnerable when you're young, and it doesn't happen so much as you get older and bigger. But it still can happen sometimes . . . like today. Hadjout must be a very special part of Algeria.'

'It is for me.' She didn't want to tell him the story of her adoption by a French settler family and searched for a change of subject to distract him. There were several photographs on a small white-painted dresser near the kitchen door. One of the pictures was of a handsome man, perhaps in his mid-thirties wearing a *burnous*. 'Who's that?' she asked.

'My father.' Again there was the sudden change of mood, obvious in his voice. It should have been a warning to her. The sleek brown muscles on his neck tightened.

'What does he do?'

'He was a soldier; a corporal. He was what the French call a "loyal Algerian", a "good Arab". They gave him a Croix de Guerre for bravery in 1944, and then in 1945 they crucified him.'

She thought he was speaking metaphorically. 'Crucified?'

'He was in hospital at Bone. He'd been wounded in France in 1944; liberating them! My mother, my brothers and myself, we were living with my grandparents in Guelma. My father was allowed to come home on sick-leave. That week there was the uprising in the Setif; you'll know all about that. Then the backlash, and the inevitable reprisals. My father and twelve other innocent men were nailed by their hands to a wooden barn and shot to death. They used bird-shot, fired from almost maximum range. It wasn't quick. It took a long time, and a lot of shots to kill them.' He paused and took a deep breath, and Maryse Rose saw that his eyes had become unusually hard, like polished black granite pebbles. 'When it was safe we went to find his body. My mother couldn't recognize him. But I found his medals in his pocket, so we knew.'

Habib's hands had been so tightly clenched while he spoke that his fingers looked as though they had been carved from old yellow ivory. As he picked up his glass of tea and drained it quickly, Maryse Rose noticed that they trembled with emotion. She felt that anything she might say would be inadequate, but knew he expected, perhaps needed a sympathetic response from her. 'That was a terrible thing to have happened.'

Habib grimaced at the revived memories. 'I was fifteen, but that day I became an old man.'

Despite Maryse Rose's earlier intention to see no more of Habib, he had begun to fascinate her. He was always exciting company, courteous and far more charming towards her than the brash Parisians. His nationalistic pride was so infectious that when she was in his company she began to find an unforeseen pleasure, and even romance, in her own Arab ancestry. Everything Habib did was backed by unlimited enthusiasm and energy. His quick humour constantly amused her, and his ability to make a few francs go a long way was intriguing. He knew a hundred bistros and back-street restaurants where the food was equal to any she had eaten in the finest Paris hotels, and their atmospheres were busy, intimate and welcoming. He had a large circle of acquaintances and friends, mostly Algerians, but amongst them Moroccans, Tunisians and Egyptians. And spicing their conversations and discussions with intrigue for her, would be occasional whispers of clandestine meetings with men whose names she had read in the newspapers or heard on the radio . . . Ben Bella, Ait Ahmed, M'hamed Yazid.

Each evening after she had been home, to shower and change, she would drive the 2CV to meet Habib in one of the many small bars beside the river. She realized now that his biggest fear was solitude and that he enjoyed noise, crowds and the company of as many friends as he could gather around his table. Sometimes they would play cards, but always he liked his conversations intense, lively and political. He had been educated by the state, and the pension his mother received had permitted him to continue his schooling long past the age when most Muslim Algerians would have been forced to seek work. Books fascinated him, and he enjoyed displaying his unusual memory for them by reciting passages from the works of socialist or communist authors. Maryse Rose was never bored by him. So much was new to her, the revolutionary theories to discuss, the ideas to expand, the policies of Algerian freedom.

He had told her only briefly that he was involved in commerce, but he never willingly discussed his work. If she questioned him he would refer to it as dull and unpleasant and his office as 'a tedious place near the Bastille'. Eventually she realized that just as she avoided talking about her own background, this was a subject which he too wished to avoid.

It was through her own carelessness that he discovered the truth about her upbringing. Her Citroen was garaged for servicing, and she had used a taxi to meet Habib that evening.

They had just finished a meal in one of the many cafés he frequented. It was late, and rain had begun to streak the window-panes. Habib paid the bill and checked the money he had left in his wallet. 'I'm afraid we'll have to walk,' he apologized. The nearest Metro station was a mile away.

'I've got some money.' She searched for her purse in her handbag.

'No, we'll walk.' He hated her to pay for anything when she was with him, and would always refuse her offers to share the cost.

'For heaven's sake be sensible, it's raining. If you won't let me pay for a taxi, then at least allow me to lend you something and you can pay me back tomorrow. Here . . .' She placed her handbag on the table, open, and held a few notes towards him.

He reached forward, but instead of taking the notes from her hand pulled her identity card from her handbag. His intention was to tease her.

'Habib!' She tried to reach the card, but he held it further away from her, then turned it, frowning almost imperceptibly as he read her name aloud.

'Maryse Rose Charpentier. I thought Rose was your surname.'

'Habib, you're a pest.' She deliberately made no comment about her name, but a sick feeling grew quickly in her stomach.

He read the card again, and this time included her Algerian address. 'Maryse Rose Charpentier. Beau Lac,

Hadjout.' He caught her eyes wih his own. They gave her no indication of his thoughts. 'No apartment number, no street number, no street. Just Beau Lac, Hadjout?'

'Hadjout's not a big place.'

He leant towards her. 'But Charpentier is a *very* big name, and you can find it on the bottles of red wine which also say *Château* Beau Lac.' His face was serious as he turned the card slowly in his hands. 'I thought you were one of us, but I realize you've let me make quite a fool of myself. No wonder you had so many strange ideas. It explains a lot . . . your expensive clothes . . . fine shoes . . . the perfumes you use . . . even your car. Everything of too much quality for a normal Algerian girl.' He looked contemptuous. 'The daughter of a French "grand colon"; you must have found it quite amusing to go slumming with an Arab.'

'Habib, that's unfair, and I'm not the daughter of a "grand colon".'

He laughed, but without humour. 'But you have the same name and you live in the same Château. Charpentier!' He said the name as though it were a curse. 'One of The Ten.' He tossed the card onto the table and raised both his hands in a gesture of hopelessness. He made a move as if to stand up. 'I think I should say, goodnight, Miss Charpentier. No doubt you can telephone for one of your father's limousines.'

She caught his wrist quickly. It had become important to tell him the truth; important that she should not lose him. 'Habib, stop. I'm not Christian Charpentier's real daughter. Yes, I admit my name is Charpentier, but I'm as Algerian as yourself. I was adopted by the Charpentiers. My parents were Bedouin. I was a foundling.'

He spoke coldly: 'Impossible.'

He was reacting just as she had feared when she had first decided to keep her background from him. 'Not impossible, only unusual. Please listen to me.' She explained desperately.

'You should have told me when we first met.'

'But would you have believed me then?'

'Perhaps.'

'Only perhaps! And you wouldn't have trusted me, would you! I'd have been one of those Beni oui-oui, those "loyal *French* Arabs" you hate so much. Everything would have been different between us. You wouldn't have talked about your ideals, you wouldn't have explained things to me. You wouldn't have tried to teach me anything. And you wouldn't even have liked me.'

He was silent for a few seconds, and then asked: 'Don't you realize that the Charpentiers are my sworn enemies?'

'Enemies?'

His body had stiffened, but he seemed poised and alert as if she was threatening him. 'Your people are the ones we fight against. The ordinary pieds-noir are nothing to us, merely numbers. But your people, your family, they have the money and the influence, they dictate the country's policies . . . the direction it should go. They control the government . . . they *are* the government . . . the police . . . the army.' He paused again before continuing. 'Do you think that somehow, during all these weeks we've been discussing Algerian problems, that the Charpentiers have been absolved from blame and responsibility? Principles don't allow convenient exceptions.'

'I've never asked for an exception.' She realized that secretly she had known one day he would learn the truth about her. Perhaps then it had offered a convenient escape for her if she required it. Now, however, she regretted she had not forced herself to tell him before.

'I understand why you haven't invited me to your home to meet your family. The Charpentiers! What could you say to them? Papa, here is my Arab boyfriend . . . accept him as an equal! In God's name Maryse . . . I've read a dozen of Charpentier's speeches to the Assembly. He's not even a liberal. He's the great "anti". I can even quote some from memory: "Algeria is a Department of France, therefore a Frenchman agreeing to Arab-Islamic independence for Algeria is . . ."'

She interrupted him. 'Is as inconceivable as if it were agreed for Normandy.' She could remember the occasion. It had been when de Gaulle had first visited Algeria. Christian Charpentier's speech had been broadcast and she had listened to it with Colette, Belle and Vincent. It had sounded stirring and patriotic, then.

'And you believe him?'

'I love him as a father, but I don't believe the words any more.' She hesitated. 'Habib, try to understand my confusion. Haven't you wondered why I question you so much? Sometimes I feel as though I am becoming insane . . . for almost twenty years I've been taught to respect and admire everything that's French. For almost twenty years I've *been* French. It's just not possible for me to become an Arab woman in the space of a few weeks. You must have patience.'

The heavy rain eased to a thick mist as he walked her home to Parc Kahn. He hardly spoke, but when they arrived he stood beneath one of the tall street lights and stared at the de L'Ormeraye's mansion as though attempting to relate her to its grandeur. A yellow ornamental lamp, haloed by the mist, lit its porch and many of the windows glowed warmly in the moist darkness. She knew that to him it was as alien as she would find a desert tent.

He had never kissed her but now she wanted him to do so, needed him to hold her in his arms. Instead, he quietly wished her goodnight, then waited until she had climbed the steps to the door before turning away and walking briskly up the street.

They had not quarrelled, but she realized that Habib had been more than simply angered by her concealment of her background. He had expected the open form of honesty characteristic of Arab women towards their men, and she had unintentionally failed him. In doing so she had behaved in the manner he found so typical of the settlers' attitude towards his race. A few weeks ago, in the early days of their friendship, this might not have seemed so important to her but now she felt miserable.

She did not want to lose him, and for the first time knew that she was in love with him. She could not even understand how it had happened, nor when. She had thought there could be only one kind of love, the wild and passionate love she had experienced with Philippe, a love which lasted far beyond a lifetime. Even now, she could feel this love for Philippe still within her. The love she felt for Habib was different . . . it had grown slowly from fascination and intrigue, but was no less possessive or consuming. Were the two kinds of love which she felt, so different in their ways that it was possible to divide the emotions equally? Surely, in time, one must dominate the other? The thought that both the men she loved were lost to her made the future unbearably bleak. She experienced, too, an extraordinary feeling of isolation as though a world to which she truly belonged had been taken from her so that no place remained in which she could exist. She had wept for Philippe, but in the present limbo there was only a vacuum.

Habib did not contact her for three days.

It was Saturday morning, one of the few mornings in the week when Maryse Rose breakfasted with her aunt and uncle. Belle had risen unusually early after a late night at a party and was puffy-eyed and without her make-up; dressed in a long satin housecoat that clung to her plump figure as she sat at the table. Beside Maryse Rose's place, when she came down from her room, was a cellophane-wrapped bunch of red roses. Attached was a small card and on it a single line in Arabic. It read simply: 'We Arabs should be together.'

Belle attempted to interpret the pleasure in Maryse Rose's eyes as she watched her read the card. Belle's knowledge of written Arabic was scant, and although she had examined the card she had not understood the message.

'An Arab dressed as a person brought it,' Belle said disdainfully, using a settler expression to describe an Arab in European dress. 'He said he wanted to wait, but of course I told the maid to send him away. He didn't have the manners to go to the tradesman's door. They never learn!'

Maryse Rose glared at her.

'Perhaps he works for one of your friends,' suggested her aunt, calmly. 'The flowers are quite beautiful.' She smiled at Maryse Rose. 'It's a very romantic bouquet, my dear. Perhaps we can have the pleasure of meeting your beau?'

The note and the flowers had given Maryse Rose a slightly inebriated feeling, as though she had drunk a glass of champagne on an empty stomach. She wished she had been downstairs when Habib had called, and was angry with Belle. 'I'd like you to meet him . . . all of you. But it'll be difficult if Belle orders him away whenever he calls.'

'Whenever . . .' Belle's eyes widened in horror. 'My God! You're friendly with an Arab!'

Maryse Rose kept her voice calm. 'Why not? I am an Arab.'

'Not a proper one.'

'Why? Because I don't wear a *haik*?'

Belle looked desperately at her aunt. 'Aunt Isabelle, you must do something before she ruins all of us. What will people say? She disgraced us at home, and now she's trying to disgrace us here. You can't let her bring an Arab into this house . . . you know they're all thieves. He'd steal everything . . . your jewellery. And they're murderers.'

Claude de L'Ormeraye had been silently eating, but now he looked up quickly. 'That's quite enough, Belle.' The admonishment in his normally mild voice surprised his wife as much as Maryse Rose and Belle. Claude de L'Ormeraye had never before involved himself in the arguments which sometimes developed. He smiled at Maryse Rose. 'Your young man will be welcome in my house,' he told her. 'In fact, I would personally like to meet him very much.'

Despite her uncle's willingness, the two men did not meet. Habib's mind was unable to accept the proffered hospitality, and although he now admitted Maryse Rose's Arab parentage, the environment in which she had been raised, and still lived, continued to disturb him.

Maryse Rose became Habib's mistress just as she had fallen in love with him, in a gentle, unplanned and almost mysterious way that was so natural that later even the time and manner were blurred. Maryse Rose could remember only that it seemed he had always been part of her, that the touch of his lips against her breasts, the delicious excitement of his body inside her belonged not only to the present but to a past which seemed to reach back into the dark mysterious recesses of eternity.

Maryse Rose and Habib did not discuss a future for themselves but she felt that one existed, understanding that it lay beyond the ambitions he held for his country's freedom. Nor did she allow herself to question his occupation. There were no signs of work in his apartment, and he appeared never to visit the 'office' he had once mentioned. Telephone calls he received while she was at his apartment were invariably from friends who wished to contact him for social reasons; some she met, but most he saw privately whilst she was at the hospital. His life seemed romantically enigmatic to her.

She completed her training in late August and took the final examinations in September, receiving her State Diploma a few weeks later. Although she was offered a permanent position with the International Hospital, she refused. The two years of study had been hard and she had decided she had earned a vacation before making any final decisions about her future.

Habib had suggested they might travel to Switzerland together in late October, in her 2CV and she was already looking forward to the trip. Sometimes, now, he borrowed the Citroen while she was at work.

It was a Thursday afternoon when she drove it to Habib's apartment block. It was raining lightly when she parked. She opened an umbrella and ran to the entrance.

At the top of the narrow flight of stairs, she paused and found the door-key in her handbag. But as she slid the key into the lock the door was suddenly opened, a man grabbed her extended arm and jerked her violently inside the room. A second man snatched her handbag from her grasp.

Before she could react, he said sharply: 'Deuxième Bureau.'

The first man, squat and powerfully built, spun her around by her shoulders. 'Hands against the wall.' When she hesitated, dazed by the shock, he said: 'Suit yourself.' He twisted her arms behind her back and clipped a pair of handcuffs on her wrists. The metal bit painfully into her flesh.

They acted with a brutal authority that made her afraid to question them or even demand proof of their identity. Everything was happening too quickly for her stunned mind to grasp. Even as questions formed the situation was changing, developing. Fear was the only constant emotion. The man who had said 'Deuxième Bureau' took her handbag and spilled its contents onto the table. A lipstick rolled to the floor. He picked it up gingerly, as though it might be a weapon, then he opened her wallet.

'Maryse Rose Charpentier?'

She nodded. Although her heart was racing, it seemed incapable of pumping her blood around her body. She felt very cold, as if she were about to faint.

The first man began running his stubby fingered hands over her body inside her raincoat. She squirmed as he cupped her breasts. 'Stand still,' he ordered. He ran his hands down to her waist and she was unable to prevent an involuntary protective movement. There was a sudden fierce pain in her ankles as he kicked her feet from under her. Unable to use her hands to save herself, she fell heavily and lay winded. The man turned her onto her stomach, then placed one of his knees on her shoulders, pinning her down and driving the remaining breath from her bruised lungs. With growing panic she felt she was suffocating to death as his weight stopped her breathing. Her raincoat, skirt and slip were pulled upwards and the man's hands moved between her buttocks and thighs, searching her intimately. Then his weight on her shoulders lessened and she was hauled into a sitting position with her back against the wall. She vomited, gasping frantically as she retched.

The man beside the table, tall, moustached and wearing

a navy-blue raincoat watched for a few moments, and then said: 'Get the cuffs off her, she's harmless.' While his companion freed her wrists he walked to the kitchen and when he returned tossed a towel onto her lap. He pulled one of the chairs from beside the table and sat opposite her, waiting until she had wiped her face and her breathing had eased. 'I'm Inspector Ravaux. I suggest that you co-operate with us. Where is Habib Saadi?'

'I don't know. Tell me what's happening?' The taste of bile in her mouth made her stomach heave again and she swallowed quickly. 'Please let me go to the bathroom.' The front of her clothing was stained and her condition embarrassed her.

'Later.' The Inspector's eyes were stone hard. 'You live with him here?'

'No.' What did they want with Habib, her mind questioned. It was inconceivable that he was a criminal.

'The neighbours say you are here all the time.' The man's heavy moustache hid his upper lip completely and was stained beneath his nostrils with nicotine.

'He's my . . .' She was going to say fiancé, but instead said: 'Boyfriend.'

'Where is Saadi now?'

'I came round here to see him . . . I expected him to be here.' The Inspector made no comment so she added: 'Please let me telephone my uncle.' She needed to end the helpless feeling of isolation and even a familiar voice would help her.

'You Algerians are a pain in the arse,' said the first man. He was round-faced, his nose broken like that of a boxer. There was afternoon stubble on his chin. 'A telephone call? What do you think this is, an American gangster movie? You swine get no privileges.'

For the first time the Inspector spoke quietly. 'Go and bring my car to the entrance. Wait for us down there.'

When the man hesitated, he spoke again. 'Now, sergeant.'

The sergeant frowned. 'Yes sir.'

When he had left them alone the inspector helped Maryse Rose to her feet and led her to the bathroom. He stood by the door while she washed and dried her face and hands. Her leg throbbed where the sergeant had kicked it.

She faced the Inspector, 'Why have I been treated like this? Is this the way the Deuxième Bureau always behaves in France?'

'We behave as it is necessary to behave. And terrorists are not our favourite people.'

'Terrorists? What do you mean?' Her confidence was returning as she realized the whole incident was a mistake. 'Do I look like a terrorist? Did you find a gun in my stockings? A knife? Your sergeant searched hard enough.' The memory of the man's hands beneath her clothing was unpleasant.

'We found forty kilos of plastique inside the washing machine,' said the Inspector coldly. 'Enough explosive to remove this entire apartment block from the area of Saint Cloud.'

'My God!'

'Yes, my God.' The Inspector held her eyes with his own. 'So we're determined to discuss the matter with your Mr Saadi.' He motioned her towards the living-room. 'I think you should come back in here where we'll talk in a little more comfort.'

She was interrogated for two near sleepless days and nights, at first for an hour by Inspector Ravaux in Habib's apartment, after which she was driven to the Deuxième Bureau's headquarters. She was humiliatingly strip-searched, by two women who by their personal remarks to each other revelled in their work, before being questioned by a succession of men all of whom constantly repeated the same list of questions but in a hundred differing ways; some bullied, others cajoled.

Their threats did not frighten her, and she began feeling only a strange satisfaction that Habib had eluded his pursuers. She became more determined that the answers which she gave them, although honest, would not assist in his capture.

On the evening of the first day she was allowed only a brief meeting with her Uncle Claude's lawyer. The man was confident, persuasive and loquacious, and made Maryse Rose angrier than her interrogators had by his constant references to the manner in which she had been used and duped. She did not feel ill-used by Habib, nor could she picture him as a revolutionary leader as both the lawyer and the officers of the Deuxième Bureau claimed. Neither did she believe that he had deserted her; in her own mind, he had been driven from her, and had somehow heroically managed to escape. She prayed only that he would have found a safe refuge where she might eventually join him. She did not doubt that sooner or later she would be released.

The following morning a guard led her from the cold and uncomfortable cell where she had spent the night, out into the yard adjoining the headquarters. Her 2CV stood inside the doorway of a large garage, and several men were examining and searching it. A photographer, with his camera mounted on a tripod at the rear of the vehicle, was taking a light-reading with a meter. Near the rear door of the Citroën stood Chief Inspector Drevey, who had supervized her questioning on the previous day, and Inspector Ravaux. Drevey beckoned her to the side of the car and pointed.

'What is the purpose of that?'

Beneath the rear seat a section of the pressed steel

flooring had been cut away and fitted with a hinged lid. The Chief Inspector leant forward and flicked the lid with his finger. Closed, the compartment was almost impossible to detect; with the sound-deadening felt and mat in place it would be completely hidden. She had never been aware of it before. She did none of the maintenance on the vehicle itself, and had never even looked beneath the mat.

The Chief Inspector, a stout man with florid cheeks which sagged into jowls at his neck, said: 'It is intended for smuggling. And with Algerians involved, the implications are obvious.'

Maryse Rose was aware that Ravaux was watching her closely, his eyes unblinking as he attempted to gauge her reaction to the Chief Inspector's observation. Her confidence had been maintained by her knowledge of her own innocence, and her belief in that of Habib. The allegations of the officers had seemed absurd, but now she felt the blood drain from her face, and was unable to control a tremor in her voice as she replied, 'I've never seen it before.'

The Chief Inspector spoke disbelievingly, his heavy chin quivering. 'Do you expect us to believe that, Miss Charpentier, this *is* your Citroen isn't it?'

She nodded. 'Yes,' she agreed. It was barely more than a whisper but to herself seemed to contain a volume of guilt, as though she was confessing to a crime of which she knew nothing.

'So, you have a special compartment inside your vehicle but you know nothing about it? Something like this takes hours to make and prepare; it can't be bought in an accessory shop for a few francs and just bolted in place. I demand the truth.'

'I've been telling you the truth,' she said miserably. There had been no need for her to lie but before there had been nothing to fear from them. Hopelessly she wondered if Deuxième Bureau mechanics could even have built the compartment to confuse her, to make the case against Habib and herself stronger, but she knew this was unrealistic. Only Habib ever borrowed the car, and only he could have had the secret compartment constructed. But why?

Inspector Ravaux spoke gently, almost sympathetically. 'I'm sorry Miss Charpentier, but as you can see this makes the matter very much more serious from your point of view. It seems to indicate that unquestionably you are Saadi's accomplice. You must understand that sentences for involvement in terrorism carry maximum sentences in France.'

'I'm not a terrorist . . .'

The slightly comic-opera appearance of the red-faced Chief Inspector Drevey added to the horror of the situation which was enveloping her. He stabbed a finger towards the car boot. 'That,' he said emphatically, 'is to do with terrorism. We've seen similar compartments before . . . and usually they have contained explosives. In the Algerian Department, with evidence of this nature, you could be held indefinitely. Here, in Paris, you face trial and a possible sentence of ten years; longer if the judge has relatives in Algeria and is unsympathetic to a pretty face.' He turned to a guard nearby and spoke sharply. 'Take her up to my office.' As the guard moved to obey him, he glared at Maryse Rose again. 'I want a lot more co-operation from you, young woman. I want to know every last detail about Habib Saadi; everything that you can remember about him, even down to the size and shape of his circumcision scar.'

Before it had seemed as though she was no more than an observer, a bystander to a series of ridiculous events which were taking place around her. Now she realized that her involvement with Habib, no matter what her personal feelings had been towards him, would be completely misconstrued by any French court of justice. She, like Habib, was an Arab, to be treated with contempt, mistrusted and suspected. Her love for him was being tested to its limits. Although she could not see that he had in any way used her yet, there seemed no doubt that he had intended to do so, and abominably, in the future. She could see that there had been many times in the past when she should have questioned him more deeply, but then her love and trust, and the allure of mystery which always surrounded him, had prevented her. Now, although she felt she must remain loyal to him, she could find no arguments with which to protect herself, and the terrifying thought of years confined within the bleak walls of a French prison made her depressed and miserable as she waited in the Chief Inspector's office.

It was half an hour before he arrived and the guard had not permitted her to sit, but kept her standing in front of the Chief Inspector's desk. Chief Inspector Drevey swung off his raincoat and placed it, with his pork-pie hat, on a hook behind the door before walking to his chair. He sat heavily, and folded his thick arms across his chest. 'Are you ready to begin?'

She could feel tears welling behind her eyes and attempted to conceal them. 'I swear I've told you all I know.'

Drevey pressed a button on his desk and Maryse Rose heard a buzzer sound distantly. A moment later a clerk knocked and entered Drevey's office. Without a word, and with his face expressionless, he sat himself at the end of the Chief Inspector's desk and methodically took the top off his fountain-pen and examined the nib before opening his notebook. He nodded his readiness towards the Chief Inspector.

Drevey said: 'You only *think* you have told me everything, Miss Charpentier. Now I want to go through it all again, but this time we will concentrate on the things you believe are so unimportant that you have forgotten to mention them.' He opened a dossier in front of him; it was already familiar to her. 'You may sit down. There.' He pointed a stubby finger at a wooden straight-backed chair opposite him.

He questioned her throughout the remainder of the day, stopping only for two or three short breaks when he permitted her to visit the toilet, or quench her thirst with cardboard cups of black coffee brought in by the guard. When he finally closed the dossier and leant back in his swivel chair, she felt exhausted and empty.

He linked the fingers of his hands together on his gross stomach. 'You are an extremely foolish young woman,' he told her. 'Anyone with a scrap of brains would have realized that Saadi was an Arab activist. From the first time you spoke to him you were literally playing with dynamite, and with no thought of the dangers to yourself or the extreme embarrassment the relationship must cause to your family. You did not consider for one moment the effect your friendship with this Arab might cause to a man in your father's position.' It was the first time that any of the men who had interrogated her had mentioned her family, and she realized that the Deuxième Bureau would have made enquiries in Algeria immediately they had taken her into custody. Undoubtedly the Bureau in Algiers would have interviewed her father and she knew that Christian Charpentier must have been horrified to learn she was involved with a suspected Arab terrorist. Colette would be distraught. She felt even more depressed; again, unintentionally, she had hurt them.

Chief Inspector Drevey continued. 'However, I don't see that I need hold you here. And an arrangement has been made with Mr de L'Ormeraye, and with your father, that you will return to Algeria by aircraft tomorrow morning. When you get there, the Algerian Sûreté will want to see you.' He paused. 'Think yourself extremely lucky, Miss Charpentier.'

FIVE

November 1957: Algeria

As the Air France Caravelle began its long, flat descent towards the airport at Maison Blanche, Maryse Rose could barely suppress her excitement. The apprehension she felt at the thought that in only a short time she would have to face her father, had not faded. But beneath her was the familiar azure Mediterranean she loved so much, while the sky in which she seemed to be floating was so blue, so cloud-free, that where waters and heavens met there was no distinct horizon. Ahead lay the Atlas mountains, and as the aircraft banked slightly she glimpsed Algiers, the Cathedral of the Black Madonna dominating its western heights; below the long, familiar curve of the bay, distant ships and fishing boats. She was almost home.

She could smell Africa from the steps beside the aircraft; the indescribable conglomeration of odours, the desert, sun-dried earth, parched vegetation, animals, spices, the perfume of flowers and fruits, its people. As she paused, the southern wind carried to her the scent of an entire continent bringing a flush of memories.

She had imagined that perhaps she might see Habib amongst the burnoused crowds that habitually watched the arrival of any aircraft from beyond the wire fence beside the terminal. He might signal her, might discreetly contrive to pass her a note. She recognized none of the faces and Habib if he had managed to escape from France, could not possibly know of her return to Algeria. But he might be here, in Algiers, even now walking along some boulevard which was familiar to her, drinking sweet mint tea in some café which she would recognize, bargaining with a trader or shop-keeper on the outskirts of Bab El Oued.

Her reunion with Christian was emotional, but far from reproaching her as she had expected, he embraced her warmly, holding her tightly in his arms as though her separation from him had been as long as he had been able to bear. When she attempted to apologize he stopped her, brushing aside her guilt. The incident was already in the past he assured her. He was the one responsible, by enforcing the unnecessary and long years of loneliness upon her.

Algiers had changed. There had always been military in the Department, but now there were armed soldiers in every street. Paras in their 'lizard' camouflage, long peaked caps, with sub-machine-guns balanced in the crooks of their arms, guarded cross-roads and junctions. Tanks and armoured patrol vehicles moved amongst the normal traffic. At café tables in the squares customers in civilian clothing were often outnumbered by those in uniform. Graffiti or political posters disfigured every convenient wall. Ominously, there were some buildings where the glass windows had been replaced by plywood and the paintwork blackened and blistered by fire.

In Maryse Rose's eyes even the habits of the people appeared to have altered. In Algiers itself the pieds-noir seemed to go about their business with an uncharacteristic caution, whilst the Arab population appeared unnaturally subdued. There were no smiles on Arab faces; their markets, usually a hubbub of noise, were quieter; fewer Arab children played their street games. It was obvious that despite the casual reporting in French newspapers, on the

French radio and television, the situation had greatly worsened.

In the countryside beyond the city, every estate was fortified. High wire-mesh fences, topped by strands of barbed-wire, had been erected behind which imported guard-dogs patrolled with their handlers. There were road-blocks every few miles, fir-pole and barbed-wire barriers; young military conscripts warily flagged down approaching cars, one soldier moving forward to question the drivers or check their identity cards while his comrades kept their thumbs nervously on the safety-catches of their '24/29's'.

Christian confirmed her view as she watched the passing countryside. 'Things are a lot different now. You'll have to be cautious,' he warned her. 'No Europeans enter the casbah any more, not even the market square. And it's almost impossible for the military to get in there. You must never use cafés or bars where the soldiers congregate, they're targets for bombers, and the number of terrorist incidents is increasing all the time. Any European is fair game to the FLN; it has become a very nasty business.' He smiled at her, but the smile was without humour. 'Yes, perhaps I'm frightening you, but the dangers are immediate and very real. You'll find all of your friends have stories they'll tell you; you must listen to them, and learn.'

He leant back in the seat of the car and took hold of her hands affectionately. 'We are fighting to keep our country, Maryse Rose. This is no longer a simple uprising, it's out-and-out war to the finish. There are bound to be casualties, and I don't want *any* of my children amongst them.'

Beau Lac was no longer so lush and green. The groves of palm trees remained, but beneath their arching trunks all

107

the shrubs and undergrowth had been cleared so that intruders would find no cover in which to hide. As if it were a concentration camp, a double fence, ten feet in height, had been erected completely around the grounds. Within the corridor formed by the parallel lines of wire, were tall poles carrying powerful floodlights. At the entrance, just inside the drive, a concrete guardhouse had been built. Christian's political position warranted him a military guard, four soldiers, usually a corporal and three men, who patrolled the grounds day and night.

The removal of the once-plentiful flowering shrubs and lush green bushes made Beau Lac appear starkly naked. In one corner of the once immaculate lawn was an untidy shallow trench surrounded by walls of sandbags. It could have been a defensive position or a military latrine, Maryse Rose was uncertain which.

To her relief the interior of the château was unaltered, and everything was familiar and in its place. Colette was waiting for her, and with her Vincent, Madelene and their young son Axel. Madelene was happily pregnant again, and as the bright sunlight flooded through the tall windows of Beau Lac and Maryse Rose heard the welcoming voices of her family, she felt that summer was returning to her life.

After Christian's brief comments at Algiers airport, neither he nor any of the family discussed Maryse Rose's involvement with Habib Saadi again. It was as though it had never happened, and that Habib had not existed. Maryse Rose knew that was what her parents needed to believe and in many ways it seemed a punishment in itself for she was unable to explain or justify, or even reason with them.

She attempted to talk to Vincent about it on the evening of her return to Beau Lac. Dinner had finished and Christian and Colette were listening to the day's news on Radio Algiers. Madelene had retired early to bed. Maryse Rose suggested to Vincent that they should walk in the grounds.

The floodlighting at the wire barrier was throwing multiple shadows from every palm trunk, cold and geometrical, so different from her memories of evenings in its former gentle gardens.

Vincent took her arm, linking it through his own and holding it so tightly that she could feel the warmth of his body; once it would have given her a sense of protection. 'It's horrible isn't it, but unfortunately necessary,' he said, referring to the glare of the fierce lights cutting through the palm fronds and destroying even the stars that would be glowing above in the night sky. 'And at night now it's risky to wander in the vineyards. Here, at least you're safe; a bullet can't reach the lawns through the trees.'

'Bullets?' Beau Lac had always seemed so safe a refuge for her.

'Or shrapnel.' Vincent slowed the pace to prolong their stroll. Without the paths through the palm groves the lawns seemed to have shrunk. 'It's a favourite FLN trick . . . the bastards drive past in trucks and spray the villas with machine-gun fire, or toss in a couple of grenades. It's cowardly but typical; the swine don't have the courage to come out into the open.'

'Vincent . . .' she hesitated, not knowing how she should begin to tell him about Habib. 'You do know what happened in Paris?'

'Yes, of course. You were vulnerable . . . you felt unwanted, perhaps. You were an easy prey for any jackal.'

'That's not exactly right. Don't you want to hear about it from me?'

'No. It's not that I'm unsympathetic, but because I understand how it all happened. It's best forgotten. None of us need an explanation from you, and least of all father. God knows what would have happened if the Deuxième Bureau hadn't intervened. He's still furious with Uncle Claude. I doubt if they'll ever speak again . . . I agree with him, Claude is an idiot.'

'Uncle Claude didn't do anything,' protested Maryse Rose. 'He was always kind and understanding.'

'And naïve,' Vincent retorted sharply. 'He's a typical liberal Metropolitan. They should make up their minds which side they support.' His voice softened. 'Anyway, our desert rose is back with us and Papa is bringing Belle home soon, too, so we'll all be together. I suppose that's one good thing to come out of it all; we're a family again. And at least Mama can stop worrying about you nursing.'

Colonel Henri Lefitte telephoned her three days after her arrival in Algeria. He was friendly and polite. Could she, he wondered, drop into his office the following day? There were one or two matters he would like to clear-up. Perhaps she would allow him the pleasure of taking her to lunch afterwards?

Like all the other Algerian government offices, the Sûrété Headquarters in the old Turkish palace was guarded by a military detachment as well as by members of its own security staff, and it was only after her identity card had been checked by three separate guards that Maryse Rose was permitted to enter the reception area. She gave her name at the desk, and then waited while the clerk telephoned the Colonel's department. The Colonel himself led her to his office.

He was charming, and unchanged. The last time Maryse Rose had met him had been at the fateful All Saints ball, when the Arab uprising had begun. She had danced with him then. It had been the night she had met Philippe

110

for the second time, and seeing the Colonel once again revived disquieting memories.

Henri Lefitte was wearing a lightweight grey suit, as always carefully pressed, the creases in the trousers knife-edged, while the cuffs of his gleaming white shirt protruded an exact centimetre from below the sleeves of his jacket; a crimson silk handkerchief was tucked into his top pocket. He was so deeply tanned that with his narrow, slightly hooked nose he looked like a tall Arab. His greeting was effusive. From a small refrigerator concealed in the lower section of a bookcase he produced a half bottle of Moet et Chandon, and only when he had poured them both a glass did he mention the purpose of Maryse Rose's visit.

The matter, he told her, would not normally have been one dealt with by his own department. However, once he had learned of it through Christian, he had immediately engineered total responsibility in order to prevent any further embarrassment to his old friend. Now, it was only a question of completing formalities and the file could be relegated forever to the dusty records department in the palace's vaults.

He chatted lightly for an hour and a half, about her stay in Paris, current Algerian news, and gossip of their mutual acquaintances and friends; while he did so, he flicked through the file he had received from the Paris Deuxième Bureau, occasionally asking her to confirm some apparently small item, or to enlarge on another. It seemed social and pleasant but later as he walked her to the Hotel Aletti restaurant for lunch, she realized that the Colonel had learned far more of Habib Saadi's personality, ideals and even reasoning, and of the intimate relationship she had formed with him, than had any of the Deuxième Bureau interrogators in Paris. Lefitte's casual method of questioning had been professionally insidious.

He had however given her no indication that he had

any intention of making use of what he might have learned. He had made no notes, and no written alterations to her previous statements. He had eventually closed the file which contained them, and as they left his office tossed it onto a shelf as though it were of no importance. Perhaps, she thought, the unease which she was feeling was unjustified.

It had been more than four years since she had dined at the Hotel Aletti, but not even the colour of its paintwork had been altered. The same head waiter met them at the restaurant entrance, bowed recognition to herself and the Colonel, and led them to a table beside one of the windows overlooking the harbour. The same curtains hung in the same elegant folds, the same glasses and cutlery graced the impeccable white linen table-cloths. Regardless of what might ever happen to Algeria itself, it seemed to Maryse Rose that the Aletti Hotel would prove eternal. She had celebrated so many past occasions in its mirrored hall, family anniversaries and weddings, the comings of age of Vincent, Belle and several cousins, that its surroundings were reassuringly familiar.

Lefitte insisted on aperitifs while she studied the menu, was generous with the wine throughout the meal and ordered liqueurs with their coffee. Maryse Rose felt relaxed; she had thought that the lunch with Henri Lefitte might prove to be an ordeal, whereas it had been enjoyable.

When he smoked a cigar and signed the bill, he suggested they should return to his office. It would be quite a brief visit this time, he assured her. There were just one or two minor items he would like to clear up.

He had been so polite and amicable during the interview and the lunch which followed that Maryse Rose was quite off-guard when she entered his office for the second time.

He offered her a seat, then buzzed for a clerk. When the man answered the summons, Henri Lefitte asked him: 'Have you done as I asked.' The man nodded a quick affirmative. 'Good. Now, I don't want to be disturbed . . . for any reason whatsoever.'

When the man had left them alone Lefitte walked to one of the tall cupboards which lined the inner wall of his office beside his desk. He opened a small door and fumbled briefly inside. A second later Maryse Rose heard her own voice from a concealed speaker.

'I'd never viewed things as an Algerian before, from an Arab's point of view, and I realized how ignorant I'd always been, how badly informed. The French press in Algeria is so biased and dishonest . . . Habib discovered the Arab in me, perhaps he didn't discover it but he kindled the Arab spark that was always inside me . . . we were together almost every day, every evening, often all night . . . I'd never been interested in politics before, particularly Algerian politics, they'd always seemed so dull, but he seemed to know everything and everyone, he remembered Father's speeches to the Assembly . . . of course I was sympathetic to his nationalistic ideals, anyone with common decency can see the misjustice and corruption in so much of the French system . . . it made me want to help the Arabs . . . there was far more about which we agreed, than disagreed . . . I even tried to understand why Habib believed terrorism was justified to provoke situations which would weld the Algerian people together, to fight for their freedom . . . of course it's war, and death for an Arab in a *jihad* is martyrdom; there have to be sacrifices but the majority of Arabs will survive and benefit . . . The explosives? I never knew about them; I don't know what difference it might have made if I had known. It's difficult to speculate in retrospect . . . Naturally, I felt glad Habib had escaped, he meant a lot to me and they would have destroyed him . . .' There was much more.

The tape lasted for just over ten minutes. It had been so carefully edited that the only voice which could be heard was her own. All her normal conversation with Lefitte had been removed, and the pieces that were left were only those relating to her friendship with Habib and the time they had spent together. It was obvious they had been lovers. Out of context and without Henri Lefitte's own conversation, so pleasant and ordinary and sometimes amusing or flippant, it was a terrifyingly incriminating documentary. It made her appear an enthusiastic recruit to the Arab cause, one who had not only been aware of Habib's close association with a terrorist group but who was, perhaps, willing to participate herself if circumstances had demanded it. Even her description of the discovery of the secret compartment in her car, by the members of the Paris Deuxième Bureau, sounded as though she had known of its existence beforehand.

She listened, stunned with horror. When the tape finally spun off the reel, clicking, click, click, click, she was unable to speak.

Henri Lefitte had been standing at the window, staring out across the bay with his back to Maryse Rose throughout the playing of the recording. He turned, switched off the recorder, and as the sound died, faced her for the first time. He reached into his pocket and handed her two photographs. 'We have these, too. There are several more.' His lean face was expressionless and his deeply set eyes gave her no indication of his thoughts.

To her dismay she saw that the photographs, although made grainy be enlargement, were of herself and Habib. In one, they were with two of his visiting friends, all seated on the steps of the embankment of the Seine.

'Of course, you recognize the subjects,' said Lefitte.

'Yourself, Habib Saadi, Rahmoun Kaddour and Mahfoud Belaid. A clutch of three bad eggs; Kaddour and Belaid are members of the FLN hierarchy and are on my personal list.'

She felt his eyes examining her as she stared at the photographs. She could remember the sunny day when she and Habib had walked along the river bank with the two visitors. Habib had introduced them as 'cousins'; they had been friendly company during the week they had stayed in Paris.

After an interminable silence, Henri Lefitte asked: 'Can I get you a glass of something? A brandy perhaps?' Her throat was dry and felt constricted as though a metal band had tightened around her neck. She was unable to answer him. He moved closer to her and when he was a couple of feet away leant back against his desk. 'Very useful equipment, a recording machine. We use them because people seldom relax and open-up when there's a note-book in front of them.' Without taking his eyes off her he reached sideways and picked up a bronze casket which stood on his desk; it was of Arab workmanship, antique, the top beautifully cast as a reclining lion. He held it towards her. 'Cigarette?' She shook her head, stiffly. He took one himself and lit it with a small wax match which he struck on the base of the casket. He inhaled deeply, as if he were hungry for nicotine. 'I must admit, in the kind of national emergency we face here today Arabs have been executed on far less adequate evidence.' He added quickly. 'Of course, that wasn't a statement.' He paused. 'If you were European it would be worthless; it would be thrown out of court. But the photographs are very incriminating, and another difficulty for you is your Arab parentage. You know the old proverb, "What's bred in the blood will come out in the bone". You know that's how the pieds-noir think. They will discount your upbringing, your present family. They will simply say that poor Christian Charpentier tried to domesticate a wild animal, and when it became adult it reverted to its natural savagery.' He took a long pull at the cigarette. 'There has been so much bloodshed, so many disgustingly brutal murders of settler families . . . did you know that we have had cases where young European mothers have been disembowelled alive, and their babies killed and pushed back inside them? The pieds-noir have become vengeful. You can't blame them, I suppose. If that happened to my wife and child, I'd want an "eye for an eye" . . . ten eyes!'

He pushed himself away from the desk, walked purposefully to the recorder and removed the reel of tape. He handed it to Maryse Rose. She took it automatically. 'Destroy it,' advised Lefitte lightly. 'Burn it; anything you like. As I've said, it's hardly proof of anything. As for the photographs . . .'

Lefitte dropped his cigarette into a water-filled ashtray that looked like a spitoon at the side of the desk. The stub hissed briefly, then he moved so that he was standing behind Maryse Rose's right shoulder. She could no longer see him, but his closeness made her feel even more nervous. Tension seemed to screw her nerves into tight coils, each near breaking point.

'You can see now how vulnerable you are, my dear,' he said, this time with exaggerated warmth in his voice. 'Dangerously vulnerable. Christian Charpentier's wealth will be unable to save you once you are formally charged. Neither can his political influence, nor can all his friends, including myself, help you if you were ever required to be judged by a jury of European settlers.' He rested both his hands on the back of the chair. 'However, the French have always had the reputation of looking after their own. And if you are loyal to France, then France protects.'

He was silent for a moment as though to add drama to his words. 'I want you to work for France; work for me. We can be useful to each other. As an Arab woman there are many places where you can go that are certainly inaccessible to most of my men; perhaps all of them. You have a good connection with Habib Saadi, and no doubt you are accepted and trusted by quite a few of his friends. And they will certainly think that you can be helpful to them; no other Arab woman in the country is so acceptable amongst the pieds-noir "aristocracy" as yourself. No other Arab woman has so free an access to the confidences of "The Ten", or to the secrets of our politicians.'

'I've heard a name,' continued Lefitte, lowering his voice to a conspiratorial level. 'Mouloud ben Khellil. And I want to know what he is, here in Algiers . . . their political or operational leader. And in due time, I want him, and every one of his men in my cells. A coup like that, Maryse Rose, would be *very* beneficial to both of us, but particularly to you.'

Maryse Rose was absorbing Lefitte's words slowly, her mind still numb and reluctant to accept the situation. She knew what Colonel Lefitte was demanding; that she should find Habib, and eventually betray not only him but his leader and colleagues. She had no illusions about what would then happen to them all; they would be tortured for information, and if they survived they would face the guillotine. She glanced down at the tape and photographs she was holding. The Colonel's 'gifts' were a concealed threat. He intended her to remember that he held the master copies. It was unspoken blackmail. If he were to hand over her file to the prosecutor, backing the photographic evidence with the tape recording of the 'private interview', in the inflammatory atmosphere of Algiers he would destroy her completely. Worse, he might also destroy both Colette and Christian Charpentier.

Lefitte had been silent for a while but spoke again, this time softly, his head close to her own. 'I've known you for a very long time, Maryse Rose; watched you grow from a pretty child into a very attractive young woman. It is my intention that we should get to know each other very much better.'

She felt Lefitte's hand move from the chair-back to her shoulder. It rested there for a moment and then slid down to the gentle swell of her breast. She stiffened slightly, but a strange paralysis seemed to bind and gag her, so that she could neither move nor protest as his fingers slowly unbuttoned her silk blouse and then slipped the straps of her brassiere off her shoulders. His hand cupped a naked breast, massaging her, the thumb and forefinger caressing the nipple. She felt his breath, warm and moist on the skin of her neck, then his lips touching her.

He took his hand away suddenly. 'Your body is charming, my dear. Quite charming. But this is neither the time nor the place. We will come to a sensible arrangement. Naturally, you will need a little time to get used to the idea that we will be, as it were, working together. I promise you that it will be enjoyable, and rewarding.'

A few minutes later he led her through the reception foyer to the massive oak doorway, where he bowed and kissed her hand. 'I shall telephone you,' he promised, making it sound as though she had requested him to do so.

Maryse Rose was so shaken by her meeting with Lefitte, and so pre-occupied by his odious demands that the road from Algiers to Hadjout seemed to unwind ahead of her like a blurred grey silk ribbon. The urgent howl of the klaxon of an oncoming truck forced her to swerve violently and attempt to concentrate on her driving, but it was impossible. She stopped the car on a shoulder of grass

118

above steep brown cliffs which overlooked a small shingle bay. Two hundred yards out on the clear sea, a solitary fisherman in a small dinghy was attending a string of lobster-pots. Beneath the cliffs a flock of birds were diving, their hurtling bodies dotting the pale green shallows with circular patches of white foam. She stood on a narrow peninsula watching them. Momentarily she felt it would be easy to join them, to launch herself from the cliff-top, her arms stretched back like their folded wings, arcing outwards and downwards into cool depths where she could hide forever.

She sat on an outcrop of rock just below the crest of the cliff, hunching her body so that she could bury her head in her arms. The aloneness which she had not experienced for months, had returned. Now it was worse. Before it had been caused by her loss of Philippe and the separation from her family and friends in Algeria. Today seemed to finally prove that the world she had once believed she was a part of, did not exist for her. It was their world, that of the pieds-noir and there was no room within it for her. It was just as Habib had told her so many times; she was no more realistically part of a European family than a caged lark they might buy in a street market, and which amused and entertained them for only as long as it sang.

For the first time since she had learnt that Habib had fled his Paris apartment, she longed to be with him again. She needed reassurance that she belonged somewhere, to someone; that there were people who would accept her totally, and in whom she could trust and believe. She wanted to hear Habib's laughter, his fierce argument, his arms, strong, around her; to feel the supple muscles of his body as he made love to her, and to hear his gentle breathing when they lay, hot and exhausted beside each other in the encompassing safety of the night.

She forced herself to think of Henri Lefitte, and as she did so the dull, leaden, sickly feeling returned. If she had been the real daughter of Christian Charpentier, Lefitte would never have dared to threaten her. But as an Arab woman, as he so clearly pointed out, she became prey to any settler who chose to exploit the situation in which she had unwittingly placed herself. She realized she had been foolish to believe it had all ended in Paris; if Lefitte had not taken advantage of her, then there would have been someone else amongst the Algerian Sûreté staff.

She could see only two alternatives, to accept Lefitte's proposals or leave Algeria yet again. The former was so repugnant to her it was unthinkable, yet the second could only promise a lifetime of melancholic banishment somewhere beyond the reach of French justice.

'Hello.' The greeting was so softly spoken she did not recognize the voice. She looked up, warily. Vincent stood a few feet above her on the cliff-top. He walked down the gentle grass slope, and sat beside her on the rock. 'I didn't want to shout in case I startled you,' he explained. 'Didn't want you falling off.' He read the puzzled look in her eyes. 'I was coming back from the Algiers road and saw one of our cars at the side of the road. I thought it might be Mama. It's not a very sensible place to stop on your own, there's an Arab bidonville only a few hundred yards along the road. You can be certain that some of the inhabitants will be FLN sympathizers and one or two might like an opportunity to make a name for themselves.'

'I'm an Arab,' said Maryse Rose tautly. 'They wouldn't harm me.'

Vincent frowned. He knew Maryse Rose in all her moods, but her voice sounded uncharacteristically bitter. 'That's a strange thing to say.'

'Well, am I an Arab or a European? You answer me.'

'Does it matter?'

She felt the anger which had been submerged beneath her hurt, fear and shame surge upwards. 'Damn you Vincent! And damn Mama and Papa! Of course it matters.' Her eyes filled and tears blurred her vision. She was no longer able to control them as they seemed to burn hot furrows down her cheeks.

It had been many years since Vincent had seen her cry, and she had been a child then. Now he felt embarrassed and confused. He tried to put an arm around her shoulders but she shrugged him angrily away. 'What have we done?' he asked.

'Done?' She turned quickly, her eyes wild within her tears. 'Don't you all know? You tried to make me one of you. You tried to turn me into a pied-noir.' She reached for him with both her hands, holding his upper arms, her fingers digging into his flesh with the urgency of the movement. 'Look at me Vincent. What do you see?'

Vincent sounded bewildered. 'I see you.'

She was almost shouting, now. 'You see an Arab, damn you, Vincent. A Bedouin woman. An Arab dressed as a person!'

Vincent spoke calmly. 'I see my sister, Maryse Rose. And I love her, very much.' He drew her towards him. For a few seconds she fought him, but then her strength left her. He held her close against him while she sobbed, her breath drawn in deep, convulsive gasps.

Gradually the tears and the anger and bitterness, faded.

'You'd better tell me what's been happening,' Vincent suggested gently.

'You wouldn't listen to me a few days ago.'

'But I'm listening now.' He let her sit upright but kept hold of both her hands, his eyes finding hers.

She talked for over an hour; all her thoughts and emotions, of her feelings on losing Philippe, and later on meeting Habib. How she had loved them both in quite different ways, and of her fears, of Habib's warning to her, and of the brutal interrogation in Paris, and then, finally, the full horror of her meeting with Colonel Henri Lefitte. As she told Vincent every detail of the interview she felt his hands tighten ominously, and saw his eyes harden with fury.

When she had finished, Vincent spoke for the first time. 'I shall kill that bastard.'

She knew his threat was real. The European settlers considered family honour above all else. She shook her head, quickly. 'No, I understand how you feel. I have the same feelings, but we'd lose you. Everything we have as a family would be destroyed.'

'Then you must go away. I won't have that man touch you again. Not ever.'

She felt the tears well again. 'I won't go. I've been away from here far too long; a lifetime. I can't leave Algeria again. It's . . . it's like dying; dying slowly, just a little every day.'

'We didn't know you loved Philippe so much.' Vincent tried to smile, but was trapped in her emotions. 'We . . . Papa and I, as I told you the other night, we wanted to protect you.'

'You should have stopped protecting me years ago; all of you. I should have learnt about the real world little by little when I was a child, when I was more resilient; while I was learning about everything else. I thought the real world was Beau Lac, the beach parties, our own friends, our family. The real world is quite different.'

Vincent leant forward and kissed her forehead. 'You're right.' He stood and lifted her to her feet. 'Come on, I'll drive you home. Someone can come back for the other car.' When they reached the cliff-top he paused. 'Will you trust me to have a chat with Papa?'

'You know I'll always trust you. But what good can it do now?'

She did not know what Vincent would plan to do about Lefitte, only that somehow he would find a way to help her. In her mind the incident had begun to assume the proportions of an incomplete nightmare still threatening her, in which some indescribably evil spirit pursued her through claustrophobic darkness. Even to dwell on it briefly brought back a cloying physical sickness. Each time the telephone rang she experienced a feeling of dread, and in an attempt to escape the fearful anticipation which increased whenever she was alone in Beau Lac she spent as little time in the château as possible. Once she would have passed the hours revisiting the favourite places of her childhood. But the beaches, coves, and ancient ruins where she had so often played were no longer safe. She walked in the vineyards and orange groves within the estate but the fear travelled with her and was her only companion, so there were times when she felt that she was being forced towards madness.

A week passed but the tension had not lessened. On the Saturday morning, at breakfast, Vincent seemed unusually cheerful.

'I'm taking Madelene to the pistol range at Khemis,' he announced. 'There's a course beginning there. I think it's sensible that she should know how to handle weapons. A lot of women do now.' He stared across the table at Maryse Rose. 'I think you should come, too. It would be a day out for us all . . . pleasant. We could stop somewhere for lunch afterwards,' he added encouragingly.

The thought of their company was inviting, but guns had never interested her. 'No, I don't think so.'

To her surprise, Christian unexpectedly supported

123

Vincent. 'I'd like you to go along, Maryse Rose. I think it's important.' He read her thoughts. 'It's not guns that kill, it's the people who use them. There are too many such people in Algeria and you must know how to protect yourself.'

'I think you should go with them, dear,' said Colette, adding further weight to Vincent's invitation. 'And Madelene will probably need moral support. I shall take Axel shopping with me into Algiers.'

Maryse Rose sensed that a further refusal would only bring firmer persuasion from all of them. 'All right,' she agreed, but noticing the quick glance which passed between Vincent and Christian, she had the uncomfortable feeling that somehow she had been drawn into a conspiracy.

Khemis was almost sixty miles from Hadjout. Had it been possible to travel in a direct line across the coastal mountain range it would have been little more than thirty, but the road bent eastwards, first in the direction of Blida and then swinging through almost a hundred and eighty degrees until it followed the high plateau of the Bled towards Mascara and eventually Oran almost three hundred miles west along the coast.

It was spectacular countryside, heavily forested, with the slopes of the Massif de l'Ouarsenis rising to the south. Wet season rivers, bordered by dense thickets of bamboo now trickled stealthily through shaded conduits beneath the roadway. In another month they would become raging torrents, powerful enough to rip away their banks and destroy the bridges as the autumn storms of the high plateau fed them.

Vincent drove while Madelene chattered incessantly beside him, skipping from subject to subject without a moment's pause.

Maryse Rose, sitting behind her, let the sound of her sister-in-law's voice, blending with the hum of the engine of the powerful Citroen and the growl of its tyres on the loose road surface, wash over her. It was hypnotic, as was the endless forest through which they drove. For the first time since her interview with Lefitte her mind felt empty and her body relaxed. The soft velour seats seemed to draw her into them and hold her. She slept deeply.

She awakened as the car pitched over deep pot-holes. There were military guards before a high wire gate; a soldier beside Vincent's window examined their identity papers before waving them through. A sign indicated the civilian training area.

The camp and ranges were set in a narrow valley in which all the trees had been cleared for a distance of half a mile beyond the perimeter wire. The ground was naked, raw, and as Vincent parked the vehicle Maryse Rose could hear the sharp sounds of gunshots and smell the acrid scent of cordite in the still air. Set apart from the ranges, and to the right of the parking area, were a dozen wooden barrack rooms with curved, corrugated iron roofs painted white to reflect the sun. Closer was another group of buildings, one with a low verandah.

The majority of the vehicles in the parking area were military but there were several civilian cars. Guards patrolled the perimeter wire in pairs, while between the barracks soldiers strolled, sunbathed, played cards or chatted in groups. Three hundred yards away beyond the buildings, a squad of men, stripped to the waist but carrying back-packs, drilled on a parade ground of oil-bound dust to the screamed orders of a non-commissioned officer.

Vincent, Madelene and Maryse Rose were directed to an office where they again produced their identity cards, and were required to sign indemnity forms. When the formality had been completed they were led across the flat plain of the camp to the pistol ranges. Each range had a sheltered firing point roofed with corrugated iron, but open on the side which faced up the range; the entrance to the firing point was a narrow doorway.

Inside, the noise was deafening. A line of civilians, men and women, were firing at targets at the far end of the twenty-five metre range. The iron roof reverberated. Behind each trainee stood an instructor. There was an officer loading pistol magazines from boxes of ammunition on a table at the back of the range. As they approached him, he turned and faced them.

It was Philippe.

SIX

Philippe's mind, pre-occupied by the task he had been completing at the loading bench, did not respond as quickly as her own. Maryse Rose's recognition was instantaneous, her reaction defensive and animalistic. She ran from the challenge imposed on her already tightly stressed emotions.

In the bright sunlight she hesitated only momentarily, the protective instinct for mental survival driving her from habitation towards the distant safety of the green forest. It was an impossible goal; beyond the rifle and machine-gun ranges and the brown earth embankments of their target trenches and butts, the land rose steeply away to the high perimeter fence reinforced by a dense barrier of coiled barbed wire.

She ran blindly, her thoughts as scattered as a flock of birds startled by the broken twig beneath the foot of a careless hunter.

She heard warning shouts, but ignored them. A hundred yards to her right she glimpsed khaki figures gesticulating wildly.

Hands clawed at her clothing, her arms, she fought them off; hysteria adding to her strength. She stumbled and fell heavily on her knees, and for a while remained motionless, her hands clutching the earth, her head lowered between her arms, fighting to control the vio-

127

lent trembling of her body as reason slowly returned.

She knew it was Philippe she had fought, and could not face him. 'Please go away,' she begged him.

'No.' There was no tenderness in his voice. 'Do you realize where you were running? Another few yards and you would have been in a mine-field.' His voice was angry. 'Have you ever seen what a mine does to someone?' She felt his hands on her arms, powerful, lifting her. 'Get up, Maryse Rose.' He steadied her. 'This isn't Tipaza, this is a wartime military camp.'

She forced herself to raise her head, but avoided his eyes. His face seemed slightly narrower than she had remembered, fine lines scored his tanned skin and the long scar down his cheek was no longer so clearly defined.

He began leading her back towards the barrack area several hundred yards away; she had not realized she had run so far. There were a group of soldiers ahead of them, and he waved them in the direction of the firing point. He was holding her wrist as he might have held that of a wayward child, and she could feel the sharpness of sand on her skin making his grip feel coarse and rough.

'Why didn't you write to me?' she asked, anger surfacing through the fear.

'I wrote. You know I wrote.' He didn't look at her.

'Yes, before; when you were in the mountains. But never afterwards, not after The Citadelle.'

His voice was severe again. 'If you're trying to embarrass me with imagined wrongs it won't work. Two years is a long time in a war . . . more than a lifetime for a lot of men. You learn to forget dead friends, and dead romances.'

'If it died, then you killed it!' she said bitterly. 'I wrote to you from France. I wrote every day from Paris, for several weeks. You never replied; not once.'

He stopped and faced her, releasing her wrist. For the first time she found she was able to meet his eyes. They were more penetrating than those of her memories. 'We both wrote.' He grimaced awkwardly, the scar pulling at his face muscles. 'You don't believe me? We both know we're not lying but neither of us can prove it. I knew you'd gone away, but I didn't know where, so I wrote to you at Beau Lac.' He paused. 'I realized your mail might be intercepted, but not my own. That would be a Court Martial offence. Obviously I overlooked your family influence.'

Maryse Rose said nothing. She realized that Philippe was being truthful. He *had* written to her, but his letters had never been forwarded. The memory of the anguish she had experienced sickened her even now.

'Did you know I'd be here, today?' His voice was softer. She shook her head. 'I wouldn't have come.'

'I suppose not.' He hesitated, thoughtfully. 'Have you hated me so much?'

'I never hated you,' she admitted. 'Not for a second. I was just very hurt.' She could not tell him how deeply, nor how miserable those first long months of loneliness had been for her. 'Did they put you in prison?'

Her question made him smile for the first time. 'No. I didn't really steal the Jeep. They knew that. I was only reprimanded. I lost seniority of rank.' His face stiffened again. 'I was stupid thinking they'd ever allow us to be together. Soldiers day-dream too much on patrol.' Just as they had always done, his eyes seemed to penetrate her mind. 'Did they make it very bad for you?' His use of the word 'they' encompassed everyone.

'We're a Catholic family.'

'The priest? A confession?' He didn't expect her to answer him. 'And then they sent you away in disgrace! I thought all that went out with the end of the World War. But I'd forgotten this is Algeria, and you're the daughter of one of "The Ten".'

'It was nothing to do with that,' she said with unnecessary defence.

'It has everything to do with it. The country has its own upper class, guarding themselves as if they were a French royal family.'

'Not always.' She thought of Lefitte. 'Sometimes it's impossible even for "The Ten".'

Philippe caught the change of tone in her voice and recognized a faint hint of despair. 'I never thought we'd meet again. I'm sorry I startled you.' He could remember her wide-eyed expression when she had recognized him, like that of a hare desperate to escape from a hound.

'I didn't run away from you.' Maryse Rose began walking again, slowly.

'What then?'

'Memories. The reality of the present . . . the future.'

'Do they all frighten you so much now?'

'Yes.'

'Why the future? The war?'

She shook her head, reluctant to reveal her fears to him.

They were now only thirty yards from the pistol range and the irregular metallic shots made the still air vibrate, probing like blunt knife points into her skull. Vincent and Madelene were somewhere inside the building, and she realized they must have known that Philippe would be here. They had planned it all. Christian had known, too . . . and Colette; that had been the conspiracy she had sensed that morning! Again she was being manipulated. She felt resentment and remembered Habib's words. 'I'm a puppet,' she said, abruptly.

'I don't understand you.'

'It doesn't matter. Tell my brother I'll be in the car.' She turned towards the parking area, hoping that Philippe would not follow her.

130

'Wait.' His voice was urgent. She hesitated. 'Can I telephone you?'

She had anticipated his question and had intended to refuse him. Unexpectedly she was unable to do so. 'Everything is too complicated.' She paused and then asked quickly: 'Do you know that I'm an Arab?'

He seemed puzzled. 'You're Christian Charpentier's daughter.'

'Adopted. It's a long story.' Now he knows, she told herself. But did it matter any more?'

His grey eyes were once more delving into her mind. He repeated his question. 'Can I telephone?'

She was afraid again. 'No. Not yet. I'd like time to think.'

During the return journey in the car, she would not respond to Vincent's apologies. It seemed to her that despite the assurances he tried to give her, the family had sought a way to be rid of her and the problems she had caused them all.

Only much later, when she was alone in the peaceful solitude of her room was she able to understand their motives and accept that they had acted in a way they had hoped would please her. It was probably too late; two years too late. As Philippe had said, a lifetime. And in that lifetime, for her, had been Habib.

It had been Habib who had been in her thoughts during the days that had passed since her arrest in his Paris apartment. Philippe had been no more than a fading memory in recent months, and she had always felt that somehow, at sometime, Habib would contact her again. Whenever she visited Algiers, or even the local market at Hadjout, she wondered if he might suddenly appear at her side. She would have welcomed his tactile presence, the urgent enthusiasm of his conversation. He would be risking his life attempting to see her, but romantically it was what he might do.

Now, however, Philippe had returned to her life, and no matter how illogical it seemed to her when she considered her feelings towards him, there was an unplumbable depth to the renewed emotion she was experiencing. Somehow, with Philippe, it was impossible for her to separate recent from past memories; they were irretrievably interwoven in her mind, so that even the rough grip of his hand on her wrist in the military camp had a sensuous relationship with the first erotic moments in the moonlit bedroom of The Citadelle, when his fingertips had awakened the eager passions of her womanhood.

Colonel Lefitte telephoned on the Tuesday morning. He did not ask to speak to Maryse Rose, but left a brief message for her with Ismail. It stated simply: 'Hotel Moulin, rue Bretonnière, 4 pm. Today'.

She had begun to hope that perhaps she would not hear from Lefitte, and that he might have reconsidered the cruel propositions he had made to her, but the blunt command made his intentions quite clear.

She had not mentioned Lefitte to Vincent since she had first told him of the Colonel's advances. Nor did she believe that he had discussed that aspect of it with Christian, who would surely have wanted every minutest detail from her. All the fears, and the deep sense of dread she had experienced in Lefitte's presence returned. The thought of Lefitte removing her clothing, touching the most intimate parts of her body as he had fondled her breast, revolted her.

She rang Vincent at his Algiers office, praying that he would be there and able to take her call. She almost wept with relief at the sound of his voice. To her dismay, when

132

she had read Lefitte's message to him he said abruptly: 'Then you must go to see him.' She began to protest but Vincent stopped her.

'Trust me. You'll be quite safe.'

Vincent's reassurances gave her no comfort as she drove into the city, and her apprehension grew as she turned off the main boulevard along the rue Delacroix. She could not remember the Hotel Moulin; there were countless small commercial hotels in the area, and the rue Bretonnière was one of several small roads off Delacroix.

The afternoon traffic was already heavy, and it took her a quarter of an hour to find a parking space three hundred yards from rue Bretonnière. She felt she was walking to the gallows. She was already late and it was 4.15 as she turned the corner into the small street. It was clogged with stationary vehicles and pedestrians. Thirty yards ahead she could see the hotel sign, a large windmill outlined in neon tube that would be illuminated as darkness fell. Below the sign, on the pavement and in the road, the crowds were even denser. She could hear someone shouting but was unable to distinguish the words. She pushed her way forward, until a young paratrooper, his sub machine-gun under his arm, stopped her.

'Keep back, Miss.'

She could see several paratroopers and gendarmes now, attempting to keep sightseers away from a group of men kneeling beside a crumpled body on the roadway.

'What's happened?' she questioned the nearest soldier but he ignored her, turning his attention to a section of the crowd who were pushing closer.

A man beside her half-turned: 'The Kabyle smile,' he said ghoulishly, using the French military slang for a cut throat. 'You can see the blood on the road.'

'That's nonsense,' interrupted a woman to her right.

133

'His throat's not cut. Besides, it was Europeans who beat him, not Arabs.' She adjusted her coloured head scarf fussily.

'He was probably only a pimp, then,' suggested the man. 'There are enough of them in this area.'

'I saw it all,' the woman said, authoritatively. 'He was walking towards the hotel when a car pulled up alongside. Two men jumped out . . . pieds-noir . . . they beat him unconscious with their pistols. I screamed for the police but it was all so quick. The police have taken my name and address as a witness,' she added confidentially.

From further along the road beyond the crowd Maryse Rose heard the penetrating bell of a Renault ambulance and a moment later the vehicle, directed by policemen, edged into sight. Two attendants clambered out, carrying a stretcher. The paratroopers and gendarmes standing beside the unconscious victim moved aside. She caught a glimpse of the man's battered and bloody face as he was lifted onto the stretcher and carried to the ambulance. He was unrecognizable.

One of the paras, a sergeant, began shouting as the vehicle moved away, the shrill sound of its bell cutting through the babble of the crowds' conversation. 'It's all over . . . move along now . . . be on your way . . . clear the road . . .'

The compacted traffic followed in the wake of the ambulance, as the crowd quickly dispersed and the patrolling soldiers moved on. In moments Maryse Rose was almost alone. An Arab porter from the Hotel Moulin swilled a bucket of soapy water across the bloodstained pavement and began scrubbing it with a broom. Brown suds filled the gutter.

For a while the incident had distracted Maryse Rose, but now her earlier apprehension returned, heightened in the aftermath of the violence. Inside the dark foyer of the hotel, in its lobby or bar, Colonel Lefitte would be waiting for her.

It took all her courage to climb the few shallow steps, and enter. Apart from a clerk behind the reception desk on the right of the foyer, it was empty, the still air smelling faintly of furniture polish and disinfectant. A large and ornate chandelier, out of proportion to the small foyer, hung from the ceiling. The room was octagonal and panelled with long mirrors in gilt frames so that for a moment she seemed to be standing in an enormous hall that extended forever in every direction.

The clerk looked up, interested, and then coughed loudly to draw her attention. 'Madam?'

She walked closer to the desk and spoke nervously. 'I have an appointment with a Colonel Lefitte.'

The clerk, a short, dapperly dressed man of about forty-five assumed a theatrically apologetic expression. 'I'm afraid we have no guest of that name.' He paused thought-fully. 'But, of course he may not be staying here. Perhaps you would care to wait in the lounge.' He waved towards a gap in the mirrors which led into a corridor. 'You'll find a bell for service, if you'd like coffee, or tea.'

The lounge was eerily silent, apart from the ominous ticking of a tall mahogany clock which stood in one corner of the room. There were two dozen leather armchairs placed around low coffee tables on which stood brass ashtrays. The windows of the room overlooked a small courtyard shaded by one spindly date palm, beyond which rose a high wall with a spiked grill on top.

It was four-thirty. She stayed until the hands of the clock reached five, when it struck the hour with an off-key, tinny sound. Then she left.

She felt only a little less apprehensive on her return to Beau Lac. The fact that Lefitte had not appeared at the hotel added a sinister element, and it occurred to her that he might never have intended to meet her there but had in some way been testing her. Perhaps, concealed, he had even watched her nervous arrival, and had left satisfied that she would obey his future instructions. More disturbing was the thought that he might be deriving pleasure from her fears; a cat playing with a captive mouse.

Colette met her in the hallway, excitedly brandishing a letter. 'Oh, there you are. Where have you been?' She did not expect or wait for a reply. 'A letter from Belle. She's flying back on Saturday.' Her voice was excited. 'All together again. It will be lovely. Did you see Axel in the garden? I suppose he's with the *fatma*.'

Neither Christian nor Vincent returned from Algiers in time for dinner that night. Christian was dining with a group of fellow Deputies and would stay in Algiers, while Vincent, according to Madelene, was involved in the inauguration meeting of a new club which he and a number of his friends had decided to start. Just what the purpose of this club was Madelene did not know, but Vincent had informed her it was to be quite exclusive.

Maryse Rose had hoped she would be able to talk to him that evening but it was only much later, when she was almost asleep in her bed, that she heard the sound of his car in the driveway of the chateau.

He awakened her early the following morning with a soft knock on her bedroom door. He was already dressed, his white shirt crisp, his pale grey business suit sharply pressed. 'Can I come in?'

She peered at him sleepily over the bedclothes. He sat himself on the edge of the bed.

'You obviously didn't see Lefitte yesterday.'

She pushed herself up onto an elbow. 'How do you know?'

He held the morning newspaper towards her, folded

into a narrow oblong. 'He won't be keeping any engagements for a very long time.' Maryse Rose tried to focus
her eyes on the print as Vincent continued. 'Someone
made a thorough job of it . . . outside the Hotel Moulin.'

Instantly, she could picture the bloody body being lifted
onto the stretcher, and there was horror in her voice as
she asked: 'Vincent . . . you didn't?'

He interrupted her and smiled grimly. 'No, but I'd have
liked to do it personally. The bastard deserved it and I
don't doubt there are a hundred men in Algiers with
every reason to kill him; his job isn't one that makes
friends. Strange it should be pieds-noir though, and not
Arabs.' He leant towards her and kissed her lightly on the
forehead. 'I must be off to work.' Near the door he stopped
and turned towards her again. 'Have you heard from
Philippe?'

'Not yet.'

He grinned at her. 'He shouldn't waste time.'

If Vincent had expected her to derive satisfaction from
the news of Lefitte's beating, he was wrong. The savagery
of the attack which she had almost witnessed was
described in gruesome detail in the *Echo*. There were
conflicting witnesses' reports on the exact number of
attackers, it might have been two or three, but Lefitte's
injuries were severe, and he was still in intensive care,
and even if he survived was likely to remain in hospital
for many weeks. The brutality shocked Maryse Rose, for
although she hated Lefitte she could not forget the years
when she had known him and his wife Suzanne as regular
visitors to the château. Nor did she feel greater hope for
the future. It was no more than a respite for her. Lefitte
would be well again and it was unlikely that he would
forget her. All that had happened was that an unpleasant
meeting had been postponed, and at sometime she would

have to face him again. For the next few nights horrific dreams eclipsed her thoughts of Philippe, and she awakened in terror in the darkness of her room from nightmares in which she was relentlessly pursued by a grotesquely disfigured phantom.

Belle arrived back in Algeria late on Saturday afternoon. Maryse Rose had not wanted to meet her at Maison Blanche airport, but Colette had insisted that all of the family should be there. Belle barely acknowledged Maryse Rose's presence, and made no effort to conceal her dislike even during the excitement of her homecoming. For a time Maryse Rose found herself on the edge of the family group as though she were no more than an acquaintance or servant. Belle's behaviour was so blatantly rude that later, when Maryse Rose was alone with Vincent, he questioned her about it.

'What's been happening between you two?'

Maryse Rose shrugged. 'It's no different.'

'Of course it's different. I know she's always been difficult, but now she acts as though she really hates you.'

His observation hurt her. 'Perhaps she does. Perhaps she has a right to.'

'That's nonsense. Childhood jealousies are one thing, but she's an adult now. She should try to act like one.'

Maryse Rose found herself defending Belle. 'Some people can hide their feelings, others can't. Belle is just being honest. I can understand why she feels as she does towards me. Everything I've ever done affects her.' She caught Vincent's quick frown. 'It does, Vincent, and far more than it has ever affected you. When I've made mistakes, Belle has always had to pay for them. It's a penalty of us being girls ... sons have an easy time, you're forgiven everything, but what happens to one sister is always reflected in the treatment of the other.'

'That cuts both ways,' insisted Vincent, determined not to pardon Belle so easily.

'It does, but Belle and I think differently. We're bound to think differently. Remember, I'm the intruder, and if it hadn't been for me in the family, Belle . . .'

Vincent stopped her. 'Belle is just a spoilt brat.'

'No . . . not unless we all are. Remember how you used to quote Dumas when we were children. "One for all, all for one." But you never meant it as he did. We used to laugh about Mama, and the ridiculous lengths she'd go to making sure each of us received exactly our share of everything. I've even been woken in the middle of the night to be given an ice cream because Mama suddenly remembered that Belle had been allowed one that afternoon. If one of us had new shoes, the other received the same, even if we didn't need them. And dresses, coats, toys, pets, the ponies . . . everything. And the same went for Mama's affection. One kiss here, and then one for each of the others.'

'I'm going to speak to Belle.'

'Please don't,' Maryse Rose insisted quickly. 'The world is quite big enough for Belle and myself.'

'But is Beau Lac?' Vincent's blue eyes, so like those of his father, Christian, questioned her.

'Quite big enough,' she repeated, positively.

She was less certain that evening when dinner had finished and they were together in the drawing-room. Axel had been put to bed earlier, and now that the evenings were chilly a fire had been lit in the grate of the ornate marble fireplace, and the red coals were casting their warmth across the room. Ismail had served drinks, and Vincent relaxed, a balloon of Armagnac in his hands, leaning against the mantelpiece with his back to the fire. Christian and Colette sat on one of the sofas, Madelene, now heavily pregnant, beside her, Maryse Rose on another. Belle had left them a few minutes earlier, but now returned to the drawing-room with a long roll of paper in her hands.

'I thought you'd all be interested in this.' She unrolled the paper as though it were a parchment scroll and held it towards them. 'It's a photograph of Maryse Rose's boyfriend.'

It was a police poster showing the photographs of the heads and shoulders of a dozen young Arabs, some in European dress, others in their traditional clothing. Belle pointed at one. 'This is Habib Saadi. A handsome boy isn't he.' She laughed. 'He's become quite famous. His photograph is on every *pissoire*. Ten thousand new francs for information leading to his arrest.'

Maryse Rose was stunned. She recognized the photograph as a reproduction of one which had stood on a chest of drawers in the bedroom of Habib's apartment. Originally it had been of Habib and his mother, but the woman had been cut from the picture. Once, Maryse Rose had teased Habib about it. He had looked so much younger then, barely needing to shave. It had been taken when he was seventeen, on the first anniversary of his father's murder. His mother's face had been serious, her eyes filled with sadness; a slender woman who looked almost fifty but who was probably little more than thirty-five. Habib was the oldest of her children.

'You malicious bitch!' Vincent shouted the words. He strode across the room and tore the poster from Belle's hands. For a moment it seemed that he was about to strike her and she flinched instinctively, but he turned away, screwed the paper into a ball and tossed it into the fire.

Christian was on his feet instantly. 'That's enough.' His eyes expressed uncharacteristic fury.

'Enough from whom? From me, or from Belle?' Vincent glared defiantly at his father.

'Enough from both of you. I won't tolerate this uncivilized behaviour in my house. You're not Arabs bickering in a street market.' A quick change of his expression indicated he had recognized his unfortunate choice of words. His cheeks coloured slightly, but he attempted to cover his embarrassment by reinforcing his anger. 'Belle, you will apologize to Maryse Rose at once. And Vincent, you will do the same to Belle and to your mother and myself.' He had not given Vincent such a curt order since his youth.

Vincent paled. 'I don't regret defending Maryse Rose. Belle has been acting disgracefully towards her.'

Christian's eyes narrowed dangerously. 'You will apologize or you will leave my house, tonight.' Colette attempted to intervene but his fierce expression warned her to silence.

'I'll apologize.' Belle's voice was pitched close to hysteria. 'I don't care. I apologize to everyone.' The situation had developed far beyond anything she had foreseen. 'I'm sorry Maryse Rose. I'm sorry, Mama. It was intended as a joke. I apologize, Papa.' She ran from the room.

Christian stared coldly at Vincent. 'I'm waiting.'

Madelene spoke anxiously. 'The children Vincent . . . Axel and the new baby when it arrives . . . they have to stay here in Beau Lac, where it's safe for them. For their sake, Vincent.' Less than an hour previously they had all listened to the news on Radio Algiers. The murder of a French settler's seven-year-old son by Arab children with whom he had been playing, had been reported. It seemed to Madelene that her husband's pride was a small thing to sacrifice for their children's security, but she understood Vincent's feelings. Without her prompting she knew he would never back down. The two men were far more alike than they would ever admit.

Vincent met his father's icy stare evenly, knowing his father realized that without Madelene's intervention he would never have complied with the demand. It was unlikely too that in his anger his father had considered his grandson or the unborn child, due in only a few weeks. Vincent forced himself to remove the tension from his voice. 'I'm sorry, Papa.'

There was a tense silence as Christian seated himself again, while Vincent poured himself another large Armagnac from the decanter, then Ismail spoke from the doorway, drawing their attention. 'There is a visitor, M'sieur.' He addressed himself to Christian. 'A Lieutenant Viard. Do you wish me to show him in?'

For a moment Christian hesitated, searching his mind to identify the name, then he looked at Maryse Rose, questioningly. 'Would you like him to come in?' His voice was quite normal, almost gentle.

Her mind was incapable of cohesive thought, still numbed by the events of the past minutes. Automatically she said: 'Yes, Papa.'

Christian nodded towards Ismail.

Instantly Maryse Rose regretted her decision. How could she invite Philippe into this room, to meet her family after all the problems her relationship with him had already caused? And at this unpleasant time when the atmosphere of the room was so tense it was almost visible. Colette was sitting stiffly, white-faced, and Madelene was close to tears with relief. Christian had spoken calmly, but she knew that his emotions must still be close to the surface, while Vincent was tense and uncomfortable, obviously regretting that he had been forced to accept some kind of masculine defeat.

She stood, intending to intercept Philippe outside in

the hallway or corridor, but before she was able to do so Ismail ushered him into the room.

Philippe was in uniform, wearing a pistol holster on his belt as though he were on duty. He bowed towards them all then smiled grimly at her and walked quickly forward until he was standing in front of Christian. Christian pushed himself to his feet as Philippe held out his hand. Christian shook it briefly, his face expressionless. Colette stared up at Philippe with a faint look of astonishment on her face as he turned towards her, took her hand and kissed it nodding recognition to Madelene and Vincent. He said nothing to Maryse Rose but turned towards Christian again.

He spoke very formally. 'Sir, I came here this evening to seek your permission.'

My God, thought Maryse Rose. He's going to ask if he can marry me, but I don't even know my own feelings anymore.

It had simultaneously occurred to Christian that this might be the Lieutenant's intention, and he was taken aback. To his obvious relief Philippe said. 'I wish to court your daughter, Maryse Rose, sir.'

Vincent laughed, stiffly, but Philippe ignored the interruption.

'I'm very much in love with her, sir, and I would like the opportunity to convince her that she should marry me.' Philippe paused. 'I have two weeks leave, sir. If I do not succeed by the end of that time, then I'll not trouble her or your family again.'

Christian said: 'Well . . .' slowly. Maryse Rose recognized a slightly amused look in his eyes that a short while before had shown only anger. He looked towards her, seeking some indication of her wishes, then spoke to Philippe. 'It is not entirely up to me, Lieutenant Viard, but I'll agree if that is what my daughter wants.' He looked at her again.

The ease with which she was able to answer him surprised her. 'Yes, Papa.'

To her amazement, Philippe stiffened slightly and began an obvious move to leave. Then he said to Christian. 'In that case, Sir, I'll telephone her in the morning.' He bowed. He had not spoken a single word to Maryse Rose.

'Just one moment, young man.' Colette frowned up at him. 'I shall need to get to know you, too. She's my daughter as well as my husband's. I suggest you come to dinner here, tomorrow. At eight o'clock.'

'Yes, ma'am.' For the first time, Philippe smiled openly at them all. 'I hope I haven't disturbed your evening too much. Goodnight.'

'I'll see you out,' said Vincent. He walked quickly beside Philippe. When they reached the front door which Ismail opened, Vincent smiled and held out his hand. 'Well done Lieutenant,' he said. 'I sincerely wish you luck.'

For the first time in many months Maryse Rose dreamed of Philippe. The next morning she could not remember the dream but wakened feeling unusually comforted and secure. In retrospect, his approach to her father amused her; it had been so unexpected, so correct and old-fashioned. Had he informed her in advance of his intention she would have forbidden it, dreading Christian's reactions. But unwittingly Philippe had chosen a maoment when her family were most vulnerable, and his arrival had been a welcome distraction for them all. Afterwards, when he had left, they had treated it as though it were an everyday occurrence for a suitor to call on her, with only Madelene and Vincent subjecting her to the mildest teasing. Belle had remained upstairs in her room. At breakfast, however, she had gone out of her way to be polite to Maryse Rose so that it occurred to her that

144

after all there might have been a little profit in the family's unpleasant argument.

Thoughts of Philippe occupied Maryse Rose's day. The present minutes drove away the past months, diminishing them and everything they had contained. She could feel Philippe's arms around her in the romantic moonlight of The Citadelle as though he had held her only hours before, and the years of separation had never existed. When she questioned her billowing emotions it seemed clear to her that she had never ceased to love him, and that she had mistakenly allowed her fears and loneliness to mask her true feelings.

As the day passed she experienced a growing sense of excitement, so that as she bathed and dressed that evening it was as though she had become a girl once more, anticipating a tryst with a man she knew she had loved forever. For the first time in almost two years she wore the Arab bracelet he had given her on the day when they had become lovers.

The dinner was a success. Philippe was so charming that Maryse Rose was certain the entire family had warmed towards him. Only at the end of the evening, when he had wished goodnight to her family, were they alone for a brief few minutes. He took her hand, the first time he had touched her, as they walked together towards his car.

'Was it terribly difficult for you?' she asked.

He laughed. She had not heard his laughter since the day they had run through the sea together, drenched by the rain, beside the Tipaza beach. 'Yesterday was difficult. I've felt less nervous leading a charge against the enemy. I half expected to be grabbed by my collar and marched out of the grounds.'

'You were very brave.'

He laughed again. 'I decided it had to be done properly. Better to face them now . . . I'd have to do it eventually.'

145

'You're very sure of yourself,' she admonished him, gently.

'Admit defeat, and you're defeated.' They had reached the door of his car, a Peugeot saloon painted military green. 'I've got a present for you.' He reached inside the vehicle then held out his hand towards her, palm downwards. 'Here . . .'

She took the concealed gift. It was an orange.

'Peel it.'

Uncertain of what he was expecting from her, she dug her thumbnail beneath the soft skin, and stripped it from the fruit.

'And now bite it,' he ordered.

Suddenly she understood, and bit slowly into the sweet flesh. 'There's no rain . . . no salt spray from the sea.'

'And no Roman temple.' His voice was little more than a whisper, as though he feared he might be overheard. He touched the tip of her nose with his finger, then ran it lightly down her body from her throat, between her breasts, to her waist. 'You tasted of oranges, from here to here.' Before she could speak again his lips against her own brought the same swirling and tempestuous emotions that she had experienced when he had last held her in his arms. The same remembered sense of intoxication began to flow through her. Just as she began to feel that in some impalpable manner their minds and bodies were becoming one, he drew away from her.

'Vincent calls you the Desert Rose.'

She nodded.

'It's very appropriate.' He leant forward and kissed her forehead. 'Tomorrow afternoon?'

'Please.' She held his hand as long as possible, reluctant to lose the contact as he climbed into the car.

She watched as he drove slowly past the guard at the gate. She saw the man salute, and then the vehicle was lost from sight as it turned onto the road. When Philippe had been close to her the night air had seemed warm, but now, as she stood alone its wintry chill made her shudder.

She was living again, each new day welcomed by a thrill of anticipation for the pleasure she knew it would hold for her. The times when she was apart from Philippe appeared simply as moments during which she could savour recent memories, reliving his embraces, and cherishing the tender words he had spoken during their last meeting. Everything seemed as fresh to her as the growing warmth of spring sunshine after the depressions of a long winter. But, before, as lovers, they could have wandered along woodland paths in the green valleys of the familiar mountains, or found seclusion amidst the sand dunes of lonely beaches. Now there was danger in solitude; the sniper's bullet, the mined track, or the assassin's knife.

For Europeans, even Algiers itself had shrunk itself during the past two years, already known as 'the Battle of Algiers'. To venture into the casbah would be suicidal, even if it were possible for a European to pass through the military checkpoints on its entrances where troops searched every male Arab, or ran metal-detectors over the heavily clothed bodies of the women. No pieds-noir would risk a visit to the small markets around the casbah's perimeter; it was too easy for a razor to slash in the jostling Arab crowd, and its user, perhaps a child, to scuttle away into the crowded background.

Few ventured anywhere without weapons of their own. An Arab tradesman, with his barrow-load of fish, could be a terrorist. The street-sweepers, the water-sellers, chewing-gum salesmen, the labourers who mended the roads, the beggars and newspaper vendors, were all the enemy. No European would stroll along any road, knowing that an Arab was walking a few steps behind him; when this happened they stepped aside and slowed down, until the Arab was in front where they could watch his actions.

Many of the places Maryse Rose had visited as a teenager, were now closed or being rebuilt as a result of bombings. The milk bar near Saint Eugene beach where she had often drunk milk-shakes as a child had been bombed, as had The Cafeteria – a favourite meeting place for students – and the Otomatic in rue Michelet, and its neighbour the Coq-Hardi. The Casino where she had often danced, had suffered a similar fate. The casualties had been horrific.

But for the moment the war of the city appeared to have been won by the French. Thousands of Arabs had been arrested and imprisoned. Many had been guillotined; others had been shot by troops in pitched street-battles and riots. FLN bomb factories had been discovered and destroyed.

However, despite all the problems that remained, there were places where lovers could invent a privacy even though in the company of others. There were still many pleasantly secluded bars and clubs, the cinemas and theatre. And for Maryse Rose and Philippe there were the deserted evening vineyards and orange groves, within the wire fortress of Beau Lac, to which they could return at the end of a day.

It was the last night of Philippe's leave, and despite him telling Christian that he intended to ask Maryse Rose to marry him, he had not done so. He had booked seats that evening for the opera, and reserved a table at a nearby restaurant. She had expected him to suggest they should meet that afternoon, as they had done on every day of his leave, but when he left her on the previous night he had said nothing. It had worried her. Perhaps, she thought, she had in some way disappointed him. The day was unusually long and disquieting as she waited for him.

He called for her at Beau Lac at a little after 7.00 pm, and they drove together to Algiers. There was a strange lightness to his conversation which made her feel as if she were in the company of a friend rather than a lover, as though their relationship were moving backwards rather than progressing towards the climax she had begun to expect. During the intervals at the opera, and later in the restaurant, it was no different.

By the time they returned to Beau Lac she was filled with a sense of dread, convinced that when Philippe left her that night to return to his barracks and duty she would never see him again. The feeling of hopelessness which he had driven away during the past two weeks was already pressing its way back into her mind.

He parked the car out of the floodlighting and in the shadow of one of the tall palms. He made no move to get out, but sat silently.

'Do you want me to go inside?' she asked quietly, when he made no move to put his arm around her.

'No.'

'What then?' She was conscious that her voice sounded thin, small; that of a disappointed child.

He did not reply, but reached across her lap and took her hand. She felt the hardness of metal as he slid a ring onto her finger. She faced him quickly. She could see his face in the half-light, his eyes sparkled and he was grinning.

She pulled her hand away from him and examined it. On her finger was a diamond engagement ring. 'You idiot,' she said furiously. 'You've been teasing me all evening. I thought you'd stopped loving me.' Her body felt as though she had slid into a warm bath. Beau Lac's floodlights reflected in the stones of the ring. 'It's very beautiful.'

He took her hands again. 'It's not yours yet. It's the prize for answering a question correctly.' His voice was serious.

'No more teasing?'

He shook his head. 'No more. Just the question.' He was gripping her hands tightly as though he feared she would run from him. 'Will you marry me?'

She said: 'Yes,' softly, and as he drew her towards him felt warm tears of happiness on her cheeks.

It seemed that nothing could spoil her contentment in the weeks leading towards her January wedding when Philippe would be able to take a few days of leave, and they could begin their lives together. But disaster struck at Beau Lac.

With Christmas less than a week away and the family's celebrations for Maryse Rose's coming of age already planned, 4,000 vines and two of the orange groves were destroyed. Financially, the damage would make only a fractional difference to the Charpentier Company profits even though it would take three or four years before newly planted vines would bear fruit in any quantity, and much longer for orange trees to mature. Far more disturbing was the knowledge that the damage had been done by Arab workers who had been trusted employees of the family for many years, some since Christian Charpentier's own youth on the estate.

The damage was done during one night, and reported by the estate manager the following dawn. The Arab guards whom Christian had armed with shotguns, had fled, as had the foreman, his wife and children and the few labourers still permitted to live near the vineyard.

The estate itself was deserted, the gates in the wire fencing, left open. The destruction could not have been the work of the estate workers alone, for it was obvious from tracks in the damp soil that there had been many people involved. Hundreds of the vines had been slashed through near the root, the others ruined by fuel-oil and weedkiller. The surface roots of the orange trees had been drilled, the deep holes packed with potassium nitrate, trunks had been ring-barked with machetes.

Despite threats and questioning by the gendarmerie, the inhabitants of the Arab bidonville where most of the workers had lived were silent. The culprits had slipped away into the maquis to join the guerillas of the FLN, their passport to acceptance the success of their raid on the Beau Lac estate.

Two nights later the Arab bidonville was burnt to the ground. Several car-loads of pieds-noir parked in the road a hundred yards short of the pathetic village built of packing-cases, flattened oil-drums, discarded tarpaulins and scraps of waste material. The raiders were armed with shotguns and Molotov cocktails made from a mixture of petrol, rubber solution and detergent. They lit the petrol-soaked fuses of the Coca-Cola bottle bombs and hurled them amongst the crowded dwellings. Then, as the inhabitants ran confused from the spreading flames, fired indiscriminantly at anything that moved.

Less than ten minutes later when the gendarmes of the nearby post arrived, there was no sign of the pieds-noir attackers. By morning the bidonville was smouldering wreckage, amongst which lay the bodies of eleven victims . . . four of them children. There were twenty-three wounded.

That day the military authorities doubled the number of soldiers guarding the grounds surrounding Beau Lac.

*

On the morning of Christmas Eve, Christian gathered his family together in the drawing-room of Beau Lac. He had returned from Algiers late the evening before, and now it was obvious from his solemn expression that he had some kind of unpleasant duty to perform. He waited until they were seated, and then said flatly: 'I'm afraid that I have had to make a difficult decision.' He paused for a moment as if to add emphasis to the warning in his words. 'Today I am dismissing all our Arab staff.'

'Papa!' Even Belle was unable to stifle her surprise.

Christian smiled at her, sadly. 'It can't be helped, Belle. I've discussed it with your mother and we both agree it has become necessary.'

Maryse Rose said: 'Surely not Ismail, Papa? He's always been here.' Ismail had played with them in the gardens when they had been children. He had dressed their cuts and bruises when the *fatma* had been busy elsewhere, comforted them if they had been scolded. He was as much part of Beau Lac as herself. The thought that he was to be forced to leave shocked her.

Christian tightened his lips. 'Ismail is quite elderly. In his case I should have said retired rather than dismissed. And of course his son will continue to work in our offices in Algiers. I've already spoken to him and he agrees that it is for the best. Ismail will get a good pension, and accommodation in company property near his son's family. As for the others, they will receive compensation.'

'But why must we get rid of them all?' questioned Belle incredulously.

Vincent answered her. There was a faint hardness to his voice indicating his agreement with his father's decision. 'We can't trust them.'

'Don't be ridiculous,' Belle glared angrily at Vincent. 'Of course we trust them. They're house servants, not field-workers.'

'It's not what they may want to do, Belle, but what they can be forced to do,' explained Christian. 'All of them have families, children perhaps, fathers, mothers, brothers and sisters; people they love. But they know the FLN are quite ruthless. If they are forced to choose between one of their close relatives being horribly murdered by the terrorists, or agreeing to their demands, we can't be certain of their decision. And neither myself nor your mother are prepared to risk your lives in those circumstances.'

Belle's voice was unusually tremulous. 'How can we live here without servants?'

Christian glanced at Colette. His wife's face was pale, and her eyes moist. 'It is possible we may close Beau Lac at some time in the future.' He said quickly. 'But not immediately. It will depend upon the way the future unfolds. However, new staff will be here later today.'

'New staff? Who are they?' Belle sounded as if she were about to burst into tears.

'They're French, dear, Metropolitans,' Colette attempted to make her voice comforting. 'Your father interviewed them last night in the city. I expect they will soon fit in.'

'I hate Metropolitan servants,' Belle complained. 'They're so arrogant.'

It was the first time in her life that Maryse Rose had ever heard Belle defend an Arab for any reason, but Christian would not be swayed. By eleven that morning the Arab staff had been informed, and waited in the parking area beside the château with their possessions heaped beside them; rolled carpets, odd items of furniture that they had acquired over the years in service, their ornaments, bed linen and clothing. In less than three hours their lives, previously so ordered, had been changed forever. Their farewells were a combination of amazement, sadness and resentment. Old Ismail appeared to have aged forty years since he had served dinner, unsuspectingly, the previous evening. Now his hands shook as though he suffered from ague, the lines on his gnarled face seemed deeper than ever, and his eyes had become as misted as those of an old dog. He had served the Charpentier family for almost forty years and had received less than half a day's notice.

When they had been driven away in Charpentier Company trucks, to be taken to the villages or homes of relatives, the château felt deserted. Although the staff had been unobtrusive they had always been there, softly passing doorways, dusting or cleaning, in the background had been their conversation, hushed but always present, mingling with the distant hubbub of the kitchens, and the cook's occasional burst of song.

The dreary atmosphere of sadness did not change for the family with the arrival in mid-afternoon of the new servants. They were strangers who complained of the state of their accommodation, and for a time wandered about Beau Lac as if they were sightseers. For Maryse Rose, and Belle, they were even more impersonal than the waiters in the Algiers restaurants, or the chambermaids of hotels in which they had stayed.

For once the two women were in agreement, Beau Lac would never be the same.

Christmas passed in social idleness, with its usual round of visits to the homes of friends, the services at the Hadjout church, and a luncheon to celebrate Maryse Rose's coming of age, at a small much-favoured restaurant set high above the city.

Philippe telephoned Maryse Rose every day, stretching his calls until she could hear shouted complaints in the background from fellow officers in the mess at the Khemis barracks.

154

After the short vacation she filled her time with the thoughts and preparations for her wedding. Colette had wanted it in the cathedral in Algiers, but Maryse had known Philippe would hate it; eventually it was agreed it should take place in Hadjout.

Although the first days of January dragged by slowly for Maryse Rose, the long hours punctuated only by her conversations with Philippe, suddenly time accelerated and there was soon little remaining in which to complete all her preparations.

Had it been peacetime, with Philippe's regiment carrying out its normal duties, there would have been accommodation for them both after the ceremony in the married quarters of the barracks, or a nearby house. Now this was impossible. The army was as much at war as it had been in Indo China, and wives were an incumbrance. To rent a private house near the barracks was too dangerous; the families of French officers had already become special targets for the terrorists. And to buy or rent an apartment in Algiers seemed pointless as she would be alone for much of the time. However, unsatisfactory it might seem, it made sense to remain at Beau Lac until the country's problems were resolved. Perhaps that would not be too long, she thought optimistically.

She awakened on her wedding morning, the 24 January, to bright sunlight, and the night-wet earth already drying in a light Mediterranean breeze. As she stared from the window it changed her sombre mood instantly to one of eager excitement. At ten o'clock the hairdresser arrived from his salon, and by eleven-thirty she was being helped into her wedding gown by its designer and her fussy seamstress. The exquisite cream handmade dress of Italian lace, full-skirted and delightfully feminine, swirled like a mist around her as she pivoted before her mirror; fine seed pearls decorated the closely fitted bodice and captured the golden reflected rays of the sun. As the hairdresser placed the matching lace and pearl headdress on her upswept bouffant hair and tidied imagined faults in her immaculate coiffure, the two normally blasé Metropolitan maids who had helped with her preparations, watched with the satisfied smiles of master craftsmen surveying their work.

Belle had agreed to her mother's suggestion that she should be Maryse Rose's maid-of-honour with ill-concealed annoyance, knowing that her refusal would be unacceptable to both her parents. She hated the thought of playing second-fiddle to Maryse Rose, both in appearance and circumstance, reminding herself that had it not been for Maryse Rose, she herself might have been a bride by now. But regardless of her feelings, it was more than she dared to spoil this special day. She consoled herself with the conviction that she was taking part only to please her mother.

Although Maryse Rose was unaware, both civil and military security officers mingled with the guests and bystanders who crowded the street and church for the ceremony, but despite Christian's secret fears there were no incidents to mar the day.

Maryse Rose saw only Philippe, tall, handsome in his dress uniform, accompanied by his closest friend, Captain Paul Sandrin, whom she had met only briefly the previous week. The two men waited for her, unable to resist the temptation to turn their heads as she walked up the aisle on Christian's arm, and she could see a warmth of love in Philippe's eyes as he watched her.

The day passed quickly, as though it was a fleeting dream. In the sunlight, and with the gardens filled by guests, it seemed for a while that Beau Lac had returned to its former splendours. Only beyond the palm grove did the war continue to exist; beyond the high barrier, the barbed-wire and the patrolling guards.

Much later Maryse Rose and Philippe escaped to the gentle solitude of their rooms and were alone at last. And then it was as though the distant hours of passion they had experienced together in The Citadelle had never existed and they were shyly discovering each other for the first time.

She lay content beside him as he slept, remembering the emotions that he had created for her and which still lingered in her mind. Her body was enjoying the relaxed sensation of fulfilment. The night was silent, the room lit by faint starlight, and she could see him only as a dark silhouette.

For a long time she watched him, the gentle rise and fall of his chest reassuring, comforting.

She reached to touch him, but as she did so he wrenched his body away from her, groaning as if in agony, his flesh hot, tormented, his thoughts trapped within some nightmare. His fear startled her. She tried to calm him but could not penetrate his terror. He fought her protective arms.

She switched on the bedside light to waken him, but his dream persisted. He turned from her, and for the first time she saw his naked back, glistening with sweat . . . strange scars patterning the muscles across his shoulders, each mark almost identical, leaf-shaped, the length and breadth of her smallest finger.

At first she thought the marks were created by shadows, but as he moved restlessly, so they moved.

He had always faced her when he was naked . . . in the shower at The Citadelle . . . when they lay beside each other . . . in love making. She had never realized it before, but perhaps he had deliberately shielded himself from her?

The nightmare was passing. Now he lay more quietly. Beneath him the sheet was damp, and the pillow soaked with his perspiration. She wanted to hold him in her arms, comfort him until real sleep returned, but was afraid to do so.

SEVEN

June 1958: Algeria

Despite the air-conditioning in the Citroen the dust was being swirled in thick clouds from the gravel road by a crowded bus ahead and percolated into her car. Belle could taste it on her lips, and knew that it would already be dulling the sheen of her freshly set hair. The road had become a casualty of the endless war; there had been plans to hard-surface it years before, but the civil funds were now committed to the reparation of war damage and the maintenance of security.

To aggravate her further, on the outskirts of the city there were two separate road-blocks within two hundred yards of each other. The first was manned by a patrol of 'Lizards', paratroopers in their distinctive uniforms with a small-patterned camouflage that was strangely reptilian, the second barrier by gendarmes. To Belle's annoyance the road-blocks appeared to be doing the same job of work, the men at both asked the same questions, examined her papers, briefly searched the car and then waved her through. At each check-point there was an almost identical crowd of Arab travellers, most on foot, a few with bicycles. The settlers received preference while the Arabs waited impatiently.

Once past Bab el Oued she encountered the heavy city traffic with its endless delays at lights and crossings, so that it took her a further half hour to reach the residential estates on the hills above Algiers. It was more than two years since she had last visited the area but it had changed little, only the barbed wire or iron spikes above the walls of the gardens and the guards behind the closed gates, indicating that the war existed even in this seemingly peaceful suburb.

The apartment block was one of half a dozen, set in a vast landscaped amphitheatre so that every dwelling had its own balcony overlooking the great sweep of Algiers bay, and catching the sun during all the daylight hours. Surrounding the white concrete buildings were gardens, still carefully tended, with rows of tall date palms lining the narrow roadways. Each block had its own patrol of guards, and beside the shaded entrances stood uniformed security men, machine-pistols cradled in their arms, their faces robotic with boredom.

The parking area was empty. At this time of the day the apartment residents were at work. The units had been built for bachelor Metropolitan civil servants employed in the Algerian Department, or for the occasional use of the senior management of contractors or business companies visiting the country at the invitation of the government.

Belle brushed out her hair and then carefully inspected her make-up. As she opened the vehicle's door the heat of the late June day met her as an almost solid barrier after the dry coolness of the air-conditioned Citroen scented with her musky perfume. She straightened her silk dress, which was already beginning to cling in the humid afternoon warmth, and checked the seams of her stockings before walking quickly to the nearest of the apartment blocks. The guard saluted her with no change of expression on his tanned face, and did not question her. There were no carpets in the foyer and the sound of her heels echoed from the depths of the long corridor which serviced the nearby apartments. She took the lift to the fifth floor.

The windows in the corridor faced south towards the mountains, overlooking the residences of nearby embassies. In the distance, to the right of the building, was a football ground requisitioned by the military and now used as a storage depot for the military equipment shipped out to the port below.

Outside one of the apartment doors, Belle stopped and searched her purse for the key; it hung from a short length of gold chain attached to a small gold pendant, shaped as a heart and inset with a diamond.

The apartment was empty. It consisted of only four rooms; a lounge-diner with windows which led to the balcony, a bedroom, bathroom and small kitchen. It was luxuriously furnished, its marble tiled floors overlaid with thick hand-woven carpets, the armchairs and the sofa of light tan calf-skin, the table, bookcases and cocktail cabinet of rich mahogany. The hessian-clad walls were decorated with a collection of ornate silver and gold-inlaid weapons; Arab flintlock pistols, swords and daggers.

She walked into the bathroom and checked her make-up again. With a feeling of disgust, she noticed there were already perspiration marks on her dress, and wished she had chosen cotton rather than silk today, but she had wanted to look spectacular and seductive. She returned to the lounge, opened the cocktail cabinet, mixed a shaker of martini and poured herself a drink. In the base of the cabinet was a record-player. She searched through a stack of records, placed one on the machine and switched it on. She checked her watch. It was three minutes to noon. She sipped the martini, then opened one of the balcony windows. As she did so, she heard the sound of the door opening behind her, and turned, smiling a welcome.

It was Henri Lefitte.

Although she had anticipated the excitement of their lovemaking time had dulled the memories of the exquisite pleasure she received from his hands, lips and body. With other men she was forced to play the innocent, but with Henri Lefitte she could openly release the constricted passions which seemed held like floodwaters within her. Henri made her other lovers seem no more than school-boys, inept and inexperienced. She had been only sixteen on her first visit to this apartment. It had appeared to her so daring, so adventurous. Henri had been the first man to appreciate her as a woman, and throughout all the years that had followed, the initial sense of romantic adventure had never diminished but had frequently been heightened by the secret knowledge they shared. There had been delicious self-satisfaction when they had been together in the company of others, and humour in the formalities that masked their clandestine intimacies.

She had hoped to see Lefitte much sooner after her return to Algeria and had been horrified to learn of the attack which had taken place, and which she had feared would leave him disfigured. She had resisted the temp-tation to contact him in hospital and had waited anxiously until he had been discharged. Then she had telephoned him on his private office line.

The scars showed on his face, a criss-cross of fine lines below the temples and on both cheeks. She decided they were not too ugly, more like Germanic duelling scars; manly.

She deliberately turned her back on him and stared casually out of the window. 'I've mixed you a drink.'

She heard a glass chink. 'Martini, American style.'

'Of course.' She knew what he would do next, swallow the first glass in one deep swig, pour the second then walk softly behind her to gently kiss her neck. A moment later she felt the touch of his lips and the faintly electric sensation of his moustache against her warm skin.

'It's been too long.' Henri Lefitte's voice was like the purr of a cat.

'Have I changed?' She felt his lips again.

'Yes.' His breath was scented with cachou.

'I'm older.' She deliberately added resentment to her voice, tempting a compliment from him.

'And you're more beautiful.'

She moved away from him, into a bar of sunlight which slanted through the windows. 'And how has Suzanne been keeping?' She knew he disliked her mentioning his wife when they were alone together.

'Quite well, thank you, Miss Charpentier.'

She still had her back towards him. She put her glass on the arm of the chair beside her, then reached behind her neck and ran the zip of her dress down to the swell of her buttocks. She shrugged herself from the silk, letting it fall to the carpet around her ankles. Then she unclipped her bra, tossing it onto the chair before sliding her briefs down her thighs and stepping out of them. Slowly she removed her suspender belt and rolled off her stockings. She faced him, knowing the sight of her naked body would quickly arouse him.

Henri Lefitte's eyes examined her. There was an earthy femininity in her heavy but firm breasts and the broad swell of her hips, reminding him of neolithic terracotta goddesses; primitive, erotically sexual. To please him she had cut her pubic hair so short that it barely shaded the divided triangle between her thighs. The memory of the first occasion he had revealed her in such a manner excited him now. He could remember how she had lain passively and trusting, her knees raised and apart as he had carefully shaved her. She had been a girl then, and it had been little more than pubescent down, as soft as the fur of a young animal.

Henri Lefitte waited, knowing that this sexual game they had so often played together was important to them both. She came towards him slowly, tantalizing herself as well as him, dropping softly to her knees as she reached him, as if she were his slave. Then she released his belt and unbuttoned his trousers. He did not help her. She took the firm column of his erect penis between her moist hands and guided it to her lips. For long moments she teased him with her tongue before taking him so deeply into her mouth and throat it was as though she was devouring him. Now she could enjoy the physical control she had established over his body and emotions, stopping only when she sensed the first torturing thrill of nearing orgasm rise as a shudder within him. Then she drew him down beside her, their roles instantly reversed by his eagerness and hunger, writhing beneath him until his climax tore itself from deep within him as a cry of agony that matched her own.

Much later, as vehicles began returning to the car parks below the apartments and the shadows of the date palms lengthened, he questioned her. His voice deliberately gentle, maintaining the same quiescent satiety their bodies were experiencing.

'What has been happening at Beau Lac?'

Belle had showered and dressed, and was making-up her face in the bedroom mirror. Henri Lefitte sat on the edge of the bed, watching her.

Belle pressed her lips together on a piece of tissue before replying. 'Nothing has happened at Beau Lac.'

'Maryse Rose is married.' He made it sound no more than a light observation.

'That's not important.' Belle glanced at Lefitte, angrily. 'Please Henri, I don't like people staring at me when I'm doing this.'

Henri Lefitte stood and walked to the window. The sun

was beginning to slip behind a bank of distant cloud on the horizon, turning the evening sea into a vast lake of liquid gold. 'And how is her lieutenant?'

'Boring,' said Belle, languidly. 'We see very little of him. He was posted to the Aurés in May.'

'Her boyfriend, Habib Saadi, is in Algiers,' Lefitte said casually.

Belle swung to face him, quickly. 'In Algiers? My God, why don't you arrest him? What if he wants to kill me?'

Henri Lefitte smiled at her discomfort. 'He doesn't know about you Belle. We're like the newspaper reporters, we never divulge our sources. Yours was a useful tip-off.' He paused. 'Though passed on a whim rather than evidence, I suspect.'

Belle pouted at the gibe. 'But I still don't understand why you allow him to roam Algiers.'

'Because it suits me to. If I bring him in, oh yes he'll talk for me, but he won't know very much yet. He's far more use to me on the streets. He doesn't make a move without my knowledge.' He paused. 'Now suppose you tell me about Vincent.'

'He's angry with Papa.' She shook her hair back off her face, glad that the conversation had moved to a different subject. It had taken her quite a long time to convince herself that she had acted out of patriotism.

'Why?'

'A Company thing . . . Charpentier business.'

'And why should that make Vincent angry?'

'Because Papa has been selling off parts of the Company, and Vincent is furious. He said it wasn't necessary because the Arabs will never win. He's right of course, but there was a terrible row. Since then, Vincent spends most of his evenings at his new club.'

Henri Lefitte looked thoughtful, the muscles of his lean face tightening almost imperceptibly. The tone of his voice was harder as he answered. 'Yes, I've heard of this "club". But I don't know *all* of its members . . . besides your brother, of course. It interests me greatly.'

'I don't think it's so very exclusive, despite what Vincent claims.' Belle stood and brushed a trace of face-powder from her dress. 'Georges Suinot is a member. You must know him, he's one of Vincent's old schoolfriends. And Pascal Chollet . . . Guy Dekint . . . Rene Junal. A few others, I don't know everyone's name. They don't often come to Beau Lac.'

Lefitte ran his finger lightly down the ridge of his nose. Once it had been straighter. In hospital it had been painfully held in place by sticking-plaster while a metal brace behind his lower teeth had supported his broken jaw. The scarring of his face would be permanent and would always show; the memory of the vicious assault he could conceal but not forgive. He repeated the names, as if to imprint them in his mind. 'Suinot, Chollet, Dekint, Junal. Yes I suspect I may have met a couple of them!'

For Maryse Rose the year had begun with so much happiness that in her mind the harsh realities of the war had been diffused. In the first weeks of their marriage she had seen Philippe frequently. The barracks at Khemis were little more than an hour's drive from Hadjout, and his duties as range officer enabled him to leave the camp on Saturday mornings so that he could arrive at Beau Lac before lunch. The circumstances had seemed to her no different to those of many other wives whose husbands were forced to work away from home during the weekdays, but the few hours spent together until mid-afternoon on Sundays had become precious, and the guest-wing of the château their private apartment from which it seemed seldom necessary to emerge. Then, only

Philippe's more frequently re-occurring nightmares had marred the time they spent in each other's arms.

As on their wedding night his dreams appeared to relive a terror so unspeakable his conscious mind could not, even now, reveal it to Maryse Rose. His groans of pain, his agonized body bathed in an icy malarial sweat, resisted all her efforts to calm or comfort him. He would wrench himself violently from her touch, while the gentlest of her caresses would contort his already tense body as though an electric probe had been forced into his flesh. Her softly spoken words of comfort never penetrated the horror which enclosed his tormented mind. Afterwards he lay on the dampened sheets, his eyes wide but unseeing as the nightmares retreated. Sleep, when it came at last, was a coma into which he slipped exhausted, and whilst his awakening seemed to contain no memories of the terrors which had assailed him, he would resent her questions.

In May, unexpectedly and with only a few hours notice, Philippe's company had been posted to active duty in the Aurés, a desolate and mountainous region close to the Tunisian border. In parts it was heavily forested and traversed by deep canyons and gorges. The French troops there patrolled continuously against a growing army of rebels; the fighting was brutal.

Suddenly, the war which had seemed to barely touch her enveloped every aspect of her life: it was no longer possible for her to ignore. Headlines in newspapers, naming some new outrage or act of terrorism, seemed bolder. The lists of casualties, seemed longer and more pronounced. The radio news items became terrifying moments of anticipation as she waited for the region of military activity to be identified. Even car drivers greeted each other by sounding their horns 'Al-ger-rie Fran-çais'. The war could never be forgotten.

Although she received letters from him, usually in batches of three or four, it was twelve weeks before he returned for a short leave during the first week of August. His appearance startled her. Although he was deeply tanned by his weeks of patrol in the fierce heat of the mountains, there was a strange unhealthy pallor beneath the surface. He was edgy, quick-tempered, and although she knew he was exhausted this did not pass even when he had slept for the first twenty-four hours following his arrival at Beau Lac. More difficult for her to accept was his silence. Before, their conversation had always been easy, amusing, lightened by his quick humour or softened by his endearments. Now, if he spoke at all, it was seldom more than a curt answer to her questioning. Other times he seemed to ignore her completely.

She had been longing for his return and the gentle passions of their love-making. During those first exciting weeks of their marriage there had always been time, even on the briefest of his visits to the château. Often they had both experienced such a compelling urgency that their haste to fulfil their sexual desire had seemed almost indecent. Now he did not seem to want her, and nor did her body appear to arouse him.

She had wanted to feel his arms around her, cradling her reassuringly as they lay resting, enjoying the warmth of his body close to her own during the uneasy darkness of the nights. To her dismay it was as though he now found her repulsive, avoiding even the merest touch of her hand. At first she found herself accepting the guilt, feeling a deep sense of shame that she could no longer make herself attractive for him. But as the days passed she realized that the problem lay within Philippe and that unless she could persuade him to reveal it, it must inevitably destroy them.

Philippe was persistently evasive, but on his last evening at Beau Lac, Maryse Rose was determined to succeed. For the whole of his five-day leave he had insisted they took their meals in the solitude of the apartment. Colette had been surprised that neither he nor Maryse Rose had joined them on even a single occasion, but had assumed it was only because of their need to be alone together after his long absence.

Philippe spent his last day of leave in the gardens, lying on a sunbed and sleeping or listening to a portable radio. Maryse Rose was with him, but there had been little conversation. Now, during dinner, she talked cheerfully, as though there was no difficulty between them despite his abrupt answers. She encouraged him to drink almost two bottles of the château's best vintage wine, and when the meal had been completed and a house maid had cleared the table and left them, she sat herself on the carpet beside his knees as he relaxed in one of the armchairs.

'Philippe, what's been happening to us?' She wanted him to touch her, but he leant back in the chair and closed his eyes.

'Nothing has been happening.' His voice was flat and there was an ominous finality to his statement.

'That's exactly what I mean. Nothing has been happening.' She took hold of his hands, but there was no movement in response.

'I'm just tired.' She knew it was only an empty excuse.

'Darling, it's not fatigue. It's . . . it's everything. You don't want to talk. You don't even want me to be near you.'

He began to push himself from the armchair. 'I want to get to bed early. I have to be in Algiers by six am.'

She was unable to restrain her desperate anger, forcing him back into the chair with both her hands against his chest. 'No, Philippe, no! Can't you see what this is doing to me . . . doing to us? You have to tell me. We have to talk.'

'I don't need a damned interrogation.' His voice was as angry as her own, and for a moment she thought he was about to strike her.

'Then do you need a damned wife?'

He brushed aside her arms and stood, his eyes hard. 'You're part of a world that doesn't exist anymore. Dancing on beaches, champagne parties in your gardens, horse racing and luxury yachts.'

'I exist.' She faced him. 'I'm here. I haven't changed. I have the same needs . . . the same love. What's your world? What's the one you don't want to share with me?'

He turned his back on her and said: 'Death.'

'Death?' The word startled her. She tried to turn him towards her, but he shrugged her arm away. 'Is that what you think is the whole world? Our world? My God . . . Philippe darling . . .'

He interrupted her. 'Go to bed. I'll sleep out here.'

'No, Philippe, we're man and wife. I love you. And I want you.' A cold sense of panic was beginning to build inside her. She was losing him to something she could not even understand.

He faced her. 'Maryse Rose, I don't want you.' His words struck her like a blow.

'But why?' Her voice was that of a bewildered child.

'Christ Almighty! Do I have to spell it out to you?'

'Yes.'

'Do you know what we do out there in the mountains?'

'I read the newspapers. I listen to the radio.'

He laughed harshly. 'You read the newspapers.' He raised his voice to almost a shout. There were small beads of perspiration on his forehead and the muscles of his jaw were taut. 'We fight, damn you. We fight and we die.' The level of his voice dropped but it was icily cold. 'Paul is dead.'

'Oh, I'm so sorry, Philippe.' She could remember him at their wedding; a short, stocky man, perhaps a year or two older than Philippe, with a quick laugh and charming sense of humour.

'Do you want to know how he died? Do you want to know how Captain Paul Sandrin ended his war . . . and Sergeant Aubin, and Corporals Berthoud and Tredez . . . and the others? Do you know what we say to each other when we go out on patrol? We don't say "good luck" any more. We say "take care of your balls . . .". Well, Paul didn't take care of his.' Philippe was shouting again, now. 'You want to know the details of how Paul lost his balls? We're not out there fighting against human beings, we're fighting animals. Being shot, or blown to pieces is a clean death for a soldier. But, you don't get a clean death out here . . . unless you're lucky.'

'I don't think it was any different in Indo China.' She was trying to calm him.

'You don't think! It was a damned sight cleaner war than this. At least out there the torturing was done by men. Here, it's the damned women who do the dirtiest work. Women! I'm insulting half the human race by calling them that. They stand on the hills and watch us . . . they stand at the entrances of their villages, and in the doorways when we pass . . . and they watch us like vultures. You can read their minds. They're waiting for us, their hands like bloody claws, henna and tattoos. They're waiting for the time their men drag us, wounded, into their villages, so they can stake us out and push brambles up our tools like pipe-cleaners. And when the bitches can't get any more enjoyment out of that game they slit open our scrotums and pull our balls off, one at a time, and then, just for a final joke, they stuff them into our mouths and sew up our lips. Oh, Paul had a great time of it. And half a mile away we could hear them . . .' He imitated the high-pitched 'yill-yill-yill-yill', that the Arab women used as a signal of their excitement, or to call to each other across the mountains.

Suddenly, Maryse Rose understood. In his troubled mind, she had become one of those Arab women. When he had watched them in their villages, it had been her face he had seen. And when Paul had been killed, it had been her hands which had done the butchering. Hurt and frustration swirled into fury. She slapped him as hard as she was able, repeating the blows with both her hands as he staggered backwards; fighting him when he gripped her wrists, until she had no strength left in her body.

She had split his lip and a thin trickle of blood ran down his chin. The skin of his cheeks were parchment pale, accentuating the long furrow of brown scar tissue.

Her anger had gone, leaving her feeling weak and empty. She forced her eyes to meet his and hold him steadily. 'I'm not one of them, Philippe. Yes, I'm an Arab, but I'm your wife, and I love you.'

He let go of her wrists, then lowered his head slightly. 'I'm destroying us.'

'No. Not you. The war is trying to destroy us, but we can't let it.' She felt her strength returning, and realized that perhaps she had managed to penetrate the barrier which had been separating them.

He held her hands more gently, now. 'When I was out there . . . every day . . . whenever there was time for private thoughts, I wanted you. I wanted to be with you.' He paused. 'At night, in my imagination we were together, and we made love. I could remember every smallest detail of you . . . how you looked naked, how you moved, spoke . . . even the warm smell of your body. I could remember how you look when you're asleep . . .

172

silly things, like how you awaken in the mornings, how you put on your bra, how you brush your hair. I made you so real in my mind, that sometimes I talked to you. All I wanted was to come home to you. But when I did, I could only see ghosts, and everything was wrong.' He hesitated. 'It was my patrol that found Paul and the others. It was . . . very bad.'

'When was he killed?'

'Last week. Two days before I came home. We were supposed to be coming on leave together. I'd planned for us all to meet up . . . have a meal . . . get drunk.'

'You should have told me about him sooner.'

'I was going to . . .' He looked embarrassed, and lowered his eyes. 'Then it became impossible.' He paused, searching for the words to express his feelings. 'Emotions become confused. Perhaps, when you experience an emotion totally it's indistinguishable from others; like fear becoming exhilaration in battle . . . like love and hatred . . . they're all close neighbours.'

She moved nearer to him, and he put his arms around her. 'Perhaps you have been fighting too long, even for a soldier.'

'A few months . . .'

'No,' she reminded him. 'Not months. More than six years. First in Indo China, and then here. It's too long.'

'They were different wars.'

'But the same battle.' She found her handkerchief and gently dabbed the blood from his lip. 'There's nothing shameful about being afraid. And every night, even here with me, something terrible happens to you. I've tried to ask you about it before, but you shut me out. I can't just be part of all the pleasant things in your life, I need to be part of everything. And perhaps if I can share your nightmares, together we can drive them away.'

He was silent for a long time, and his arms around her

173

seemed to tighten as if he needed the assurance her body longed to give him. 'I can't tell you what happened, because I don't remember.' He hesitated before continuing. 'God, I've tried hard enough.' His temples were moist with perspiration. He bit his upper lip, and shook his head slightly. 'Before Dien Bien Phu . . . I was one of a patrol; there were eleven of us, all conscripts except the sergeant. Afterwards, there was only me.'

'Afterwards?'

He spoke reluctantly. 'I recovered consciousness in a field hospital. It was all blank. Nothing inside my head. They told me I'd returned on my own . . . three days after our patrol went missing. No-one else came back.' Sweat was now beading his face as though he had been exercising heavily. 'I had a fractured skull . . . concussion . . . and the wounds. It occurred to me that I might have survived because I turned and ran while the others fought . . . I mean, the wounds were on my back. I don't even know how they were caused! I've had the nightmares ever since, but when I awaken I can't remember what's in them. Only that sometimes I wish it weren't necessary for me to sleep at all.'

She felt him shudder as though a sudden chill wind had blown across his body. 'Please kiss me.'

He held her for a long time, his lips against her own, and felt his body slowly relax. She desperately wanted to feel the intimacy of their naked flesh, not at this moment in a sexual way, but so that it could reinforce the communion she had at last established. It seemed so fragile, still so immature that even a careless breath might destroy it and tear Philippe away from her once more.

As though he read her thoughts, he picked her up in his arms, lifting her as though she were weightless and carrying her to the bedroom. But although he undressed her tenderly every frustrated desire of his past months seemed to explode uncontrollably at her touch, so that his passion smothered all but the most animal of her own needs.

Later, he slept peacefully beside her, and for the first time during his leave the nightmares did not return to torment them. For a long time, Maryse Rose lay awake. The night was warm, and moonlight filtered through the curtains at the windows. The sheet beneath her was damp, and she could smell the erotic scent of their mingled perspiration. Very faintly, against the upper part of her arm, where it touched his chest, she could feel his heartbeat. She was conscious of an unfamiliar womanly sensation; something new, something more satisfying than anything she had ever previously experienced. At first she was unable to identify it. It was not physical, yet nor did it exist solely in her imagination. Then, in the dark, soft silence, she understood. During the sweet moments when he had lain, still inside her, whispering his love for her, within her a new life had begun . . . a life they had created for each other. Although scientifically her instant knowledge might be denied, she was certain, quite certain. And as she stared down the length of her body in the grey, dimmed moonlight, it seemed to be surrounded by a faintly glowing and magical aura. She had the feeling that she lay at the very centre of the entire universe.

The weeks passed with Maryse Rose experiencing growing feelings of joy. As she had expected, her period had not occurred, and shortly afterwards she had begun to have brief but daily bouts of morning sickness. She had told no-one yet and there was the delicious sensation of a jealously-guarded secret held within her own body.

She had counted the days in her diary, finding a new thrill in the knowledge that in late April, just as the green

Algerian spring began a change towards summer, she would hold their child for the first time in her arms.

Every day she found some new purpose in her life to excite her in some unanticipated manner. Subconsciously she cosseted herself, lingering in the comfort of her bath, taking more time than was usual to prepare her make-up, relishing the more exotic of her perfumes, while her mind built then discarded a thousand plans for her future with Philippe and their child.

Reluctantly, she realized that she must have her pregnancy confirmed. It seemed at first almost blasphemous that someone other than the man she so dearly loved would have this priceless knowledge first. But she accepted that this was unavoidable, comforting herself with the thought that the confidence of a doctor was, after all, no different to that of a priest.

The thought of the intimacy of the medical examination made her nervous, so that as she drove to the Saint Pierre clinic she was unaware of the small and rusty Fiat van which pulled away from the roadside as she left Beau Lac, and followed her into Algiers. When she parked at the clinic, the Fiat remained in the street a hundred yards short of the entrance.

She was surprised how little time the examination and tests took. As they had requested she had brought a urine sample with her to the clinic. She had expected to wait at least twenty-four hours before she would know the result, but less than thirty minutes after she had given the sample to a nurse, a smiling young doctor called her back into his office.

She already knew the result, but when she was seated he leant forward confidentially. 'Well, Madame Viard, there's no doubt the test is positive. And, I can see no reason why you shouldn't produce a perfectly healthy baby. As far as we can tell, everything is fine. And now about diet ... and what you can do to help things along ...'

As she left the clinic she paused on the marble steps at the doorway. The grounds, the car-park and the street beyond seemed filled with an extraordinary kaleidoscope of colours far brighter than any she had ever seen before. The branches of trees were alive with birds, and hung with the ripening fruits of late autumn. Every wall seemed to be draped in blossom, while above, the sun shone from a sky of a rich, pure blue. Only one thing was missing to make her happiness complete ... Philippe. She prayed that somehow, wherever he might be at this wonderful moment, he might sense just a part of her thoughts and share her joy.

She had intended to return immediately to Beau Lac following her visit to the clinic, but now she remembered that in the Maison Lafayette there was a department which specialized in all the items she would need during early motherhood. She would not buy them yet, she told herself. That would be tempting the devil, but there was no harm in looking ... examining the things she might later wish to purchase.

She began to walk towards her car. As she did so, the Fiat van which had been waiting in the street started its engine, revved it noisily then accelerated into the parking area. With its wheels squealing on the hot tarmac, it swerved alongside her and the passenger door was flung open.

The driver leant towards Maryse Rose. 'Get inside.'

Startled, she pulled back.

The man spoke again, this time his voice was more urgent, his command more hurried. 'Maryse Rose. Get in ... quickly.'

'Habib!' She could see his face now, his eyes wild and his skin glistening with perspiration. There was several days' growth of stubble on his chin.

177

'Please, get inside. We can't talk here.'

'No, Habib, no.' She glanced around, nervously, half expecting to see a patrol of gendarmes hurrying towards them. Habib's sudden appearance had confused her, taking away much of the decisiveness she might otherwise have had. It showed, in the uncertainty of her voice as she refused him.

'Don't argue.' Habib leant further across the passenger seat. 'We have to talk. It's important.'

Apprehensively, she climbed into the vehicle and closed the door. The Fiat smelt of oil and exhaust fumes. Its seats were grubby, the upholstery scuffed and torn. There were tools on the floor by her feet, while the van behind her seemed to be filled with broken chicken crates.

Habib revved the engine again and drove the van into the road, ignoring the angry horns of the traffic into which he forced the vehicle. The Fiat swayed perilously on the corners, its suspension soggy, its steering worn. He did not speak until they reached the outskirts of the Arab quarter to the east of Bab el Oued, and then he pulled onto a rubble-strewn building site where a number of dilapidated cars stood for sale. An old Arab waved at Habib as they entered, then wiped a bundle of rags across the bonnets of the parked cars, optimistically.

Habib switched off the engine, and then leant towards her as though to kiss her. She pushed him away. 'Habib, you're a fool. Take me back to the clinic, at once.'

He blew out his lips. 'That's a fine greeting after all this time.'

'What am I supposed to do? Throw myself into your arms?' Her dark eyes were as wild as his own. She tossed her hair back from her face with nervous anger.

'That might do for a start.' Habib grinned at her.

'Habib, I'm married now,' she said in desperation.

His face became serious. He paused for a moment then said: 'It's something I hadn't planned for.'

'Planned!' She laughed, shrilly, almost hysterically. 'You hadn't planned for my marriage! You conceited idiot. But I suppose you planned my arrest . . . and my interrogation by the Deuxième Bureau. Obviously you planned the forty kilos of explosive they found in your refrigerator. My God! Your planning might have taken me to the guillotine.'

Habib frowned, his eyes narrowed as she spoke. 'Forty kilos of explosive? Did you see it?'

'Of course not, they'd taken it away. They told me about it. Plastique.'

Habib said: 'Then they lied to you. There was no plastique in my apartment.'

'And I suppose you weren't a terrorist.'

He shrugged. 'A terrorist is someone who causes terror. If I terrified the Deuxième Bureau, then I suppose I was a terrorist. But I swear there was no explosive.' He paused, his eyes holding hers. 'Do you really think I would have risked your life by keeping explosive in that stuffy, overheated apartment? And if you remember, our refrigerator didn't work . . . and for a damned good reason. There were almost four million francs inside its cooling system.'

She had calmed a little and was regaining her confidence. Habib had always been open with her and she always felt she would know if he lied. She did not believe he was lying now. 'Four million francs! Then why should they claim it was explosive? And where could you have got four million?'

'Donations . . . subscriptions . . . whatever you like to call them. I collected it all. Myself and my friends.' He pursed his lips and then shrugged. 'It was what I was doing in France. That was my business.' He spoke wrily. 'I was collecting funds from brother Algerians who pre-

179

ferred the safety of France to the dangers of pursuing their freedom in Algeria.' He paused, thoughtfully. 'Another few days and it would have been safely in Switzerland. As it was, those damned police almost got me executed by the FLN as a traitor. It takes some explaining that you've lost four million francs of the party's funds. It was a difficult time.'

She was puzzled now. 'But why would the police claim they'd found explosives?'

Habib grunted, disgustedly. 'A few kilos of explosives are far easier for a policeman to come by than four million francs, and even if it were split four ways it's a lot of money. A million buys a good villa . . . two reasonable houses . . . a small farm. A million buys luxury. Who knows what the hell happened?' He stared out of the window of the car. 'Do you know I was tipped-off that they were about to raid my apartment? I received a telephone call half an hour before it happened. I wondered at the time who my friend was . . . he spoke with a Parisian accent. Now I think I know . . . a flic!' He turned towards her again. 'I tried to warn you but I couldn't locate you. I don't think it would have made any difference anyway. They would have known where you were living, who you were. Probably they knew everything about you.'

'How did they find out about you in the first place?'

Habib grimaced. 'God knows! But not every Algerian supports us. There are different groups . . . at times they work against each other. Perhaps I just pushed someone too hard for a donation. It's easy to upset people, especially when they're so far away from Algeria; they're braver then.' He put his hand on her arm, and she did not draw it away. 'Did the bastards make it very bad for you?'

She nodded, silently. 'It was bad in every way. Frightening at first; violent. Humiliating. It involved everyone . . . my family. My father hasn't spoken to Uncle Claude since then. Yes, it was bad for me.'

'I'm sorry,' said Habib, softly and she could recognize the genuine sincerity in his voice. 'I should never have involved you.'

'You didn't,' insisted Maryse Rose. 'If anything, you seemed to have gone out of your way to keep me out of things. I didn't really know anything. They questioned me a lot, but I don't think they learnt anything of value, because I knew nothing.' She suddenly became aware that his gaze was beginning to embarrass her, as if he was deliberately trying to remind her of the relationship which had once existed between them. 'Habib, I must go now. Please take me back.'

He restarted the Fiat but was reluctant to return her yet. 'I've only been here a few weeks. I was in Berne . . . then Cairo. I was worried about you.'

'It's been a year, Habib. Life doesn't stand still. Now please . . .'

He rammed the van into gear with a jolt that spun the wheels and jerked Maryse Rose back into her seat. 'Five minutes for a coffee, then . . .'

'The last time I agreed to that, it turned out to be far more than five minutes.'

'That's what I was hoping.'

'This time the answer really is no.' She made her voice serious. 'I'm not only married now, but I'm also pregnant.' Instantly she regretted her words. Philippe had been the one she wanted to tell first . . . now she had spoilt that pleasure for herself, and felt in some way she had been a little unfaithful to him.

Habib's voice was flat, unemotional. 'Congratulations.'

He drove in silence until she questioned him. 'Why did you want to see me today?' He shrugged. 'But it's so dangerous for you. They had posters up for you in France. Colonel Lefitte knows all about you . . . he wants to catch you.'

Habib said: 'Colonel Lefitte,' contemptuously. 'That pig! Plenty of us owe him one. Yes, he might like to get me into his cells for a little entertainment, but his speciality is amusing himself with our women couriers. One day, though . . .' He left the threat unspoken.

'You haven't answered me,' she persisted.

He didn't reply to her immediately, then cleared his throat in an embarrassed way before speaking. 'I just wanted to see you again. I didn't know you were married.' He slowed the van and pulled it into the kerb. They were now only a short distance from the clinic, and he kept the engine running. 'My feelings haven't changed,' he said, almost accusingly. 'And I didn't find anyone else.'

'We made each other no promises in Paris,' she reminded him.

'No,' he agreed. 'But I made a foolish assumption.' He paused. 'Who is he?'

'French . . . a soldier.'

He grimaced. 'Then I hope we never meet each other in the *maquis*.' As she opened the door and began to climb out, his voice stopped her. 'If you ever want to find me . . .'

'No, Habib, don't tell me.' She looked back at him. 'Just be careful.'

As she walked away in the direction of the clinic she heard him call: 'Ask Mouloud at the car lot.'

Her unexpected meeting with Habib seemed to have drained her mind of all its purpose, and her body of its strength, so that instead of visiting the Maison Lafayette she drove straight back to the château. The afternoon was hot and airless, and even the high-ceilinged rooms of Beau Lac felt stuffy and uncomfortable, and she longed for the rocks at Tipaza and the touch of cool sea breeze on her body. Apart from the servants, the château was empty. Madelene, Axel and the new baby, Yvette, were at the swimming club, Belle on some social assignation, and Colette playing bridge with her friends.

Alone, in the shade of one of the palms, Maryse Rose wrote to Philippe. For weeks she had been planning the contents of this letter, the way she would tell him her exciting news, how it was now confirmed, her own feelings towards the child she was carrying and her deep love for its father. She wanted him to share every thrill, every moment of joy, every smallest revelation. But as she tried to write, thoughts of Habib intruded and confused her.

Later, she had dinner with the family but told them nothing of her visit to the clinic. Her emotions felt as exhausted as her body, so that when Colette questioned her on her day she was aware her answers were guiltily evasive, as transparently untruthful as those she might have used as a schoolgirl to avoid her homework. Belle watched her with a stare of curiosity that was so blatant Maryse Rose felt herself blushing and unable to meet her eyes. When the meal had finished, she excused herself quickly and went to her rooms, conscious that the subdued conversation she had heard as she climbed the stairs could only be about her.

It was still early, and although she was fatigued her mind was restless. She re-read her letter to Philippe, but decided she could not improve upon it. It seemed too much of an effort to begin one of the many books on the apartment's shelves, so she turned on the radio, slipped out of her dress and lay on the bed. She attempted to fix her mind on a mental image of Philippe, but it was impossible; the image faded each time she relaxed, to become that of Habib . . . not the Habib today, but of the months they had spent together in Paris. She could hear

183

his voice, his ideas as effervescent and clear as the waters of a mountain spring.

The absurdity of her thoughts made her angry with herself. She found a packet of Philippe's Bastos and lit one clumsily. She had never smoked, and the harsh African tobacco of the cigarette bit into her lungs, choking her. She stubbed it out.

With growing desperation, she searched the apartment until she had found every photograph she had of Philippe, and of their wedding. Then she studied them closely, dwelling on each for an unnecessary length of time in the hope that somehow she could force away the intruding memories of Habib. But as the evening lengthened she realized that trying to forget was only another form of remembering.

Henri Lefitte lay across the upper part of Belle's body, supporting himself on one elbow. Her breathing had quickened until now it almost matched the rhythm of his fingers deep in the moist cleft between her broad thighs. The control he could exercise over her most intimate emotions, and her body, gave him satisfaction; it was an ability he mentally likened to a musician's skill with an instrument. He smiled when she gasped as his fingertips found the most sensitive parts, and then gradually increased the tempo until her body responded beneath him. He toyed with the idea of stopping just before she reached the climax of her orgasm, but could picture the angry scene which would follow. The August afternoon had been too pleasant to tease her; their lovemaking had been inventively enjoyable.

Belle groaned, then shouted wildly, forcing her hips upwards, arching her back in an ecstatic spasm. He turned slightly, watching her brown nipples rise like small erections, a faint blush darkening the smooth skin of her upper chest and throat. He let his hand rest between her thighs, but eased himself beside her. 'Good?'

Belle's thoughts were settling like light snow on a mountain. She did not reply immediately. 'Yes. It was very good.' She winced as he withdrew his hand.

He lay back on the bed and waited. She seemed to doze for a while, and then turned towards him, her hands seeking him. He stopped her. 'No more.' She frowned disappointedly. He laughed. 'The insatiable Miss Charpentier . . . you mustn't be too greedy.' She pouted at him as he rolled sideways and stood beside the bed. He blew her a kiss.

They showered together, and as they stood towelling themselves afterwards Lefitte said casually: 'Maryse Rose has been meeting Habib Saadi.'

Belle froze; a plump renaissance statue. 'Meeting Saadi!' There was disbelief in her voice. 'Saadi? Are you sure?'

Lefitte continued to dry himself, enjoying the rough sensation of the coarse bath-towel against his skin. 'I told you we were keeping an eye on that particular melon. She saw him the day before yesterday.'

'The day before . . .!' Belle remembered Maryse Rose's behaviour when they had been at dinner together that night. Now she understood. 'The little bitch!'

Lefitte laughed. 'Sisters!'

Belle responded furiously. 'She is *not* my sister. You know I hate you to say that. I can't help it if my parents were stupid enough to collect stray dogs.'

Lefitte became serious. 'Are you a patriot, Belle?'

Belle was still angry. 'Of course I'm a patriot. What a ridiculous question to ask me.'

'Good. Then you'll help me.' Lefitte began dressing. 'I want to know every move that Maryse Rose makes.' He did not explain that following Habib Saadi's meeting with

185

Maryse Rose the Arab had not returned to the house where he had been staying, but had disappeared into the labyrinth of the casbah. Lefitte's agent had been unable to locate him since. And to increase Lefitte's annoyance, he had received information only that morning that Saadi had become far more than just a small-fry terrorist; according to the Deuxième Bureau he was being rapidly promoted within the FLN, and it was suggested that he had received special training in Egypt to take control of a company of *moussebiline* in one of the FLN 'regions'.

Belle stared at her reflection in the bathroom mirror. The mystery which often seemed to surround Henri Lefitte's work had always been part of his attraction for her. To become even a small part of it was irresistible. 'That's not difficult.'

'It may be more difficult than you think,' Lefitte warned her. 'I need accurate information . . . every day. Whenever she leaves Beau Lac I want to know about it. And if you learn she is planning any visits to Algiers, then I must know about them in advance.'

'Of course I'll do the best I can. But why?'

'Can you think of a better situation for an FLN sympathizer than as a member of a respected French household . . . the household of an important member of the Assembly? Think of the possibilities, the confidences, even the documents your father may bring home with him. And the private telephone conversations that can be overheard and reported.' He paused as Belle walked thoughtfully into the bedroom. He raised his voice slightly. 'The most despicable Algerian Arab traits are ingratitude and disloyalty.'

As Belle drove back along the coastal road towards Hadjout Henri Lefitte's words repeated themselves in her mind. 'Ingratitude and disloyalty . . .' In the circumstances they seemed very applicable to Maryse Rose. True, she had been released by the Deuxième Bureau in France after her arrest, but that was far more likely a result of Christian Charpentier's influence than Maryse Rose's innocence; Henri Lefitte had made that quite clear. And as Henri had said, ingratitude was despicable. Had it not been for Colette and Christian, Maryse Rose would have perished years before in the desert heat . . . she owed them everything, her home, the luxury she experienced, her education and even the very clothes she wore each day. The financial settlement Christian had made on Maryse Rose as a wedding gift, had been stupidly generous . . . more than enough, even if she were unmarried, to live in comfort for the rest of her life. Unmarried? But she *was* married . . . and to a French officer. And while her husband risked death each day fighting to protect lives and property, she was continuing her illicit and disgusting liaisons with a dangerous terrorist! That was disloyalty in its most base form.

The afternoon sun was low, reflecting from the bonnet of the car. Belle slipped her sun-glasses down off her hair and over her eyes. Philippe, she admitted to herself, was an attractive man, in spite of his scar . . . in fact, like those of Henri, it added to his masculinity.

As the road unwound ahead of her she thought about Philippe. He was lean and muscular, and she had secretly watched him when he had been sunbathing in the gardens. His slender hips gave him a trim, athletic appearance. He might be quite interesting as a lover. It was a shame he was wasting himself on an Arab. He had such unusually grey eyes. Perhaps his background was questionable, but that was no fault of his. He had bettered himself . . . he was totally loyal to de Gaulle, and to France. All the soldiers were, especially the officers.

187

France meant nothing to an Arab, other than a place where they could go to earn, steal or beg money.

By the time Belle arrived back at the château she was determined that Philippe must learn of Maryse Rose's unfaithfulness. Maryse Rose, Madelene and Axel were playing ball on the lawns. Yvette, Madelene's seven-month-old daughter was asleep in her shaded carriage. Belle acknowledged them briefly as she entered the chateau. She had to find Philippe's address, and knew it would be on one of his letters to Maryse Rose; somewhere in their rooms in the guest-wing.

EIGHT

The secondary road from Sour-el-Ghoziane was no more than a broad loose-surface track which ran from Bou-Saada in the south, across the Atlas mountains to the outskirts of Algiers. In many places it was impossible for Maryse Rose to drive Vincent's big Citroen at more than ten miles an hour. There were countless pot-holes, their depth masked by lengthening shadows from the evening sun, and the heavy military lorries which regularly used the road had cut sharp-sided ruts which trapped the car's wheels and made the steering-wheel buck and twist violently in her hands.

There was a discomforting air of apprehension in the silence of her two passengers, Arab clerks from the Charpentier depot at Sour-el-Ghoziane. She had thought she would be grateful for their company on the drive back to Algiers, but instead they were making her nervous. The road was notoriously dangerous at this late time of the day, and only three weeks previously a civilian vehicle had been machine-gunned by FLN rebels and one of its passengers seriously wounded. Maryse Rose had planned to leave Sour-el-Ghoziane no later than mid-day, but a fault which had developed in the Citroen's ignition system that morning, and the subsequent delay while it was repaired, had kept her in the small township for another three hours.

She was unaware that Christian Charpentier would never have allowed her to make this trip to the depot had he known of it, but he had flown to Marseilles two days previously and would not return before the weekend. Even Vincent had refused her at first, until her persistent argument had changed his mind. He had mentioned at dinner that a substantial amount of money needed to be taken to the township for the payment of local traders, and she had quickly volunteered. She had been bored by inactivity, and aware that soon her pregnancy would confine her even more. The opportunity to travel beyond Algiers, even for a few hours, was too inviting to miss. Vincent was reluctant to accept her offer, but she had been persuasive. Eventually, he had agreed, but made her promise to leave the Sour-el-Ghoziane depot by noon at the latest, and to ensure that the manager telephoned him in Algiers as soon as she had done so. She had heard the man ask for the Algiers number even as she had walked from the office. It had been the man's suggestion that she should take the two Arab clerks with her. They were middle-aged, well-educated men who had worked for the Charpentier accounts department at the Head Office in Algiers for many years and had been auditing the depot's books for the past week. Their presence in her vehicle would be of assistance if the vehicle were stopped by an FLN unit, and in any case the two men were due to return to Algiers the following day by bus.

The early morning drive to Sour-el-Ghoziane had been more tiring than she had anticipated. Like most of the country's interior routes the road had been neglected except where repair had become essential. Even then, the work had been half-heartedly undertaken by labour recruited from the few roadside villages, strongly influenced by the attention of *cadres* of the local FLN. Nevertheless, Maryse Rose had found the journey pleasant and exhilarating. The sky had been cloudless, the mountain air clean and refreshing after the oppressive autumn heat of the coastal plain. She had experienced a welcome feeling of freedom and release.

It had been three weeks since she had written to Philippe telling him of her pregnancy, and he had not yet responded. It did not worry her. She wrote to him almost daily, and had done so since his posting to the Aures. He received her letters only when he returned to the base. She knew he would reply as soon as he heard the good news, and it had been enjoyable contemplating his reaction. She had been able to visualize his face, at first serious with concern for her well-being, and then warm with the thoughts of pleasure that a family would bring to them both in the future.

As she drove, the sun began to drop below the western mountain range, adding to the sense of isolation but making the driving a little easier as the valleys became dusk-shaded. The scenery was losing its bright colouring and the rocks on the mountainside which had previously glowed in the afternoon sunlight now appeared sinister and threatening. She attempted a conversation with the Arab clerks, but their minds were pre-occupied with the dangers of the countryside through which they passed. They were city Arabs, agoraphobic in their outlook, comfortable in crowds amidst noise, and naturally distrustful of space. Their replies were no more than grunts of acknowledgement; they would not be happy again until the Citroen drove once more between the tall apartment blocks, civic buildings, department stores and offices of Algiers.

The road wound into a shallow gorge. Within feet of the vehicle's wheels, to its right, was a narrow verge which dropped away almost vertically to the bottom of the valley and a dry river-bed two hundred and fifty feet below. On the left of the road the ground steepened upwards into dense scrub through which grew sparsely-leaved, skeletal trees. Wet-season streamlets had ploughed the road surface at right angles so that the Citroen, even with its excellent suspension, plunged and bucketed like an unbroken horse. Maryse Rose reduced the speed to little more than a crawl, realizing that even the smallest mistake could be fatal.

The view of the road ahead was limited as it followed the sharp contours of the gorge, and as Maryse Rose drove the Citroen around a sweeping left-hand bend a soldier in camouflaged combat denims stepped quickly from the scrub at the roadside and waved them down with the muzzle of a sub-machine gun. As if to reinforce the order, a second soldier appeared from behind a rock at the edge of the gorge, his 24/29 rifle aimed directly at the Citroen's windscreen.

She experienced brief moments of indecisive panic before determining the soldiers were French, and with a feeling of relief slowed the car to a halt a few yards from them. The two men were unshaven, their tanned faces dark beneath several days' growth of beard. Their foreheads, cheeks and arms were streaked with black and green camouflage cream, and even if one of them had been Philippe she would have been unable to recognize him. The men carried backpacks, and wore grenade-pouches; bayonets or knives hung in scabbards at their belts. Their regimental insignia was indistinguishable.

As the car stopped, four more soldiers appeared on either side of the road, their weapons threatening, their camouflage disguising their features so that they seemed more like the weird forest characters of a Walt Disney fantasy than human-beings.

The soldier who had signalled the car with his sub-machine gun now used it to indicate he wanted the occupants of the vehicle to get out. When they had obeyed he spoke abruptly, in barely comprehensible Arabic: 'Hands on roof.'

Maryse Rose smiled reassuringly at the nearest of the two Arabs. 'Don't worry.'

Instantly the soldier aimed his sub-machine gun at her and screamed an order. 'Silence . . .' He jerked his head at one of the soldiers at the side of the road. The man nodded, then hung his rifle over his shoulder before moving behind Maryse Rose. She felt herself blanch at the unpleasant memories his searching hands revived, but unlike the sergeant of the Deuxième Bureau he contented himself by running his hands only over the looser parts of her clothing before moving on to the two Arabs. He searched them thoroughly, and then turned towards the man with the sub-machine gun. 'All clean.'

The soldier waved them towards the roadside.

'Our documents are inside the . . .' began Maryse Rose.

Before she could finish the sentence, the nearest man slapped her hard across the side of the face. The blow momentarily dazed her, the pain filling her eyes with tears. He forced her to the side of the road with the muzzle of his 24/29 against her breastbone. Her realization of growing danger controlled her anger. These were not bored conscripts manning a blockade within the city and counting away their hours of duty until they could relax in the bars or dancehalls, but were hardened fighting men, cautious of their lives, and explosively lethal in this wild, threatening environment.

She watched silently as they searched the interior of the Citroen.

Two of the soldiers opened the boot of the vehicle and tossed the Arabs' suitcases onto the road. While one man prodded inside the boot with the muzzle of his rifle, the other unfastened one of the suitcases and tipped out the contents. He stirred the pile casually with a booted foot, and then Maryse Rose saw him take something from his pocket and drop it in the centre of the heap of clothing. Even as her mind questioned his action, he turned quickly and called to the man with the sub-machine gun. 'Over here, corporal . . . a grenade.'

Growing horror began to fill Maryse Rose's mind. She had seen the man deliberately attempt to incriminate one of the innocent Arab clerks.

Disbelief momentarily silenced her as the corporal walked to the rear of the Citroen, squatted for a moment beside the Arab's suitcase and picked up the object. She could see it now, cylindrical, khaki-painted. The soldier beside him said: 'Russian.'

The corporal nodded agreement and faced Maryse Rose and the two Arabs. He spoke in French his voice deep with contempt. 'You filthy Arab pigs!'

Maryse Rose began to protest. 'That's nothing to do with us . . . that soldier, I saw him . . .'

The man who had slapped her swung his rifle butt violently sideways into her ribs. She felt them crack. Pain lanced through her chest like the keen blade of a spear, making her cry out in agony. At once the thought that she must protect her unborn child dominated her. She folded her body forward, clasping her arms across her stomach, the broken ends of her ribs grating as she moved and making her gasp with pain. She fought waves of dizziness which swept over her. The man grabbed her by her hair and pulled her upright. Beside her the two Arabs stood, wide-eyed, muted by fear.

The corporal shouted an order at the Arab men. 'Get in the car . . .' When they hesitated, the soldiers guarding them drove them into the front seats with their rifle butts.

The corporal kicked the passenger door closed and then took four slow paces backwards. Maryse Rose suddenly realized his intention. She began screaming as he opened fire with his sub-machine gun. A long burst of shots echoed through the valley. Glass splintered and shattered, thin shards arcing from the vehicle. Lines of dark holes stitched its metalwork. The head of the nearest Arab disintegrated in a scarlet mist. The corporal continued firing until the mechanism of his sub-machine gun jammed on its empty magazine. The echoes of the shots faded in the distant hills.

One of the soldiers walked quickly round to the driver's door, glass splinters crunching beneath his rubber boots. He aimed his rifle inside the vehicle and fired a single shot, then ejected the spent cartridge. The corporal ignored him, sliding the empty magazine from his weapon and replacing it with a fresh one. The faces of his men were expressionless.

Maryse Rose's brain relived over and over again the appalling seconds in which the two innocent men who had been accompanying her had been so brutally murdered. It had been so bloody and obscene her mind was attempting to deny its reality.

'What about this one?' The voice of the soldier who had struck Maryse Rose questioned the corporal unemotionally.

'Kill her.'

One of the men, tall and heavily built, spoke quickly in a harsh Marseilles accent. 'Why don't you go and see if the road is clear, corporal. We'll catch you up in five minutes.'

'Five?' There was laughter from the other soldiers of the patrol.

The man with the Marseille accent spoke again, his voice tinged with inappropriate humour. 'Be reasonable, corporal. We only want to fuck the bitch to death.' There was laughter again, which the corporal silenced.

'Shut up.' He glanced at the fading sky and then studied

his watch. There were two hours until full darkness when they would bivouac for the night somewhere in the scrub. There was normally little traffic on the road at this time of the day, and apart from the two official military whores back at the base, both fat and in their late thirties, the men had been without female company for almost six weeks. Five of his section had been killed in that time, including the sergeant with whom he had served in Indo China. It made no difference to him now what happened to this Arab woman, so long as she was killed afterwards. 'I've already given you my orders.' The men looked disappointed as the corporal looped the sling of his sub-machine gun over his shoulder and unbuttoned his grenade pouch. He pulled out the Russian-made grenade which one of his men had claimed to have found amongst the Arabs' possessions, and tossed it to a nearby soldier. 'Afterwards, use this on the car. And get the damned thing off the road.' He turned and began slowly walking away. The men watched him. He called to them without looking back. 'I'll wait half an hour. God help anyone who isn't with me by then.'

They had discarded their rifles, and removed their packs and webbing. They stood facing her like hungry wolves, in a semi-circle a few feet away. As terror had thrust its way through the incapacitating numbness which had first held her, she had tried to beg them to release her. But each attempt to speak had brought a blow, until now she knelt in front of them, her head and body throbbing with dull pain, her blouse and white cotton slacks spattered with blood. One of her eyes was already so swollen she could hardly see through it, and the taste of blood in her throat made her want to vomit. They seemed to be waiting, as though she were a prostitute who would disrobe for their pleasure.

Deep shudders of fear shook her body; fear not for herself, but for her child. She tried to speak again, but one of the men stepped quickly forward and pushed her onto her back with his boot against her chest. Like a pack of ravenous animals they moved together so that the weight of their bodies smothered her wild struggles, pinning her to the scrubby ground. Laughing and joking they dragged her excitedly to a smooth rock which stood above the rapier-like grass a few yards away. Their webbing belts pinioned her feet, spread wide beneath it, while two of them holding her arms stretched her helpless across the weathered stone as though she were on a medieval rack. She screamed again, but one of the men wedged a filthy handkerchief in her mouth.

The thick-set soldier who had spoken to the corporal, stood between her widespread legs, and drew a combat knife from its sheath. Grinning at the waiting men, he melodramatically tested its edge with his thumb, then slowly inserted the point of the knife under the cuff of her sleeve and sliced the razor-sharp blade through the fragile cloth to her shoulder and then to her collar. The men howled in anticipation. Theatrically, he repeated his action on the opposite side, and with the flourish of a showman removed the entire front of her blouse. She tried to drag herself from the men's imprisoning hands, but they were too strong. Her back felt as if it were breaking.

Encouraged by the others, the man cut the waistband of her slacks at her hip, and carefully ran the knife down the leg to her ankle. Again, the men shouted their approval. She could feel the chill evening air against her exposed flesh. Her heart pumped blood explosively as though it would burst. The man cut the seam on the other leg, then paused. He waved the knife slowly above her like a magician's wand, shouted 'Voila . . .' and snatched away the cloth.

She could see their hungry eyes examining her near-naked body, but her struggles were futile. The soldier bent forward and hooked the point of his knife under her bra between her breasts. He pulled the edge upwards, then flicked the material aside with two quick movements. The men jeered.

'Not big tits.' The man's accent had thickened as though he had been drinking. 'But big enough.' She felt him cut through the silk of her panties between her thighs, and then downwards from the elasticated waist. He hesitated again, deliberately prolonging the moment to goad the passions of his comrades as if he were undressing a strip-tease artist at some coarse stag party. He drew the soft material from her, exposing her completely.

She wanted him to kill her quickly, now, but knew it would not happen until they had all been satiated. She tried to pray, but the words became jumbled amongst the confused emotions of fear, humiliation and outrage, which churned within her.

The men of the patrol were silent as he straightened himself, unhooked his belt and let his combat trousers fall to the ground. His legs were grotesquely hirsute. He pushed his khaki underpants down his thighs; his penis was erect, thick and heavy. She felt his fingers, their nails soiled and bitten, probe the sensitive female lips that the rock beneath her forced towards him. He laughed. 'Dry as an old bone!' He spat noisily into the palm of his hand and wiped the frothy spittle onto himself.

He entered her violently, driving himself deep inside her with one surging movement of his sweating body that seemed to rip her flesh apart. Behind the cloth gag, she screamed, unheard amongst the man's jeers.

She attempted to will herself to die, to become unconscious so she could escape the agony and shame. But there was no simple palliative for the torture of her mind and body, and only when it seemed it had become unendurable did an unspeakable loathing for her antagonists begin to grow and shield her. She forced herself to watch them, to lock her eyes on theirs, to attempt to drive the hatred she was experiencing, knife-like, into their minds. With one she succeeded, so that he became unable to meet her fierce stare, and stood, unfinished and ashamed. And while the others continued he left them and sat alone above the deep valley.

Only when the lust and imagination of each of the other men was completely spent, and their coarse sexual humour withered towards boredom, did they finish with her. She was no longer capable of movement, as if each line of motor nerves had detached itself from her brain. They left her lying across the rock, now on her belly, as they dressed. Despite the camouflage cream smeared on their faces, and the unshaved beards she would never forget them, nor the smell of each individual man. It had been seared into her mind, as indelibly as the brand of a white-hot iron.

Pain had become one dull, heavy sensation as if her entire body was being compressed within a huge vice. She could breathe more easily now that the filthy rag had been removed from her mouth, but she was incapable of sounds. Only her eyes moved, to follow the actions of the men.

They completed strapping on their equipment, shrugged it into more comfortable positions on their shoulders, and found their rifles in the grass.

The heavy man who had stripped her walked towards her, and swung her over his shoulder as if she were a sack of chaff. She had no strength to resist although she knew she was about to die.

He opened the rear door of the Citroen, and heaved

her inside. She slumped across the seat, motionless. Above her the once pale blue roof-lining of the vehicle was blotched red. The hand of one of the Arabs was dangling a few inches from her face. She could smell the mortuary scent of visceral fluid, blood and urine.

A front door of the vehicle was opened, and a soldier reached inside and released the handbrake, then the vehicle swayed several times and began to move. She heard its broad tyres crunch on the loose-surfaced road.

As the grey Citroen began to gain momentum at the edge of the steep drop to the dry river-bed, one of the soldiers pulled the pin from the Russian hand-grenade. He held the clip until the car's front wheels reached the edge of the gorge, and then tossed the grenade into the vehicle. It landed on the lap of one of the murdered Arabs.

The soldiers watched as the vehicle gathered speed, hit a large rock which spun it sideways, to crash and roll through a dense patch of undergrowth and saplings. A second outcrop of rock launched the vehicle into the air as the slope beneath it steepened. For a moment the Citroen seemed to hang motionless above the rocks, and then as the grenade detonated it exploded into an expanding ball of orange fire. Burning debris bounced and ricochetted amongst the boulders while a thick column of hot black smoke began to rise from the valley in the still evening air.

At first the sounds and the indistinct voices, barely penetrated the green darkness she assumed was death. Within its comforting folds there was no more pain, no memory. For an eternity she drifted without thought, aware only that there was pleasure in the emptiness of the void. Figures, white, wraith-like, moved at the perimeter of her misted vision, their features hazed. Sometimes, they touched her gently, their hands phantom hands, their whispers, flickering shades which danced briefly candescent in her mind. Her return to life was reluctant.

With life came fear.

Suddenly.

A pale star within her green darkness expanded to blinding light. The whispers magnified to roar like stormwinds. Blurred vision sharpened so that the vague shapes took form above her. Instinctively, she fought again, until her defiant senses reasoned that the hands which held her were softly feminine, the body scent faintly of fragrance and not of acrid male sweat, the voice that of reassurance and not aggression. At last she lay still.

The eyes of the woman who held her wrists, were concerned. 'I am Sister Marguerite. You are quite safe now my dear.' The slender hands released Maryse Rose's wrists. The nun, barely older than Maryse Rose, leant forward and brushed strands of lank, damp hair from Maryse Rose's bruised cheeks. 'Soon, with rest . . .'

Maryse Rose interrupted her a sudden thought projecting far beyond all others. 'My baby?'

The nun lowered her head and was silent for a moment before she replied. 'I'm so sorry. You know how we will have tried.' She held Maryse Rose's hand between her own. 'It was our priority, but we were helpless. It is the Lord who decides . . .'

The melancholy hours of night were filled with grief for her, through which flowed incessant changing patterns of emotion, each for an instant dominating its predecessor. It was impossible for her to hide herself away in sleep, for pain waited on the threshold of unconscious movement to waken her, whilst memory tortured her again behind closed eyelids. Interwoven with her sorrow, was guilt at her own foolishness in venturing beyond the city, and a resentment of her body's inability to save the child she had so much desired; Philippe's child. She had failed him, and there were moments when the dominant need was to cleanse herself of the guilt, and of the filth that seemed to coat her body, even within her most intimate parts. She despised the men who had raped her, murdered her unborn child, but also herself for failing to resist them; she would never be able to forget their eyes feasting on her nakedness, nor the manner in which their bodies had deliberately shamed her for their own amusement. She had been no more than a form of masturbation for them, of less value than a prostitute.

During that night and its long dawn, and throughout the first full day of her consciousness the sisters helped her, comforting and reassuring her. They knew little of what had happened to her, nor of how she had survived.

On the afternoon of the following day, she learnt more in an interview with a captain of the Algiers gendarmerie. The interview was almost as humiliating as the rape itself. Just as she had been interrogated by the Sûreté and Deuxième Bureau in Paris, the captain insisted on the repetition of the most minute and intimate details, all of her words recorded by a subordinate who accompanied him. To her dismay, she realized that although it had happened less than thirty-six hours before, there was already an air of fiction and exaggeration to her story, and at times she could see disbelief register on the faces of the two men. Only the presence of the young nun gave her the courage to continue.

She had survived miraculously. An Arab truck driver carrying a load of animal hides to the city had seen the smoke in the valley and stopped to investigate. A truck making the passage through the mountains at that late time of the day was in itself unusual, and more so that a driver would risk halting his vehicle in such a dangerous region. The captain of the gendarmes suspected the man's motive to be that of potential loot. He had discovered Maryse Rose lying in the broken saplings and brush through which the Citroen had rolled before exploding above the chasm. The captain seemed surprised that the truck driver had not left her there to die, but had carried her unconscious back to his vehicle and then driven her towards Algiers with the intention of taking her to the first hospital he could find who would be prepared to admit an Arab woman. He had been stopped for a routine search by a police patrol twenty miles further along the road and Maryse Rose had been identified later that evening when Vincent had become concerned that she had not arrived in Algiers.

The captain of the gendarmes was unsympathetic. Maryse Rose had behaved foolishly by driving at that time of the day in such a notorious region. It was his opinion that she should consider herself lucky she had survived at all; to him her injuries did not appear serious. Her broken ribs, concussion, odd cuts, scratching and bruising, even the loss of her unborn child, were little enough payment for her foolhardy behaviour. Naturally, he would investigate, but the chances of ever bringing the guilty men to justice was nil. If the French army could not deal with gangs of FLN killers, then there was considerably less chance for the gendarmerie.

'FLN?' She thought she had misheard him. 'They were French soldiers,' she insisted. 'I told you they were French.'

'No. Not French.' The captain looked quickly at his subordinate, a sergeant, as though seeking confirmation. 'Certainly not French soldiers. The FLN are very active in that area. There have been other incidents . . . a shooting. Extortion in the villages. The bullets found in the wreckage of your car were nine millimetre . . . a common size.

But the fragments of grenade were certainly Russian; quite different to those used by the French army.'

'But they didn't speak Arabic . . . only one of them badly.' Maryse Rose's voice was rising and the nun attempted to calm her. 'I know Frenchmen from Algerians . . . Good God, I'm Algerian myself.'

'They tricked you,' said the captain, with conviction. 'Anyone can pretend to speak a language badly. Arabs who have worked in France, and many in Algiers, speak good French. And they steal their uniforms off the French soldiers they murder.' He paused as she stared at him, with disbelief. 'You are still very confused, Madame Viard. When your memory of the incident returns, you will see that I am right.'

'Memory . . .!' she screamed at him. 'You think a woman can forget who raped her? Do you think I will ever forget the men who violated me . . . the faces of the men. I can still smell them all . . . the stink of animals. Do you think I don't remember the men who killed my baby?'

The two gendarmes stood, the captain swinging his chair back into its place against the wall near her bed-head. He spoke to the nun. 'We have all the information we need for a report. It is a pity we can't bring the men to trial, but you see our problem. How can we catch terrorists out in the maquis? . . . an impossibility.' He glanced towards Maryse Rose. 'She'll recover. I've seen it before. It could have been much worse; she could have been killed. They usually slit their victim's throats.' He put his kepi back on his head and straightened it carefully. 'Thank you for your help, Sister.'

When he had gone, Maryse Rose wept uncontrollably. The man had made her doubt herself, although she knew that every word she had told him had been the truth. And he had treated the entire incident as though it were no more important than a traffic offence. He had been quite unable to comprehend the humiliation, pain and anguish she had experienced, still experienced. Rape without a murder and by a criminal he could easily apprehend, did not interest him beyond the necessity of writing his report.

To retain her sanity, she knew she *had* to be believed. She understood that had the men been Arabs they were unlikely ever to be apprehended, but they were French! And French soldiers who would return sooner or later to their base. They would even come to Algiers for their leaves! She could identify them . . . they were *not* faceless men. If the gendarmes would not believe her, then there must be someone prepared to make a proper investigation. Perhaps Philippe would know who? Philippe *must* know . . . he would want it done, to seek justice for herself and their child.

It was important to be believed by someone . . . anyone. Even the nun was non-committal. Why wasn't Philippe with her now? He was her husband . . . surely the army would have contacted him in this kind of emergency? Where was Vincent? Colette? Even Belle?

A priest visited her later, an elderly man, stooped, his hair bleached white by age and a lifetime of the African sun. Years before he had been a missionary and tropical diseases had shrunk his body until it was little more than a frail skeleton. His fingernails had grown long, and horny.

She repeated her story to him, and while she spoke he was silent. Occasionally he nodded, the slow, even nod of a porcelain mandarin. He sat, his bony hands clasped on his lap, and when she described the degradations she had been forced to suffer he raised his eyes slightly as though her words might somehow soil him.

'Father, you believe me?'

He tightened his clasped hands. 'My child, it is not up to me to believe. If you can feel in your heart that it is the truth, then that is sufficient to guarantee God's understanding. Lies do not hurt God, only the one who speaks them. I think we should pray together . . .'

'You don't believe me, even though I've told you the truth!'

The young nun looked at her, startled, as though she was committing blasphemy.

'What I believe is unimportant,' said the priest. 'But through God I can offer you peace and comfort in prayer, and I can help you to accept the Holy Father into your body, and thus seek a new grace. And later when your husband returns, you must see your own priest, together, and he will show you how, in the light of God, you may rebuild your life.'

'Tell me that you believe me, Father,' Maryse Rose insisted. The priest looked at the nun and raised his shoulders in a gesture of hopelessness. 'You're no different from the gendarmes . . . no different to them.' Tears of frustration filled Maryse Rose's eyes; without belief she could not see how she could begin to heal herself. 'You don't want to believe that the men you think are protecting you are capable of this kind of atrocity. You don't want to believe that the stories of torture . . . the burning of villages, the napalm, the rapes you read about are true; you claim its socialist propaganda. The French are your damned heroes. You even like to call yourselves French, although not a quarter of you have French blood in your veins! Everything evil is Algerian . . . Arab . . . Muslim. And I am a liar because I'm an Algerian, and I dare to accuse good French catholic soldiers of abusing me, tormenting me, raping me, abusing me . . . trying to murder me . . . murdering other Algerians . . .'

'I believe you.' The voice which interrupted her was calm, unexpected. Vincent stood inside the door of the small room. She had not seen him enter. He spoke firmly to the priest. 'I think it would be better if you left, Father.'

The priest seemed relieved at Vincent's suggestion, and stood, making a brief sign of the cross above Maryse Rose's bed, before hurrying away.

'You can leave us alone,' Vincent told the nun, abruptly. 'I'm her brother. The one who has been telephoning you. Vincent Charpentier.'

'Of course, Monsieur.'

When they were alone, Vincent sat on the edge of Maryse Rose's bed and took her hands. 'I've been with you every second since they found you.' He smiled at her apologetically. 'In spirit, anyway. They wouldn't let me see you at first. I nearly drove them mad, telephoning every hour . . . Today they began hanging up on me!'

'Did you hear everything I told the priest?' Maryse Rose asked.

Vincent nodded, grimly. 'Yes. And I do believe you. There are bad eggs in every basket, and the French army is no exception. I've seen a few myself in the past . . . met a few more recently. I'm very sorry such a terrible thing has happened to you, Rose.' He only used the single name when he wanted her to feel particularly close to him. It was something he had done since her childhood, and she was glad of it now. He kissed her forehead. 'Those men will pay for it, I swear to you. I'll find them if I have to devote the rest of my life to it.' He looked distastefully around the bare room. 'I'll get you out of this place as soon as I can. It's like a cell in a morgue.' He paused and lowered his head. 'Christ, I feel sick about it all. If I hadn't agreed to let you go, it wouldn't have happened. The trip was far too dangerous. I should have gone myself.'

'It would have been all right. But those soldiers they

wanted to kill . . . that was what was so awful. They wanted to kill and abuse Arabs . . . any Arabs. They just didn't care. Those two poor men. It was so brutal.'

'Soldiers lose their powers of reasoning when they've been fighting for too long,' Vincent said, quietly. 'I'm not making excuses for them, but it becomes impossible to identify the real enemy. Once I watched a man machine gun an entire herd of cows, for no reason whatsoever. Afterwards, he just said he wanted to hear the bullets thudding into flesh.' Maryse Rose shuddered, and Vincent apologized quickly. 'I'm sorry. Blood is the last thing I should talk about. Getting you back to the château is far more important.'

'I'm not sure I want that,' said Maryse Rose, softly.

Vincent looked puzzled. 'What do you mean?'

'Just a feeling. I'm not sure that I want people around me for a while.'

'Mama isn't people . . . nor Madelene. Not even Belle, really. I'll contact Philippe's commanding officer. He will arrange compassionate leave for him. You have to be with people who love you.'

'Then why isn't Mama here now?' asked Maryse Rose.

Vincent looked uncomfortable. 'Mama is . . . well, you know what Mama is. Of course she's concerned, just as much as I am . . . or Madelene.' He sighed deeply and raised his eyebrows. 'Mama wants to wait until Papa gets home . . . two or three more days. The gendarmes came round and explained things to her. She didn't . . . none of us knew about the baby until they told us. Mama is very sad for you. Papa doesn't know about the baby yet. I spoke to him this morning. I didn't want to get in touch with him until we found out how . . . how you were.'

'I suppose he suggested I went to Paris again,' said Maryse Rose, wrily.

'Not exactly. He said something about a private clinic in Gstaad, where the air would do you good.' He apologized again. 'Remember, Papa is old-fashioned, and he doesn't really understand how people feel.'

'Vincent, you believed me but I don't believe you.'

Vincent seemed surprised. 'About what?'

'About Mama. Why isn't she here? I'd rather you told me.'

Vincent moved uncomfortably, and blushed. He was silent for a few seconds. 'She doesn't feel that it would be good for you if we make too much of it. We argued . . . Madelene doesn't agree with her. Damn! I told her that things aren't undone by ignoring them. She's lived such an encapsulated life that things like rape only happen to servant girls . . . no, I don't mean that in reference to you, but she just can't conceive what it must be like. She thinks that being raped by half a dozen men is just like having sexual intercourse that number of times with Papa. It's uncomfortable, maybe it's boring, but nothing more. And she's lost babies herself . . . she thinks losing babies is normal . . . oh God, I don't even know what she thinks, exactly!' He gripped her hands more tightly. 'Madelene packed you a bag. It's outside. She said she hoped you wouldn't mind her going through your things. She put in some clothes, odds and ends, your make-up. Said it was what you would need. If you want more, then telephone her. I'll bring it tomorrow. There's some money, I think.' He paused, staring deep into Maryse Rose's eyes, and knowing she was still thinking about Colette. 'I'll make Mama understand, Rose . . . tonight, when I get back. It isn't that she doesn't care. We all do.'

He stayed for half an hour, until the nun returned. Then, reluctantly, he stood to leave, promising he would return the following evening. When he had kissed Maryse

Rose goodbye he searched in the breast-pocket of his suit. 'I almost forgot. This came for you today. A letter from Philippe.'

She did not open Philippe's letter immediately. She knew by the date of the military postmark that its contents would be painful for her. Philippe would have been delighted by the news of her pregnancy, and would be sharing all the joy she had expressed when she had written to him. Like herself, he would have begun to plan their future together. Perhaps, at this very moment, in the evening dusk, he was sitting outside a mountain bivouac, his thoughts of her and the child he believed she was carrying for him . . . the child she had lost. Somehow, soon, she would have to tell him . . . so impersonal in a letter. How could she express all her feelings. At this moment, she needed him, to hold her in his arms and comfort and reassure her.

She lay for a long time, his letter held in her hands between her breasts. She was alone now, the room silent. Above, a single light-bulb, harsh, made the room naked and featureless. Her body throbbed with dulled pain. Sounds in the corridor beyond her room faded, so that the sense of solitude she was experiencing deepened. At last she tore the flap from the envelope and unfolded the pages.

Maryse Rose,

A soldier's greatest strength in wartime is his faith. A few dates, a drop of wine, sufficient ammunition and trust in his colleagues, carry him through the days. But when he is alone at night it is the thoughts of those he loves that refreshes him, and their loyalty that sustains him.

*I remember our conversation on the final evening of my
last leave. You loved me, you told me. You were my wife,
you said, and being an Arab didn't matter. There were
many more things you swore to me as we lay together,
and I believed you then. I blamed myself and the war for
having hurt you.*

*Yesterday, five of my men died in a fellagha ambush. I
thanked God that I had survived so that soon you and I
might be together again, but when I returned to camp and
received my mail I wished that I had been one of those
buried in the maquis.*

*You have lied to me continuously since your return from
France, and where you have not lied in spoken words you
have lied by silence.*

*I could have tolerated the knowledge that you had a lover
there, in fact I had no right to prevent it. But to have had a
lover who is an enemy terrorist, fighting the people whom
you claimed to love is beyond my comprehension. Perhaps
I could have forgiven even that, but to learn that while I
am away you are still amusing yourself with him, is
despicable.*

*I am not interested in either you or the child you are
carrying. I most certainly do not wish to see you again.
I will apply for a separation during my next leave. Enjoy
your Arab lover without a French husband on your
conscience.*

Philippe.

At first her mind would not accept the contents of the
letter. Even in more normal circumstances it would have
sickened her and carried her into the depths of despair.
Now, it was as though the dreadful violence and degradation she had suffered had never ended, and this was yet

one more part of the torture to be inflicted upon her; far more cruel and wounding than all her previous experiences.

She could admit only one of his accusations, that of her silence. In the earliest days of their reunion her happiness had driven Habib Saadi from her mind. Later she had not known how to tell Philippe, fearing that the love she had rediscovered was still fragile and might be lost. After their marriage, it had seemed unnecessary to discuss it, for it was now the past, while their future together lay ahead, and her love for Philippe had by then become so passionate and unquestionable that it had seemed as impregnable as a fortress.

For a time, the shock of Philippe's letter numbed her. She had anticipated joy, warmth, love and comfort in Philippe's letter, whilst it contained only hatred and accusations. And adding to her distress was the knowledge that someone close to her had maliciously betrayed her, and by doing so had destroyed all that she held most precious.

She lay awake until midnight when one of the night-duty nuns gave her a sleeping draught. The drug worked slowly, so that she felt she was falling hopelessly into a swirling, dark whirlpool from which she would never emerge. She tried to scream her fears, but it seemed that the rag which had silenced her in the mountains had once more been forced into her throat.

She was sedated for another twenty-four hours, during which time Vincent visited her again and sat silently beside her. He touched her but there was no response. Beneath the olive skin of her cheeks, the bruises had begun to darken, so that her features seemed distorted and mottled by shadows. Alone with her, Vincent gently pulled her bedsheet down from her shoulders and examined the swollen flesh, the imprints of fingers, the scarred angry tissue. As he covered her again the muscles of his jaw and neck were tight with fury and his eyes reflected the light as coldly as black sapphires.

The chimeric dreamworld in which she had been forced to dwell failed to diminish the memories of her ordeal, or the lance-like distress of Philippe's rejection. On her awakening, the hospital room itself and the bed in which she lay, became part of the wretchedness from which she knew she must escape.

The need to cleanse herself, to somehow decontaminate her body was compulsive. Movement was agonizing but she refused the assistance of the nuns, resenting the touch of their hands. The sight of her body reflected in the speckled glass of the bathroom mirror startled her, and with a shudder of revulsion she saw that some of the bruising was still identifiable as the marks of hands; worse, they returned horrific memories so that each scar became linked to a specific obscenity she had been forced to endure. She adjusted the temperature of the shower until the water almost scalded her skin, then washed herself repeatedly until she became too exhausted to continue. Afterwards, rather than return to the bed which she could imagine was still soiled by the touch of her own body, she dressed, and the touch of clean clothing appeared to refresh her mind.

During the quietest time of the afternoon siesta, when the nun who was on duty dozed in the quiet of a small office near the general ward, Maryse Rose left the hospital. Its corridors were deserted as she walked painfully into the bright sunlight of the street outside. She had spent the past hours in careful thought, and knew she would never be able to return to Beau Lac; like the hospital itself, it no longer offered sanctuary for her.

She signalled a passing taxi and ordered him to take

her to the rue Marengo on the outskirts of the suburb of Bab el Oued.

She had not anticipated how the casual glances of passers-by would embarrass her; they seemed to know she had been defiled. Despite the heavy make-up she had used to conceal her bruises, she felt they were conspicuous and imagined questions forming in the minds of those who saw them. She felt dizzy with the exertion of walking, and the weight of the suitcase tugged at her ribs making every step an individual agony. She rested for a while in a small café, grateful for its poor lighting and the glass of mint tea which briefly stimulated her, then she continued until she reached the building site near the Grand Mosque.

There were no Europeans in the area, and the eyes of the Algerian men and women followed her as she passed. She knew they thought she was a prostitute. She had tried to dress simply, but the selection of clothes which Madelene had chosen for her had left her no choice. By the standards of those who lived in this poor area she was obviously wealthy, and wealth here, for a woman, was an indication of her profession. With her bruised features, they would assume that her pimp or a client, had beaten her, and like a wounded dog she was returning to hide herself until she had healed. She could recognize their contempt.

The two lines of cars in the lot were no more than the rusting salvage of vehicles the neighbouring pieds-noir of Bab el Oued had abandoned at some dump. Optimistic prices, scrawled in Arabic numerals on pieces of cardboard, were propped against their dusty windscreens. In one corner of the lot three teenage Algerians were dismantling a vehicle, using a small donkey to draw the rope of a winch that was hauling an engine and gearbox from an old Peugeot. Amongst the line of cars, an elderly man in an oil-stained *gelabeiah* was leaning over the engine compartment of a dilapidated Renault Dauphine. He looked up as she approached, his deep-set, beady eyes, automatically appraising her value as a customer.

She spoke to him in Arabic: 'Are you Moumoud?'

He smiled before nodding. His lips thin and cracked, his few teeth yellowed and stained by nicotine. 'You are interested in buying a car? There is a good selection.' His dark eyes examined her clothes. 'We have a Buick . . .'

She stopped him. 'I want to contact a friend. He told me you'd be able to help. His name is Habib Saadi . . .'

The hours passed, fragmented and confused by her exhaustion, so that later had Maryse Rose been asked to describe the room of the Arab house in which she had waited for dusk, or the tortuous route by which Moumoud then led her into the old city, it would have been impossible for her. Somehow they avoided the military barricades, and once inside the casbah's ancient walls were joined by other guides, men she would never recognize again, silent, carrying guns which shone blue-black in the moonlight reflecting from whitewashed buildings. The only sounds were her own footsteps, so it seemed she was accompanied by agile phantoms who slipped noiselessly from shadow to shadow ahead of her.

The guides paused at a huge wooden door. She turned to thank Moumoud but he was no longer with her, and when her eyes sought the guides again in the half-darkness only one remained, a tall man, cloaked by a hooded *burnouse* so that he was faceless. The hinges of the great door were greased, and it opened easily despite its size. Once inside a small courtyard the man took her suitcase from her and then searched her. Fatigue blunted her automatic mental protest, but the man's hands were unlike others she had felt and sped over her as light and impersonal as the fluttering of a moth, so that she was uncertain as to whether he touched her at all.

He led her into a corridor beneath the building, and then up a narrow flight of stairs. He opened another door on a small landing, and when she had stepped past him closed it silently behind her. For a moment she thought she had been imprisoned alone, for the room was lit by only a single desk-lamp on a crowded table, so that she could see nothing beyond the dissected pool of light it threw on the table-top and the uneven floorboards near her feet.

A paper rustled and moved on the table. She saw a man's hands briefly in the light, the fingers elegantly slim. A chair, unseen, grated on the wooden boards.

'Maryse . . .' Habib spoke her name with a warm tenderness. He moved towards her, still no more than a silhouette, and stopped a yard from her. There was a hint of uncertainty in his voice when he spoke again. 'They told me you needed to see me. How can I help you?'

She did not answer him. After a moment he walked back to the table and tilted the lamp so that it shone full in her face. She lowered her head quickly but the harsh light exaggerated the bruises on her face and neck.

Habib swore softly in Arabic, strode quickly to her and gently lifted her face in his hands. She could feel them trembling with emotion. 'Who did this to you? Your husband?' She shook her head. His fingers seemed to burn her where they touched her skin. He released her and flicked a light-switch on the wall beside the door. A light-bulb hanging from the ceiling filled the room with a cold yellow light. Although she had dropped her head again she knew his eyes were examining her, and the same feeling of shame she had experienced earlier, returned. She felt that amongst her wounds he would also

216

see the obscene filth that still seemed to fester within her body.

'Habib, please don't.'

His voice was taut with cold fury. 'Who did this to you?'

She had seen him angry, but knew this was a far deeper and far more dangerous emotion; one she had never encountered in him. It held the threat of a terrible and primitive violence and revenge. 'French soldiers . . . in the Aim-Bessem pass. They killed the two Algerian men who were with me.'

She knew from his face that there was no need for her to describe in detail what had happened to her. He understood the brutality and degradation and she was grateful.

'When?'

'A few days ago.'

He turned his head towards the door and shouted so loudly and unexpectedly that she winced. 'Hassan . . .' The door opened almost immediately, as though the man who had brought her had been standing on guard, outside. He had tossed back the hood of the *burnouse*; a young man of perhaps twenty, a neatly-trimmed moustache curving down each side of his mouth. Habib said, curtly: 'A French patrol. Two days ago in the Aim-Bessem pass . . . I want to know their regiment. I want the patrol identified; the name of their officer and NCO's, the names of the men. I want to know everything about them. Most of all, I want to know their future movements. Use the radio.' The young man nodded, his face expressionless. When he had left them alone, Habib faced Maryse Rose. 'We'll find them. They'll go back to their base. They'll drink in a bar and they'll talk. They always do. And we have ears wherever there are French soldiers . . .' He paused. 'Damn their souls!' His voice became more composed, calmer, and his eyes questioned her. 'But I don't understand why you've come to me. Your husband?'

She spoke so softly it was no more than a whisper, and despite all the hurt she had felt, she was unable to tell him how she had been rejected. 'It's not worked out.'

For a moment he seemed puzzled. 'But when I followed you to the clinic . . .' Realization silenced him briefly. 'Your baby!' He saw tears form in her eyes and groaned with anger, banging his fist against his thigh. 'My God, and they wonder why we hate them so much.' His eyes examined her face again, searching far deeper than the marks and bruises on her skin. 'You're too ill to have come here tonight. You need medical attention . . . and rest.'

She tried to smile at him. 'Just rest . . . and peace.' She had no more reserves of strength, and felt herself sway as though she were about to faint. He helped her to a small iron bed set against the wall at one end of the room.

'Lie here. In the morning a doctor will see you. And when you are stronger we can talk about the future.'

She shook her head, determinedly. 'I have to talk tonight. Tomorrow . . .' She did not finish the sentence, but saw that again he understood. Tomorrow it would be impossible to discuss. She lowered her voice. 'I haven't come here to throw myself at your feet, Habib. I could have returned to Beau Lac; I have enough money of my own for independence. I'm here because I'm an Algerian woman . . . and I want to fight.' She paused, nervous of the emotions which her thoughts were bringing closer to the surface of her mind. 'Dear God, I knew so little; I thought real fear was what I had experienced in Paris . . . and then with Lefitte. But it wasn't. Fear is much more . . . it's total helplessness; blind frustration . . . it paralyzes and degrades and humiliates, and you can do *nothing* to save yourself. I've seen death before, but only the kind of death that is humanely acceptable . . . death containing at least vestiges of respect. But malicious and sadistic death! The Arabs with me were innocent men . . . good men, with wives and families. And the reason for killing them was manufactured by their murderers. They didn't even bother to look at our identification papers; they didn't care who we were. And I learnt what it is like to be an Algerian woman . . . an Arab woman . . . with no protection, and no human rights as an individual.'

'You want revenge?'

She shook her head firmly. 'No, not revenge. At first, yes . . . but then I realized I must fight for respect . . . for personal pride. For all the things you tried to tell me are missing from the lives of the Algerian people.'

Habib slowly tapped a Bastos from a crumpled packet, struck a match and drew deeply on the cigarette. 'You will never be able to kill, Maryse. You will never be able to fire a bullet into a man's body, or throw a bomb, or even carry explosives for us. To do those things requires a lifetime of the humiliation and degradation you have only briefly experienced. Or it needs a madness and desperation that you will be incapable of feeling towards your enemies.'

'Because I am a woman?' she asked angrily.

'Because you are a Charpentier! No matter what has happened, you will never be able to lose everything that you have learnt and felt and experienced with them. If you aim a gun at a French soldier, at the crucial moment, the fraction of a second when you must decide whether he lives or dies, the ghost of a Charpentier will step between yourself and the target.'

'I understand that, but I don't need to kill in order to fight. I'm a trained nurse. I can fight by keeping the *moussebiline* alive. You once said there was a need for medical help.' Was he trying to force her to beg to be allowed to join him?

'If you can still go back to Beau Lac, then why not work legally in the regroupment camps? Algerians are starving to death less than twenty-five miles from here. You could help Arabs, and the French would even give you medical supplies. You would lose nothing . . . and you would be helping.'

'No!' She was almost shouting at him now. 'That's not what I want to do, Habib. Don't you understand? I can't be neutral or passive any longer.'

He smiled. 'Good. That is what I need to know for certain. It's too easy to permit you to make decisions that you will regret afterwards, and there can be no turning back once you are part of us. The mountains are not the cities, Maryse, and the military laws of the *moussebiline* are enforced by the gun and the rope. Are you prepared to work in the *djebel* . . . the mountains?'

'Yes, of course.'

'And do you know what it's like there?'

She shook her head. 'I know it won't be pleasant.'

Habib laughed, grimly. 'Pleasant!' His voice became serious. 'It's ten times worse than anything you may have heard about the regroupment camps. This has been a long winter and it is still freezing in the mountains. The men have inadequate clothing, and there's so little food that at times they are too weak to carry their weapons. It's no better in the summer because then there's a shortage of water. When a man is wounded, he's treated on the spot and he lives or dies by the will of God. We have very few medicines or drugs, and conditions are primitive. There are no modern operating theatres, and a sick man is lucky if he's given an aspirin. Sometimes they prefer to kill themselves rather than endure a slow death. You will be hunted by the French all the time, and if they catch you, then what you have already suffered will seem like nothing compared to what may happen to you. There

220

will be days when you will pray to God for sleep and rest, and nights when you will pray just as hard that you can keep yourself awake. You will catch lice and fleas, and they will be a reminder that you have kept yourself alive just a little bit longer.'

She understood that he had been testing her. 'I still want to help.'

He ground out his cigarette against the welt of his shoe, and then stood. 'Then you are very welcome here, Maryse. But it will be several weeks before we leave for the *djebel*.' He lifted one of her hands to his lips and kissed it softly. 'My tent is your tent, my food your food. I will get you a warm drink to help you rest.' He left her for only a few minutes, but when he returned she was already asleep, still in a half-sitting position on the bed. She groaned softly but did not awaken as he gently lifted her legs onto the mattress and covered her with a blanket. He turned out the main light and adjusted the one upon the table so that she lay in shadow. For a long time he sat watching her. Much later, as the stars faded in the dawn sky above the old city, he wrapped himself in a *burnouse* and lay on the wooden flooring across the door-way of the room.

NINE

Algiers: The Casbah. May 1959

The flat roof, with its low crenellated walls, stood a little above the neighbouring houses of the Casbah. To the north there was an almost unobstructed view of the wide bay, and beyond the barracks-like apartments of Bab el Oued to the west it was possible to see the affluent French villas which lined the coastal road, gleaming in the spring sunshine. Habib Saadi sat within one of the crenellations of the thick walls staring through a pair of binoculars. From his viewpoint he could see nothing of the barbed-wire barriers which guarded the entrances to the Casbah, but he had been watching the progress of a small military convoy along one of the distant boulevards. Its destination was unimportant to him. He was doing no more than killing time.

In less than four hours he would be leaving Algeria for Tunisia by a complicated route. With identification papers and a passport in the name of Mostefa Ferradj, he would first sail to Barcelona. There he was to be supplied with Moroccan documents and travelling as a Moroccan national would fly first to Rome, and two days later via Sousse in Tunisia, to the inland airfield at Gafsa where he would be met and driven to a *moudjahiddine* camp on the old caravan track of Oued el Kebir close to the Algerian frontier. Had it not been for the war and the necessity for secrecy by the FLN, all but the final forty miles of his journey could have been made by train from Algiers railway station, less than twenty minutes walk from where he was now seated.

Behind Habib Saadi, hanging from a rope suspended between two bamboo poles lashed vertically to the crenellated wall, was a line of washing, the damp garments barely moving in the soft sea-borne breeze he was enjoying after the stuffy atmosphere of his room. Beyond the washing, in one corner of the square roof, was a chicken-coop with a small run. Inside, half a dozen thin fowls scratched hopefully for maggots in the three inches of dung which carpeted its floor.

Hassan Ben Yahia had climbed the narrow stone staircase to the roof parapet several minutes previously. He had said nothing to Habib, but had lit a cigarette and then leant against the wall, peering down into the narrow street below. Sound drifted upwards. The casbah was never silent during the day, and music from a dozen different radio stations of the Maghreb mingled discordantly, penetrated by shouted conversation and the sounds of iron-tyred carts rattling on the cobbles.

The two men were not friends. Hassan Ben Yahia had commanded this cell until Habib's arrival from Cairo. He had been ordered to accommodate Habib, his superior officer within the FLN, until Habib received his instructions to proceed to his post in the *djebel* as a Lieutenant in Wilaya 3.

It was now May, and to fire Ben Yahia's discontent, during his entire stay with the cell Habib had automatically assumed control. Ben Yahia's resentment had grown when Habib repeatedly vetoed the cell's plans, so that for the past five months they had done virtually nothing except act as messengers and a post office for more active groups. In Ben Yahia's opinion it was no way for a young and ambitious member of the FLN to make a name for himself, and he was convinced that once the war ended the prizes would go to those who could show that they had earned them. Spending most of his nights driving a disguised radio van around Algiers and avoiding the attention of French military patrols might be dangerous for him, but he felt it contained little romantic appeal for those who might be chosen to judge him at some future time.

Hassan Ben Yahia dropped his cigarette butt into the street below, watching it spiral between two pedestrians, then he strolled lazily to the chicken-coop. He took a handful of maize from a tin beside the coop and dropped it through the wire mesh. The birds scrambled for the grains.

The wall beside the coop overlooked a square courtyard at the rear of the building. In the centre of the courtyard was a round fountain, and against one of the walls, a fig-tree, thin trunked, stretching its head eagerly towards the light. In its sparse shade sat Maryse Rose, reading. She was always reading, thought Ben Yahia, and she contributed nothing to the work of the cell. True, she paid for her keep, and in fact there was a small profit for them from her board and lodging, but she was a liability. It was madness for Saadi to trust her; one word in the wrong place and the cell members would end up as guests of the Operational Detachment, specialists in the more painful forms of interrogation. It was difficult enough for the cell members to maintain their cover, even in the casbah; which, to assist French security was divided into units, each building individually numbered and under the watchful eye of some Muslim ex-soldier whom the French authorities considered loyal. Some were loyal, and it was Ben Yahia's scheme to execute a number of these.

Ben Yahia looked at his watch. It was a few minutes before eleven o'clock.

'Is waiting so difficult, Hassan?' asked Habib, his voice tinged with sarcasm. He was quite aware of Ben Yahia's feelings towards him. Perhaps, he had admitted to himself, he might feel the same if the circumstances were reversed. It was a little like finding, as a child, that your schoolmaster had been billeted in your house, to cast a disapproving eye over whatever you might do.

'Inactivity is always difficult,' replied Ben Yahia. He reminded himself constantly that he must have patience. Sooner or later Saadi would be instructed to leave. It could happen even during this visit to Tunisia. 'She makes me nervous.' He jerked his head towards the courtyard.

Habib knew he was referring to Maryse. He laughed. 'Why? She's only a Bedouin woman, a Berber, despite her former name.'

'If she was the Charpentier's donkey I'd be nervous. You should never have permitted her to stay. Every time she leaves the casbah . . . even when she leaves the house to go to a market, I sweat until she returns.'

'And then you sweat for the next twenty-four hours, until you're sure that a French patrol won't come running along the street to hammer at our door. I've seen you,' Habib said coldly. 'I've told you she's completely trustworthy.'

Ben Yahia put his hands in his pockets and angrily kicked a large piece of red tile which lay on the bitumen-coated flat room. The tile shattered with a sound like a pistol shot against the far wall. 'So you keep saying. But you keep quiet about the other Charpentier . . . her brother . . . the OAS Ultra. He's about as safe as a mad dog. Her entire family are fascists.'

'Pick a new subject, Ben Yahia. We've discussed this one a hundred times before.' Habib lifted the binoculars to his eyes again, and focused the lenses on the balcony of a house some hundred yards away. An elderly man sat reading a newspaper, by his side was a linnet in a reed cage. Habib knew he was an informer, paid by the French.

'Take the woman with you,' said Ben Yahia, abruptly.

'Don't talk nonsense. What would she do, wait on her own in Barcelona?'

'Why not? Does it matter where she waits for you?'

'And what if I return by a different route? No, she stays here. I'd trust her with my life.' As the days had grown into weeks, and then months, it had pleased Habib to see how Maryse had fought to overcome her physical and mental wounds. At times he knew the memories returned to torment her, uninvited, and unexpectedly, triggered by some obscure association. But she was strong again now, and like himself ready to take her place amongst the *fidayine*. It would be good to be with her in the mountains. Perhaps there, she would become a complete woman again, for him.

'Every man has a right to choose whom he trusts with his life,' observed Ben Yahia, bitterly. 'And we don't choose her.'

'*You* personally don't choose her.' Habib corrected. He lowered the binoculars and faced Ben Yahia. 'After what's happened to her, if the French used the *magneto* on her now she wouldn't talk.' He stared hard at Ben Yahia. 'But what about you? You've never been tested. How silent will you remain when they fasten the terminals to your penis and generate a few thousand volts?'

'They have to catch me, first. And that's what I'm trying to prevent.' Ben Yahia was angry.

'Not judging by the schemes you suggest.' Habib said sharply, then paused and spoke in a more friendly tone. 'I know how frustrated you feel. It was no different for me at first. I was always angry, in Paris. It wasn't until I was in Egypt that I realized how necessary my work had been. But every plan we use here has to be considered on a great many levels. Yes, I agree with you that it would be helpful if there were no informers in the casbah, but if you begin to execute their "old soldiers", then you'll force the enemy to come in and retaliate. This isn't the only FLN cell in the casbah; you must always remember that. The bomb factory is far more important . . . also the new arsenal. And at least we know the present French informers. If we kill those, they will be replaced by some we do not know. There are always traitors who can be bought and sold, even in a *jihad*. Comfort yourself with the thought that one day we will have an accounting; save the bullets for then.'

Maryse Rose walked with Habib through the narrow lanes and alleys of the old city towards the eastern entrance where the steps led down from the Market of the Lyre to Briand Square and the theatre where so often as a girl she had been taken by Christian and Colette Charpentier. Then, it had been the casbah which had seemed so alien and she would never have dared venture alone into its mysterious streets. Now it was different. In the Arab quarter, she felt secure and protected, and it was only when she ventured beyond its walls that the new sense of her vulnerability returned. The combat denims of many of the French soldiers who thronged the boulevards and pavements outside the bars and cafés made her feel uneasy, and their coarse humour, which at one time might only have faintly annoyed her, now seemed to threaten her.

She knew she was unrecognizable, even to those who had been her closest friends. For the past months she had worn nothing but Arab clothing; long loose dresses and a concealing *haik* draped as a shawl over her head and pulled across the lower part of her face. Although it had seemed strange at first, it had given her an anonymity she welcomed. It was as though she had been reborn; her identity had also been changed. With so many Algerians still employed in the government offices, it had been little trouble for Habib to obtain new papers for her. They gave her names as Melila Bachir, and even should the French authorities care to check the details they would find it impossible. Her place of birth and the village in which she had supposedly lived, had been bombed out of existence by their own military forces. She was no more than another untraceable refugee, sheltering with distant relatives within the walls of the Arab city. Now, even Habib and the other members of the group called her Melila; a new name to her new life.

Only occasionally had she experienced pangs of regret at her decision to isolate herself from her family, and her former way of life. There were times when she missed Vincent, and longed to hear the sound of his voice and his affectionate teasing. She had telephoned him the day after leaving the hospital, and for the first time in her life she had lied to him. It had been difficult. She had told him that she was leaving Algeria for France and that for her peace of mind and health she must find a future for herself far away from the country which now held so many terrible memories for her. She had asked him to explain her feelings to Christian and Colette, and had promised to write to them all as soon as she was settled. The letters had never been penned, and the knowledge that they must be worried about her saddened her, but she was aware that the truth would give them even more pain. Although Christian and Colette might understand her fears and perhaps be able to relate her experience to her present reasoning, they would never accept her decision. For the Charpentiers there was no way of life acceptable in Algeria but that of the settlers. Their Algeria was one in which the *status quo* was maintained and the present links with France forged in permanence. An independent Algeria, where native Algerians could vote on equal terms with the colonists was anathema and they would view Maryse Rose as no more than a traitor to themselves and France.

As though in compensation for the loss of Philippe and her family, the bond between herself and Habib had strengthened, so that the quiet love she had felt for him during her stay in France now contained far more complex elements. He had demanded nothing in return for her dependency on him in the past months, and the comfort and reassurance she had so badly needed had been given selflessly and without even the vaguest of hints that one day he might exact some form of payment. He had been physician and friend, and the latter in its most classical of forms. She had become aware too, that he had been suppressing his own feelings towards her, concealing them regardless of their intensity for fear that they might cause her further hurt.

He had changed since the time they had shared together in Paris. Then he had been wild, impulsive, sometimes irresponsible and uncaring, whereas now he had matured and become a man. It showed even in the way in which he moved, or spoke, and although he had previously been good-looking in a boyish way, his new maturity had accentuated the best of his Arab features so that he had become far more handsome and masculine.

On their way to the quay, an incident at the military barrier at the entrance to the casbah tested his self-control. Three young French conscripts guarded the barbed-wire barrier; the oldest no more than nineteen. Normally there would be a sergeant or corporal with them, but for the moment they were unsupervised. They had been ordered to check identity papers and the occasional basket or suitcase that might be used to carry weapons. As usual there was never time to search them all. Now, however, the young soldiers were amusing themselves by teasing the Arab women. As each woman reached the barrier one of the men glanced at her papers, while the other lifted the hem of her dress with the foresight of his 24/29. Although the clothing was never lifted more than knee height, for the Algerian Muslim women it was a grossly insulting experience. But the more voluble their complaints the longer the inspection lasted. From the ribald comments of the conscripts, so fresh from their training barracks in France that they were as yet untanned by the Algerian sun, they were unaware that the majority of the Algerian population of the department were bilingual.

The crush of the crowd at the barrier prevented both Habib and Maryse Rose from seeing what was taking place until it was too late to turn back. Instantly, Habib realized how it might affect Maryse Rose. He stepped between her and the soldier with the rifle, hoping she would be allowed to pass through the barrier behind him unmolested, but the conscript pushed him back into line with the muzzle of the weapon. Habib glanced quickly at Maryse Rose and saw the horror of her memories in her startled eyes. The third of the conscripts began searching Habib's suitcase.

Suddenly Maryse Rose realized that Habib would attempt to kill the soldier who carried the rifle rather than allow him to touch her. The colour had drained from the olive skin of Habib's temples, and the muscles of his jaw had tightened. Like an animal about to spring on its prey he had unconsciously moved his weight so that he was balanced on the balls of his feet, and his hands had opened like talons.

The third soldier who had been crouching above the

opened suitcase stood and pushed it towards Habib with his foot. 'Go . . .'

Habib hesitated. His eyes were on the soldier with the rifle who had moved in front of Maryse Rose. She knew that unless she acted immediately Habib was certain to intervene. At the very least he would be arrested, and it was possible that one of the recruits might be unable to resist the opportunity to enhance his reputation amongst his colleagues by shooting Habib on the spot. She spoke quickly in Arabic. 'Do as he says. They can't hurt me here.'

Her stomach had begun to cramp, and she knew she was perspiring heavily.

To her relief, Habib moved reluctantly a few yards along the street, but then stopped. His eyes narrowed dangerously.

The young conscript shouted at her. 'Come on, Fatima, show us your beautiful legs.'

The tone of the youth's voice, and his arrogant manner sickened her, but she spoke just loudly enough for her voice to carry the distance that separated them. 'You can see them anytime . . . and a lot more.' She was deliberately husky, seductive. The conscript's pale blue eyes met her own, surprised. 'I'm a hostess,' she added.

He was interested. 'Where?' He was round-faced, freckled. His hair cropped above protruding ears. He was little more than a boy.

She invented a bar. 'The Pelican. Boulevard Saint Jacques. You can meet me there, after seven.' Perspiration trickled uncomfortably between her shoulder blades. She was aware that Habib was staring at the soldier.

It had been three months since the young conscript had slept with his fiancée in Lille. He ran the tip of his tongue along his upper lip. 'I'll be there tonight.' He eyed

231

her Arab clothing and the *haik* which covered the lower part of her face. 'But how will I know you?'

'I'll remember you,' she promised, truthfully.

He smiled and then waved her past him with the rifle. When she was a few feet away he raised his voice slightly. 'I'm Georges, Georges Charlot.'

Habib was waiting for her, his eyes surprised and questioning. 'He didn't touch you, the little bastard.'

'No . . .'

'Then what did you say to him?'

She forced herself to laugh, lightly. 'He thinks he has met a new girl-friend.'

Habib only grunted, but she noticed a few moments later that he was walking far closer to her than usual so that there were times when she could feel the touch of his body against her own. In France he would have taken her arm, but here, while she was in Muslim dress, custom forbade the public intimacy.

He said little as they walked together, but at the entrance to the docks, he stopped and faced her. 'Thank you.'

'For what?'

For the first time since the check-point, he smiled at her. 'For using your brains. I wasn't using mine.' His voice was suddenly serious. 'Take care while I'm away. I don't want you hurt again.' He paused, then lifted her hand towards his lips but at the last moment turned it, so that his kiss was in the centre of her palm. She felt an unexpected thrill. For a few moments he stood looking at her, silently, and she realized that his eyes were telling her his secret emotions. For the first time since she had gone to him she wanted him to hold her in his arms and caress her once more as a lover. It was a desire that only a short while before she had never expected to feel again. Gently she pulled the *haik* away from her face. He did

232

not kiss her but his fingertips softly touched her cheek for a moment. Then he left her, walking quickly across the wharf towards the quayside immigration offices. The eyes of a pair of strolling gendarmes followed him briefly as he joined the queue, but were distracted by a group of children chasing a football across the parking area. She lost sight of him when he entered the building.

For an hour she stood watching as the final passengers joined the ship and cranes loaded cargo and vehicles into the holds. Then, as the dockworkers released the ropes and hawsers from the vessel and the cream hull began moving slowly away from the quayside, she turned towards the old city, choosing a longer route to the northern entrance to avoid the unwelcome attentions of the young French soldiers.

Hassan Ben Yahia watched the *Tassili* leave. From his vantage-point on the flat roof of the building, with the binoculars, he could see the deck officers on her bridge as the ship manoeuvred slowly about in the harbour before aiming her bow north west into the open sea. There were passengers lining the *Tassili*'s port rails, but at this distance it was impossible to identify them. Perhaps Habib Saadi was amongst them, but unlike those who would be working in Spain or southern France for the next two or three years, he had no need to imprint this last sight of the homeland on his mind. Habib Saadi would be back in Algeria in two or three weeks at the most.

Ben Yahia was twenty-two years old. Born in Sidi-Bel-Abbes, a small town some sixty miles south of Oran, he had grown up amidst a population who had an intense resentment for the French. Sidi-Bel-Abbes was the head-quarters depot of the Foreign Legion, and the Legion dominated every aspect of the local Algerians' lives. Although Algerian born, to his shame Hassan Ben Yahia was not one hundred per cent native. His father had been an unknown legionnaire, his mother a Bedouin. The soldier could have been any of the many nationalities who joined the Legion, but his only legacies to his son were a paler than normal skin for an Algerian, and hazel eyes. Ben Yahia hated his illegitimacy, and the physical differences he was unable to conceal. From his early childhood he was teased by other children. They had called him 'The Berber Pig'. Apart from the colour of his eyes and skin, neither his looks nor manners had justified the cutting insult, but he had been forced to tolerate it until he had grown strong enough to discourage his tormentors. He had earned a local reputation for explosive reflex-violence, and spurred by the goading he had been forced to endure he had studied with an aggressive determination until he had become what the French liked to name an 'évolué', an educated Arab. He had then read mathematics at Algiers university, and had become a qualified teacher. He could have found employment in a government school, but chose instead to teach in a small, privately owned Muslim college within the casbah itself. The principal, a Mullah who was learned in the sacred law of the Koran, encouraged his staff to participate in what he saw as a holy war of Moslem liberation. But more importantly the Mullah, Hadj Ahmed M'Ouzegane, was the main FLN link between several of the casbah's cells, and was the only means of communication between Ben Yahia's own group and the next echelon of command within the FLN. Habib Saadi's ability to by-pass the Mullah was yet another reason for Ben Yahia's resentment.

He watched the *Tassili* until the afternoon sun reflecting from the sea through the lenses of the binoculars began to make his head ache, and the ship was barely visible. Habib Saadi had gone, at least for the time being. It was just possible he might never return, if the commander of

Wilaya 3, Mohand Ou El-Hadj, decided to smuggle his latest lieutenant into the region across the Tunisian frontier.

If that were the case, Ben Yahia thought, Saadi's woman could be told to leave.

He shaded his eyes from the sun for a moment, then searched in his jacket pocket for his sun-glasses; they were mirrored, completely concealing his eyes. He pushed them on, then contemplatively bit a thin sliver of nail from the middle finger of his right hand and spat it into the street below. If Saadi failed to return the Charpentier woman became Ben Yahia's problem, and telling her to leave was not necessarily the safest thing for him to do. If she was in fact untrustworthy, it might encourage her to go to the Sûreté with information about the cell. She would be rewarded by the French.

He could kill her, he thought. It would be relatively easy to smother her and dump her body into the sea from the cliffs. The French would not bother to carry out an autopsy on an Arab woman. They would simply report that she had drowned. She would be identified by her papers as Melila Bachir, not Maryse Rose Viard or Charpentier. No-one but Hassan Ben Yahia and Habib Saadi knew her real identity.

He could then send a message to Saadi saying that the woman had become deranged, and despite all his efforts to help her had committed suicide. It was a plausible solution.

But not the right one! Ben Yahia pushed the bridge of the sunglasses higher up his nose; when he frowned the glasses tended to slip lower. Whatever his personal feelings regarding Saadi and the Charpentier woman there was a war to be won, and most of the real fighting was being done in the *bled* or the *djebel*. Killing a qualified nurse was like throwing a consignment of grenades into the Mediterranean. There was little enough medical help for the FLN *djoundi*, and skilled nurses willing to risk their lives in the mountains were rare commodities. If she could prevent just one *djoundi* bleeding to death, or rotting slowly with gangrene, then he, Hassan Ben Yahia, had no right to prevent her.

Hassan was not incapable of self-analysis. He was aware that his mistrust of the woman stemmed from his dislike of Saadi. In fact, he admitted to himself, for a Bedouin woman she was extremely attractive; many of them disfigured themselves in an ugly manner with facial tattoos. Her accent, too, was far less grating than that of many Arab women and her occasional use of cosmetics in a European manner was pleasantly sophisticated. He was uncertain of her relationship with Saadi. It was obvious that they were not lovers, and yet their affection was greater than that of a normal friendship between a man and a woman. Like brother and sister? No, not even that. Something quite different.

Brother and sister! The thought developed in Ben Yahia's mind. Melila was a Charpentier. Saadi had told Ben Yahia about her background when she had first arrived and needed new identity papers. And in the confines of the old house with its thin floors, he had overheard many of their conversations; there was little that Ben Yahia did not know about her now.

That damned Charpentier brother of hers! Perhaps not a real brother, but a brother by adoption. 'Vincent Charpentier . . .' Ben Yahia repeated the name silently. It was like a curse.

He had seen the man once, at a pieds-noir rally, wearing a brassard on his right arm decorated with the Celtic cross of the French National Front. Ben Yahia had listened to all the speeches from behind the curtained window of a second floor apartment; the vehemence had been frightening, and the presence of Vincent Charpentier, the son of one of the country's best known politicians and wealthy businessmen, had lent credibility to the rabble-rousing oratory.

There had been four men standing together on the balcony before the excited crowds of pieds-noir that day; Jean-Jacques Susini, a pale, ill-looking Corsican; Jo Ortiz, a stocky, broken-nosed Spaniard who was leader of the illegal para-military militia; Colonel Thomaso, founder of the pieds-noir so-called Home Guard which was linked with the disappearance of guns, ammunition and grenades from the barracks of the territorial units; and Vincent Charpentier, suave, educated and intelligent . . . perhaps the most dangerous of the four.

Charpentier's organization was coldly efficient. In October of 1957 a grenade had been tossed into the window of a room above a carpet shop on the outskirts of Bab el Oued. Its explosion ignited a large store of chemicals which the FLN had intended for making bombs. Two Arabs had died in the fire, and one of them had been Hassan Ben Yahia's cousin.

Afterwards FLN intelligence had identified a new right-wing colonist group as responsible for the killings and the frustration of their plans for a new bombing campaign. And the group had been formed by Vincent Charpentier who from his personal wealth was equipping his men with the most modern weapons, believed to be shipped into Algeria amongst the goods imported by the Charpentier Company. The new organization had grown rapidly with Vincent Charpentier's skilled management.

Hassan Ben Yahia would have liked to kill any of the men he had seen on the balcony on the day of that rally; particularly Vincent Charpentier. He had clenched his fists in frustration as he had listened to the speeches. A sporting rifle fitted with a telescopic sight would have

237

been the answer, but Ben Yahia had been unarmed at the time. And even had he been carrying the pistol which was hidden in his room at the casbah, it would have been incapable of the accuracy necessary to hit one of the men at that distance.

Since then, they had seemed impossible to kill. The four men were never alone in public, and even when they were addressing their supporters were known to wear bullet-proof vests. Their chauffeurs were all ex-military, mostly paras or legionnaires, armed and trained in security methods. The houses in which the four leaders lived were as heavily guarded as military barracks, and to enter their places of work was an impossibility for an unknown Arab. Further protection for the men was the efficiency of their own intelligence systems, which the FLN believed to be as good as those of the French government agencies.

Ben Yahia mused. To kill Vincent Charpentier would be regarded by his superiors as an indication of his potential. It would be impossible for them to ignore; it would lead to his promotion within the FLN, but more importantly it would establish his reputation for the future. Instead of being regarded as little more than a radio-operator, Ben Yahia would be seen as a man of initiative, with the courage and ability to act in a practical manner.

He knew he was day-dreaming. To be certain of killing any one of the men required the fire-power of a complete FLN section, and even such trained soldiers might not be sufficient unless they were fully armed; equipped with heavy machine-guns and perhaps a few land-mines . . . electrically detonated mines at that. It would take time and patience, for none of the four men used the same route regularly or travelled at specific times of the day. They had made themselves completely unpredictable, frequently changing the vehicles they used or the style of clothing they wore.

Below in the courtyard the heavy street door shut with a thud that was audible to Ben Yahia on the roof. The door was a century and a half old, made of the black heart-wood of a mahogany tree that had stood in a West African jungle for five hundred years. The thick panels of the door were iron-bound, and studded, its locks built to withstand a battering-ram should the old city be attacked by the sea-pirates that had once ravaged the ancient coast. If necessary, the locks could be reinforced by solid iron bars which fitted into recesses in the walls on either side of the door within the courtyard. It gave Ben Yahia, and the members of his cell, a sense of security at night. If they were raided by a French patrol, the door would keep the soldiers or police out for sufficient time for the cell members to be warned, and to escape through the passages which linked the old house to its neighbours. But the French patrols seldom entered the casbah, and if they did it was usually just before dawn when most of the inhabitants of the old city were sleeping. A successful daytime raid was an impossibility, for a warning would be passed through the casbah quicker than a patrol could run.

Ben Yahia walked to the interior wall of the roof, and looked down into the courtyard. He saw the Charpentier woman pause by the small pool for a few moments, as though examining her reflection in the surface of the water. She straightened herself, pulled her *haik* back off her head and shook out her hair before turning to stare up at him. He stepped back quickly out of sight, and then regretted the movement. It made it appear as though he had been spying on her. Angry with himself he kicked the side of the chicken-coop, so that the scrawny birds exploded from their dung dust-baths in a noisy panic.

*

239

Even before Habib's departure for Tunisia, Maryse Rose had begun to feel impatient. For weeks she had been eagerly anticipating their orders to proceed to the Aures; now there was further delay. The leaders of the FLN were notoriously fickle and she was beginning to feel her skill at nursing was being wasted. The FLN leaders could change their minds yet again, and it might yet be months before she was able to escape the claustrophobic atmosphere of the casbah and work in the refreshing freedom of the mountains.

Habib's absence brought her a renewed sense of despondency which at times conjured memories of Philippe's rejection. During the first months she had protected herself with an exaggerated hatred for him which she had based on his spurning of their child, but she knew the emotion was false and concealed the passions of the love they had once shared and which she had believed was inviolable. Now she was incapable of analysing her feelings towards him, for they changed repeatedly with memories she was unable to dismiss. In Habib's company the memories faded, but her present solitude was a tempting bait for them, attracting them to her mind.

She was grateful for the friendship which Hassan began to show towards her in Habib's absence. It surprised but pleased her, for although he had always been polite it had been obvious he resented her presence as much, if not more than that of Habib. But with Habib away, Hassan's attitude appeared to have changed. Before, he had taken his food alone rather than with the other members of the cell in the one communal room of the building. Now he joined them all, and there had been several occasions in the last few days when he had sat chatting with her in the courtyard, or had strolled with her in the streets of the old city. And although his questioning had sometimes brought her sad reminders of the life she had discarded, she was glad of his company and the distraction it offered.

It was the fifteenth day of Habib's absence, and the sun was already lost below the western horizon where the Atlas mountains softened into easy forest-clad slopes that fell towards the evening sea. High clouds trapped and reflected the last red sunlight, and above the casbah flocks of doves wheeled and swooped towards their roosts beneath the dull green-copper domes of the ancient mosques and palaces. Lights had begun to glow behind the narrow windows and in the markets the traders were lighting flares. The slow, hot air which rose from the streets had become tainted by the scent of kerosene.

Hassan Ben Yahia sat at the table in his room. The room was identical in shape and size to that of Habib's on the floor above. The ceiling was beamed, supporting uneven oak planks and whenever Habib was in residence Ben Yahia could hear him pacing the floor at night, coughing or clearing his throat; the sounds were a constant aggravation. Now, apart from the music of distant radios, all was silent in the house and Ben Yahia was feeling elated.

He was studying a gold wedding ring.

The fine engraving which he had just discovered within the metal band was an exciting and unexpected bonus. It read 'Philippe et Maryse Rose. Janvier 1958'.

Until half an hour before the ring had been in a small, suede-leather jewellery bag in Maryse Rose's suitcase. Ben Yahia had stolen it.

He had remembered the ring the previous day. Its unique design, fluted edges and minute engravings of roses, was ideal for his purpose. He had seen it amongst her possessions when he had searched her suitcase on the night of her arrival in the casbah. Then he had been looking for weapons, or some indication that she might be a French spy.

The ring had become an important part of Ben Yahia's plan.

It was a basically simple plan, and its simplicity was its strength. He was convinced it would work.

The thoughts which he had been casually examining following Habib's departure had gelled towards reality. What he had gleaned from Habib during the past months of Maryse Rose's history, and confirmed in his recent conversations with her, had convinced him that she might be the one weakness in the defences of the man responsible for the murder of his cousin. Ben Yahia's Arab pride had temporarily masked his other motives.

The woman was to be the bait, Vincent Charpentier the prey, and Ben Yahia himself, the predator.

In any normal circumstances, the trap would fail. But the circumstances were conveniently abnormal. The woman and Vincent Charpentier shared a unique relationship. The man, as a boy, had saved her life, and by Arab custom and probably that of the pieds-noir, this gave Charpentier a responsibility for her that he would be unable to ignore. If the location which Ben Yahia selected for their supposed rendezvous was one which held some emotional memory for them both, then Vincent Charpentier would deliver himself to his executioner. And only the previous evening the woman had unwittingly revealed the killing-ground; a temple within the ruins of the ancient Roman city of Tipaza, where she and her brother had frequently played together in their childhood. Ben Yahia had recognized its significance in the misting of her eyes as she described it.

If the note to meet her was sympathetically worded, then Ben Yahia knew that Vincent Charpentier would come alone. He put the wedding ring on the table and removed the cover from a portable Olivetti typewriter.

It was Monday afternoon, and to Madelene's surprise Vincent had returned early from the office. He seemed nervous, somehow excited and she knew at once that he was concealing something from her. Men were so transparent with their secrecies, she thought, resisting the temptation to question him. So much of his life was hidden from her now that there were times when she wondered if he even needed her and the children, though he would refute her accusation. Even if he could accept it, he would blame it on the war; the part he had chosen to play in it frightened her. For her peace of mind she deliberately distanced herself from the organization he had formed. He had called it a 'club', but when it had grown to rival similar organizations, all claiming to defend the settlers' rights, it had begun to be mentioned in the newspapers and Vincent had been named its leader. She had been fearful for his safety, and Christian Charpentier had been furious with his son. For weeks the two men had not spoken, but at last Christian had appeared to relent. Secretly, perhaps, Madelene believed, he envied Vincent the more active role he was playing. The politics of the war had become increasingly frustrating for the members of the Assembly.

Vincent spent only a few minutes in the garden with the children before going to his room and changing into casual clothes. Then he joined Madelene again, glass of beer in his hands. He sat beside her in one of the garden chairs.

'I've heard from Maryse Rose.' He made no attempt to conceal the excitement in his voice.

'Thank God.' Madelene smiled at him. 'I'm so pleased,

darling. I know you've been worrying about her. Christian and Colette will be delighted. Where is she?'

'Here, in Algeria.'

'In Algeria? Then why . . .' She left the question unfinished. 'Is she coming home?'

Vincent shrugged. 'I don't know. Perhaps.' He paused. 'She may be in trouble.' He found the ring in his pocket and held it towards Madelene. 'This was with her note.'

'Her wedding ring! Why send that? Surely she would never take it off her finger . . .'

'After what Philippe did to her, I'm surprised she even kept it. I imagine she wanted to authenticate her letter to me.'

'Would that be necessary?' Madelene looked puzzled.

'It might be. She wants me to meet her.'

'But you wouldn't refuse.'

'Of course not.' Vincent slipped the ring back into his pocket. 'But I might have suggested a different place to meet, somewhere a little more public . . . safer.'

Madelene's eyes widened. 'Then you mustn't go.'

Vincent laughed at his wife's fears. 'Do you think our desert rose intends to murder me?'

'Of course not, but you must be sensible. I know you miss her badly, we all do, but it's silly to take risks . . . silly for both of you to take risks. What are you going to do?'

Vincent drained his beer and then pushed himself to his feet. He looked down at his wife and smiled. 'I'm going to meet her, and I'm going to try to persuade her to come back home.' He stooped and kissed her on the forehead.

It was a little after five-thirty when Ben Yahia parked the borrowed 350cc Moto Guzzi motorcycle between the small fish market on the Tipaza quay and the hull of one of the fishing boats which had been hauled out of the water for repainting. The wharf was busy and crowded. Nets which the families of the fishermen had been repairing during the day were being loaded back into the boats in preparation for the coming night's fishing. The boats themselves rocked lazily in the soft swell alongside the harbour wall, while the crews checked their acetylene lights, recoiled their long-lines and anchor ropes, stacked boxes of bait, greased winches or refuelled the engines. There was an oppressive stench of fish and rotting seaweed in the air, while a thin fog of diesel fumes from the boats' exhausts drifted across the quay.

Ben Yahia had not anticipated the sense of fear that had developed in his mind as he had ridden towards the small town on the motorcycle. Throughout the day he had experienced only a growing excitement, during which he had stripped and cleaned the American Smith and Wesson revolver twice, and then unnecessarily polished and greased its heavy .455 bullets. He had never fired the weapon. It had been rusty when the cell had been given it two years previously by the Mullah, Hadj Ahmed M'Ouzegane, and was a relic from the World War; probably discovered long ago by a Bedouin in the wreckage of some abandoned military vehicle. One of its wooden handgrips was missing, exposing part of the mechanism which operated the revolving cylinder, and Ben Yahia had bound it with electrical insulating tape. He had only seven rounds of ammunition for the revolver; its calibre was rare in Algeria. That was one reason why he had never practised firing the revolver, the other was he had been uncertain that it might not explode in his hand.

It had been some months since Ben Yahia had ridden a motorcycle, and the Moto Guzzi, like the revolver, had seen better days. Without any form of rear-suspension, and with a defective silencer, it had viciously battered his mind and body on the rough coastal road from the city. He had ridden through three check-points but had been stopped only once, and the bored gendarme, although he had looked closely at Ben Yahia's papers, had fortunately not bothered to open the tool-box beneath the rider's seat where the pistol had been hidden. But Ben Yahia's nerves had been stretched to their limit. Now, on the quayside, he felt like shouting to relieve the tension which had built in his mind, and whenever someone looked towards him, even though they might be only the fishermen or their children playing on the wharf, their eyes seemed to have knowledge of the deed he was about to commit.

A young Algerian, thirteen or fourteen-years-old, watched as Ben Yahia pulled the Moto Guzzi onto its stand. He gave the boy two francs to guard the machine, and promised a further five when he returned. It was extravagant, but worthwhile. Without this precaution Ben Yahia knew that parts of the Guzzi, if not the complete machine, might disappear in his absence. They still might, but there was less chance of such a disaster. The youngster sat himself in the saddle and made a pretence at riding the machine. To limit his enthusiasm, Ben Yahia removed the spark-plug lead before leaving.

He walked through the crowd, the revolver now wrapped in a rag inside a canvas shoulder-bag marked with a red-cross, until he was on the edge of the quay, then he retraced his steps a few yards and jumped down onto the rocky shore on the western side of the wharf.

The brown rocks were coarse and abrasive, but easy to negotiate as long as he avoided those coated with fine weed close to the water's edge. Three hundred yards along the shore a tree-covered headland rose above the surrounding land. It was enclosed by an eight foot wire fence, topped by a single strand of barbed wire. Within were the ruins of the Roman town, standing amongst gnarled olive and orange trees. The wire fence served only to protect the ruins from the attention of children of the nearby port, and was unguarded. When he reached the wire Hassan waded into the sea, waist deep, and swung himself around the metal post which had been sunk into a concrete block beneath the surface of the water.

When he had visited the ruins a couple of days before he had entered from the road on the south. From the sea they were unfamiliar, and it took him a further quarter of an hour to reach the gently sloping area where a pathway led towards the colonaded ruins of the temple. The early evening air was warm and still, and the atmosphere of deserted ruins brought a strange tingling to the hair on the back of his neck. Somehow, even in daylight, it was ghostly rather than romantic for him, and adding to the tension he was experiencing were memories of ancient superstitions. He wished now he had chosen some other place.

Beside the ruins of the temple was an arched doorway, and close to it a stone bench. Nearby, was an open tomb still partly shielded by a stone slab which had been dragged half off the structure by long dead tomb robbers. Ben Yahia intended to hide within the tomb, but now it occurred to him it might have other occupants; it was a trap for scorpions and snakes.

He glanced at his wristwatch. It was five minutes to six o'clock. There was no time left to find another hiding-place! With a shudder he lowered himself into the darkness. The tomb was less than five feet in depth and floored by rubble and shattered masonry. He did not dare move his feet for fear of disturbing anything which might be lurking beneath the crumbling rock.

His hands were shaking so violently he had difficulty unfastening the strap of the shoulder-bag. He unwrapped the Smith and Wesson, and was unable to resist examining its cylinder to check the bullets again. His fingers seemed unable to operate the catch which secured it, but at last the cylinder swung open; the rounds were in place. He closed it with a metallic click that was so magnified within the confines of the tomb he was certain it must have been heard for fifty yards. The weapon seemed to have doubled in weight.

Sweat trickled uncomfortably down his neck.

Albert Limouzin, Vincent's chauffeur and bodyguard, drew the heavy Mercedes off the road and parked it on the grass verge some hundred yards short of a cream-painted villa which overlooked the sand dunes and partly excavated Roman cemetery to the south west of the ruins of the Roman town. He did not know the purpose of Vincent's visit to Tipaza but as they had driven through the fishing port he had experienced an intuitive sense of danger.

Limouzin was thirty-eight-years-old. He had served three five year contracts with the Foreign Legion, the last as a sergeant training recruits in un-armed combat. He was Algerian born, and had joined the Free French forces two years after the liberation of the country in the World War. He had been with them on the victorious march into Paris with General de Gaulle, and had later won a Croix de Guerre on a crossing of the Rhine.

Limouzin turned in his seat and spoke abruptly to Vincent. 'I don't like it, Monsieur.' Albert Limouzin's head was shaven, his scalp tanned a deep brown and mottled by dark freckles.

'What don't you like?' Vincent had told him nothing, other than that he wanted to be driven to the Roman town at Tipaza. Now he resented Limouzin's intrusion into the excitement he was experiencing at the thought of meeting Maryse Rose after so many months.

Albert Limouzin pursed his lips. 'Just a feeling,' he admitted.

Vincent stared past Limouzin's bulky shoulders, along the road ahead of the parked Mercedes. There were no other vehicles nearby, only a farm truck three hundred yards away loaded with empty grape baskets, its driver gesticulating furiously, arguing with an Algerian labourer at the rear of the vehicle. Vincent had expected to see a car or taxi parked somewhere close to the entrance to the Roman ruins, but it was possible Maryse Rose could have walked from the port, less than half a mile away. She might even be a little late for their meeting. Perhaps, though he hoped not, she could have changed her mind. He had already considered the arguments he would use to convince her she should return to Beau Lac with him.

Limouzin climbed heavily from the vehicle and opened the passenger door at Vincent's side. The chauffeur was frowning. 'Do we wait here?'

Vincent said: 'No, Albert. You wait here. I'm meeting someone, alone. I'll be no more than half an hour.'

'You're unarmed, m'sieur.' There was concern in Limouzin's voice.

'This time it doesn't matter; it's my youngest sister.' Vincent began walking towards the entrance.

Albert Limouzin watched Vincent until the thick groves of olive trees hid him from sight, then he reached into the car and drew an automatic pistol from the glove-compartment. He pulled back the breech-block and slid a round into the breech before pushing the weapon into his waist-band beneath his jacket. He hooked his thumbs into his belt, leant back against the side of the Mercedes, and waited. Although his body appeared relaxed, his eyes showed intense concentration.

*

The wild olive trees which lined the path and clothed the ancient ruins, creating sunlit glades within which stood ornate columns, half-ruined tombs, theatres, and the foundation of villas, had seemed magical to Maryse and Vincent as children. The gnarled roots which sprawled over hewn stones like serpents, the twisted trunks and interwoven branches laden in autumn with miniature blue olives, had given the trees fairy personalities. To walk through the grove and the jumbled buildings with their carvings and inscriptions, to the open sunlight surrounding the ruined temple on the soft, final slope towards the clear green sea, had made their visits an adventure they had always enjoyed. Sometimes, the place had been deserted, so that they had felt it was their own, and had run and shouted and laughed and played, gloriously uninhibited. They had loved this ancient place.

As he walked the path, Vincent remembered the past. Sometime soon, the country would be peaceful again. The present uprising would be ended, and the times they had once experienced might return. Childhood seemed so far away, now.

He knew exactly where he would meet Maryse Rose. Beside the ruins of the temple was an arch, once part of a doorway. Within it they had always placed their clothing, their picnic hampers; there they had sat in the shade when the sun had been at its midsummer hottest.

He quickened his pace a little, in anticipation. Beau Lac had seemed empty since she had left.

The light cotton shirt which Ben Yahia was wearing was clinging to his body. Sweat, like salt tears, ran from his forehead into his eyes, blurring his vision. His body prickled uncomfortably as though he was standing in a nest of red ants. The tomb had trapped the day's heat like a brick oven, and its air was heavy and oxygenless; suffocating.

The barrel of the cumbersome Smith and Wesson revolver rested between two pieces of stonework less than six inches from his face. The tape which he had bound around its butt had softened in the heat so that it stuck to his hand.

The overlapping slab of broken stone which lay on the top of the tomb concealed him, but gave him an unobstructed view of the arched gateway less than ten feet away. His field of vision was narrow; he would not be able to see Charpentier until the man walked past the tomb. Nor would he hear footsteps on the soft sand of the path. If he missed with his first shot, there might be no chance of a second; there was plenty of nearby cover behind which Charpentier might throw himself. And Ben Yahia had also noted his own vulnerability; in the event of Charpentier returning his fire the tomb was likely to become his own. There was no way for him to escape other than into the open ground above where Charpentier would be able to kill him easily.

Ben Yahia's stomach heaved. He put his hand quickly to his mouth and swallowed hard, tasting raw bile. He wiped the sweat out of his eyes with the back of his hand, and then blinked to clear his vision.

A shadow appeared to grow upwards from the base of the stonework of the arch ahead of him and Ben Yahia almost fainted with shock. The shadow appeared distorted, monstrous, a jinni leaping from the ground. Ben Yahia's heartbeat thudded in his ears.

The glade had not changed in the few years since Vincent had last visited it. The olive trees were so ancient themselves that time now meant nothing to them; they had been mature a century ago.

At the entrance to the glade, Vincent paused. He could not see Maryse Rose, but beyond the ruined temple the ground sloped away and it was possible she was standing at the water's edge or within the arch itself which was open only on the side which faced the sea. He had his left hand in his pocket, holding her wedding ring.

For the past months of Maryse Rose's absence, a truth which he admitted he should have realized years before, had been troubling him deeply. He was in love with her, and knew that he had always been; from the day he had discovered her beneath the desert rocks. But the sense of kinship which had masked his feelings for so long had dissolved, leaving him to face the revealed emotion. And now he was afraid he would be unable to conceal it from her; they knew each other's moods so well. Nor could he see how it would be possible to untangle the web which must continue to separate them. He could not hurt Madelene, or risk damaging the lives of their children. But Madelene must already suspect his unintentional coolness; their lovemaking had become mechanical and infrequent. He used the organization as an excuse to return late to their bed, knowing that when he touched her body his mind would focus not on her but on another woman.

In a few moments he would be with Maryse Rose again, and wondered if it was even possible for him to face a lifetime without her.

He walked hesitantly towards the archway.

The shadow of the jinni became a man, tall, slender, elegant in immaculately pressed cream trousers and white sports shirt. He was less than eight feet away from Ben Yahia, his back towards him. His hair was short, lighter in colour than that of most settlers. Ben Yahia could see fair hairs on the man's tanned forearms. Was it Charpentier?

Ben Yahia's view from below ground level distorted the man's body so that he seemed extremely tall with unusually long legs. Ben Yahia aimed the revolver at the man's torso, and attempted to squeeze the trigger. The spring of the Smith and Wesson's action was so strong it was impossible; his damp fingers slipped on the metal of the trigger. He took hold of the weapon with both hands.

The man turned to face him. Ben Yahia pushed himself back into the shadow of the tomb, straightening his arms and squeezed the trigger of the revolver with all his strength as he did so. It was Vincent Charpentier. Ben Yahia recognized the pale blue eyes, the slightly angular face.

The explosion of the revolver in the confines of the tomb deafened Ben Yahia. The revolver bucked violently upwards in his hands.

He had expected the bullet to make a neat clean hole; probably the wound would be bloodless. Instead, Vincent Charpentier's head disintegrated in a mess of shattered bone and torn flesh. For a moment the headless torso remained standing, blood spurting across the brown sun-weathered stone of the arch in obscene patterns, and then it crumpled to the stained earth.

Hassan Ben Yahia screamed in horror.

Albert Limouzin heard the shot and the scream which followed. He swore loudly, drew his automatic and began running in the direction of the sounds. After fifty yards he slowed to a cautious walk. There was no doubt in his mind that his employer was dead; if it had been necessary, any terrorist worth his salt would have used a second shot. There was a chance that they might have saved ammunition by finishing the job by cutting Vincent Charpentier's throat rather than by shooting him, and that might account for the scream, but it was very unlikely

that an unarmed man would have survived. Albert
Limouzin had lived through too many battles to have
illusions. He was concerned now with balancing his reputation as a bodyguard against his own survival.

He moved cautiously along the narrow path, his dark
eyes searching the small olive groves he knew could give
cover to an entire section of FLN terrorists. It took him
ten minutes to reach the glade where the temple stood.
He could see Vincent's body, the white shirt stained
crimson with blood. Limouzin knelt behind a broken
column until he was certain the area was deserted.

He did not examine the body immediately, but searched
the surrounding buildings to ensure there was no-one
concealed by the sloping beach. Then he returned. Vincent lay on his stomach in an untidy heap, his legs curled
beneath him in a foetal position. Albert Limouzin did not
need to touch him. Most of Vincent's head was missing.
Pieces of bone, brain-pulp and scalp splattered the ground
behind him.

Albert Limouzin muttered: 'Jesus Christ!'

Knowing that the body must be left unattended while
he reported the crime, he searched it and removed the
wallet containing Vincent's identity papers and cash. Vincent's left hand was clenched inside his trouser pocket.
Limouzin eased it out and prized the fingers open. They
contained the wedding ring which Limouzin examined
closely. He then found the note.

Before he drove to the gendarmerie at Tipaza, he parked
the Mercedes outside a bar and made three telephone
calls. The first was to Andre Chatelain, Vincent's second-
in-command, informing him of what had taken place,
and suggesting that a 'ratonnade' would be appropriate
that evening. The second was to the editor of the Echo
newspaper, and the third was to Radio Algiers.

*

Vincent Charpentier's murder was announced on Radio Algiers in a news bulletin at ten pm that night and the 'rat-hunt' organized by Chatelain began in the Bab el Oued district of Algiers shortly afterwards. Gangs of young pieds-noir motorcyclists swept out of the always volatile area into the streets of the neighbouring Algerian township, attacking anyone they could find. Riding furiously up the narrow alleys and passages, their pillion-passengers armed with machetes, knives and razors, they hacked and slashed the terrified Arabs indiscriminately.

They were followed within minutes by an angry mob of settlers on foot, determined to avenge the murder of one of their leaders. Charpentier was a name every settler had known since childhood, and recently, Vincent Charpentier had become one of their heroes. The rioters tore open the Algerian shops, looted the contents, and ignited the buildings. They set fire to cars parked in the streets, tore cobble-stones from the roadway, and hurled them into the houses. More methodical than the motorcyclists, they hunted fleeing Algerians like packs of wolves and those they caught they beat or stamped unconscious and then hanged from telegraph poles or any convenient tree or street sign.

At the far side of the city at Maison Blanche, a complete Arab tenement block was burnt to the ground with several Algerians trapped inside. Settlers in trucks drove through the bidonvilles tossing home-made petrol bombs amongst the pitiful shacks built of cardboard boxes, corrugated iron sheets and flattened oil drums. At Agha, two Algerians caught by a group of pieds-noir youths were tied to the doors of the railway station and stoned to death.

There were few official attempts to control the riots. The gendarmerie barricaded the main thoroughfares with their vehicles to keep the rioters from the central areas of the city, but kept away from the dangerous mobs rampaging in the Algerian quarters.

The 'ratonnade' continued until almost dawn, when exhaustion drove the pieds-noir back to their own districts. A pall of smoke drifted above the eastern and western suburbs of the city like an autumn sea mist.

TEN

A thousand yards ahead of the *Tassili*'s bow a troopship from Marseilles began the delicate manoeuvre which would take her stern-first alongside the quay in Algiers harbour. As she did so the mate of the *Tassili* gave an order to the bosun who rang the bridge telegraph and signalled 'engines slow' to the engineers below decks. The throb of the engines died away as the ship sliced through the water, carried forward only by her own momentum, her wake diminishing.

The Algerian passengers, travelling either third-class on the open decks of the vessel or second-class in the lower saloons, crowded towards the rails of the ship. They were almost home. Some had been watching since dawn an hour before, to catch the first sight of the distant mountains as the sun rose above the eastern horizon. It was five-fifteen am.

The ship's tannoy system crackled, then gave a shrill whine which was followed by the voice of the *Tassili*'s captain. He spoke first in French, and then repeated his brief speech in a nasal Arabic.

'A radio message from the port authorities in Algiers has stated that following the murder, yesterday evening, of a leader of a French political organization, there have been a number of serious disturbances during the night in the suburbs of Algiers. Passengers disembarking at Algiers are advised to travel through the city in groups, and to keep to the main boulevards in which there are military and police patrols.'

There was a murmur of startled conversation from the Algerian passengers, lost as the bridge telegraph rang again and the vessel's screws churned the green water once more. Near Habib Saadi someone turned on a portable radio and searched through the stations with the instrument on full volume. There was no news bulletin, only a weather forecast on one station, and early morning chat and music on the others.

The war was in its fifth year and there were few passengers who had not at some time experienced riots as either participants, or victims. They had no doubt now of their role in present disturbances; the murder of a leader of a pieds-noir organization would mean that the settlers would be seeking revenge. The mist the passengers had seen above the suburbs was the smoke of dying fires, and the excitement that many of them had been experiencing at the thought of meeting their families and friends once again now became apprehension and concern for their safety.

Habib Saadi was more curious than distressed by the news. He ignored the questioning conversations of his fellow passengers as the ship docked, and followed the crowd through the immigration halls. There were more soldiers than usual posted at the dock entrances, and he could see military patrols at all of the main intersections of the roads. Apart from the soldiers and the gendarmes, there were no signs of rioting near the port. It was too early yet for the streets to be crowded by people on their way to work in the shops and offices, and there was little traffic on the roads other than the normal trucks on their way to and from the markets.

He bought a newspaper at a kiosk on the corner of the opera house square, and then stopped abruptly as the headlines caught his eye. 'Vincent Charpentier murdered!'

There were two photographs with the text. One, of Vincent Charpentier taken on the deck of a yacht at an early season regatta, the other of Maryse Rose . . . standing beside a French officer. She was in her wedding gown. Habib barely recognized her. She was clasping a bouquet of flowers, and holding the officer's arm. Her hair was swept back, softly bouffant, crowned by a white lace headdress. He had seldom seen her looking so happy.

But according to the caption beneath her photograph and an individual headline above it, she was implicated in the murder and wanted by the Sûreté for questioning. Her wedding ring, arrowed in the photograph, and a note from her suggesting the rendezvous, the newspaper explained, had been found clasped in the dead man's hand.

Habib ran.

He was stopped at the casbah barrier by a soldier who looked at him in disgust and said scornfully: 'You're safe now, melon. You can walk home from here.'

Habib ignored the insult. The streets of the casbah were already filling; labourers from the old city began their day's work far earlier than the office workers of the suburbs. Habib pushed through them where the streets narrowed.

The door of the old building was still locked when he reached it. He hammered on it until he could hear the bolts being drawn within and the clang of metal as one of the iron bars was placed beside the door. It was the woman house-keeper, Fadela.

'Where's Ben Yahia?'

Her eyes widened as she saw the perspiration on Saadi's face, and his sweat-stained clothes. 'Still in his bed. It's early yet.'

Habib stood in front of the door to Ben Yahia's room and put down his suitcase. He took a small step backwards and then kicked the door as hard as he could. It burst off its hinges with an explosion of shattering wood; dry splinters of worm-ridden timber showered the room. Habib strode to the bed as Ben Yahia sat up quickly, his face taut and terrified. Habib grabbed him by the hair with one hand and dragged him from the bed onto the floor. Ben Yahia squealed in pain as Habib hauled him to his knees.

'What do you know about this?' Habib held the newspaper in front of Ben Yahia's face and let go of his hair.

There was a startled voice from the doorway. 'What's happening?' Habib glanced over his shoulder. Two of the cell's members, Ahmed Lacgheraf and Mohamed Noureddine stared at him. They were the youngest members, barely twenty.

'Fetch Hadj M'Ouzeganc,' Habib ordered, angrily. Neither of the men moved. 'Do as I say,' shouted Habib. 'Fetch him at once.' As both men turned, he added: 'Not you Noureddine. You wait here.' He turned back to Ben Yahia. 'Well?'

Habib's anger suggested a lie would be safer than the truth. 'I don't know anything.' Ben Yahia shrugged vaguely, and then rubbed the top of his head where Habib had held his hair.

Habib kicked him in the face, knocking him violently backwards so that he crashed against the edge of the table. He lay stunned for a moment, blood pouring from his broken nose and split lips. Habib gave him no time to recover, and with surprising strength lifted him bodily and hurled him across the room back on to the bed. One of its legs collapsed so that Ben Yahia was wedged between the thin mattress and the wall, facing Habib.

Ben Yahia's face seemed to be on fire, and his mouth was full of blood. He had not anticipated Habib's return so soon after Vincent Charpentier's death, and had thought that even a few hours would have been enough time for the FLN leaders to have recognized the courage of his action and rewarded his initiative. Habib Saadi's return then, would have been of no consequence to him. He had been relieved to hear Habib's order to Lacgheraf to fetch Hadj M'Ouzegane and knew the Mullah would soon put Saadi in his place. He struggled into a sitting position and began wiping his face with the corner of a blanket.

Habib tore it out of his hands. 'Did you kill him?'

Ben Yahia was recovering from his initial fright and the pain of Habib's assault was easing. His confidence was returning. 'There was an opportunity, so I took it.'

'On whose orders?' demanded Habib, his face still pale with fury.

'No-one ordered me.' Ben Yahia hauled himself painfully to his feet. Hadj M'Ouzegane would arrive soon and he did not want the Mullah to see him with his face covered in blood. He stumbled towards a shelf where there was a wash-basin and a jug of water. 'I do not need to be ordered to kill the enemy.'

'So you stole Melila Bachir's wedding ring and used her to trap Charpentier?'

Ben Yahia sounded scornful. 'Melila Bachir? Maryse Rose Charpentier. Why not? Is it suddenly an illegitimate act of our war not to use subterfuge? You are a fool, Saadi.' As he began to put water into the bowl, Habib swung him round by his shoulder and hit him again with all his strength. The bowl and basin shattered as Ben Yahia fell.

He was barely conscious. Habib pulled him into a wooden chair which stood against the wall, jerked his own belt from his trousers and fastened it around Ben Yahia's upper arms and the back of the wooden chair. He struggled weakly as Habib tore strips from the blanket

261

and pinioned his arms behind his back and his ankles to the chair leg.

Habib stood back when he had finished, and looked quickly at Noureddine who had been watching from the doorway. The youth had decided there was no point in interfering. He had known nothing of Ben Yahia's action. 'Were you involved?' Habib asked him.

Noureddine shook his head vigorously. 'No.' Why had Ben Yahia called Melila 'Maryse Rose Charpentier' Noureddine wondered. For his own safety he decided to disassociate himself as much as possible from Ben Yahia, as it was still unclear what the outcome of Habib Saadi's fury would be. 'I was with Ahmed and Melila, last night. We remained indoors . . . the rioting was bad. We could hear explosions.'

'Does she know about Charpentier's death?' Habib asked.

Mohamed Noureddine shook his head; again. 'No, Habib. We didn't listen to a radio last night. We talked, then we went to our rooms.' He paused. 'She still sleeps.'

Ben Yahia sat silently now, his eyes fixed on Habib Saadi. The sooner the Mullah arrived the better. Then Ben Yahia would have Saadi and his woman thrown out into the street.

'Where is the pistol you used?' Habib demanded.

Ben Yahia ignored him.

'It might be sensible to answer him, Ben Yahia,' Mullah Hadj M'Ouzegane stood in the doorway. Ahmed Lacgheraf peering past his shoulder. The Mullah was a small man, lightly-built. Nearly seventy-years-old, his eyes were deeply set, and the skin of his face furrowed and lined.

Ben Yahia said: 'Thank God! This man is insane. Order him to release me.'

'Of what is he accusing you?' asked the Mullah quietly, ignoring Ben Yahia's request. He moved forward into the room, and automatically gathered his robes a little closer to his body.

'Executing Vincent Charpentier,' replied Ben Yahia.

'And did you?'

'Yes, of course,' said Ben Yahia, lifting his face a little as an indication of his confidence. Now Saadi would see how others considered the importance of his action. In a few minutes their roles would be reversed, and it would be Saadi who was forced to eat dirt.

'Without any authority?' demanded the Mullah.

'There was no time to seek approval. The opportunity arose, so I took it.'

'There was no time?' The Mullah sounded surprised. 'And yet you see me every day? Surely it was necessary for you to plan the execution carefully and at length?'

Hassan Ben Yahia hesitated before replying. 'I . . . I thought that the fewer people who were aware of my plan the less likely that it would be frustrated. Charpentier was an important target.'

'So you thought I might prevent you, and therefore you made all the decisions yourself?'

'I didn't exactly think you'd stop me,' said Ben Yahia, a little of his confidence fading. The arrival of the Mullah was not yet proving as helpful as he had hoped. At least, not yet. 'I thought there might be some deliberation that would waste time. Opportunities like this pass very quickly, and should not be ignored.'

'So how did you get the wedding ring from the Charpentier woman?'

'She's here in the house,' said Ben Yahia with satisfaction. 'Saadi calls her Melila Bachir, but I knew she was a Charpentier. I took the ring from her room.' He tried to smile, but the pain of his split lips made it impossible.

263

'And you typed a note in her name and sent it with the ring to Monsieur Vincent Charpentier?'

'Yes.'

'Which accounts for the fact that it is she they are looking for today, and not yourself.' The Mullah looked at Habib. 'The newspapers are full of it, and there was a lengthy news report two hours ago on Radio Algiers.' He turned back to Ben Yahia. 'According to the radio, Hassan Ben Yahia, forty-seven Algerians were killed in the riots of last night. There were disturbances in Oran and Philippeville as well as here. Forty-seven Algerians, Hassan Ben Yahia, in exchange for the death of one Frenchman! Now answer Habib Saadi's question. Where is the pistol I issued to this group?'

Ben Yahia stared at the floor near the Mullah's feet. The Mullah seemed unexpectedly to be siding with Saadi. 'It was necessary to dispose of it.'

'How?'

'I threw it into the sea,' admitted Ben Yahia, uncomfortably. He wished now that he had risked carrying it back. The pistol had been the Mullah's former property.

The Mullah shook his head, sadly. 'Pistols are hard to obtain, Ben Yahia. Men risk their lives to get them for us. In the *djebel*, sometimes there is only one weapon between four men.' He looked at Habib. 'This woman, Melila Bachir, she is the nurse?' Habib nodded his reply. 'She is the Charpentier daughter who is of Algerian origin?' This time the Mullah answered his own question. 'I have read of her. I was unaware she had joined us, but it is good. It shows there is strength in our blood. What is she to you, Saadi?'

Habib hesitated. 'We met in Paris, where she was studying nursing. We were friends . . . good friends.' He did not want to explain fully to the Mullah. 'I like her.' He paused. 'No, I must be truthful, Hadj, my feelings are very strong for her.'

264

'Strong enough for them to colour your judgement on a matter of FLN business?'

'Of course not.'

'I believe you,' said the Mullah. He faced Ben Yahia again. 'You have convicted yourself of two crimes . . . that of taking action without the authority of senior officers of the Front de Liberation Nationale, which has resulted in the deaths of forty-seven of your people, some of whom were fellow members of the FLN. Secondly, you chose to throw away a weapon which had been entrusted to you on behalf of your complete cell; a weapon which might have been used to far better purpose in different circumstances. Presumably you also threw away what ammunition you did not use.'

'It was necessary,' said Ben Yahia, his voice rising. 'What was done was done for our cause. And Arabs are always being killed by those damned pieds-noir.'

'Not when we can prevent it,' corrected the Mullah. 'We do not tolerate people acting on their own behalf. You cannot possibly know what other damage your action may have caused. The settlers may have completed their reprisals, but the French authorities have not yet even begun. It has been necessary this morning, to make arrangements to close down one of our most important arms factories as a result of the likelihood of searches by the military. And many other things have been put at risk. We did not want the hornets' nest stirred into activity at this moment, as Habib Saadi is aware. It does not suit us, and it has endangered our complete programme.' He lowered his voice slightly, and stared hard at Hassan Ben Yahia. 'With the authority of the Front de Liberation Nationale, you are sentenced to death.'

Ben Yahia's eyes widened in disbelief. 'I am an honourable man, Hadj. I would do nothing to harm the cause. I

265

demand a proper trial where I can put my case before the people.'

'It has been put,' said the Mullah. He turned to Habib again. 'The matter is now in your hands. It is possible that the Bachir woman may care to exercise her family right to justice, and I have no objections. Will you be remaining in the city?'

Habib said: 'No. We leave in a week.'

'That is good. May Allah watch over you in the mountains.' He turned to leave.

'Hadj . . .' Ben Yahia's voice was desperate, his eyes pleading.

The Mullah ignored him, but spoke to Ahmed Lacgheraf. 'In future *you* will report to me. Come this evening after prayer.'

When the Mullah had left Ben Yahia was silent for a moment, and then said: 'Of course, he's quite wrong. I'm entitled to a military trial. You'll arrange it Habib.' He deliberately used Habib's first name. 'I'm useful to them. I can use a radio. I can fight in the *bled*. I'll be glad to leave Algiers with you, the war is stale, here.'

Ahmed Lacgheraf caught Habib's eyes. 'What shall we do with him. Shall we fetch Melila?'

'No. She's Christian.' Habib knew it was wrong to involve her in an FLN decision of this nature. 'We settle it now, ourselves.'

Ben Yahia began speaking again, but now in a whining voice. Had he been able to move from the chair he would have been on his knees begging them. 'My mother . . . remember my mother. I send her money. It's all she has. I was working for the cause . . . for the same God, Habib . . . Ahmed . . . I've always worked well.'

Habib looked at Mohamed Noureddine. 'Stand outside the door.' The youth looked as if he were about to be

266

sick. 'If Melila or Fadela come, keep them away. Ahmed, twist the hem of the blanket into a rope.'

Ben Yahia's eyes followed Ahmed Lacgheraf as he tore the hem from the blanket, put one end beneath a foot and began rolling the other between his hands. At last he took the two ends. The strip of blanket twisted like a live snake into a double-stranded rope two feet in length. Ahmed did not know what Habib intended to do with it, but handed it to him. It seemed likely that Habib was going to use it to secure Ben Yahia more tightly. Instead, he looped it around Ben Yahia's neck and knotted it over his spine.

In terror, Ben Yahia realized Habib Saadi's intention. 'Habib . . . please . . .'

Habib said: 'Shut your mouth, you beg like a child.' Ahmed watched him, his mouth wide open, as Habib selected a sliver of wood from the debris of the shattered door and pushed it between the rope and the back of Ben Yahia's neck. Ben Yahia began struggling, but Habib wound the sliver of wood until the rope tightened around Ben Yahia's throat. Ben Yahia tried to scream but the breath was trapped in his lungs. His face deepened in colour and his tongue began to protrude; his eyes bulged. He struggled wildly but Habib's belt around his shoulders and chest held him to the chair. Urine stained the front of his trousers and began to drip onto the floor beneath him. His body writhed with one final convulsion, and then relaxed. Habib held the cord twisted around his neck for another full minute before releasing it. Hassan Ben Yahia was dead.

Ahmed watched in horror. He had never seen a man strangled to death before. He had heard of the method used at FLN executions but had never expected to witness one. A year previously he had slashed the arm of a French motorist who had been foolish enough to drive through the Algerian quarter with his window open, but that had given him only satisfaction when blood had spurted to discolour the interior of the car's windscreen. This had seemed far more brutal and cold-blooded, even though he did not doubt the justice of the Mullah's decision. The Mullah was a holyman, he had experience which Ahmed would never have thought to question. He spoke in a whisper. 'What will we do with him now?'

Habib felt suddenly exhausted. The entire business since he had first arrived at the house had taken less than half an hour, but seemed to have lasted a week. He wanted to wash, then sleep. He looked at the body. He could smell excreta. 'Put it on the bed and cover it. Then repair the door. Tonight, late, put the corpse out in one of the streets, a long way from here.' He removed his belt from around Ben Yahia's body and fed it back into the loops at his waistband. Mohamed Noureddine had put his head around the side of the door and was staring at the dead man, with a terrified expression on his face. 'Better still,' added Habib. 'Push the bastard into one of the sewers.'

He did not know how Maryse Rose would react to the news of Vincent Charpentier's death, and he could think of no way he could protect her. Death was such an individual thing, easy to accept for some but psychologically devastating to others. Was it religion, environment or ancestry which determined reaction, he wondered briefly. Maryse Rose was Arab by blood, but Christian, not Muslim. As a Muslim, he knew she would have expressed her grief but cushioned it by the knowledge that it was Allah's will and therefore not only unquestionable but inevitable. The grief, which was a form of self-indulgence, could then be quickly overcome. And death was commonplace in an Arab's life, and sometimes preferable to the existence in which they found themselves. The Koran taught them that death brought reward far in excess of worldly comfort and wealth to the right and godly. Habib was not religious, himself, and he had decided long ago that he would put his trust in socialism when the time came. But he regretted now that he knew little of the Christian teachings regarding death, only that there was supposed to be a place for Christians just as Mohammed the Prophet had decreed for Muslims.

He was glad that Maryse Rose's room was at the back of the old house. With its thick walls it was unlikely that she would have been disturbed. He knocked softly at her door.

She opened it a few moments later still wrapping a gown around her shoulders. Pale after her sleep, she seemed no more than a child to him.

'Habib!' She threw her arms around his shoulders and drew him towards her. He could feel her soft breasts through the material of the gown, pressing against his chest. He held her, and could smell the warm, feminine scent in her hair. He let her hold him, kissing her neck before leading her back into her room. He pushed the door closed behind them.

She was excited, and repeated his name several times. 'Habib, Habib, Habib . . . did everything go well?' She asked. 'Did you like Barcelona? Were you seasick?' She was teasing him, pleased by his return. 'I've been hoping you'd be back this week. It's been a long time, almost three weeks.' She had a small camping stove in her room, fed by a cylinder of gas. She struck a match, lit the stove, and put a pan of water on the purple flame. 'Did they give you breakfast on the ship? Would you like rolls? They're a little stale; yesterday's. I'll make tea. Sit on the bed, it's more comfortable . . . there were riots last night. Was it safe on the streets this morning?' She found her watch on the stool beside her bed. 'Good heavens, it's so late, I'm ashamed. I should be dressed . . .'

He interrupted her. It was wrong to allow her excitement to continue. It would be harder for both of them the longer he left it. 'Melila . . .' She looked at him curiously. He seldom used that name when they were alone although he would always use it in public. 'Vincent Charpentier was killed last night.' She looked at him, disbelievingly. 'That was what the riots were about. They announced it on the radio . . . someone wanted maximum impact.' He read the questions in her eyes. 'No, it wasn't the FLN. It was a stupid act by a senseless individual. It'll serve no-one any good.'

There seemed to be no blood behind the delicate skin of her face, and her eyes were suddenly moist. Habib wished there was some way he could comfort her.

'I must telephone my parents. I must go to them . . .' She stood as though to begin dressing, then turned off the gas-stove. Her actions were automatic rather than controlled.

'You can't,' said Habib, softly. 'It's impossible.'

There were tears on her cheeks. 'You'll prevent me?'

Habib shook his head. He had never seen her look so beautiful, but the shock of the news had already turned her eyes into deep wells into which he could no longer penetrate. 'I wouldn't stop you, but you can't contact them.' He tried to find the words to explain to her, but eventually held the crumpled newspaper towards her. 'You'd better read this.'

He watched emotions change her face as she read the page. When she spoke again it was with a tremor in her voice, and so softly he could hardly hear her. 'But who?'

'Ben Yahia.'

She whispered: 'Dear God!' She let the newspaper fall to the ground. 'But I must still go to them . . .'

Habib made his voice firmer. 'No. Don't you see what will happen? All the evidence the police have points to your involvement. Perhaps they'll believe you if you say you didn't kill him, but you will never convince them you are completely innocent. You're not one of them, remember? You know how their system operates. And it isn't like Paris, this time. This isn't France. Your friend Colonel Lefitte will be the beginning, and then he'll hand you over to the Operational Detachment. They don't care who you are. They'll torture you until you talk.'

'But I know nothing of use to them.'

'You would tell them about me, here in the casbah. And about Ahmed and Mohamed . . . and Ben Yahia, and this house. And everything you say they will see as yet more proof that as a member of the FLN you helped kill your brother. They will even make you invent things which are not true, and when you are brought for trial you will have signed a full confession.'

'You know I wouldn't tell them anything.'

He knew that the thought of the atrocities of which both sides were guilty horrified her, but it was important now she understood the dangers she would face if she visited her family or surrendered herself to the authorities. 'I know you would try to be silent. But do you remember Fatima Hussaini?' He paused. 'When you were raped it was very bad for you, but the soldiers were only playing with you. Torture for information is quite different. They hung Fatima Hussaini by her wrists, naked, with her legs either side of a trestle. Then they kicked her backwards and forwards until the sharp edges of the wood wore through her flesh to the bone. When they were tired of that, they pumped her full of water and jumped on her stomach.' Maryse Rose was staring at him with the same look of horror and near disbelief that he had seen on Ben

Yahia's face when the Mullah had pronounced his death sentence. The muscles in his throat tightened, but he knew he must continue if he were to save her. 'In the end after many hours, they killed her. They thought she had been carrying messages for us, but in fact, she was guilty of nothing. It won't be any different for you. You can never return to them, now. Promise me you won't try.'

She was swaying on her feet as though she were about to faint. He took her hands and drew her down onto the bed beside him.

'If I had been here it wouldn't have happened; I could have prevented it. I know how much Vincent meant to you.' She was avoiding meeting his eyes, but he held her face gently and turned it towards him. 'You're very important to me . . . far more important than I can ever make you understand. France was only the beginning for us. Allah's kismet is often hard for us to comprehend, but it is always part of his schemes for us.' She was not crying, and her face now seemed expressionless. 'Would you like me to stay with you?'

She said: 'No,' and then watched him leave.

When the door closed behind Habib, she stood and walked to the one window in the walls of the room. It was only a foot in width, protected by a vertical iron bar set into the sill and the lintel. It was high enough in the building for her to see beyond the wall of the courtyard into the street. Two hundred yards up the hill, a woman was pushing a loaded handcart towards the market; a man, probably the woman's husband, rode side-saddle on a donkey a few yards ahead of her. In front of one of the arched doorways to another courtyard a group of old women squatted beside baskets of rice, shouting conversations to their neighbours in shrill, crackled voices.

272

Algerian students in European dress mingled with Arabs recently arrived from the desert or the hills.

It was impossible for her to imagine a world, even this one, in which Vincent no longer existed, somewhere. The previous evening, as the streets had begun to quieten, she had been strangely drawn to the roof of the building. For a long time she had stared towards the west as if something, or someone, demanded that she should search her memory one final time. Distantly, she had been able to recognize the low coastline behind which lay the fertile vineyards and orange groves of Hadjout. She had remembered Beau Lac, not surrounded by its barbed-wire defences, but as it had once been, with the grove of soft palms, flowers and fragrant shrubs and the family together on its lawns. The memories had been strong enough for her to recall the scent of the gardens on summer evenings, and for her ears to hear the laughter. She knew now that it had been Vincent reaching out to her.

The tears which had filled her eyes a little while before would no longer flow. The emptiness which she was experiencing permitted no relieving flood of grief, and as she stepped away from the window she could see her own reflection in a small mirror which she had hung on the cracked plaster of the wall. She did not recognize the woman who faced her; sallow-skinned, the eyes suddenly dull and aged, the face no more than a hollow mask behind which there was nothing but a void.

During that day, alone in the room, she prayed for grief and for the sorrow she knew she should feel. But it was not until the sky faded from evening gold towards the purple of dusk that the real sadness began to grow within her, swelling until it filled her, bursting from her body as uncontrollably as the storm-driven waves of a winter ocean. In her mind she cradled Vincent as he died, as he slipped away from her forever into the unimaginable darkness of time.

Habib heard her weeping, each sound an individual wound which seemed to cut deep into his chest. Unknown to her, during that night he shared her sorrow as much as if Vincent Charpentier had been his own brother.

The funeral of Vincent Charpentier would have been impossible for Maryse Rose to ignore even had she wished to do so. With the encouragement of the leaders of the various settlers' organizations he had become a martyr, and she a symbol of Algerian treachery. As Habib had warned her the pieds-noir had already decided her guilt, and the right-wing newspapers and the radio pandered to their audiences with features that vilified her as a murderess whilst praising Vincent as a national hero. Less than twenty-four hours after Vincent's death a hundred thousand francs was being offered by the leading businessmen of Algiers, men whom she had known all her life as friends of her family, as a reward for her capture. Such a large amount of money was a fortune to most Algerians, and despite her changed identity, Habib was aware that it must only be a matter of time before she would be betrayed if she remained in the city. But she would not yet leave with him, and ignored his pleas.

To Habib it seemed as though Maryse Rose was punishing herself for Vincent's death. She had insisted on reading all the exaggerated reports, studying the countless photographs of the Charpentier family and herself which had been ferreted from the newspaper libraries; incidents of her past social life in the company of Vincent and her adoptive parents, reached back to her childhood. To Habib's amazement, she listened, pale but seemingly unmoved to a lengthy interview with Belle on Radio Algiers. Belle's hatred was vicious and unjust.

Maryse Rose would have been unable to explain her own feelings to anyone; the hatred had inexplicably become an anaesthetic which temporarily deadened and overwhelmed her grief. She could no longer associate herself with the woman described in the newspaper articles, or in the radio interviews. This Maryse Rose was someone she did not know, had not known could even exist. And the hatred was as unreal for her as the woman they depicted.

Regardless of what kind of funeral Christian and Colette Charpentier would have chosen for their beloved son, the settler community saw it as yet another opportunity to manifest their solidarity and signify their continuing claims for a French Algeria. From dawn, crowds of pieds-noir began to line the rue Valée up which the funeral cortege would drive towards the European cemetery overlooking the wide sweep of the bay. Within the cemetery itself, they thronged the path which led from the gates to the ornate tomb of the Charpentier family; a tomb built of imported rose marble, mined in the quarries of Cararra in Italy. Twelve feet square, and almost as many in height, the rose tomb with its ornate carvings and recessed panels had been intended by the founder of the Charpentier Company to house generations of the family's dead, in deliberate affluence.

Maryse Rose had risen early, and left the old house in the casbah. She knew that Habib, had he known, would have attempted to stop her. She walked through the narrow lanes to the southern gateway at the boulevard Victoire. Today the guards at the barriers had been increased in number, as the volatile emotions of the pieds-noir at neighbouring Bab el Oued smouldered close to flash-point. It would be considered a miracle by the military government, if the day ended without further rioting.

The only comments made to Maryse Rose by the

soldiers at the barriers were a warning for her safety. Algerians were recommended to stay within their own quarter, and to remain indoors. No Algerian shops would open beyond the walls of the ancient city. She was risking her life to venture amongst the impassioned settler community.

She ignored the soldiers' advice, and continued along the avenue Mal de Bourmont until she was able to enter the cemetery from the south, close to the barracks of the Garde Mobile. She knew the location of the Charpentier tomb, as it had been a place of annual family pilgrimage on the Day of the Dead. Then, like Belle and Colette Charpentier, she had carried bunches of chrysanthemums, so that even as a child she was unable to see the bright flowers on market stalls without them bringing an instant picture to her mind of the long rows of graves and mausoleums that bordered the paths of the cemetery, and the impressive rose tomb which dwarfed its neighbours.

She had avoided the mass of settlers by the route she had chosen, but as she neared the tomb she could hear their voices like the rumble of a distant storm. Moving through the graveyard to the slightly higher ground she was at last able to view the tomb, and the crowds which surrounded it. They were unlike any other mourners she had ever seen; it was obvious that for most of them it was a political gathering. Many carried banners, displaying the insignias of the illegal organizations, the Celtic crosses, the double cross of Lorraine within a diamond. Most wore armbands above which they had sewn black bands of ribbon as if Vincent Charpentier had been a member of their own families. Below, a hundred yards beyond the tomb where two of the paths crossed and the ground was more open, a band was playing, alternating between solemn funeral music and military marches.

It was noon before the crowd which now stretched as far as she could see towards the boulevard de Verdun and the rue Valée, stirred and seemed to compress itself, heaving like the coil of some vast snake on the narrow highway. The service for Vincent Charpentier had taken place at the cathedral of the Black Madonna, and now the hearse, its roof draped in wreaths and tributes and followed by a long procession of cars, forced the waiting crowds aside. They followed it, a densely packed and uneasy mob which seemed to spill through the ornate gates of the cemetery in the hearse's wake.

Although they were close to her now, they ignored the solitary Arab woman who watched from beside one of the unimportant gravestones. Their attention was on the cortege.

The hearse stopped forty yards from the rose tomb, and the attendants alighted. Behind the hearse the doors of the family mourners' cars opened.

For a moment Maryse Rose's heart seemed to pause as she recognized Christian, as she saw him help Colette from a car, supporting her with his arm. He seemed smaller, almost frail, his shoulders stooped and his back bent pathetically, as if the weight of his family's grief was too much for him to carry. To her dismay, Maryse Rose could not see Colette's face, hidden beneath a black lace veil. The mourners paused as Vincent's coffin was lifted from the hearse, while the crowd of settlers nearest them rippled with indecent anticipation, as six of Vincent's oldest friends, all of whom Maryse Rose recognized, supported the coffin on their shoulders. Each mourner brought Maryse Rose greater sadness; her former aunts and uncles, those she had thought of as cousins, intimate friends; Belle, comforting a weeping Madelene, and behind them with Vincent's children, Colonel Henri Lefitte and his wife. There were many others whom she knew.

And then, as the coffin reached the rose tomb, she saw the priest; the man who had married her to Philippe in the church at Hadjout!

She wanted to throw off her Arab clothing, cast aside the *haik* that concealed her face, and run to them. She wanted their grief to be her own, to share their sorrow with them. She needed to feel Colette's arms around her as they comforted each other. She felt her mind drawn irresistibly amongst them.

She made an unconscious move forward to join them, but a hand, its fingers like small bands of steel, gripped her arm. 'No, daughter.' The voice was thin and the command given in Arabic. She attempted to pull herself free, but the man, an Algerian, held her strongly. He was old, his face gnarled, and his clothing no more than rags. He pulled her back behind the gravestone. 'They will not welcome you, today. It is not the time for servants, no matter what the death may mean to you.' As she stared at him, he smiled, and answered her unspoken question. 'I clean their cemetery. As a consequence, I am invisible to them. But they may see a *fatma* . . . it would be unwise of you.' He spoke reproachfully. 'You should not even be here, woman. Why not go home? Mourn with them there, if you have a need.'

She did not leave the cemetery, but waited amongst the gravestones until it had emptied. Then, when she was alone, she walked slowly to the rose tomb. The flowers of the wreaths scented the air around it. She ran her fingers gently over the newly carved name on the panel beside the bronze door, as though Vincent would feel her touch. It seemed impossible to her that this grotesque stone monument, so ostentatious and vulgar, should hold within its musty darkness the body of the man she had loved for all her life. Unknown to him, as a child, she had worshipped him almost as if he had been a god. It had been Vincent who had been the hero of her first romantic dreams and fantasies, and as she had become a woman it had been to him that she had wanted to give herself. Even when he had been lost to her he had become the prime against which she had measured all other men, including Philippe.

Why had he been forbidden to her?

There seemed to be no human answer.

She remained at the tomb until long after nightfall, when a soft yellow moon rose above the eastern mountains to flood the cemetery with its gentle light. There were moments when, as she sat on the cool marble steps, she knew Vincent was beside her, hidden in the deep shadows. Sometimes, as light as the evening breeze, she felt his touch or heard the whisper of his voice, and then knew that he had returned her love.

ELEVEN

The Hodna Mountains: Spring 1962

The *douar*, Ksar el Oujmene, seemed part of the mountain itself. Built on a small plateau five thousand feet above the valley the village was reached by a single narrow footpath, while its stone houses were scattered amongst the rubble of a cliff which towered above, sheltered from the icy winter winds. It had been mortared and shelled several times, so that many of its original buildings had been demolished and few were left unscathed by the French attacks. Its inhabitants now lived in little more than caves, roofed by twisted sheets of rusted corrugated-iron. The mountains, their lower slopes clad with dense forests or blackened by fire, were raw and harsh, their craggy peaks desolate and snow-clad from January to March each year. At times the French Alpine troops patrolled the high passes and peaks, but to attack the village from above was impossible for them.

The *douar* was the base camp for Habib Saadi's company of FLN guerrillas, but the strength of the Katiba varied almost day by day. Casualties reduced the number of *moussebiline* but the normal replacements which slipped past the French Commando de Chasse in the valleys were now being reinforced by *harkis* who were deserting from the French Algerian regiments and bringing with them their weapons and ammunition.

The winter of 1960-61 had been disastrous for the FLN. The weather then had been the most appalling in the country's records, and the conditions for the guerrillas operating in the *djebel* unbearable. At the time Maryse Rose had believed it impossible to survive. For several weeks the snow-bound *katiba*, to which she was attached as medical officer had been forced to exist in a narrow gorge concealed within the inhospitable forest. Men had melted ice in their steel helmets over smouldering heaps of damp wood and bark. Even their poor fires had been a luxury lit only when the low cloud of the *djebel*, or its snowstorms, hid their smoke from the French patrols who sometimes passed within a hundred yards of the camp. The wounded lay on beds of wet tree boughs and moss, sheltered only by rough bivouacs through which the bitter winds had driven freezing snow. When French patrols were nearby the wounded men who were unable to stifle their moans of pain were gagged; some had suffocated to death.

Few of the *moussebiline* had suitable winter clothing, and the traditional Algerian winter cloak, the *cachabia*, had not been designed to cope with the needs of mountain guerrillas. When it rained, the felt *cachabias* absorbed the water like sponges, and if the weather then turned colder the damp material stiffened and froze solid. There had been no supplies available for the *katiba* throughout the entire winter, and the presence of the Commando de Chasse had made movement difficult. The men had been forced to eat crushed wheat and grass stewed into a soup, and had become so weak that many had frozen to death where they lay. There had been no medical supplies, and those that had been issued to Maryse Rose when they had left the Ksar el Oujmene base in the autumn were soon used. She had known there was a lack of medical equipment amongst the FLN troops, but had been horrified to learn that she had to carry out amputations in such primitive conditions with no more than a cut-throat razor and a sterilized hacksaw blade. Her sutures had been shoe-maker's thread, her forceps electrical pliers. A serious wound was a certain death sentence. If the *moussebiline* moved on, they were forced to leave behind those unable to walk, for to attempt to carry the wounded meant certain discovery by the French patrols.

Then, there had been little good news to lift the men's flagging morale. But as the winter of 1960-61 ended, the news, beamed to their transistors by radio stations operating from abroad, revived the determination and spirits of the *moussebiline*. It was obvious now that Algeria was becoming ungovernable for the French, and De Gaulle was coming under international pressure to end the war and agree to a totally independent Algeria governed by its majority.

By the following year the French military could no longer dictate the course of the war, nor influence the peace which might eventually follow it. In France itself acts of terrorism by the settler-formed Organisation Armée Secrète had increased until the French people themselves became sickened by the carnage. Everything was playing into the hands of the Algerian freedom fighters, and if they could maintain the pressure from every direction, they could only win.

It was late February 1962, and the weather was gradually improving. Spring had already arrived on the coastal plain where the mountains protected the fertile land, and even at the altitude of Ksar el Oujmene it was noticeably more pleasant. The stone shelters were warmed each day by the sunlight on the corrugated iron roofs, and wild flowers were colouring the distant grazing meadows of the valleys; in a few weeks the heat of the sun would scorch the grass brown, the *chergui* would bring more of its acrid dust from the Sahara to cover the freshness of the forests, and the roofs of the stone huts would blister the skin at a touch.

The *douar* covered an area of little more than four acres within the hanging-valley. Scree and debris which had fallen from the cliff above had weathered over centuries into infertile sand, but there were small patches which had been improved with the dung of the herds of goats or thin sheep which the original inhabitants had kept, and within these 'gardens' it was possible to grow a few poor vegetables. Most of the *douar*'s population had been moved to resettlement camps by the French, and apart from two or three families the village was occupied only by the *katiba* of the FLN. For many of the *moussebiline*, Ksar el Oujmene was the nearest thing to civilization that they had lived in for the past seven years of war.

A winter stream, fed by the snowfields, replenished three deep tanks which had been dug into the impervious rock of the mountain. Used carefully, when the stream dried-up the stagnant water lasted throughout the summer. There was plenty of firewood in the forests below, and as the number of French patrols in the area had recently diminished it had become possible to use the fires for warmth as well as cooking. There were reasonable stores of food in the *douar*. A small flock of goats had been driven across the mountains prior to the first winter snows, and these were now grazed above the tree line. A lorryload of rice had been found amongst the vehicles of a military convoy successfully ambushed. And sometimes the *harkis* who arrived almost daily in the village, brought with them canned food they had stolen from the French military stores before deserting their regiments. The *moussebilines* were not getting fat, but this winter they had not starved.

Maryse Rose was the senior of the two medical officers now attached to the *katiba*. The previous autumn she had been joined by a young Algerian girl who had begun her medical training in a clinic in the desert trading town of Bou-Saada. The girl, Iaicha Zighout, was barely sixteen and unqualified as a nurse, but even the small amount of medical knowledge which she had obtained was useful, and Maryse Rose had been grateful for her help and company. The two women shared a common background; both were Bedouin in origin. But unlike Maryse Rose, Iaicha had joined the FLN with the intention of revenge; her entire family had been wiped out in a French military 'ratissage' against her home village in the foothills of the Ouled-Nail mountains. It had been a reprisal raid, a pacification operation by the French when it had been learned that the village had been sheltering and feeding the FLN guerrillas who had been regularly cutting the telegraph cables between Laghouat and Algiers. The air-raid had been over-kill; there had been less than a dozen guerrillas, none of whom had been in the village when it was bombed. Over forty villagers had died, and amongst them Iaicha's parents, sisters and brothers, aunts, uncles and cousins, and grandmother.

What Iaicha Zighout lacked in skill, she made up for in her determination to heal the wounded *moussebiline* as quickly as possible so they could return to their fight against the French she hated. No matter how exhausted Iaicha might feel, she would attempt to conceal her fatigue until Maryse Rose ordered her from the shelters that were used as the *katiba*'s field hospitals. Then the girl would sleep for only a few hours and be back at work as soon as she awakened, her hair still dishevelled and uncombed, her hands often raw with the cold and her cheeks as pinched and hollowed as those of an old woman. With the typical characteristics of a Bedouin woman Iaicha

Zighout would be loyal to the FLN to her death, and as unforgiving to the French for as long as she breathed.

There were only three injured men at present in the field-hospital's shelters. One of these was suffering from a broken leg which occurred when the man had slipped while climbing to one of the *katiba*'s lookout posts high on the cliff above the *douar*. It was an uncomplicated fracture and the man was already able to move around the village with the aid of crutches. The other two men were suffering from battle wounds received a fortnight previously in a clash with a French patrol. One had been injured by fragments of an F1 grenade which had exploded behind him, the other by a 7.5 millimetre bullet from a MAS 36 which had ricochetted, spinning from a rock, to tear a large piece of flesh and most of the man's left shoulder joint from his body. The man injured by the grenade would live to fight again now that the shrapnel had been removed from his body, but the other man would not survive. There was still a shortage of drugs and he had lost far too much blood. Plasma was impossible to obtain so far from a city or large town, although it was often required.

It was early evening, and there was little more medical work that needed to be done. Iaicha was in the shelter with the wounded men, she would remain there, talking with them or simply watching them until Maryse Rose called her away.

Maryse Rose had walked for a hundred yards beyond the *douar* to a point where the cliff rose steeply, and it was only possible to continue with the help of ropes which had been pinned to the rocks. Two hundred feet above her, in a low cave set behind a narrow ledge, lay the *katiba*'s look-outs, resting on their elbows and scanning the distant valleys with their binoculars. They watched for signs of French patrols, or for the regular signals sent in morse from home-made heliographs or bits of mirrors, by the *katiba*'s *moussebiline* on the distant hills. Messages could be relayed across the mountains, providing the sun was shining, almost as fast as those by radios of the French army.

There was a niche in the rock where the path ended, worn smooth by the hooves of countless goats that had played there throughout the years, and the rock caught the last of the sunlight and held its warmth. Maryse Rose liked to sit there, alone with her thoughts at her day's end. Distantly, above the range of hills beyond the deep valley, she could see the hawks and buzzards riding their thermals, circling as they patrolled the hidden glades and crags. Sometimes wild goats, or slender horned gazelle broke cover to cross the valley paths or meadows, or the black choughs dived from their nests on the cliff to play their violent, noisy tumbling games in the disturbed air-currents that swept the bleak rock face.

The men of the *katiba* had learnt that these evening moments of solitude were important to Maryse Rose. Only rarely did they disturb her. Later, she would join them for their evening meal, or sit watching them as they gambled with cards for dried beans or even grains of corn. They gambled incessantly whenever they were off-duty, with cards, dice or the toss of a coin, even on the number of times a petrol lighter might ignite in succession.

She saw little of Habib. Like Iaicha and many of the *moussebiline*, he was spurred by a fanaticism which Maryse Rose had never herself experienced. He was continuously restless, unable to relax, working every hour he was able to keep himself awake; planning throughout the nights, out patrolling with the *faoudj*, or translating the coded messages received by the *katiba*'s radio. Sometimes he left *douar* for weeks at a time, visiting the headquarters' base in the Massif de l'Aurès.

When, as at present, he was in Ksar el Oujmene, there were times when he seemed to barely notice her and would arrive in their shelter after midnight, to throw himself on the mattress beside her. He would be asleep in seconds; by dawn she would be alone again.

She could not remember when they had last made love, or even when they had first become lovers again. It had been sometime during that first harsh winter, when they had lain close, seeking a respite from the fierce cold in the warmth of each other's body. Afterwards, with his weight still on her she had felt the fine snow driving through the rough thatch of tree branches onto her face. The efforts of their love-making had exhausted them both, then it had been animal, somehow desperate and final as if some deep instinct had demanded an act of reproduction before death. She had known she was infertile for she had ceased to menstruate throughout that winter, and her body had awakened only when she had reached the *douar*, and the food supplies improved.

At times it was impossible for her not to regret the loss of her former life at Beau Lac. As her hands had hardened and the soft curves of her body had become sharp and angular, her legs thin and scarred, she had been unable to prevent herself comparing the present to the past. She was no longer feminine. Even the guerrillas looked on her as one of themselves, and did not bother to moderate their coarse humour in her presence. She was another man amongst them, a *moussebiline* who had been beside them as they fought. On patrol in that first year she had excreted where they had excreted, stripped naked and washed with them in the same streams, slept amongst them in the rocks or forests, stank as they stank, starved with them.

287

Now the evening view across the valley to the far hills was her escape. She flew with the eagles, seeing through their eyes far beyond the mountains to the distant plains bordering the hidden blue sea. There for a while she could enjoy her memories, the sound of gentle waves, the liquid warmth of their caress, the soft comfort of silk garments against her body, the perfumes. Somewhere, even now men would be standing dressed elegantly in tuxedos, glasses of iced Pernod or whisky in their manicured hands, their women luxuriously gowned and fragrant, legs clad in sheer nylon, diamonds sparkling on their fingers as they sipped champagne. Somewhere there would be music from a hidden orchestra, filtering through blossom-laden shrubs; somewhere people still laughed with pleasure and found contentment.

Her thoughts this evening were interrupted by shouting, a voice shrill with boyish excitement. 'Melila . . . Melila . . .' One of the *moussebiline*, Chouki, a youth of fifteen, ran towards her up the narrow path. He had accompanied the patrols unarmed until he had managed to pick up a French light machine-gun, and had refused so vehemently to hand it over later that Habib had been amused and permitted him to keep it. Now he carried the weapon everywhere, a long bandolier of machine-gun belting draped over his narrow shoulders, so that he seemed to Maryse Rose more like the caricature of a corsair than a real soldier. To his annoyance he had been unable to find a uniform small enough to fit him although he examined those on all the French dead. His blood-stained combat jacket once the property of a 'Lizard', reached to his knees and was belted with a short length of hemp rope. Beneath it he wore tattered shorts, and his thin legs and feet were bare. He was grinning widely, waving to her as he ran. 'Melila . . .!' He reached her, but continued to jump up and down like an enthusiastic boy

at a football match. 'They're here . . . back . . . the patrol
. . . what success! Two trucks, they destroyed. They've a
new heavy machine-gun . . . grenades . . . everything.
And more food. Canned beef, and tea. Luxuries . . . soap
powder. Only one of our men is dead . . . Hani . . . a
bullet in his brain . . . very quick. God's will! But fourteen
Frenchmen . . . all killed. And prisoners, Melila. They've
brought back prisoners. Eight of them. Two of them
wounded . . . but prisoners at the *douar*!' He grabbed her
wrist, pulling her to her feet. 'Come and look at them,
Melila. They're shitting themselves with fear.'

As she followed him down the track, from the compound of the *douar* came the nerve-chilling 'yil-yil-yil' of
the women, their strange piercing cry echoing from the
cliff to the distant hills where it would be heard in the
still evening air by the *moussebiline* of the *katiba*'s outposts.
The cry was a signal the women used to call to their flocks
of goats, their children, each other or their menfolk. It
could be a sign of jubilance, a warning . . . a threat.

Besides herself, there were only four other women
in the *douar*; Iaicha, and three older women who had
returned with their husbands and children when the
French military and the Blue Caps had rounded up the
remainder of the village's inhabitants and despatched
them to the hated resettlement centres.

Now, the four women, watched by the amused *moussebiline*, were taunting the prisoners; a wretched group of
frightened men most of them no more than twenty years
of age, who knelt or squatted in a tight group in the dust
of the compound, their hands tied behind their backs by
ropes which were looped up around each man's neck,
tethering him to a neighbour. Behind them, coated with
grime and blood, lay two wounded men on rough
stretchers made of blankets and tree boughs.

Iaicha was holding a curved pruning saw which was

normally carried by those who went foraging for wood. Using the tool like a sword, she was swinging its gleaming teeth closer and closer to the throat of a prisoner while one of the older women held him by the ears and twisted his head backwards to expose his neck. The man's eyes were wide, bulging like those of a terrified rabbit, and he had begun screaming, adding to the pandemonium of shouts of encouragement from the audience of *moussebiline* and the women's shrill vibrating cries. Children were throwing stones at the two wounded men, who seemed barely conscious and unable to protect themselves.

Chouki, still leading Maryse Rose by the arm, pulled her into the circle of *moussebiline*. 'Look at the Frenchmen,' he shouted to her. 'Not so frightening now are they, without their machine-pistols and their rifles? I've heard them scream before. They always scream like babies.' He was laughing so much there were tears on his cheeks. 'Iaicha will make them squeak.' He raised his voice to an even high pitch. 'Iaicha . . . don't spoil it for us by cutting their throats. Saw off their pricks, first. Make them eat them.'

The *moussebiline* laughed with them. Chouki was their favourite and they tended to treat him as a mascot.

Maryse Rose wrenched herself from his grasp so that the boy's light body spun away from her. He lost his footing and fell backwards against the side of one of the shelters, his machine-gun and ammunition belts rattling on the stones. She pushed Iaicha away from the young soldier and turned to face the *moussebiline*. 'What are you, animals?' They were suddenly silent. 'If you have to kill these men, why kill them here? Why torture them?'

One of the guerrillas answered her. 'We knew the women were bored. We've brought them a circus.' There was laughter again, but it was more subdued. The men had known Maryse Rose for a long time, but had never seen her so angry before.

'You've fought for seven years to win this war, and it's almost over. How do you want men of other nationalities to speak of you when it's finished? Do you want them to say, these Algerians are honourable? Or do you want them to think you cowards?'

'The French kill us,' protested Iaicha loudly. 'They murder *our* families. They torture us. And haven't you seen our children fighting with dogs so that they can get some scrap of food out of French rubbish bins? Why should we treat them differently?' She pouted angrily.

Chouki was kneeling, wiping grit from the breech of his machine-gun. His eyes flashed, and his lips were drawn back in a furious snarl. Melila, whom he had always liked, had made him look weak and foolish in front of his friends. 'Kill them. Let Iaicha cut off their balls.'

'Killing in battle or even when the battle has just ended, is one thing. But to kill in cold blood, hours afterwards, is dishonourable. These men surrendered to you. It means they put a trust in you. You owe them that debt.' Maryse Rose stood her ground between the prisoners and the women.

One of the older *moussebiline* spoke gruffly. 'If I owe the French anything, it is a knife across their throats. The same way we kill a goat or sheep.' The other men of the *katiba* shouted their agreement.

'Silence . . .' Habib Saadi strode through the circle of men. He held a pistol in his hands and for a moment Maryse Rose thought he was about to shoot the prisoners. He stared down at them contemptuously for several seconds before facing his men. 'They are not to be killed.' There was a groan of disappointment. 'Those are my orders. If they are disobeyed, those responsible will be executed.' He scowled pointedly at Chouki. 'Do you all understand?' The men nodded. 'And they are to be fed

291

the same rations as ourselves. That too is an order.' He turned as if to walk away, but then paused and spoke again. 'But if any patrol brings in more prisoners then they will share their own rations with them. Is that quite clear?'

Later that evening when the sun had set behind the mountains and the meal had been finished, Habib sent for Maryse Rose. His command post was more of a dug-out than a hut. On one wall a map of the *wilaya* was held in place by four wooden pegs driven into gaps in the stonework. The radio was on a low bench beside the *katiba*'s code books and log. Habib sat behind a table built of ammunition boxes studying a second more detailed map on which he recorded the movements of French patrols. The only light in the dug-out was from a kerosene lantern resting on the rough table beside his map. A cup made from an empty detonator can, filled with tea sweetened with wild honey, steamed beside his elbow. He looked up, then pushed himself backwards until his shoulders were resting against the wall before speaking to her.

'Why did you interfere?'

Tonight she answered him in French rather than the Arabic they always used. 'Humanity.' She met his questioning eyes. 'And pride.' He cocked his head little. 'I'm as much an Algerian as the rest of you. Why is it necessary for us to continue to act as savages?'

'Is that what you think my guerrillas are?' She could see rising anger in his eyes. Even amongst the men his short temper had become notorious. Few dared to cross him.

'Of course not. But the years of war have dehumanized all of us. We have to end the senseless killings.'

'So we can live happily together? The Algerians and the French as brothers?' He drew a small goat-skin purse of tobacco from his breast-pocket and rolled a thin cigarette. He ran the tip of his tongue along the brown paper and then handed the cigarette to her. She lit it while he made another. The coarse tobacco bit into her lungs and brought saliva into her mouth. Once, the taste would have sickened her; she had never liked cigarettes until she had joined the *moussebiline* in the *djebel*, but at times it had been the only comfort available to them. Habib nodded towards another ammunition box beside the table. She sat on it as he slid the can of tea towards her. 'The French are leaving.'

She misunderstood him. 'The prisoners?' Had he agreed to release them?

He laughed, softly. 'The pieds-noir. I spoke to one of the new *harkis*. Every day the ships are crowded with the colonists, running to France, Spain, Italy . . . even Malta. They are selling their businesses, transferring their money.' He took a long pull at his cigarette, and held the rich smoke in his lungs for several seconds before releasing it. It was as though he were feeding on the nicotine it contained. 'So you see, *they've* already decided we can't live together. I know it, and you know it too. They could live with us for only just so long as they were the bosses, and we made money for them. The sooner they've all gone, the better for our country.'

The war and the years in the harsh mountains had prematurely aged him, Maryse Rose thought. Already his dark hair was salted grey at his temples, and his face was lined. He was not yet thirty-three. 'Everything has changed,' she said softly. 'In Paris you used to speak of equality. One man, and one vote. In those days I don't remember that it was your intention to drive the pieds-noir out of the country.'

'They've driven themselves away. They had the opportunities; they lost them.' He angrily stubbed out the cigarette on the wall beside him, then ground the red sparks into the dust with his foot. 'But the war's not over for them yet.' His eyes seemed to sparkle with enthusiasm in the light of the lantern. 'If we weaken now, in these last weeks, everything we've already gained will be forfeit. We have to be stronger than ever, and we have to fight harder. The orders I've received say "no quarter . . . maintain the pressure." And that is what I shall do with this *katiba*. And our discipline is important, Melila. This war against the French will not end cleanly. Even when they have gone, we will have to continue to fight for what we have won. If we look like a corpse, vultures will come to feed on us. We will need the *moussebiline*, and their loyalty and spirit. And I do not want it weakened in any way.'

She realized that he was criticizing her interference with the prisoners, but something else disturbed her more. He no longer wanted the war to end. Somehow, its violence, unpredictability and continual challenge had become a drug for him. Perhaps he was even afraid of peace and a normality it would bring, but which he had never experienced. There would be thousands like him, and like Chouki to whom a scene of beauty was a battle-field filled with the bodies of dead enemies he could plunder. 'I shall need to attend to the French wounded,' she said, determinedly.

For a moment she thought he was about to refuse her. 'Give them a little of your time, but that's all. We have no drugs for them . . . insufficient for our own wounded. And we'll need everything, soon enough.' His eyes met hers again, and softened a little. 'Our friends of the Commando de Chasse intend to pay us a visit. I had an intelligence report this evening. We're becoming a little too successful for them.'

'They'll attack the *douar* again?'

'That's what they'd like to do, and trap us all up here. Fortunately, their men drink in the evening, and talk too much at the bar; and the barman is one of us. This time, we'll go out and meet them. The entire *katiba* will fight, not just a patrol.'

She was horrified. 'Habib, it's madness. You could lose half the men . . . all of them, perhaps. And there's no need. You could move the *katiba* further into the mountains for a few weeks. We have the provisions. You've never fought the kind of battle you're suggesting. What will it prove?'

Habib's eyes hardened. 'If you require me to tell you what it'll prove to the French, then you're not yet as much an Algerian as the rest of us, Melila.'

The French prisoners, including the two wounded men, were being held in a small compound at the edge of the *douar*. In peaceful times the compound, little more than seven yards square, was used for the penning of the villagers' goats or sheep when they were brought into the village for slaughter, or in the case of the sheep, for shearing each spring. Now it was used as a corral for the *katiba*'s donkeys, when the beasts were not being used by the forage patrols. Its walls had been repaired after the last bombardment and stood some five feet in height. Chouki had appointed himself one of the guards and sat with his machine-gun on the tin roof of a neighbouring shack from where he could see the entire compound. Another of the younger *moussebiline* stood beside the narrow entrance with a 24/29 resting over his arm like a sporting rifle. He was juggling one of the French FO grenades, its light-steel shell already polished bright by the fabric of the pouch in which it was usually kept. The *moussebiline* carried all their weapons and ammunition with them everywhere, sleeping with their pistols, rifles, submachine-guns or mortars beside them, guarding them as jealously as their forefathers had guarded their ornate, long-barrelled muzzle-loaders.

It was only an hour after dawn, but the *moussebiline* had always adjusted their way of life to suit the hours of daylight. The air was still chilled by the night, and in the compound the prisoners were huddled close together on the dung floor. Their combat jackets and boots had been removed, and while some of the men wore khaki vests above their trousers many were naked from the waist upwards. A million flies, attracted by the smell of dung, tormented them.

Maryse Rose visited the compound alone. Iaicha had refused to accompany her. Maryse Rose could have insisted but had decided it was pointless; if Iaicha was unwilling to help the two wounded men voluntarily then she might do them more harm than good. A tourniquet or a bandage deliberately fastened too tight could be as much an implement of torture as the saw Iaicha had carried the previous day.

Maryse Rose knew that Chouki and the other *moussebiline* would watch her closely, and report whatever she might do to help the wounded men. Even had she decided to ignore Habib's orders that no drugs should be used, it would be almost impossible for her to do so without his knowledge. The *moussebiline* always gossiped; there was often little else for them to do. Everyone's actions or words were discussed, however trivial they might be. There was no privacy in the *douar*; within a *moussebiline katiba* everything but a person's most secret thoughts were shared.

Chouki returned her greeting reluctantly, avoiding her eyes and barely nodding his acknowledgement. He shifted his position slightly on the corrugated-iron roof so that the muzzle of his machine-gun followed her as she walked towards the wounded men. The other French soldiers watched her warily; few of them recognized her as the woman who had saved their lives the previous evening. Their minds had been too numbed by fear. Most were uncertain as to what had happened. They stared at her combat suit with its green shoulder patches and red crescents. It was obviously an official uniform . . . the first FLN uniform they had seen on a woman.

Their eyes followed her as she squatted beside the nearer of the wounded men. She carried her medical bag and a water-flask. The wounded man, a sergeant, had been struck in the arm by a bullet which had then driven through his chest into his lungs. It surprised her that he had survived the night. The man was unconscious but with the attention of a skilled surgeon in a base operating theatre he would probably have survived. Here he had little chance. The chest wound had been covered by a military wound-dressing which was solid with congealed blood, and when she removed it the wound frothed and made a sucking noise as the man breathed.

There was a movement beside her. One of the prisoners, rubbing his arms vigorously to warm them, knelt by the wounded man. He seemed very young, little more than twenty-years-old. There was several days of beard on his chin and cheeks; an indication of how long his patrol had been operating away from their base. His beard was almost blonde, his eyes hazel, and his hair had been so closely cropped that it was less than half an inch long above his forehead, and of no greater length than his thin beard growth over the remainder of his scalp. He reminded her of the Tin-Tin cartoons she had read as a child.

'Are you their officer?' she asked him.

He shook his head quickly, surprised that she questioned him in clear French without an Arab accent. 'No, miss, a corporal.'

'I'm afraid this man will die.' She had lowered her voice, in case somehow her words might penetrate the mind of the unconscious man. 'I can do nothing to help him. He needs proper surgery, and even so I think it would be too late to help him now. All I can do is to clean and re-dress the wound.'

'Can't you give him morphine?' asked the soldier. 'And antibiotics?'

'He can't feel anything. But in any case, we have none. If he were one of our men his friends would help him out of this world.'

'You kill your wounded?' The young soldier was horrified.

'You leave us no choice,' answered Maryse Rose, coldly. 'I don't like it either, but it's often the kindest thing to do.' She began cleaning the wound with a piece of cloth and water from her flask. 'We don't have helicopters like yourselves to take our wounded men somewhere for good treatment. And if we ever have any drugs they are used on those most likely to survive.' She bound the wound with a clean bandage while the young soldier supported the man's shoulders. She noticed the man's hands were trembling.

'Do they intend to kill us?' he asked, nervously.

She answered his question honestly. 'I don't know. Last night, their officer said not; but as the circumstances change . . .' She did not end the sentence.

She moved to the side of the second wounded man, and as she did so the young soldier said: 'This is our officer. He took a piece of grenade in his knee . . . and was concussed . . . but his wound is not too bad.' He sought her eyes. 'Surely he will live?'

'A light wound for you, can be a fatal one for us,' she reminded him.

The wounded man's trousers had been split to his

thigh. His right knee was thickly bound in blood-stained bandages, and had been splinted with a short length of a tree branch. As she began cutting away the dressing, the man groaned. Automatically she glanced at his face, and felt an ice cold shock spread itself throughout her body. The officer, like the young soldier, was unshaven but his heavy growth of dark beard was dissected by a long scar. She knew instantly it was Philippe.

Even as she stared disbelievingly at him, his eyes opened and met her own, then quickly searched her face. He pushed himself onto his elbows, wincing with pain. Maryse Rose's body seemed paralysed; she attempted to will movement into her limbs, but was unable to do so.

'Maryse Rose!' His voice was an exclamation of recognition.

For a moment she was unable to speak, but then she replied in Arabic. 'Lie back, you will make your wound worse. My name is Melila. I am the *katiba* medical officer.'

He responded in the gutteral Arabic that had so much amused her when they had been together. She had often teased him when he used it in the markets. Now, the once-familiar sound of his voice wrenched fiercely at her intestines. 'Do you honestly believe I could forget you . . . the one thing I have ever really loved in my life? Do you think I could forget a face I see every time I close my eyes?'

'You are mistaken. We have never met before.' Somehow she managed to force herself to turn away from his gaze. She hunched above his wounded leg, knowing that he was continuing to stare at her. She pulled the dressing free from his flesh quickly, hoping that the sudden pain would distract him, even momentarily. Over the past years of her nursing, in training but particularly in the cruel conditions of the *djebel*, she had become used to the

299

most terrible injuries. Men had died screaming in agony as she attempted to ease their suffering, she had learnt to ignore their torn flesh, their shattered white bones, their amputated limbs, their blood and viscera. Now, the sight of Philippe's wound and his lacerated tissue beneath her fingertips brought her an unaccustomed sense of horror and despair.

'I've searched for you since the day you left,' Philippe said, this time in French. She attempted to ignore his words, but the old fascination of his voice continuously drew her mind back to him. 'I don't blame you for hating me. I was so wrong . . . so despicable. I was insane. I believe I wanted to punish myself by destroying the most important thing in my life.'

The passages within her throat seemed to have swollen, so that even had she wished to speak she would have been unable to do so. There were tears building behind her eyelids but she lowered her head to conceal them. She finished tying the new dressing quickly and then stood, turning her back on him as she did so. As she walked from the compound, she heard him say her name once more. 'Maryse Rose . . .' It was not a plea for her help, nor even for her admission to her identity. It was a statement, into which he somehow managed to insert a thousand unspoken words.

She walked through the *douar* as though she were in a trance, failing to hear the morning greetings of the *moussebiline* as she passed them. They watched her, curiously. Beside one of the small huts, a group of men squatting around a cooking-fire waved to her, then followed her with their eyes until she was beyond their sight, hidden by the piles of rubble, before passing comments between themselves.

The goat-seat of primeval rock beneath the look-out posts had already collected the warmth of the early sun, and as she sat, staring across the morning valley, comforted her a little with its sense of timeless immortality. She had never expected to see Philippe again, and yet only minutes before she had touched him and heard his voice. Now she could remember the last time he had held her in his arms, in Beau Lac. And after that strange, terrible period, when she had felt she had lost him, that night he had returned to her and their bodies and emotions had re-discovered one another, and their child had been created. The emotions she had experienced then were clearer in her mind now than the recent terrors and hardships of the war.

She had tried to hate him in the past, but understood now why it had been impossible. Regardless of how he had treated her she had never lost her love for him. Although it had been buried beneath her own horror, by hurt and by cruelty, it had continued to exist. It was something far beyond her control, something within her and yet independent of her will.

The rattle of scree on the path a few yards away made her turn. Habib, and a stranger dressed in a clean combat uniform, stood a few yards away. The stranger, an Algerian of similar age to Habib, was smiling. He was a slender man, a little effeminate in the way he moved. He was clean-shaven, which was unusual amongst the *moussebiline*, and his face and body were plump as though he had recently arrived from a town or city.

Instead of Habib introducing her to the man, he said to the Algerian: 'This is your nurse, Melila.'

The man remained a few paces away from her. He smiled again. 'Good. I'm sure we will work together extremely well.' His voice was condescending. 'I have heard excellent reports about you, Melila. I hear you have done good work for the *katiba*; it is recognized at headquarters. Soon, if you wish, it will be possible for you to receive more training, and higher medical qualifications.' He paused. 'After the war has ended, of course.' He took a pace closer to her and stared at her face. 'You are pale. Do you suffer from malaria? Never mind, I shall examine you, and the other woman.' He realized Habib's introduction had been incomplete. 'I am Doctor Abdelmalek Bouderba.'

It took Doctor Bouderba less than a minute to examine the *katiba*'s entire stock of drugs. Apart from aspirin, sulphur powder, potassium permanganate crystals and the several containers of dried herbs used by local tribespeople for the treatment of various ailments, there was only a litre of pine-scented disinfectant.

He sorted through the crude home-made instruments that Maryse Rose used for her surgery, and to her amazement was congratulatory. 'Good, Melila. You have most of the things you need. I have brought a few odds and ends with me, but I am certain I will be of most help to you in the introduction of some new and important techniques.' He stepped back and looked at the equipment which Iaicha had laid out on the ammunition boxes which served as an operating table. 'I believe, according to Major Saadi, that I have arrived at a very opportune moment. I gather he is planning an action. Excellent! We too, will be able to plan.'

It was dusk before she was able to gather sufficient courage to visit the prisoners again. The thought of having to face Philippe's eyes once more and hear him speak to her, filled her with apprehension. Her mind seemed to have divided itself, so that part of her screamed silently a need to be with him while the remainder warned her of the anguish such contact must bring.

As she walked towards the compound the vast colonies

of bats which found shelter in the crevices and caves of the rock-face above the *douar*, hunted their evening prey low above the roofs of the village. The *moussebiline* had finished their prayers and most were now completing the nightly ritual of stripping and cleaning their weapons.

At the wall of the compound three young children were throwing lumps of dried goat dung at the prisoners, watched by several of the *moussebiline* who were lounging beside the entrance, their rifles slung across their shoulders. The prisoners themselves did not appear to have moved since she had visited them earlier that day. Beside them there was a five gallon water container, and a bucket which looked as if it might have contained boiled rice or barley. At least, Maryse Rose thought, the *moussebiline* had obeyed Habib's instructions. She found herself loath to enter the compound despite the necessity to examine the wounded soldiers, but as she stood near the gate the young Frenchman who had spoken to her that morning hurried to her.

Even in the past few hours his face seemed to have hollowed and aged. He began speaking before he reached her. 'The sergeant . . . he's dead, I think.' He glanced in the direction of the group of *moussebiline* resentfully. 'I tried to make them understand, but they don't care. I asked them to send for you; they wouldn't listen.'

She followed him to the stretcher. The man lay on his back, his lips parted so that he seemed to be grinning. Even at this late time of the day, flies crawled over his lips and cheeks and coated the blood-stained bandages around his chest. She rested her fingers on the artery at the side of his neck, then looked at the young Frenchman. 'It was to be expected.' The soldier grimaced hopelessly. 'I'll arrange for his body to be removed,' she promised him.

'Perhaps you'll also ask if my men can have some of

their clothing returned? The nights here are still cold.'

The voice was Philippe's, and without thinking she answered him in French. 'I'll do my best for them.' She forced herself to turn towards him as he spoke again.

He was smiling at her. 'So you have decided to speak to me in my own language. I suppose it's a beginning!' He dropped his voice slightly. 'It's ironic that after almost three years of searching for you, I've ended up as your prisoner. I realize I always was . . . at least, I realized too late that was what I wanted to be.' She attempted to ignore him but he continued. 'I've wondered all day what I should be saying to you in these circumstances . . . about the guilt, the sadness, how I've despised myself; how desolate my life has been without you.' He jerked his head towards the *moussebiline*. 'I hope they'll give me time to apologize properly. All I can say to you is that I realized how much I love you . . . too late perhaps, but my feelings haven't changed. I still love you Maryse Rose, and if I died here, at least I shall be dying near you.'

She hissed at him between her clenched teeth. 'Be quiet. Don't you realize how many of them understand French?' If they had already heard him, the word would spread quickly around the *douar*. She did not know how Habib might react if he learnt that one of his prisoners was her husband. She had already learnt that he was more capable of vengeance than mercy towards soldiers of the French army.

As she dressed Philippe's wound again, he spoke in a whisper. 'Green doesn't suit you.' He reached forward suddenly and caught her hand. His unexpected touch made her gasp.

'You fool!'

'What have I to lose? If they decided to go ahead and kill me it won't be pleasant anyway.' He released her hand, but his eyes examined her. 'You're still very beautiful. A little thin, but beautiful.' His voice became more serious. 'Do you know what they intend to do with my men?'

One of the *moussebiline* was watching her closely and had moved nearer to them on the other side of the wall. She tried to speak without moving her lips. 'I don't know what will happen to them. It's so near the end of the war now. Perhaps, with luck . . .'

Philippe only grunted as she stood. She looked down at him and spoke loudly in Arabic. 'Try not to move your leg. I will return tomorrow.' She saw the *moussebiline* turn away, disinterested.

The *douar* slept little that night. By one am, the *moussebiline* were awake and assembled in their sections. Their NCO's checked their equipment, and issued extra ammunition and grenades. Additional stores were loaded onto the *katiba*'s donkeys and mules, while the section commanders received their final briefing from Habib. A convoy, consisting of a complete company of French Commando de Chasse were expected to leave their base at M'Sila shortly before dawn. Their objective was the capture or neutralization of Ksar el Oujmene. Unsuspecting that the knowledge of their proposed raid was already in the hands of the FLN *moussebiline* they would drive their vehicles into a deadly ambush; the largest that the *katiba* had ever mounted. The site of the ambush, already well reconnoitred by Habib and his section commanders the previous day, was a narrow defile on the mountain road, seven miles from the *douar*.

The *moussebiline* were excited by their prospects of success. This was to be no 'hit and run' attack . . . it was a trap into which their hated enemies were delivering themselves. The odds amused them. There would be approximately one hundred and thirty of the Commando

305

de Chasse, four sections of thirty men, each commanded by a junior lieutenant. There were only sixty-seven *moussebiline* on the day's count! But the element of surprise in the FLN ambush pointed to certain victory. The *moussebiline* did not consider the likelihood of their own deaths, each man convinced that by evening they would return to the *douar* as heroes.

Before he left with the men, Habib spent a few minutes with Maryse Rose. The *douar* was already growing more silent as the sections moved away down the mountain track. The village was in darkness, lit only by starlight and a half-ripe moon which hung above a distant bank of low cloud. The mountains were no more than silhouettes, and the *chergui* had strengthened its gusts, hissing through the rocks and buildings of the *douar*, tugging at the men's clothing and headcloths, swirling the light dust from beneath their feet.

Habib did not like the emotions of partings, and discouraged them. He was casual now as she walked beside him through the village. He lifted his head, testing the wind against his cheeks. 'This will be good for us. It'll help. Trees sway in the wind, grass becomes a moving sea. The wind will help conceal the men; it distracts the French gunners. Sound is difficult to locate with accuracy. God is with the men, today.'

She did not want him to risk his life but knew he would respond angrily if she cautioned him. 'There is a dog following the third section,' she warned.

He swore softly. The *moussebiline* did not like dogs, and usually killed those who hung around the villages they occupied. But somehow, just as the *katiba*'s replacements trickled into the *douar* so did other dogs, some following the deserting *harkis*. They could betray an ambush. 'I'll see it's dealt with. We have enough time to prepare ourselves well.' She could see his teeth glistening in the

306

moonlight as he grinned. 'You'll be able to hear our music. I'll see they play you a special tune . . . the victory march!'

She took his arm and moved a little closer to him. He had fought so many times, and while others had died he had always returned unscathed. He boasted it was God's will, and not simply the luck of war. But while he was out with the patrols, she had often prayed. It had been easier when she had accompanied them; there was seldom time for fear when bullets crackled through the trees, mortar bombs exploded, and shrapnel screamed from the rocks beside the men.

'We will have fifty per cent casualties,' he said, as though the figure was merely a statistic for the *katiba*'s records. He was normally correct in his estimates. When he stated that four men would die in a certain attack, he was usually right. 'Much will depend on our initial assault. If we can knock out their gunners and mortar crews, it will be easier.' He stopped and faced her. 'Tonight the radio news was good. There seems a likelihood of a ceasefire very soon, but when it happens I want this *katiba* to be strong.' He held her shoulders with both his hands, so that she faced him. 'I know you believe I love this war, but it's not so. I love only its aims. But as I've already told you, we'll have to fight for our peace even when this war is won. It's not been discussed with the *moussebiline*, but the FLN will need them if it is to be the leading political party. The tigers will eat the sheep . . . and the FLN must be a tiger.' He leant towards her and kissed her cheek. For a moment he let her hold him. 'Have patience, Melila. One day you will have your apartment in Algiers . . . with a bath, and hot water.'

She watched him until the darkness swallowed him, and the sounds of his combat boots on the pebbles were lost in the gentle moans of the *chergui*.

'I will need two operating tables,' said Abdelmalek Bouderba. 'They must be set close together. Melila, you will be responsible for the selection of those who require the most urgent attention . . . the wounded men with the greatest loss of blood, but otherwise the best chance of survival. Iaicha will do exactly as I say. After the first one or two patients, she will be able to manage on her own, and you and I will work together.' He paused and then asked: 'How many prisoners do we have?'

Iaicha answered him. 'Seven. One has died.'

Doctor Bouderba said: 'A pity. We will surely need all of them. In fact we need more.'

Need them? The way in which Bouderba had spoken raised the hairs on Maryse Rose's neck. Did he mean to help the wounded men, or something far more sinister? 'Why do we *need* the prisoners?' she asked him, flatly.

'Transfusions,' said Bouderba.

Already she was beginning to experience a growing feeling of revulsion and disbelief as though some part of her mind had already received his explanation. 'There *is* no plasma . . . unless you brought it.'

The doctor smiled at her benevolently as though he were a stage magician about to pull a white rabbit from a hat. 'We already have what we are likely to need . . . blood. Seven prisoners equal twenty-eight litres of blood.'

She was unable to prevent herself reacting in horror. 'But that's an impossible suggestion . . .'

Bouderba misunderstood her and smiled again. He fluttered his hands in apology. 'Of course it's an emergency measure, Melila. But this is war, and we are out in the field. We are bound to lose some of the men when their bodies react against an unsuitable blood type, but others will survive who would die without a transfusion. We have found that the survival rate justifies the risk.

The techniques are relatively simple, and I have all the necessary equipment. I have explained to Major Saadi that in future, especially when you have received casualties, it will be sensible to bring prisoners back to the base alive, rather than to execute them on the battleground.'

She felt as though the blood had been already drained from her own body. 'That is disgraceful! Bestial! This is a field hospital, not an abbatoir. What kind of doctor are you? Didn't you swear an oath?'

Abdelmalek Bouderba looked momentarily stunned by her sudden outburst, but recovered quickly. 'I shall be saving the lives of my people . . . of your friends.' He was angry. 'Which do you think is less painful, dying by having your testicles ripped from your body and your bowels torn out, or slipping away into unconsciousness and peaceful death through loss of blood?'

TWELVE

Only five armed *moussebiline* remained in the *douar*. Three were members of Habib's *katiba*, while the other two men were strangers who had accompanied Doctor Bouderba as guides. One of the three *katiba moussebiline* delegated by Habib to guard the prisoners was the man who had broken his leg in the fall from the look-out post; a second was an ex-*harki* who had arrived at the village only the previous evening and was too exhausted to accompany the section to which he had been allocated. The third was Chouki Negazi.

The youth was in a sullen and dangerous mood. He had spent much of the early part of the previous night cleaning his machine-gun and boasting to the older *moussebiline* of the exploits he intended for himself in the coming battle. Always amused by his youthful brashness, the men had encouraged him at first, then teased him good-humouredly. Just as his section had prepared to leave the *douar*, Habib had sent for him and ordered him to remain behind to guard the prisoners. No argument that the boy had been able to produce had changed Habib's mind. To the young *moussebiline* it now seemed that the insult he had first endured from Maryse Rose when the prisoners had been brought to Ksar el Oujmene had been compounded by the man who was her lover. It was no secret that she was Habib's woman, but her unique position had been accepted by the men since the first day she arrived at the *katiba* with their new commander.

310

They had come to respect her when she had shown she was prepared to share their dangers and sacrifices. Chouki Negazi realized she had deceived him; until recently he had thought she was his friend but now she was stealing his manhood from him. He had not yet killed one of the enemy, and in the past he had been treated like one of the mules, fetching and carrying the supplies of the patrols. Today had been his opportunity to prove his real value to the *katiba*, the opportunity had been taken from him by Habib Saadi and his woman, Melila.

Chouki Negazi's machine-gun was loaded and cocked, with the safety-catch in the 'off' position. It rested on its bipod, aimed at exactly the centre of the wounded French officer's head. The *moussebiline*'s finger was on the trigger, he knew he had only to squeeze a little, and the man would die instantly.

Maryse Rose did not continue her argument with Abdelmalek Bouderba. It was pointless. She knew that neither the ethical nor moral aspects of draining the blood from the prisoners of war would change his mind. He made it quite clear to her that he considered their death in such a manner a just retribution for their participation in the war. Had the young Frenchmen considered their country's war wrongful, he had said, they could have refused to fight; others had done so, even conscripts. But they had been prepared to sacrifice themselves in order to *take* Algerian lives, therefore they might be sacrificed to *save* Algerian lives.

'You may help or not as you choose,' he told her finally. 'In the case of the latter decision, you will be reported to the *Wilaya* command for disciplinary action and will face a military court.' He made a slight but characteristically womanly movement of his head as an indication of his indifference, and then added: 'The penalty for the refusal to obey the order of a senior officer such as myself, is death.' She had no doubt he would carry out his threat, and it was unlikely that even Habib would be able to save her.

The preparations for the use of the field-hospital had been completed; as usual there had been very little that could be done. Drums of water were put on the fires to boil, and the surfaces of the 'operating tables' wiped down with a little of the disinfectant. The blades of the instruments had been stropped sharp by one of the *moussebiline* the previous day. All that now remained was to wait for the first of the casualties to arrive back at the *douar* when the battle ended. And if they followed the normal pattern, they would arrive one or two men at a time, having scattered into the dense bush and forest after the attack, making their way to the mountain by secret tracks the enemy had never discovered.

Although her mind could now accept brutal death in the field hospitals, or even in the heat of battle, she had been unable to reconcile herself to it in other circumstances. Once she had witnessed a *moussebiline*, armed with a rare sniper's rifle, kill a French sentry at a distance of more than five hundred yards. It had appalled her, although the man had looked only like a falling tree-trunk. Twice, she had seen executions in the *katiba*. They had been men whom Habib had sentenced to death; one for theft of food, the other for cowardice. Every member of the *katiba* had been forced to watch, and there had been no exceptions. The two men had been hanged. The sight of their bodies kicking and twisting on the ropes had been nightmarish. And she was quite aware that the *moussebiline* killed the French wounded and seldom took prisoners; it was something over which she could exercise no control, but sudden outbursts of firing were usually

312

followed by screams that penetrated even through her hands as she held them tightly over her ears.

She had realized that her feelings would have been little different even if Philippe had not been amongst the condemned prisoners. The thought of the hideous manner in which they were to be used nauseated her. She was determined that if it were possible, she would prevent it, even if later she would be punished. Briefly she had contemplated killing Doctor Bouderba; there was a pistol in the hospital tent and she had been taught its use. But she doubted if she was capable of such an act even in these circumstances, and if she were, the prisoners would still be in the *douar*'s compound wiht the *moussebiline* guards; it would be impossible for her to kill all those. When the men of the *katiba* returned from the battle and learned what she had done, they would certainly torture the prisoners to death, and it was unlikely Habib would prevent them. He would be forced to order her own execution.

The situation for the prisoners and herself appeared hopeless, and although she sought desperately for a solution she could find none.

The first sounds of the ambush reached the *douar* like the mountain thunder of an autumn storm, faint but distinct in the noon air. The eyes of the *moussebiline* guards left behind in the village turned automatically towards the distant forests. They fidgeted nervously, knowing their friends were already within the chaos of the battle, envying them the aggressive challenge, the exhilaration of fear, and the overwhelming thrill of survival with triumph.

The hills, cliffs and gorges of the *djebel* exaggerated the explosions, multiplying them, overlaying one upon another until they were disguised as one continuous rumble. An ambush was over quickly, but today, the

313

thunder rolled for almost three hours, died and was resurrected again and again.

The *moussebiline* guards chain-smoked cigarettes, hawked and spat into the dust beside their feet, but did not speak. Occasionally, as their minds became entangled in the unseen fighting they would finger the blades of their combat knives, or work the bolt of their rifles, loading and reloading.

At last there was silence.

It was still unclear in her mind as to how she might help the prisoners, but she knew there was little time. In less than two hours the first of the *moussebiline* would arrive back at the village, and they might be carrying wounded men with them. Once the work began in the field-hospital building she would be helpless. The village would soon fill with the returning men, and their mood could range from jubilation to misery. Their temperament was invariably unpredictable after battle.

The field-hospital was empty when she entered. She found her shoulder bag and quickly checked its contents. There were a number of dressings. She added a small packet of permanganate of potash that was nearby on a shelf, then she filled her water-bottle. She remembred the Colt pistol. It was still in its place in one of the ammunition boxes she used for storing the few medical reference books she had brought with her from Algiers. The Colt was a heavy weapon, wrapped in a piece of oiled cloth. There were five bullets in the magazine which was kept in its butt. She pushed the automatic into her shoulder-bag and covered it with the dressings.

'Where are you going?' Bouderba's voice made her start. He stared at her shoulder-bag from the doorway. Iaicha stood a little behind him, her arms folded across her chest.

Maryse Rose straightened herself. 'I am going to the prisoners. I shall tell the guards we will require them one at a time, and that if possible they are to be kept calm. They must not believe they are being taken away for execution or they may attempt to escape. In which case some of them, if not all of them, may be killed.' She kept her voice calm. 'They would be of no use to us then.'

To her relief, Bouderba relaxed, and smiled. 'Good woman. I realized you would understand. I knew from your reputation that I'd be able to count on you.' As she moved past him, he put his arms briefly around her shoulders in a congratulatory manner forcing her to suppress a shudder. 'We'll make an excellent team, Melila.'

She was twenty feet from the prisoners' compound when she heard the noise in the valley. She did not recognize it at first; it was reminiscent of the poorly silenced tractors used in many of the pieds-noir vineyards.

She saw the first of the military helicopters hanging low above the pine tops as it followed the hidden track almost three miles from the village. It seemed motionless, like a kestrel above some concealed prey, its rotor blades catching the late afternoon sun so that the machine seemed to be encircled by a saintly halo. Its lack of movement as she viewed it from above was an illusion, and a moment later she could see that it was flying directly towards her. She lost sight of it behind the nearest range of hills, then, as the sound of engines increased, much closer now, three of the machines appeared in formation against the skyline.

For seconds the mesmerizing sound and ominous appearance of the three helicopters held her. Twin white puffs of smoke appeared beneath each of them, and moments later, even as she realized their significance, the *douar* about her erupted in a vast single explosion of crimson flame, screaming metal fragments and hurtling debris. The blast tossed her against the wall of the compound. Dense smoke swirled and billowed, its rank fumes choking her. Winded, her eardrums throbbing with pain, she stumbled through the compound gate. The *moussebiline* guards, if they had survived the explosions were hidden within the smoke. She found the prisoners kneeling together in the shelter of the wall. They had dragged Philippe beside them.

She shouted at them in French. 'Get out. Run downhill into the forest. Head south west. It's your only chance.' They seemed stunned. She dragged one to his feet and thrust him in the direction of the gateway. Others followed. 'Go . . . go . . . go . . .' Her voice was hysterically shrill, the smoke had already begun to disperse in the evening breeze.

Philippe sat with his back against the crumbling wall. He added an order to her own. 'Do as she says. Run . . .' The men obeyed him.

A second fusillade of rockets hit the buildings of the *douar*, shaking an avalanche of rocks from the cliff-face, the shrapnel moaning and shrieking amongst the rubble.

She used all her strength to lift Philippe, looping his arm around her shoulders, taking almost his full weight upon herself. He shouted in agony, biting his lip until blood ran from the corner of his mouth. She half-carried, half-dragged him from the compound.

The smoke-laden air, stinking of cordite propellant and explosive, was filled with sound. Above, combining with the roar of the helicopter engines and rotors was the staccato chatter of machine-guns. Bullets ricochetted whining, humming from the shattered buildings, churning the torn earth and making the loose scree dance as if it were alive.

Towards the edge of the village the smoke was clearing to a thin mist. Philippe groaned as every movement jarred

316

his wounded leg. They had hobbled less than a hundred yards and already Maryse Rose was exhausted by his weight. To reach the tree line seemed to be an impossibility. The machine-gunning had stopped and the noise of the helicopters was fading as they rose higher above the gorge and swung away across the valley. In a few moments the smoke would clear completely and Maryse Rose and Philippe would be exposed to the view of any of the guerrillas who had survived.

A few yards ahead of them a grotesque silhouette appeared within the mist of smoke, momentarily unidentifiable, magnified by the fractured sunlight behind it. Maryse Rose's heart sank; they were already trapped by some of the returning *moussebiline*. The breathless voice of the young French corporal reassured her. 'Here, quickly. I have a mule.' He seemed to materialize into solid human form, sweat streaking the grime of his face and chest as he dragged a frightened and reluctant animal by its bridle towards them. When he reached them, he handed the rope to Maryse Rose and lifted Philippe onto the mule's back.

Another fifty yards and they were into open ground below the *douar*. Maryse Rose ran, the mule now anxious to follow her away from the smoking debris of the *douar*. The French corporal loped beside her. There was still noise, different now, growing again.

Behind them they heard a shout of anger and then a burst of machine-gun fire. The corporal screamed, staggered briefly, and dropped amongst the rocks, blood gushing from cavernous wounds in his chest where the bullets which had struck him in the back had exited. Maryse Rose continued running, swerving the mule between boulders. She glanced behind her. Chouki stood on a pile of rubble, his machine-gun held awkwardly at his hip. He began firing again.

The Junkers bomber approached the ruins of the village on a flight-path parallel to the cliff face. From its belly dropped four dark objects, tumbling in a slow arc towards the *douar*.

A bullet from Chouki's machine-gun sliced the mule's rump like the sting of a whip, causing the already panic-stricken animal to buck wildly. Philippe yelled in agony.

The four napalm containers exploded within the *douar* with a roar of white and crimson flame that seemed to engulf the entire plateau below the cliff. Great billows of black smoke swept over the remains of the village, the intense heat of the napalm beneath them driving them upwards in a swirling maelstrom of fire. More than a hundred yards from the spreading blaze, its heat scorched the fine hairs on Maryse Rose's arms as she ran.

The sound of Chouki's machine-gun had been lost in the roar of the aircraft and the ensuing explosions. It remained silent as Maryse Rose, and the mule with its rider, reached the first of the scattered pines. The forest densened around them. Behind, a thick pall of eerie black smoke like that of a gigantic forest fire, drifted slowly towards the mountain peak.

She followed a narrow track made by the *moussebiline* wood foragers, which traced the contour of the mountain only a little below the tree-line. It ran south of the main route by which the guerrillas would return to the *douar*. Three miles from the village it ended in a small clearing beside a narrow gorge, no more a cleft in the rock surface, through which tumbled a stream. Below the clearing dense undergrowth, matted thorns and low bushes clogged the forest. She pulled the mule into the stream, let it drink for a few minutes, and then began leading it down the boulder-strewn bed.

With its source only a few thousand feet higher in the

mountain, and born of the melting winter snowfields, the water of the stream was only a little above freezing point. The cold numbed Maryse Rose's sandalled feet. It was not a new experience for her, the *moussebiline* often moved through the higher forest by means of these stream beds, but in winter the men would quickly begin to suffer from frost-bite, and that could be as fatal as a wound if it were not treated.

In places the stream tumbled towards the valley over steep waterfalls, between polished boulders, their surfaces slippery with moss and algae. They were difficult to navigate. The forest scrub pressed closely to the stream, sometimes entwined so low above it that the stream was contained within dark tunnels of thorn that tore at flesh and clothing like barbed hooks. The mule plunged and skidded over the rocks, lunging through the deeper pools, and scrambling for a foothold on the steep gravel banks. Philippe was silent, somehow containing the agony he was experiencing with every movement.

As dusk began falling, they reached a point where the stream joined a shallow river, a torrent in winter but now little more than a series of pools linked by the dying streams. In a month it would be no more than a dry wadi in which, in normal times, the peasant *fellagha* would dig their summer wells. Already the area was different; the familiar mountain peaks, the swell of hills and distant ranges were concealed by the nearby forests.

She would not permit herself to rest yet. They were no more than five miles from the *douar*, and although the returning *moussebiline* would be occupied attempting to salvage any of their equipment which remained, and might attempt to assist their wounded themselves, she was far too close to the village to be safe. They would undoubtedly move to a new base, but in the meantime they would station guards in the look-out posts. At first,

319

they would assume she had been killed . . . perhaps there had been no survivors of the vicious raid on the *douar*, but she could not be certain. And it was probable the vengeful *moussebiline* would decide to search for the escaped French prisoners; there would be no bodies in the ruins of the compound.

She crossed the main track which ran on the far side of the shallow river, and then took to the rising ground to the north in the last crimson rays of the sunset. She kept to the open ground close to the edge of the forest, knowing that the growing darkness concealed her. The day's battle with the French troops had been south west of the way she now chose, so that any of the *moussebiline* stragglers would almost certainly dissect the path behind her. The grass of the ancient meadows was long; normally, the goat and sheep herds of the *fellagha* would have cropped it close, but now it clutched at her ankles like eel-grass in a river so that she was forced to lift her feet unnaturally high with every step, the muscles of her calves and thighs aching with the effort. Her sweat-stained clothing clung to her body, while her hair was a tangled mat. The thorns of the dense scrub had lacerated her naked forearms, and torn the thin cotton trousers that were little protection for her legs.

Despite her appearance, she was fitter than she had ever been before. Her slender body carried no fat, each muscle defined and as hard as whipcord. In her early weeks with the *moussebiline* she had learnt that those who could not keep up with them as they travelled through the forests, or leapt their way from rock to rock as they traversed the high mountain passes, were left behind. They had no respect for physical weakness in either man or woman. They prided themselves on the speed they could cover distances which seemed impossible to their enemy; they could jog over rough territory for hours on

320

end and leave the searching French patrols miles behind them. In the months that followed, she had become like them.

For the next three hours she followed a narrow ridge of exposed rock that led above the tree-line of the next low mountain range. Light from the stars and the immature moon harshened the landscape. The only sounds were the hooves of the mule on the hard ground, the clatter of pebbles or the breaking of a twig, and the cry of the night animals, the foxes, owls, civets. And once, a great distance away, a single shot that echoed briefly and brought a chill of fear into her mind.

It was almost midnight when she drew the mule into the shelter of an outcrop of rock on a barren plain above the trees. Shadows turned the space between the boulders into a cave. The earlier breeze had stiffened, cutting through her thin clothing, biting into the warmth of her body. By dawn the temperatures would be close to freezing so high above the valley. She tethered the mule carefully to a shard of rock so it could not wander during the night in search of fodder, then she helped Philippe from its back.

It was difficult for her to examine his wound in the poor light, but there was wet blood on his leg where it seeped through the bandages. She re-dressed it as best she could, and then eased him back into the darkness of the shadows. She unscrewed the cap of her water bottle and gave him a drink. He spoke for the first time since they had left the havoc of the *douar*.

'Why?' When she did not answer him he embellished the question. 'Why have you risked everything?'

'There was no choice for me.' Genuine love, she now knew, was far more powerful than any other emotion. It could survive where even hatred had perished.

He misunderstood her reply. 'My men would have tried

to help me . . . Corporal Natinal was coming back with the mule. There was no need for you to involve yourself. It's almost over . . . there'll be a ceasefire any day. All you had to do was to take shelter, and wait. You could have been killed by the machine-gunner.'

'Or the napalm!'

Philippe was silent for a few moments. 'God, I'm so sick of this filthy war. It's so barbarous, so brutal, even in its death throes. Why napalm a village now? There's nothing more to be gained. It's all been so senseless.'

'It's won a country for the people. It's been wasteful, savage and cruel, but not senseless.'

Philippe corrected himself. 'Senseless for us, the French. A war of wasted opportunities. I think we all realize that now. The right words, but at the wrong times and with the wrong intentions. Lies instead of the truth. Too little offered too late. A war of clichés.' He settled himself back against the rock. 'I realized when I lost you that you'd been right. For me this was the same war I had been fighting in Indo China. Dien Bien Phu wasn't the end of that war for its veterans. We just moved to a different battlefield . . . here. And we brought with us every bad memory we had, every bad experience. When we walked into an Algerian village, our soldiers didn't see Algerians, they saw the enemy they'd been fighting before, the one they already hated . . . the one who had already killed their comrades, destroyed their own pride, self-esteem. And the hatred was a plague that infected every recruit.'

She admonished him gently. 'You should rest, not talk.'

'No, I should talk. I have two years of talking to do to you.' He paused, and she could hear his breathing, now even, as it had often been when she had lain beside him in the past. It was strangely comforting for her, now. 'I have things that must be said, Maryse Rose. About us. About the beginning of things between us.' He paused again as though searching for the correct words, and in the darkness she could picture his expression, once more remembered, familiar. 'When we first met, I didn't know you were Algerian. In nine months in a military barracks in Algeria, you learn that Arab women wear robes and *haiks* and are untouchable, or else they wear garish European clothes and no knickers. You weren't either. I didn't see any difference between you and many other of the pieds-noir girls, except that you were far more beautiful. By the time I found out, I was already in love with you . . . regardless of what else I might have felt my emotions in that respect were stabilized. But the dragon inside my head was my past, and somehow you became part of the enemy.' He lifted her hand and held her fingers to the scar on his face. 'This was always a reminder . . . and the other scars on my body.' He was silent again and then continued, his speech more broken and unsure. 'The shock of losing you, realizing how you had suffered, and how we had both lost a child we could have loved so much forced my nightmare to reveal itself to me. I remembered. There were five of us. Conscripts together in Indo China. Two of the others were boys I'd known since school in Caen. We came out of the jungle for a few hours' rest, and we were in a bar . . . a brothel. There were lots of girls. We all ended up together in a sort of dormitory . . . we'd had too much to drink. Much later, I was awakened by someone screaming . . . not an ordinary scream but something quite terrible. There were other bad noises. The girls were cutting their bedmate's throats . . . my friends' throats. The girl lying next to me missed with her knife and slashed my face. Someone switched on a light. There was blood everywhere . . . on the ceiling, the walls, the bedclothes, the floor. It takes a few minutes to die from a cut throat, and not all of my friends were dead. It was like a Grand Guignol play. I was terrified. I leapt off the bed and ran. The door was locked and as I was trying to get out all the women were stabbing and slashing at me like vultures pecking at a carcass. I don't know how I got away . . . I don't remember. A patrol found me in the mud of a rice field. I didn't remain in the army after my period of conscription because I wanted a career, but because I wanted revenge . . . against any damned enemy I could find. Maybe I needed to remind myself that I'd run away *after* my friends were all dead, and not before.'

She could remember his nightmares, the times he had shouted in his sleep, tossing and turning, to awaken with perspiration pouring from his body. Now she understood the reasons.

He continued, his voice almost hypnotic for her. 'They say that sometimes a shock can cure insanity. My shock was losing you. The letter I wrote to you was unforgivable. I realized that as soon as I sent it. I took compassionate leave immediately, but it was too late. By the time I reached Algiers you had disappeared. Vincent told me that you'd lost the baby. He despised me for hurting you . . . I didn't blame him. I searched for you for the whole of my leave. After that, when I had to return to my unit, I employed private detectives and gave them money to pay Arabs for information. I learnt nothing. No-one had heard of a woman named Maryse Rose. Everything seemed to be collapsing around me. You'd gone, and I'd driven you away. I wanted to kill myself.'

Again her emotions surprised her. She could picture his misery as he tried to find her, seeking a woman who no longer existed in the name he had used. How would she have responded then, had he found her? She could not answer herself. But now she felt touched by the sorrow he had experienced and wanted to hold him in her arms and comfort him. Instead, she moved a little closer to him, and lay beside him as the *moussebiline* lay close to each other during the freezing winter nights. 'Now rest,' she ordered him softly. 'It will be a short night.'

Even as he slept a little later, he kept hold of her hand, pressing it against his chest as a child might. She could feel his heartbeat.

She did not sleep. The sounds of the mountain and the wind mingled with her own thoughts to keep her awake. Throughout the night there had been some strange moments, dreamlike, when her mind had become aware of an alien consciousness within herself. She had quit the stricken *douar* with little idea of the direction she must travel to find safety for herself and Philippe. Now, strangely, she sensed an intuitive knowledge hovering on the very borders of her awareness, a knowledge bequeathed by her Bedouin ancestors. The mountain slopes, the cornices and crags, and the forests, were not foes as she had considered them for the past years. They were her allies.

Two hours before dawn she left Philippe and climbed to the top of one of the huge boulders which formed part of their shelter. She sat cross-legged on the rock, the mountain breeze playing with her hair, drawing it back off her face. For a long time she watched the star-filled night sky, until far beyond the eastern hills it began to lighten, and she understood she must not plan and that the future would reveal itself as it became the present.

Philippe slept as though he had been drugged, and she awakened him with difficulty. The flesh of his leg, above and below the shattered knee, was hot to her touch. She washed the wound carefully, and sprinkled it with a little of the potassium permanganate. It was a crude treatment, making Philippe wince as if she had poured neat iodine into his wound. When it was dressed, she helped him onto the mule once more.

The rim of the eastern sky was coloured by a thin band of pale yellow above the far hills as she coiled the animal's halter around her hand. She took several paces and then stopped. Her mind persisted in its warning. For a few moments she wondered if her eyes had picked out some distant movement, or if her ears had distinguished some foreign, threatening sound. But then she knew. Habib was following her. Suddenly she understood the significance of the solitary rifle shot she had heard the previous evening. It had been his signal to her . . . it had said: 'I am coming for you. I am coming to find you and the prisoner you have stolen from me. And I shall kill you both.'

They rested only once that morning when their route took them over the first range of hills and to the narrow grass meadows near the valley floor. Maryse Rose watered the mule at a shallow stream, and let it graze. Without thought, she stripped naked and bathed in the cooling water, splashing over her and feeling it tauten and refresh her body. In the company of the *moussebiline* she would have sought privacy if it were possible, but even were it not the men would have made theatrical attempts to ignore her. Now, however, she became aware that Philippe was watching her. She felt unexpectedly embarrassed, as though he were a stranger, and became ashamed of her narrow thighs and masculine buttocks, the way in which her stomach hollowed between her hip bones, and of her breasts, diminished to those of a young girl. It was not how he would have remembered her.

She did not wash her sweat-stained clothes, knowing there was no time to dry them in the sun and that if she wore them wet they would chafe her as she walked. But even though they stank she felt relieved when she was dressed and they were once again on the move.

They crossed several small tracks some no more than disturbed pebbles on the mountain slopes, and she disregarded them all. In late afternoon she paused beside a valley road. It tempted her momentarily, seeming to lead towards unknown goals. There were the marks of the tyres of heavy vehicles in its dusty surface, and in the drying grass at the roadside a discarded cigarette packet. As she pulled the tired mule once more into the thickets of the lower slopes, Philippe protested. If they struck north, he told her, and followed the road, they would be certain to reach a village. She shook her head. The danger signals had returned, and she somehow knew that the safe route lay ahead of her. She must not allow her instinctive judgements to be swayed.

For an hour during the early evening they hid while five shepherds drove a small flock of scrawny sheep past them through the sparse brush which dotted the upper slopes of the mountains. The men would have been carrying food, and might have been prepared to give her some had she approached them alone. But there was too much risk. Her torn uniform identified her as an official FLN *moudjahid*, and they would certainly mention meeting her when they reached their village. It was safer to remain hungry rather than risk capture; a lone woman in the mountains would generate speculation, and if there was an FLN unit in the vicinity of the shepherds' village, perhaps in the village community itself, they would certainly investigate.

As darkness fell she reached the first blackened wilderness of destroyed forest. Charcoal littered and coated the ground beneath stark and blackened skeletons of trees and shrubs distorted by fire. The sky had clouded and a light rain began to fall, hiding the rocky crags above the burnt ground. There was no life; nothing lived within the desolation. She remembered the burning, it had taken place the previous summer. Following ambushes by the *moussebiline* the French troops had brought their flame-throwers into the forests to destroy the hiding places. For weeks dark smoke clouds had hung above the mountains. Below, giant trees screamed in agony before exploding to their deaths in the volcanic heat. The kites, hawks and eagles had risen high above the fires, drifting from the smoke-tainted thermals towards distant and safer hunting grounds. The monkeys, boar and wild goats had outrun the flames, but the small rodents, the lizards and snakes, the myriads of cicada who filled the mountain gorges with their summer sound, had perished. The blackened rocks and earth were barren, and the mountainsides stank like the ashes of a vast funeral pyre. The *moussebiline* had simply moved on and found new places for their ambushes.

The rain increased, so that even the mule had difficulty retaining its footing on the slippery ground. A sharp overhang of rock gave them cover as the darkness intensified and a thunderstorm began to shake the mountains. Lightning split the night with jagged white spears that imprinted staccato visions of the colourless landscape on the mind like black and white photographs, so that Maryse Rose saw Philippe beside her unmoving, his paleness exaggerated. He seemed feverish, his breath more shallow as she examined him. Like an animal, she sniffed his bandaged wound; it was sickly sweet, the scent of decomposing tissue . . . gangrene. Unless he received drugs and treatment soon, he could not survive.

They had spoken little during the day and she knew it had taken all his remaining strength to retain his seat on the mule. The pain and continuous effort had exhausted him. If he received food now it would help, but there was none.

He seemed to penetrate her mind as he had so often done in the past. 'You should leave me here. It's pointless to go on. Alone you can survive.'

She corrected him. 'Alone, it would be pointless.' She moved so that she could pillow his head on her lap, feeling the coarse stubble on his cheeks with her fingertips, tracing his features in the darkness. She knew it was dangerous to think of the future, but it was impossible to ignore. There were no longer visions of them together in Beau Lac, but surely there could be other places? He had said he had continued to love her, but did he want her? There was a difference.

'Where are you leading us?' he asked her.

She could not give him a truthful answer. It was impossible to tell him she did not know their goal and that it was hidden somewhere in a mind that was scarcely more than a part of her own. 'The right place.'

'But it doesn't have a name?'

'Not yet.'

'We could call it home,' he said, taking hold of her hand and pressing it to his lips. 'Or is that an impossibility?' He kissed her hand as gently as he had once kissed so many secret places of her body, and his touch drove a flush of hot blood through her tired limbs. 'Would you ever be able to trust me again?'

'Yes.'

'But not forget?' He said it as though he were speaking for her.

'I can forget. That's something war teaches. I've learnt to remember how to survive, and how to forget pain . . . and so many other things. Loving is more important. Trust is part of loving; they mature together.'

'I love, is the most consequential verb in any language.'

He waited until sudden thunder died, before continuing. 'Will you let me court you again?'

She knew he was afraid of her refusal and had deliberately made his suggestion old-fashioned, as he had done so long ago in Beau Lac, to allow him the escape of humour should she reject him. She lowered her head and kissed him. Even the stubble was unable to disguise the memories of his lips on her own, the once more familiar scent of his skin. 'We must court each other.'

He was silent for so long she thought he was already asleep. Her own fatigue was beginning to conquer her, rolling across her mind like the heavy swell of an ocean. She knew she would be unable to resist it much longer, but that the storm itself would protect them tonight. No-one, however determined, could follow them in these conditions.

He spoke so softly that at first she thought it was no more than the winds of the storm against the rocks. 'You know that you can go home?' Had she misunderstood him? He spoke again. 'Vincent . . . it's all over. They know what really happened. They know it was nothing to do with you.' He did not wait for her to question him, understanding how the memories must be flooding back into her mind. 'A man was caught . . . the usual sweeps the Sûrété carry out from time to time. I don't remember his name . . . Mohamed something . . . it's unimportant. It came out during their interrogation . . . the forged letter, the theft of your wedding ring. Later the gendarmes found a man's body in a sewer. There were other things too, an Italian motorcycle that had been seen in the Tipaza fishmarket; a boy saw the man who drove it climb across the rocks towards the place where Vincent was murdered. It was a great shame it all happened . . . so unnecessary . . . so much more hurt for you. It was some kind of

330

mistake. A Colonel Lefitte issued a statement about it, just two days before he was killed.'

'Henri Lefitte killed!' Instantly Maryse Rose could picture Lefitte's dapper clothing, the immaculately creased trousers, his heavily brilliantined hair. She could remember the repulsion she had felt when he had unbuttoned her blouse and cradled her breast in the damp palm of his hand.

'This time it was the OAS. They fired rockets into a number of government buildings. One exploded in the Colonel's office. God, how did we ever become embroiled in a war like this?' He pressed his head deeper into her lap as though to protect himself.

He had resurrected more buried memories. 'Mama and Papa . . . Madelene?' She could not bring herself to mention Belle.

'They all moved to France. I have their address.' His voice was blending with the sound of the storm once more. 'I believe everything was sold . . . the company offices moved to Marseilles. Most of the big companies and the "grand colons" have left . . . everyone is leaving . . .'

The surface of the rock-face behind her felt ice-cold against her head and shoulders. The past had been reborn but without its former menace. The months and years she had spent in the *djebel* were losing substance. Eventually they might become no more than dreams and nightmares. Conjured into her thoughts the faces of extinct times found new clarity and although beyond the shelter of the overhanging cliff the storm raged, in her mind there was a new calmness.

She awakened suddenly, consciousness returning so brutally that for a moment she thought she had been struck by an unseen hand. The storm had died and the sun risen. The sodden, blackened ground beyond the cliff steamed in the morning warmth so that a light mist hung above the ground. The mule, standing in a quagmire of mud and charcoal dust up to its hocks, fidgeted nervously, its nostrils quivering as if it scented distant pasture and water.

It was late. She had wasted vital hours, but when she moved there was no response from Philippe. His eyelids were partly open, the pupils hidden, and there was a light frothy spittle on his lips. The flesh of his cheeks seemed to have yellowed during the night, pulling back against the bone so that the pain he had suffered while she slept was drawn on his features. For an horrific moment her body was cramped with fear. His breathing was so shallow it was imperceptible.

'Philippe . . .' She spoke his name urgently, then repeated it, more loudly. 'Philippe!' She damped her cheek with saliva and held her face close to his mouth. There was the faintest chill. To reassure herself, she felt with her fingertips for the pulse at the side of his throat. At her touch, he moved slightly. With a desperate movement she tore the lacerated cloth of his trousers open to his hip. The flesh above the wound was swollen and discoloured. A web of scarlet veins led from the poisoned flesh like the tendrils of some obscene monster clawing at his body. The used wound dressing, as she replaced it with her remaining bandage, smelt of death. She called his name again. 'Philippe . . .' She must arouse him. Somehow he must find the strength to hold himself upon the mule's back for one more day. One day was all she would need, her mind told her. 'Philippe . . .' She gripped him by his shoulders and shook him. She was filled with a sudden anger. 'Don't die . . . don't die now that we've found each other again.' There were tears running down her cheeks, streaking the dust and filth on her skin. She shook him more violently. 'Don't die! Philippe, you've been fighting for others for twelve years . . . now fight for us. Fight,

332

Philippe . . . fight.' Dear God, why hadn't he awakened her to help him?

Her voice penetrated his unconsciousness. His eyelids quivered, and then his eyes met her own. He tried to move, but lacked the strength. She drew him upwards until she was able to hold him in her arms. 'Just one day,' she promised him. 'You must fight for one more day . . . promise me?'

'I promise . . .'

She was not conscious of time as the hours passed. It was as though the poison which seeped through Philippe's body had entered her own. Her limbs were leaden, her feet heavy and uncertain. By noon the mist cleared as the breeze returned, but the distant mountains were blurred as if she viewed them above a desert mirage. Occasionally only the halter of the mule saved her when she slipped and fell in the treacherous gulleys and crevices of the blackened mountainside. Sharp scree, discoloured by heat, tore at her body. Blackened scrub splintered into sharp daggers and knives as she forced her way through.

There was no water. Before they had left the shelter of the cliff that morning, she had poured the last drops through Philippe's pale lips. Now she was dehydrated. Behind her, she could hear the mule wheezing with exhaustion, and like herself it slipped on the loose rock of the steep slopes, stumbled over boulders. Its shoulders and rump were coated with a lather of yellow foam that caught the dust and dried as ugly scabs with the heat of the sun.

At times Philippe had fallen from the animal's back. Only then would Maryse Rose rest for a few minutes while she encouraged him, sometimes with loving promises, at others with fierce threats when the nearby naked rock echoed her cries.

*

Maryse Rose became aware that she was reaching her destination as she breasted the final sharp ridge of the mountainside. The mule followed her mindlessly, its back hollowed by the weight of its burden. Philippe sagged forward, his hands gripping the animal's thin mane, blood seeping from the open wound in his leg. His chin rested on his chest, and he swayed perilously as the animal moved. She knew he was barely conscious.

Although she felt certain their journey was almost completed, the view ahead was still unfamiliar. Then, across the width of the steep valley she saw the ruins of a building on a promontory of rock. Unlike much of the valley, the shrubs and trees closer to the building were unburnt. She knew she should be able to recognize it and her mind sought an explanation.

With a chilling sense of disillusionment she realized after a few moments that the ruin of the building she could see was The Citadelle, but it was no longer the haven her mind had imagined, the place where she and Philippe had become lovers so many years before. Her subconscious had been deluded by memory; the once attractive hotel, its walls draped with the purple blooms of bougainvillea, its gardens sheltered by graceful palms, had become a victim of the war. Beyond the ruins of the building, the neglected road wound out of sight beyond a series of massive cornices.

The gorge was already shadowed by the far mountain. Distantly, to her right, she could make out the town of Chiffa, the outline of its barracks and houses vivid against the softer colours of the surrounding agricultural plain. It would be impossible for them to reach before nightfall.

The Chiffa-Medea road! Perhaps *that* was the destination her mind had chosen. As the only north-south route for trans-Saharan vehicles, it would be patrolled at least three or four times a day by French military vehicles.

Like all the *moussebiline* she knew the habits of the French army. A patrol would be made shortly after dawn each day, its purpose to check that no mines had been laid during the night. It was extremely rare for a morning patrol to be attacked; the *moussebiline* liked to have the cover of darkness before them when they struck in ambush. There would be a second, and perhaps a third patrol during the course of the day; they checked out the villages and bidonvilles, manned road-blocks and inspected trucks and lorries. As much as anything else, they reaffirmed daily the French presence. The final patrol of the day, often performed just as dusk fell, faced the greatest danger. It was the time when the *moussebiline* attacked . . . machine-gun fire from the cover of the blackened rocks ripping through the metal cabs of the trucks, shattering the windscreens, killing the drivers. Mortars which had been carefully ranged destroying the vehicles and their occupants. Afterwards the *moussebiline* would trek through the night to the safety of a distant camp.

She glanced towards the western mountains. There was a full hour to sunset, the last patrol of the day would not yet have completed its journey down the gorge. If she could reach the road . . . if she could reach the road before Habib caught up! She knew he was still behind her. Her mind could see him, moving lightly across the sombre terrain, skirting the blackened rocks, his lithe athletic body enjoying the challenge she offered him as he loped down the long hills and leapt the shallow rivers. He would rest a little, eat as he moved, drink from the streams or his water-bottle. His eyes would follow the tracks in the charcoal-soft earth, see the broken branches in the scorched thickets, the scrapes of the mule's hooves, the disturbed pebbles and scree. At times, as though some delicate cord bound her to him at even this distance, she had thought she could discern his mind probing her own.

THIRTEEN

The Chiffa Gorge: 18 March 1962

She had failed! Even as the exhausted mule plunged through the shallows of the river at the foot of the wide gorge, she heard the military trucks pass on the road high above, the roar of their engines magnified within the chasm. She stared upwards helplessly, praying that for some reason the patrol might stop amongst the ruins of The Citadelle, but the sounds of the vehicles quickly faded.

With approaching darkness a bitter wind, a remnant of the Chergui sweeping up from the Sahara desert, funnelled itself viciously through the naked gorge, spiralling dust-devils amongst the dry rocks, at times blinding her.

There was no track to follow, and she climbed the steepening side of the gorge mechanically, her mind numbed by disappointment. Ahead of her the mule scrambled for its footholds amongst the craggy rocks on narrowing ledges. To the left, a few yards away, the cliff upon which The Citadelle had been built, hung sheer above the gorge like a gigantic buttress, unassailable.

The mule reached a vertical slab of rock and stopped. She shouted encouragement at the animal, but it refused to obey her. Without warning it bucked Philippe from its back, leapt to a slightly lower ledge, missed its footing and plunged thirty feet into a gulley of loose scree. Scrambling wildly, it rolled to the edge of a precipice and disappeared from her view into the darkness of the gorge. Seconds later she heard the sickening crunch of its body landing amongst the boulders beside the river.

Philippe was barely conscious, and unable to assist her. They were so close to the goal her mind had set for her that the need to reach it was obsessional. Slowly, foot by foot, holding him by his wrists, she began dragging him up the steep slope. Whenever the chill wind slackened, she could smell her own sweat, rank, acrid. Every muscle of her body strained, knotting into cramp if she paused to rest, but she found the strength she needed in a form of madness in which the weakness of her own body was a deadly challenge to overcome.

The last sixty feet to the plateau took her more than an hour.

The moon rose with nightfall, as she built Philippe a shelter beside one of the tumbled walls. She roofed it with a piece of broken asbestos. Her clothing was filthy, bloodstained, shaded with charcoal dust, shredded and torn. During the last miles she had ripped pieces from it to pad Philippe's wounds when the staggering and lunging of the mule on the rough ground had opened them. The seam of her tunic was split from armpit to hem, exposing her left breast when she moved. The olive skin of her face, neck, forearms, hands and ankles was grazed and bruised.

She knelt beside him. He lay almost motionless, his only movement the shallow rise and fall of his chest, his temple ice-cold even against the back of her chilled hand. She had found nothing amongst the ruins with which to protect him against the wind. After a moment, she stripped off her torn tunic and laid it over him, tucking it beneath his arms as she might once have tidied the bedclothes of a patient in a hospital bed. She knew it was all she could now give him.

She left him and stood by a shattered wall above the gorge to scan the far slopes. Nothing moved in the night shadows beneath their cliffs. As the wind cut into her exposed skin she crossed her arms protectively over her naked breasts, and held herself tightly.

At first she found herself experiencing a masochistic satisfaction as she waited, willing the figure of Habib to appear on the dark horizon or amongst the moonlit crags. He had become her fate, and the confrontation she was expecting seemed to have been an inevitable part of her life. From her earliest childhood she had lived divided between two cultures, unable to totally accept either, yet each providing her with a convenient refuge from the other. Selfishly she had striven to retain the most desirable aspects of both, but it had proved an impossibility, almost destroying her and now threatening the futures of the men she loved in such different ways. Habib might kill Philippe as he lay defenceless, and by doing so would probably destroy himself if he truly loved her. She too, would be a certain victim of his vengeance.

She arched her back and stretched herself, placing her hands on her hips and inviting the cold desert wind to play across her naked shoulders, back and breasts, just as she had once enjoyed the needle-fine jets of cold showers in the lost comfort of Beau Lac. As though she had defied it, the strength of the wind faded and the gorge became silent and calm.

Her mind seemed to awaken, suddenly refreshed, and was rejecting the Arab certainty of *kismet*. She became angry with herself. Unconsciously, she had found yet another sanctuary by her acceptance of pre-ordination. Fatalism was no more than an escape from responsibility. She had already made a final choice, the gears were meshed and the wheels turning. Now, she must direct the future herself.

Feeling a new strength growing within her, she took the Colt automatic from the shoulder bag and released its magazine. To reassure herself she slid the bullets from the clip, then reloaded the weapon and laid it in readiness on a broken concrete slab in front of her. Then she sat, her back resting against the masonry, staring across the moonlit gorge and knowing that the night would be the longest of her life.

Later Philippe called to her, and she went to him. Faint moonlight glazed the perspiration on his face. He caught her hand and held it tightly as she bent her head to kiss him, feeling the destructive fire in his body with her lips. 'I'm still here,' she told him softly.

She held her head close to him to hear his words. 'There are no more nightmares, Maryse Rose.'

'I know.' Don't let him die, she prayed. Don't let me lose him now.

'I love you.' Philippe's eyes glistened in the half-darkness and she knew he was watching her.

'I love you too. But promise you will tell me every day of our lives.'

'I promise . . .'

'Now rest, my darling.'

She stayed with him, comforting him with her touch but frustrated by her own helplessness, until at last he slept again.

Amongst the ruins a pebble clattered in the debris. She moved defensively, her hand snatching at the heavy Colt, swinging it in the direction of the sound, each muscle of her body, each nerve, taut with expectancy. A mountain fox, its exaggerated ears pricked, watched her for a moment then leapt a crumbling wall into the night.

Her nerves uncoiled slowly, her body relaxing gradually like that of a desert reptile in the first morning rays of the sun. Where the fox had stood within the ruins she had once been carried in the arms of the man who lay beside her. Somewhere above, in a place now occupied only by the starlight, had been the room where their bodies had united, and where a real love that had proved itself indestructible had been born . . . that night.

'Melila . . .' Habib's cry taunted her, its source disguised by echoes. 'Melila . . . Melila . . .' She held the pistol fiercely, her eyes quickly searching the dawn rocks, the sparse bushes whose roots clung tenuously to minute crevices like spidery fingers.

It was not yet daylight, but darkness was fading to expose the broad panorama of the blackened gorge. Once it had been so colourful, so lush; for her a valley of romantic dreams.

Habib knew there was no escape for her. 'Melila . . . Melila . . .'

She could see no movement amongst the crags even as the sky above the ridge of mountains brightened. The Arab name he had given her teased her from a hundred hiding places. She turned, but his voice was behind her again, then to her side . . . to right, to left.

'Melila . . . Melila . . .'

She was tempted to reply, but knew that was what he needed; an acknowledgement of her fear.

Habib's laughter rang within the gorge. Had he come alone, she wondered? Or had his pride demanded an audience of the *moussebiline*?

For almost fifteen minutes he continued to torment her, making the name sound like an insult, adding the same kind of inflection the pieds-noir used when they referred to an Algerian. But she knew that he would end his taunts soon. He too was aware that a French patrol would pass through the gorge within the next hour.

She was afraid; not for herself, but for Philippe.

There was a sudden clatter of falling rubble behind her. She spun to face the sound. Habib stood on a corner of the wall above her, his legs wide apart, a machine-pistol in his hands. He was grinning at her. She aimed the Colt automatic at his chest.

'Squeeze the trigger,' he suggested, coolly.

The muzzle of the Colt was already wavering. She knew that in moments she would be unable to support its weight at arms length, but to her horror she understood the confidence in his voice. She was unable to kill him.

He laughed. 'You're a good nurse, but a bad *moussebiline.*' He jumped from the wall and strode through the rubble until he was only two yards from her. He turned slightly and hauled the sheet of asbestos from the shelter she had built to protect Philippe. It shattered noisily. Habib stared down at the wounded man. 'Why in God's name did you bother? He's already carrion!' He glanced over his shoulder towards the gorge, and shouted. 'Chouki . . . here's your Frenchman.' A moment later the young *moussebiline* clambered into the ruins, a MAS rifle in his hands, its pencil bayonet extended beside the barrel. Habib jerked his head towards Philippe, and Chouki scrambled quickly over the debris like an anxious terrier ordered by its master to the kill. When he neared the wounded man, the youth raised the rifle above his head as though it was the shaft of a spear, the bayonet point glinting evilly in the sunlight.

Maryse Rose screamed. 'No . . . Habib, no.'

The young *moussebiline* hesitated.

'He's my husband, Habib . . . my husband . . .'

'Stop!' Habib snapped the word at Chouki, then faced Maryse Rose. 'You're lying.' There was uncertainty in his voice, although his sharp eyes held her own.

'No. I *swear* it is the truth. Read his identity discs . . .

341

Philippe Viard. You know my papers said Maryse Rose Viard, nee Charpentier. I swear before God, Habib.'

Habib walked to Philippe's side, stooped and tore the identification discs from Philippe's neck. He read them, then threw them at Maryse Rose's feet. 'It makes no difference. Forty-two of the *katiba* died in the ambush. The *douar* was totally destroyed: only Chouki survived. You helped the prisoners escape.' He stared coldly down at Philippe. 'This garbage will be killed, and then you will return with me and face a court-martial for desertion. You have brought shame to the *katiba*, and on the name of every one of our friends who have died in this war.'

She spoke quickly. 'Is it wrong to try to save the life of someone you love? Would you have let me die if I were your wife and a prisoner in that compound . . . a prisoner they were going to slaughter like a goat?'

'It could not happen.'

'To you, perhaps no. But it *did* happen to me, Habib. It was *my* man lying in that filth; *my* man whose blood they were going to drain away.'

'And wasn't I your man? Shouldn't you be loyal to me?'

'When was I disloyal, Habib? Was I disloyal when we starved together . . . or froze in the winters? Have I ever refused to accompany the *moussebiline*? Have I ever betrayed our *katiba* to the enemy?'

'You loved me.'

'Yes, I loved you, and I still love you.'

Habib laughed scornfully. 'Love! You still love me . . . and yet you *love* him.'

'Do you think it impossible for a woman to love two men? Love is not something bought by the kilo, and then consumed in a few days, months, even years. Habib, for a woman there are many kinds of love and all of them real. I've never lied to you, and I don't lie now. You must

342

believe me that the love which we shared still exists, but it is a different love.'

'Second grade . . .!'

'No. But there is one form of love that demands far more of a woman than all the others, and it's this love which I have for my husband. I can't change it Habib. It's there inside me, as enduring as the desert or the mountains. No matter what I do, or what you choose to do, it will always survive.'

Habib was silent for a few moments, then he took a deep breath, almost a sigh. He shook his head slowly. 'To sacrifice oneself for a belief is a very Arab characteristic. Perhaps, after all, I've taught you something.' He paused thoughtfully, and then said: 'Today is the 19 of March, and a ceasefire has been agreed. The war against the French has ended.' His dark eyes held hers, and he smiled slightly. 'We used to talk about our freedom, and today we have it . . . the freedom to decide our own futures, and to make them. I can hardly deny you that privilege, now.' He lowered his eyes and she knew he was examining her body. There was a hint of humour in his voice when he spoke again. 'You are a disgrace to Arab womanhood. Make yourself decent before the French come.'

She started to thank him, but a sudden movement behind him caught her attention. The young *moussebiline*, Chouki, had raised the bayonet once more and was about to plunge it into Philippe's body. Habib saw her horror and turned quickly. 'Stop . . . at once . . .'

Chouki angrily swung the MAS towards Habib. He screamed: 'Traitor . . .' Then fired the rifle. The bullet struck Habib in the chest, hurling him backwards onto the rubble. The young *moussebiline*, his face contorted with manic fury, aimed the weapon at Philippe's head.

Maryse Rose reacted instinctively. The heavy Colt seemed to explode in her hands of its own volition almost tearing itself from her grasp. Chouki spun sideways then dropped to his knees. Very slowly he raised the MAS rifle, aiming it with a fearful determination towards Philippe. Blood pumped obscenely from a wound in the side of the *moussebiline*'s neck. Maryse Rose screamed with despair, then fired the Colt again and again until the hammer clicked on its empty breech. The bullets seemed to lift Chouki to his feet, jerking his body like the strings of a marionette. At the edge of the vertical cliff the ground collapsed beneath his weight. For a moment he was grotesquely poised, motionless, then the avalanche of rock and masonry carried him into the deep abyss below.

Habib was still alive when she reached him. The bullet from the MAS had entered his chest close to his heart. He stared up at her, with a slightly bewildered expression. 'I didn't believe you could kill anything.' Then his eyes left her and for a moment followed the outline of the mountains above the gorge. He spoke softly. 'In a few years they'll be green again.'

She nodded, trying to contain her tears. 'Very soon,' she whispered.

He looked past her towards the deep azure African sky. 'It's been a short victory, Melila.'

She shook her head quickly. 'No, Habib. It will be a very long victory for Algeria. You've given the country back to its people.'

Habib's body twisted in agony, and she heard the sound of his teeth grinding as he fought the pain. After a moment he said softly. 'If you have a son with your Frenchman, bring him back to the mountains. Show him where we fought together. Tell him the truth . . . tell him how it was, for all of us.'

Tears were burning her cheeks now. 'I promise.' Gently she smoothed his damp hair, trying to comfort him with

344

her touch, and as she did so felt his body relax into stillness and death.

The military Jeep drove slowly down the length of the gorge towards Chiffa. It was 6.30 am, and the Sous-lieutenant, his driver and the two men who manned the machine-gun mounted in the rear had been warned that not all the FLN *moussebiline* might be aware of the cease-fire. A hundred yards behind them were two Berliet trucks carrying a section of infantry from the Medea barracks. They had celebrated the previous evening; not victory, but their survival of the war. Soon, they would return to France and their homes.

The Sous-lieutenant saw movement in the ruins of The Citadelle and held up his arm to halt the small convoy. One of the machine-gunners, a corporal, stared through powerful binoculars; he was a regular soldier with four-teen years of active service in Indo China and Algeria. He had seen a lot of men die.

He swore, the muscles of his jaw tightening with anger. 'An Arab bitch with one of our men. I can see the poor devil's blood.' He dropped the binoculars and swung the machine-gun in the direction of the ruined hotel.

The Sous-lieutenant stopped him quickly. 'Leave it! Our orders are not to fire except to save our own lives.'

The corporal swore again. 'Shit!'

The young officer examined the crouching woman with his own binoculars. She was half-naked, but cradling a European in her arms. As he watched, the woman waved towards them, demanding their attention. He spoke over his shoulder to the corporal. 'Remember, your war's over, Tessier. She's signalling to us. Cover me while I go and see what's been happening . . .'

*

Beneath her feet the deck of the steamer pulsed as if it contained the heart of some vast living being. Beyond the rails the wake hung in a vast sweeping curve like a white umbilical cord linking the ship to the African coast now fifteen miles astern. Nightfall would sever it, and it was already dusk.

From this distance, Algeria seemed unchanged. The mountains, the fertile coastal plains, the cliffs, beaches, and the towns whose lights were already shimmering in the evening haze, seemed eternal. But it was no longer the Algeria she wished to remember. The white villas on the coastal road, the apartment blocks of Bab-el-Oued, the great houses of the city's pleasant suburbs were deserted. The surfaces of many streets were blackened by the fires in which the pieds-noir had burnt their possessions. The shells of vehicles they had deliberately wrecked littered the boulevards outside the shuttered cafes and restaurants. What they had not been permitted to take with them in their exodus, they had destroyed rather than allow it to fall into the hands of the victors.

She felt saddened. Over a million Algerians had died in pursuit of their liberty, and with them more than twenty-seven thousand French soldiers and civilians. Countless others had been wounded. The after-deck of the vessel was crowded with the last of the pieds-noir refugees who had delayed their departure from Algeria in the vain hope they would be permitted to remain. Now, many were in tears as they watched the familiar mountains fade into the darkness. To the west, ahead of the ship's bows, the sun dipped below the Mediterranean horizon.

Maryse Rose walked slowly along the deck towards the forward saloon where the first-class passengers were sitting quietly around the tables, or crowding its small bar. The deck lights of the ship were as yet unlit, but the

346

evening air was warm and salty clean. The interior of the saloon was smoky and uninviting. She leant against the rail and watched the bow wave rolling away from the ship as it clove the dark water.

She did not realize he was beside her until he spoke. 'Was it hard to say goodbye?' He moved closer, rested one of his crutches against the rail, and put his arm around her shoulders.

She pressed herself against him. 'Once, I thought it would be impossible. Just being there was the most important thing in my life.'

'What will you remember?' he asked her softly.

Momentarily the sadness returned. 'Champagne on the lawns at Beau Lac . . . a Roman town . . . people and laughter . . .' She hesitated. 'A marble tomb.'

'And what else?'

She faced him and put her arms around him. 'You're fishing, Philippe Viard.'

'Yes, so tell me.'

She tilted her head slightly. 'I shall remember a French officer who thought Françoise Sagan was a juvenile . . . who made me cut my arm the first time we met, and threw a glass of wine over me on our second meeting. Then he kidnapped me, took me to his secret hideout in the mountains and scandalized my family.'

He was smiling at her. 'But there was a happy ending . . .'

She nodded, feeling the satisfying warmth of contentment flow through her body. 'Yes,' she said quietly. 'An ending that was a new beginning.'